WINDOWS ON OUR WORLD

Leslie William Gates, who goes by the pen name of Les Bill Gates, was born in England in 1949. In 1972, he graduated from Keble College, Oxford University with an Honours degree in Mathematics. The following year he completed a Post-graduate Certificate in Education at Exeter University.

Les has toured the world extensively and has spent more than twelve years in the Solomon Islands and eleven years in New Zealand.

Les is a High School teacher and former Principal of King George VI National Secondary School, Solomon Islands.

Les is now pursuing a new career as an author. 'Hope', the first part of the fantasy trilogy 'Windows on Our World', is his first book. The other two parts, 'Faith' and 'Love', are in progress.

Les Bill Gates

WINDOWS ON OUR WORLD

Part 1: HOPE

**IN THE TRADITION OF THE EPIC FANTASY
NOVELS OF THE LAST FIFTY YEARS**

WOOW Books

First published by Lulu in 2007.

Copyright © by Les Bill Gates 2007

All rights reserved. This book is sold subject to the condition that it shall not, by way of trade or otherwise, be lent, re-sold, hired out, or otherwise circulated without the publisher's prior consent in any form of binding or cover, or electronically, other than that in which it is published.

All characters in this publication are fictitious, and any resemblance to real persons, living or dead, is coincidental.

Les Bill Gates
Windows on Our World
ISBN 978-1-84753-515-3

CONTENTS

		Page
Map of Manchor, Luchor and Atmos		6
Map of West Thorland		7
Map of East Thorland and Terrapo		8
Chapter 1	Arrival	9
Chapter 2	Journey to Tobin's castle	21
Chapter 3	Butterfly and Swan	35
Chapter 4	The Island	52
Chapter 5	The Northern Desert	68
Chapter 6	Bunbury	82
Chapter 7	Bo's Chasm	102
Chapter 8	Meliae and Nereids	117
Chapter 9	Homar's Forest	135
Chapter 10	The Ford and The Bridge	149
Chapter 11	Heading for Winterton	165
Chapter 12	Reunion	180
Chapter 13	Tinlin	197
Chapter 14	Hanlin Monastery	214
Chapter 15	The Council at Fort Holt	230
Chapter 16	The Keeper of Secrets	247
Chapter 17	Meetings at Southport	263
Chapter 18	Strange Beings	280
Chapter 19	Sacumed	295
Chapter 20	Return to Tobin's castle	314
Epilogue		331

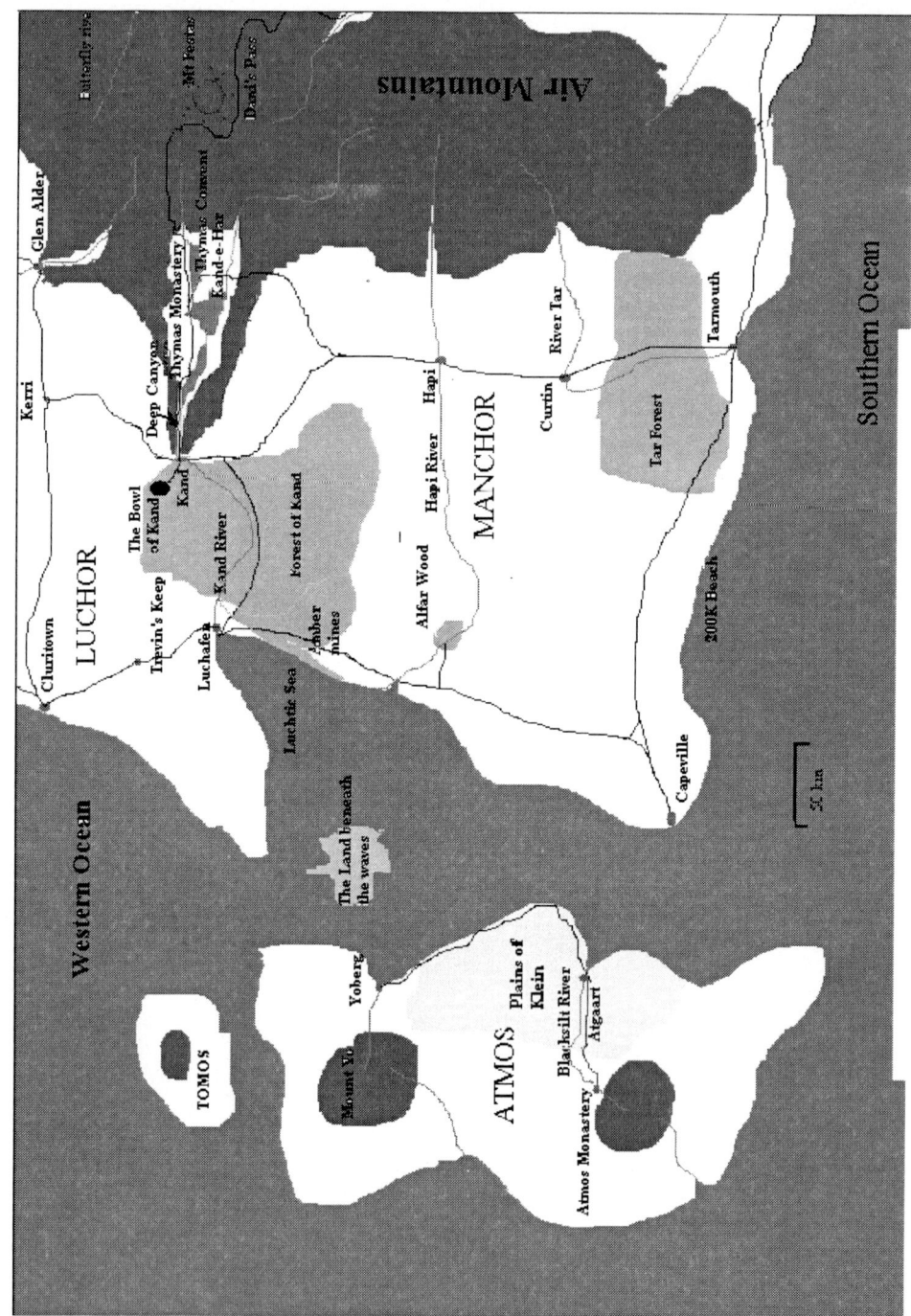

Full colour maps can be viewed on my website www.lesbillgates.com

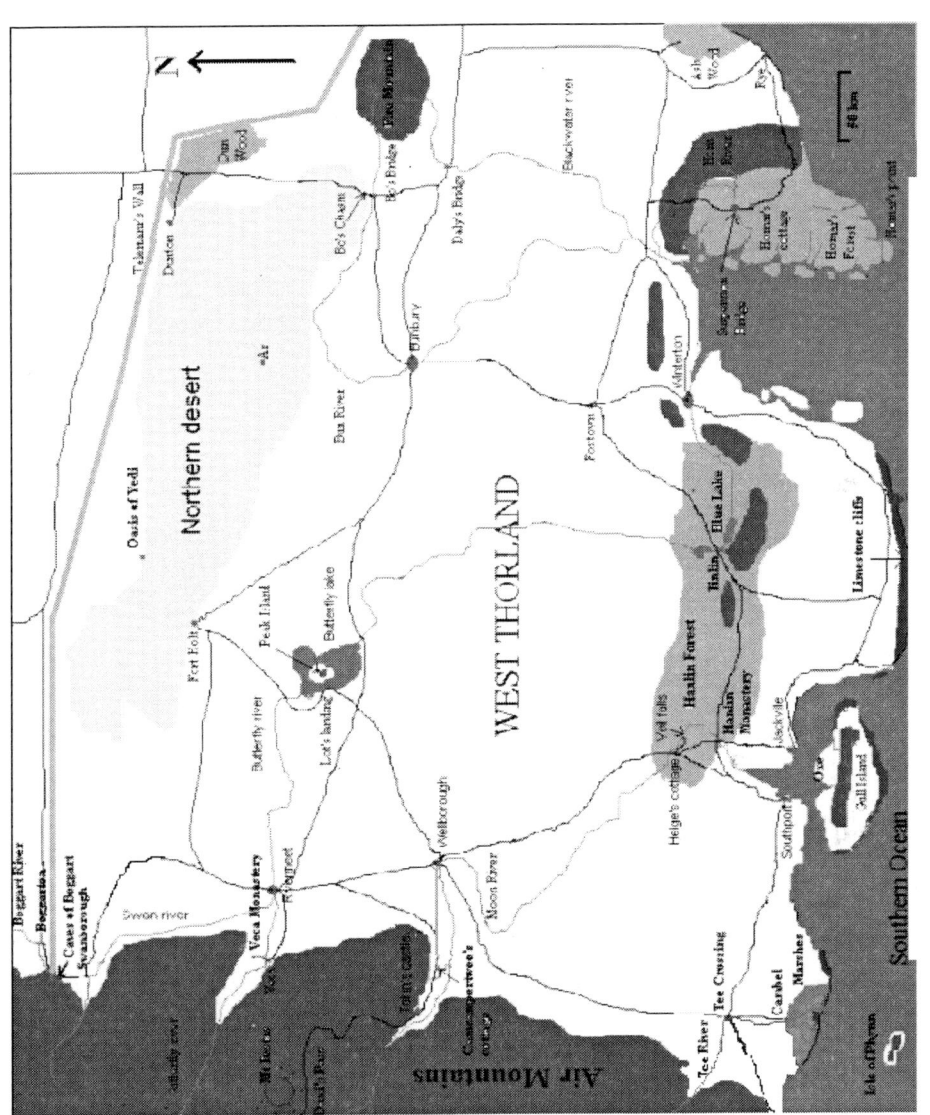

Full colour maps can be viewed on my website www.lesbillgates.com

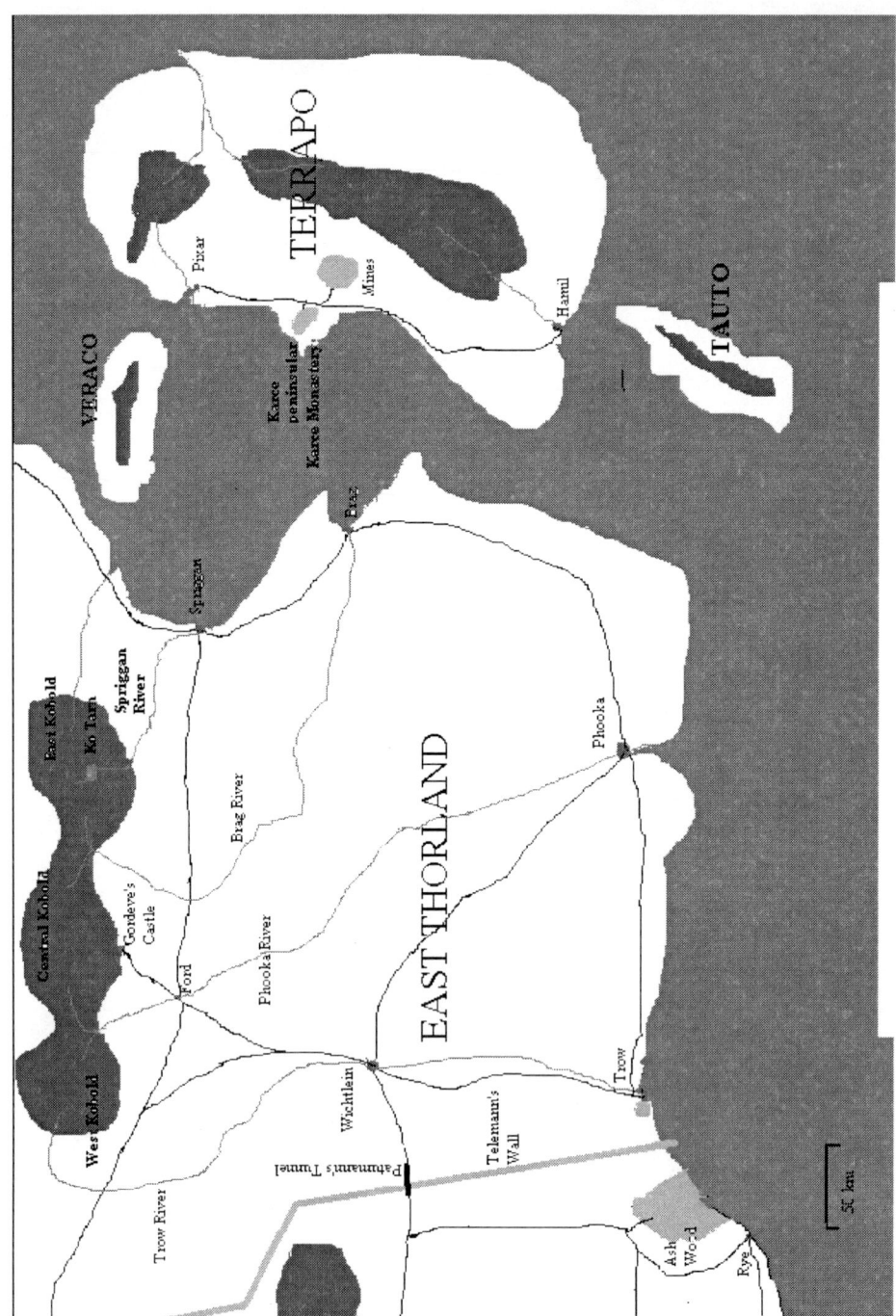

CHAPTER 1

ARRIVAL

He awoke to a morning twilight of eerie noises and bitter cold; from a dream, half-forgotten, of a river in flood, rushing waters, cries for help, a fall and a bang to his head. Yet, it had seemed more than a dream.

When he opened his eyes, flakes of snow drifting down clouded his vision, but he could just make out the silhouettes of tall, pyramid-shaped trees reaching up high above. He noticed a sharp object, maybe a stone or the root of a tree, pressing into the small of his back and he felt very cold. A thick blanket of snow covered the ground and most of his body.

As the man tried to stand up, snow fell from his clothing - clothes that were inadequate for these harsh conditions. At that moment, many thoughts passed through his mind. *Where was he, and how did he come to be there? Why was he only wearing a pair of jeans, a thin cotton jacket over his shirt and canvas shoes on his feet?* He stumbled and fell down again. Terror gripped him. His teeth began to chatter, though whether from cold or from fear he wasn't sure.

Is this the dream, and the other reality? As he lay motionless, he heard a whisper in his mind, "Squire, it's me, Quexitoxeri. Soon the time will come for the fulfilment of the prophecy. The skull shall be made whole once more, and you will rule again in the Land." *Is this the reality, and the other the dream?*

Several minutes had passed since he had awoken. Once again, he tried to stand, but his muscles seized and his bones were chilled to the

HOPE

marrow by the paralysing cold. He grabbed hold of a branch from a small tree nearby. Despite the cold, he sweated profusely from the effort of easing his way into an upright position.

The forest remained in dusky darkness, but he noticed thin shafts of light penetrating the thick canopy of trees to reach him on the forest floor, and knew that twilight was giving way to day. In these murky conditions, the only plants he could see peeping out from under the blanket of snow were some ferns and a few herbaceous plants.

When his eyes had become accustomed to the gloom, he perceived something or somebody observing him. A pair of green, luminescent eyes peered at him from behind a bush not far away sending a chill of fear through his body, but they disappeared as quickly as they had appeared. He rubbed his own eyes and looked once more, but this time saw nothing. *It's an illusion, or another part of this nightmare. I must get away from this place.*

He jumped up and down a few times to dust the snow from his garments and to try to free his limbs from their temporary paralysis. After a while, he managed to force one foot in front of the other and began to walk. He could see coniferous trees stretching endlessly in all directions and he didn't know which way to head.

Southwards the ground seemed to slope downwards a little, so he struck off in that direction. *If I can find a stream, then I can follow it and discover a way out of this forest, and maybe find some people to help me.* The snow was several centimetres thick underfoot which made progress slow, but he was thankful that it had stopped falling.

As he pursued his downwards path towards the anticipated stream, a need for survival took over urging him to put one foot mechanically in front of the other. Whenever he fell down, which happened often, he forced himself to his feet again, and trudged on. He became oblivious to his

ARRIVAL

surroundings. *It's all a dream.* An ear-piercing howl aroused him from his reverie. *Wolves!*

The man began to run as panic took over. He could hear other noises now of the wolves disturbing the undergrowth not far behind him. Pushing himself to the limit to escape from the predators, he felt his heart beating faster. A feeling of dread consumed him when he sensed the bloodthirsty animals snapping at his heels. He fell again. With his last ounce of strength, he forced himself back onto his feet.

He staggered on a few more metres until he stumbled into a small clearing in the trees. He felt more vulnerable than ever. His head darted around, looking for a place to hide. Cowering, he backed towards the nearest big tree, gaping at the leading wolf charging towards him through the undergrowth. He was a tall beast with a long, slender body covered with a sleek, grey coat and with long thin legs. Saliva drooled from his open mouth displaying a vicious set of teeth and a dark pink, lathering tongue.

I'm done for. In desperation, he picked up a stone and threw it at the aggressor. The beast yelped and backed away, but the pain seemed only to infuriate him further. He let out a deep fearsome howl, his ears pricked up and he prepared for the kill. Cringing, the man hid his face in his hands. His snow and ice-encrusted beard felt cold and hard, and gave him no solace. *I'm going to be torn to shreds.*

Amidst the fear and desperation, he heard another sound – the sound of wings beating – and felt the disturbance of the air around him. Deflated into a state of total submission by this latest horror, he peered between his fingers and was bewildered to see a giant eagle swoop down and carry the wolf away in its talons. He could hear the wolf's screams as the bird lifted the beast high into the air. A few moments later, the wolf wailed again when the eagle dropped him, and he fell far below to his death. When the other

HOPE

wolves saw what had befallen their companion, they abandoned their prey and loped away.

The man remained in his cowering position for several minutes until, realising that the first danger had passed, a foreboding of other unknown perils gripped him. Once more, he began to run for his life. Once again, his heart began to pump as he strained every sinew and every muscle to escape the danger. He kept running, downhill, down, down, and down, picking up speed and losing control. Without warning, he tripped on a sharp rock. However, his body did not strike hard ground or even the softness of new-fallen snow. Instead, he found himself falling through the air down into an abyss.

Am I going to die just like the wolf? His descent into the unknown depths lasted only a few seconds, but it seemed like several minutes. Images of darkness, silhouettes of trees, snow, and slathering wolves snapping at his heels passed through his mind. *Where am I? What's happening to me? It's all a delusion.* More images of a raging river, a screaming child, and a tree root. Whispers of a prophecy, a skull. He expected at any moment to wake up from this nightmare. He was free-falling now and anticipated that his body would soon smash into the rocks below.

Once again, his fortune changed as someone or something grabbed his clothing from above and arrested his downward plummet. Now he flew like a bird. At the same moment, he lost consciousness.

*   *   *   *   *

When he awoke, he lay in a warm bed.

He looked around and saw by the light of a candle that he was in a small room and alone. He didn't know how many hours had passed, but through a small curtainless window, he could see that there was darkness outside. He tried to call out, "Is there anyone there?" but no sound came from

ARRIVAL

his vocal cords. *I've lost my voice ... or lost my mind.* He tried again, with greater effort, and discovered that he could make a hoarse whispering sound. *It's no use. No one can hear me, even if there is someone there.*

He noticed that he wore strange dry clothes. He lay on a wooden bed, a little hard perhaps, but comfortable and warm, and several blankets covered his body. On a table beside the bed, he discovered a cup of water and some bread. *So there is somebody here.* After he had quenched his thirst, he stuffed the bread into his mouth, and washed it down with some more water. His hunger was not sated, but he felt more contented and soon drifted off into sleep once more.

When morning came and he awoke for a second time, his heart leapt as he heard the rattling of the door latch. He sat bolt upright and inched his body back towards the wall. *Wolves!* A strange woman came into the room. *Of course, it can't be wolves. I'm inside a house.* The woman smiled and he relaxed.

She was slim and, for a woman, very tall. He estimated that she must have been in her early thirties. He didn't think she was beautiful, but her striking features - thin face, sharp nose, thick eyebrows that nearly met above her deep brown eyes, and long black straight hair, parted in the middle – gave her an air of elegance. The woman wore a simple light-brown cloak with a rope tied around her waist.

"My name is Helge." The man relaxed at the sound of her soothing voice. "I'm so glad to see you're alive. When you were brought here, you were cold and delirious, and close to death. I gave you some dry clothes, put you in this warm bed, and gave you a potion of healing herbs. I've watched over you for two days and nights."

With a hoarse whisper, he asked, "Where am I? And who am I? Can you tell me, please?"

HOPE

"We call this place 'Thorland' and your name is 'The Squire', as foretold in the ancient prophecy."

"What prophecy? I have no memory of these things. How do I come to be called 'The Squire'?"

"The ancient legends of our people foretold your return to Thorland in the following verse:

In times to come when things are dire
A Saviour will come again to Thorland,
His name: 'The Squire'.
From eagle's talons he will fall,
And by his hand -
With the help of woman tall,
Twins, archer, three others and a mule -
He will reunite golden teeth with golden skull
Seeking them out in parts of the land
Yet to be revealed.
And when this is done, all will be healed.

"We believe that the time has now arrived for this prophecy to be fulfilled and that you, Squire, are the key to its fulfilment. We didn't know quite when to expect you, but the signs were that it should happen soon. There is much trouble and forces of evil are at work throughout Thorland. Spies of Gordeve are said to inhabit every town and village."

His brow furrowed. "Who is Gordeve?" he asked.

"She is the wicked wizard and sister to the good wizard Tobin"

Squire slumped back onto his pillow. It was difficult to comprehend anything Helge had told him. *Good wizards, bad wizards, female wizards?*

ARRIVAL

"Is this a dream?" he asked. "I know … you're not really here. There is no forest, no wolves, no giant eagle, no … you. Soon I will wake up and know that it's all been a hallucination."

She gave him a sympathetic smile. "You're not dreaming," she replied. "Dreams always come to an end. This will not end until the prophecy is fulfilled."

"Why me?" he asked. "I don't have any special powers. You say the ancient legends foretold that I should 'return'. I have no memory of ever coming here before. I'm not from this place … Thorland." He lay silently thinking for a few moments. *Prophecy, skull … Quexitoxeri.* "Who is Quexitoxeri," he asked.

A look of shock came over Helge's face. "What do you know of Quexitoxeri?" she asked.

"When I first arrived in this land, I heard a woman's voice. She addressed me as 'Squire' and talked of the prophecy. But I thought that also was just part of the dream."

"Quexitoxeri is the living prophet of the Creator, and the first Quexitoxeri, Sohan, was the daughter of The Squire," she replied.

"What do you mean, 'the first Quexitoxeri'?" he asked. "I don't understand."

"There have been many called by that name," she replied. "The one who spoke with you waits in Kand-e-Har on the far side of the Air Mountains."

"Waits for whom?"

"She is waiting for you, and she is also waiting for the skull."

Seeing the perplexed look on his face, she gave him a small, empathetic smile. "I understand you are confused and you don't think you belong here, but we believe that you are The Squire who lived once before in

HOPE

Thorland, and now you have returned to us. The ancient stories tell that The Squire had a small scar above his top lip on the left side. Do you have such a scar?"

Squire hesitated before replying. Why hadn't she looked for this already? Then he felt the thick growth of hair both on his chin and above his top lip. His face had remained unshaven for several days.

"Please fetch me water and a razor. I need to shave."

Helge returned after a short time with a bowl of warm water, some soap and a razor.

"I'll leave you to shave and go to prepare you some hot food," she said.

After he had finished shaving, he stood in front of a full-length mirror and examined the unfamiliar features. A pair of blue eyes stared back at him. *Is this me?* The scar over his top lip glistened in the sunlight. Despite this, his face looked round and handsome. His hair was sandy coloured, quite short and almost balding in the middle. He must have lost some weight over the last few days, but he appeared muscular and he stood erect. *I must be in my mid-thirties.* He noticed that he wore a similar cloak to Helge's, but the one she had given him was coloured grey.

Then he saw the woman standing behind him. He hadn't heard her come back into the room. Although he was not short, he noticed that she was much taller than he was.

"You were right about the scar," he conceded, "and how could you have known this unless what you say is true?"

"We are witnessing the beginning of the fulfilment of the prophecy."

"If this is a dream," he said, "then I will eventually wake up. On the other hand, if this is real, then it is my destiny to do as you ask and help save the Land."

ARRIVAL

*   *   *   *   *

Squire remained at Helge's cottage for several weeks until he had regained his strength. By that time, the snow had disappeared and signs of spring were apparent as the days grew longer, flowers began to bloom and migratory birds returned to the forest. He enjoyed the rest, but remained perplexed about the past he could not recall and apprehensive of the uncertain future than he faced.

The cottage was a simple timber structure, built in a clearing in the forest and surrounded by a strong wooden fence to keep out the wolves and other predators. Within this compound Helge had planted potatoes, beans and other vegetables. For meat, she relied on her hunting skills and in particular her prowess with the sling that she always carried with her.

Every morning he walked around the perimeter of the compound to get some exercise. Helge constantly reminded her guest about the dangers in the forest and cautioned him not to stray outside the protective fence.

Despite these warnings, there came a day when he could no longer contain his curiosity to find out more about this new world. On the lower branches of a pine just outside the gate, he spotted a splendid parrot with red and green plumage. To get a closer look, he opened the compound gate and crept towards the bird. He had almost reached the tree when the parrot flapped its wings, launched itself into the air, and flew to the branches of another tree further along the trail that led eastwards into the forest.

He pursued the parrot, intending to walk for just a few minutes, but the bird eluded him. However, it was a beautiful, sunny day and soon he had forgotten about the parrot and Helge's words of caution. Having lost all sense of sound judgement, he decided to go on a little further. After he had walked for about an hour and a half, he heard a distant rumbling sound that attracted his curiosity. As he proceeded further, the noise grew louder and he recognised the sound of rushing water.

He had walked for nearly two hours when the trees began to thin out, and the path he had followed came to the top of a small grassy knoll. He stopped in awe when, to the left of his vantage point, he saw cascading down the rocks an enormous waterfall that he estimated must have dropped 120 metres from top to bottom. *What a beautiful view.* He later learned that he had stumbled on the Veil Falls in the lower reaches of the Moon River.

Squire sat down on a small rock to rest. He filled his lungs with the fresh, moist air and felt invigorated.

Above the falls and to the right, a rainbow of myriad colours refracted the sun's light. At the bottom, a foam of cascading water obscured the rock face behind. Opposite to his vantage point, he could see a ledge that overhung precipitously above the swirling waters. As the river continued its journey towards the sea, torrents of water rushed between rocks of all shapes and sizes. Further downstream from these rapids, where the waters appeared calmer, he could see trout playing near the surface. Even further away, he saw what appeared to be a wild boar wallowing in the mud.

Squire sat enjoying these scenes for some minutes before he became aware again of a pair of luminous green eyes observing him from behind a nearby rock.

He trembled as he called out, "Who's there?"

Once again, the eyes disappeared, and he never saw them again that day.

In view of this unpleasant experience and the lateness of the hour, he decided that the time had come for him to retrace his steps to Helge's cottage. By now, he had been away for almost three hours, and he knew she

ARRIVAL

would be worried about him. He set off with mixed emotions of contentment and nervousness.

He had covered about half the distance when he heard again the sickening sound of howling wolves. Since they seemed far away, he didn't panic like the first time. Nevertheless, he began to quicken his pace. However, when he heard a disturbance in the vegetation a short distance away to his right, he sensed they were coming closer. He glanced over his shoulder, anticipating an attack from behind, but the trail appeared empty. As he turned a corner, he half expected to see a wolf on the path in front of him, baring its teeth and snarling. There was nothing there.

He was about to sigh with relief when he heard a loud grunting sound and a wild boar came crashing through the undergrowth, its tusks down as it charged towards him. It had a dark grey coat with a ridge of hair along its spine and a large head with a long, narrow snout.

Memories of that dreadful morning several weeks earlier came flooding back to him. Once again, fear consumed him and he stood petrified. *Those tusks are short and sharp like a dagger. They look like they could pass straight through my belly and out of my back.* He shut his eyes and waited. After a few seconds, he heard a thud, the animal bellowed, and then silence followed. He opened his eyes a slit and saw the animal collapsed motionless in a heap on the path. The next moment Helge appeared from her hiding place in the nearby trees. In her right hand, she held her sling, fresh from doing its deadly work.

Squire relaxed. "Am I glad to see you," he said.

"I've been following you all day," she confessed. "I was worried that you may have fallen prey to some danger. I hope that you now realise that there are many perils, not only in this forest, but also throughout this land. I beg you to never wander off on your own again." After a pause she

HOPE

continued, "Opposite the place where you sat watching the waterfall, there's a ledge. It's the same ledge you fell from after your encounter with the wolves on that first morning. That's where the eagle caught you in its talons as you fell, and brought you to me."

"I don't remember much about that first morning," he said, "but I was reminded of one unpleasant incident this afternoon. While I sat near the waterfall, I noticed a pair of green luminous eyes staring at me. I only saw them for a moment, but now I remember seeing them before on the first morning when I was very confused and frightened. It might have been an illusion, but now I'm sure it was real."

"The cougar!" she hissed. "This is very disturbing news. Gordeve's hand is already stretching out and working its evil in my forest. We can wait no longer. It's time for us to leave."

"Where will we go first?" he enquired.

"First we must travel north to Wellborough," she replied. "Then we will turn east and journey to Tobin's castle. There we will be introduced to the golden skull, and receive the instructions for our quest."

One week later, after they had packed provisions and made all necessary preparations for their journey, the two companions set forth on their quest. On a bright spring morning Helge locked up her cottage, secured the gate to the compound, and they set off on the road towards the north and to unknown and unexpected adventures ahead.

CHAPTER 2

JOURNEY TO TOBIN'S CASTLE

On a pleasant spring morning, Vineon D'Ur decided it would be a fine day for some archery practice. The sky appeared azure blue, and only a few cirrus clouds dotted the horizon. Vinny, an expert with the longbow, frequently walked to the practice range on the banks of the Moon River situated just outside the town of Wellborough.

Vinny was a portly man, of average height and his round, freckled face was topped with a thick growth of ginger hair. He usually chose to wear a green shirt and slacks, which offered him some disguise when shooting from the cover of foliage. He always carried his longbow with him and kept a quiver full of arrows, slung over his shoulder at his back.

On his way to the shooting range, he called on his three friends Reddy, Xoe and Jillijon.

"Care for a round?" he invited, laughing.

"Sure thing," said Jillijon, reaching for his bow, "though I suppose you'll win as usual, and take great delight in doing so." The promptness with which the other two followed him up the road, showed that he spoke for all of them. A few minutes later, they arrived at the practice range.

"First, we will all shoot at that target." Vinny pointed to a target attached to an ancient oak at a distance of about thirty metres. "Whoever gets nearest the centre will shoot first."

HOPE

Vinny heard the 'ping' sound of Jillijon's arrow as it was propelled towards the target, closely followed by those of Reddy and Xoe. Soon afterwards, he fired his own arrow.

"Vinny. You start, as usual," said Xoe with a wry grin.

"That might give me some advantage," Vinny replied, "but, even if one of you went first and shot a bull, I could split your arrow down the middle with mine." He laughed. "Now for number one," he said.

He moved to a marked shooting post nearby and fired at the first target at a distance of fifty metres. When all of them had fired, they walked to the target to check on their scores.

"Red, eight points," Xoe said with satisfaction.

"Yellow, ten points," said Vinny with a smirk on his face.

They continued to move together around the marked course that consisted of twenty targets altogether of different types, ranges and difficulty.

After the contest, the four companions sat by the roadside under the shade of some beech trees drinking ale and sharing a few jokes. As they did so, they saw two figures approaching on the road from the south. When the travellers were about two hundred metres away, Vinny could distinguish that one was a man dressed in a grey cloak and the other a very tall woman dressed in a light-brown cloak.

"Good morning to you," said Vinny when the two strangers drew level. "Where are you heading?"

"Good morning, sir," the tall woman replied. "My name is Helge and my companion here is Squire. We have come from my home in Hanlin Forest. We're on our way to Tobin's castle where we will begin a quest on behalf of the wizard. We've been walking for three days and have slept by the roadside, so we're hoping to find an inn in Wellborough."

"Vineon D'Ur at your service, ma'am, but please call me Vinny," he said. "I know just the place for you to stay. The proprietor of the Cat and Fiddle inn will put you up for the night and provide you with a good hot meal at a very reasonable price."

"Who won the competition?" she asked.

"He won, as usual," Xoe said, pointing at Vinny.

"By more than fifty points," Jillijon added. "He is well-known as the finest bowman in Wellborough and all around this district."

"Can you give us a demonstration, my friend?" asked Helge.

"Lady, I shoot to kill, and practise to hone my skills. I don't put on shows for strangers. However ..." He paused as a flock of geese flew overhead. "Since I am hungry, I will make an exception for you."

In quick succession, Vinny snatched up his bow, plucked an arrow from the quiver at his back, took aim, fired, and the first goose fell to the ground. Another followed a second later, then another. Soon no fewer than seven geese lay on the ground, each one shot cleanly through the neck.

"That's a fine piece of shooting, my friend," said Helge. "May I look at your bow?" Vinny handed it to her. "How do you make such a fine bow?" she asked, inspecting the weapon. "And the arrows," she added.

"It's not a simple process," he replied, "but I'll give you a short answer. I use the stripped wood of a yew sapling, which I oil with rendered deer fat. To form a tension with which to propel the arrows, I link the two ends with a cord made from the leg sinew of deer. For a grip, I use a strip of leather. The arrows are made from straight pieces of cedar, with a sharp point on one end and turkey feathers attached to the other."

Helge and Squire prepared to leave.

"Will you please do me the honour of dining with us at the Cat and Fiddle this evening?"

HOPE

Before Vinny could answer, she continued, "We'll see you there after sundown. Good day to you, sir."

Helge and Squire continued their journey towards the town centre.

*   *   *   *   *

"There it is," said Squire pointing to a sign swaying gently in the breeze. "See the sign swinging above the front door of that old wooden building with the brick chimney? That's the Cat and Fiddle."

As they passed inside, the innkeeper, who had been washing some glasses, paused to greet them. He wiped his hands on his apron and gave them a toothy smile. "Good morning strangers," he said. "I am Mr. Thom, the proprietor. How can I help you?"

"We're looking for two single rooms," replied Helge.

"You're lucky. I've got just two rooms left. They're next to each other at the back above the kitchen. Please follow me, I'll show you."

After a few minutes, they returned to the common room where they enjoyed some soup, bread and ale for their lunch. Squire looked around and noted that it was a small room with low wooden beams and a brick open fireplace, although no fire burnt on that fine spring day. It had tables enough for about a dozen patrons, but on this occasion, the rest of the tables remained unoccupied. When Squire had finished his lunch, he told Helge, "I'm going to my room for a rest. I'll see you at supper time."

Shortly before seven, Squire was disturbed by a knock on his door.

"It's supper time," Helge said.

They descended together to the common room where they found Vinny already waiting. Squire noticed that a roaring log fire now burnt in the fireplace, and the bar seemed warm and cosy.

"So, you came?" said Helge.

JOURNEY TO TOBIN'S CASTLE

"Your request was so commanding, how could I refuse?" replied the archer. "Besides, my curiosity has been aroused. I want to find out more about your quest."

Mr. Thom served them with a roast chicken, potatoes, vegetables and gravy. They spoke little during the meal. When they had finished, Helge wiped her mouth with a napkin and began telling her story. She kept her voice low.

"I'll come straight to the point, Mr. D'Ur … Vinny. The Squire and I are embarking on a very dangerous mission. When we reach Tobin's castle, our journey will have only just begun. After receiving our instructions from Tobin, we will be travelling to all parts of Thorland in search of the golden teeth that belong to the golden skull. We will meet many dangers on our journey and, although I have some skill with the sling, we will need further protection. The ancient prophecy speaks of an 'archer' joining us on the quest. I have witnessed your skill with the longbow today, and believe that you are the one. Will you come with us, Vinny?"

During the short time they had travelled together Squire had learned to let Helge take the lead, but for the first time during the course of the meal he spoke out. "I've only been in Thorland for a few weeks," he said, "but I've already witnessed many dangers. I nearly froze to death, wolves attacked me, I fell from a ledge but miraculously a giant eagle saved me, a wild boar nearly gored me, and twice I've seen the cougar."

"The cougar! I thought it was only part of legend."

Squire continued, "I'm not from Thorland but the things I've seen in the last few weeks have convinced me there is an evil in this land, and it seems I must play some part in the destruction of that evil. I don't understand any of these things, but know that we must do something to fulfil the ancient

HOPE

prophecies and to save Thorland. Vinny, we need you to accompany us. Will you help us?"

"I'm very concerned about the things you have told me, but I need some time to consider before I will agree to accompany you on this quest. I will give you my answer tomorrow morning."

The two guests retired early.

*   *   *   *   *

At the end of the evening, when the last of the patrons had left the inn, Mr. Thom prepared to lock up. He secured the front door of the inn then, carrying his candle, went to check the bolts on the back door in the kitchen.

He stood at the kitchen window and studied his reflection in the flickering light. As he smoothed his few wisps of hair, he noticed a pair of green eyes staring at him from outside. He looked more closely and saw that the eyes were not human, but belonged to the grinning face of a cat. He sensed the grin was not one of mirth, but one imbued with evil, and a chill of fear swept through him. Startled, he dropped the candle. When it hit the floor, the candle did not splutter and die, but bounced and landed on a dry sack that the innkeeper had emptied of onions earlier in the day. Within seconds, the sack was in flames and the fire soon spread to other sacks of vegetables close by. He rushed for water from the tap, but he was too slow. As quickly as he tried to extinguish the flames, more spread to other parts of the kitchen.

He began to choke as the thick, black smoke entered his lungs. Realising that he had no hope of putting out the fire, he dashed to the back door. Choking with the smoke and hampered by the overbearing heat, he struggled for several seconds before he succeeded in freeing the bolts. He rushed outside and gasped in the cool, fresh air.

JOURNEY TO TOBIN'S CASTLE

For some time he lay still on the ground before gathering his wits about him. Once he had regained his composure, he ran to the house of Mr. Pacey next door to raise the alarm. Mr. Thom hammered on the door and shouted for several seconds before the neighbour responded.

"Hang on, I'm coming," said a voice from inside the house. A man, carrying his own candle and wearing a nightshirt opened the door.

"Pacey," said Mr Thom, breathing heavily and pointing towards the fire.

Mr. Thom didn't need to explain. Pacey had already seen the bright flames lighting up the dark sky, heard the crackling timbers and smelt the sooty smoke.

"Erol," Pacey called out to his son. "Go and fetch help. Thom, you go inside and rest. I'll see to this."

"No! My inn ... I must help."

Erol appeared. "Go get the fire carriage, quickly," Pacey yelled.

Pacey got a ladder from his storeroom and pushed past Mr Thom who followed him out of the door. By the time Pacey had reached the inn with the ladder, the whole of the back of the building was engulfed in flames.

Thom tugged on Pacey's coat and pointed up to the first floor. "Quickly, there are guests in those two rooms."

Then they heard a shout. Thom looked up and saw a woman waving what appeared to be a white towel from an open bedroom window.

"Wait, I'm coming to get you," shouted Pacey, as he raised the ladder into position beneath the window ledge. With flames licking parts of the window frame, the woman threw her legs over the ledge onto the top rung of the ladder and scrambled down to safety. In her left hand, she clutched a small bag containing a few belongings and her money.

HOPE

"Quickly," said Helge. "There's a man in that room next to mine. We must save him. He's a very important man." The window of Squire's room remained shut. "He must have been overcome by the smoke and is probably lying unconscious on his bed. We have to save him."

Thom watched Pacey move the ladder to the adjacent window. The next moment he heard the sounds of approaching hooves and the furious ring of a bell, followed by a shout from Erol. Two fire fighters sat on top of the horse-drawn fire carriage. Behind them sat the boy, and a man with a crop of ginger hair.

"Quick, Vinny," urged Helge. "Squire is trapped in that room there, the one with the closed window. Can you help him?"

Without hesitation, Vinny drew an arrow from his quiver, took aim with his longbow and fired at the window. When the glass shattered, thick smoke spewed out from the hole. Within seconds, the fire fighters had erected the ladder and one of them scuttled up to the window. He hesitated only to remove the rest of the glass from the window frame before entering the room. The other fire fighter followed him up the ladder and prepared to accept the burden of the unconscious Squire onto his back.

Hastily, but with the care of a trained expert, the fire fighter carried the man down and then to a safe distance from the fire and laid him on his back on the ground. Thom rushed to Squire's side, his face pallid and drawn. He watched intently as the fire fighter administered the kiss of life. It took thirty seconds or more, but Squire was strong and soon he began to splutter. When he took his first gasps of breath, Thom knew he was alive.

Meanwhile Helge had arrived. "I'll look after him now," she said.

When the fire fighter jumped to his feet and prepared to move away, Thom grabbed hold of his sleeve and tugged. "The front of the building," he wheezed, "– there are other guests."

JOURNEY TO TOBIN'S CASTLE

He followed the two fire fighters around to the front of the inn and watched them smash down the door. He could see thick smoke had already filled the stairwell, but as yet it appeared free of flames and scorching heat. The fire fighters bounded up the stairs. Moments later, they reappeared, each carrying an unconscious guest. No sooner had they run out through the door onto the street than the partition walls collapsed and the flames spread throughout the building.

The fire fighters did their best to extinguish the flames, but it was a hopeless task. The wooden building burned furiously, and the water supplies were scarce. After a few minutes, they conceded that the building couldn't be saved and left it to burn. Mr. Thom wept as he witnessed the destruction of his fine old building.

Mr. Thom, Squire and Helge spent the rest of the night with the kind neighbour, Pacey.

* * * * *

The following morning, Vinny rose early and went to inspect the damaged inn. Where the front door had stood, lying on the ground intact amidst the ashes, the sign of the Cat and Fiddle looked up at him. He gasped when he saw the eyes of the cat in the picture had turned green and appeared to stare at him with an evil intent. Mesmerised, he found he couldn't turn his eyes away from the face of the cat. The next moment he fell to the ground and lost consciousness.

Then he had the sensation that he was rising into the air, yet his body remained on the ground. It seemed as if his soul had been set free from his flesh, and he found himself looking down at his own body from above. He began to rise higher into the air and soon he hovered high above the ruins of the burned-out inn. He began to fly forwards, slowly at first, then more and more quickly, but he had no control over his movements.

HOPE

While he raced towards the rising sun, he looked down. Below he could see fertile land – fields and meadows with farms, an occasional clump of trees, and scattered villages. After a while, he saw a large lake with a river entering from the north and exiting towards the south. A few minutes later, he flew over a vast desert. Soon afterwards, he saw what appeared to be a long winding road stretching far into the distance to both north and south. Far to the south, smoke spewed from the crater of a volcanic cone. From its slopes, another river flowed southwards towards the great Southern Ocean.

Now the land over which he flew looked barren, and he could see few villages or farms. As he travelled further to the north-east, he could see ahead of him three other high volcanic peaks bunched close together. He turned towards the middle of the three peaks, and his speed began to decrease. He started to lose height once again. Then, on the lower slopes of the mountain, he saw a castle with a moat and high stone walls. He felt himself coming in to land like a bird, and the next moment he lay on the cool grass inside the castle's courtyard – or rather, he had the sensation of lying on the grass. His real body remained several hundred kilometres away in Wellborough.

Near at hand, he observed a woman wearing a black cloak and a black pointed hat. In her left hand, she carried a black staff, carved from ebony. Her lips moved as if she wanted to communicate with him, but at first he could sense nothing except her piercing eyes boring into him. She wore nothing on her feet.

As he concentrated his attention on the thin lips, he became mesmerised by her pale complexion and a long pointed nose. Then he distinguished a muffled voice saying, "I am Gordeve, sister to the wizard Tobin. I have summoned you here so that you can carry a message to him." As she bobbed her head, he noted her hair was grey and reached partway down her back. A golden skull engraved on her hat reflected the morning sunlight.

"I have never met Tobin. How will I find him, and what is the message I must deliver?" asked Vinny.

"My brother controls the central and western parts of Thorland, those parts to the south and west of Telemann's Wall. The eastern parts are mine. Do not be concerned about how to find him. The woman Helge will lead you to him. As for the message, tell him that the ancient prophecy is incomplete. There is another line to the prophecy, which reads:

> *In times to come when things are dire*
> *A Saviour will come again to Thorland,*
> *His name: 'The Squire'.*
> *From eagle's talons he will fall,*
> *And by his hand -*
> *With the help of woman tall,*
> *Twins, archer, three others and a mule -*
> *He will reunite golden teeth with golden skull*
> *Seeking them out in parts of the land*
> *Yet to be revealed.*
> *And when this is done, all will be healed.*
> *Gordeve will rule.*

"Now go, Vineon D'Ur and deliver the message," she commanded. "I, Gordeve will rule!" She cackled.

Almost at once Vinny felt his soul rising once again from the ground and he was soon on the return journey to Wellborough, following the same route as his outward journey. When he came in to land, his soul re-entered his body and he woke to find himself lying on the ground outside the burned-out inn. No one had witnessed these events, and he had no idea how much time had passed. However, the position of the sun in the sky indicated that no time had passed at all.

Vinny seized the inn sign and hurled it into the still-smouldering timbers that had once been the beams of the common room. The sign burst into flames and Vinny heard an unnatural scream emanate from it. This assured him that the encounter with Gordeve had really happened and was the sign he had been looking for. He now knew that he was destined to accompany Helge and Squire on their quest.

* * * * *

Later that morning, Helge and Squire resumed their journey to Tobin's castle, now accompanied by Vinny. They bade their farewells to Mr. Thom and Pacey. Helge insisted on paying the innkeeper for their night's accommodation – a small compensation for the loss of his inn. Reddy, Xoe and Jillijon also came to see them off and bade their friend an emotional farewell. Vinny carried his longbow and, as always, a quiver of arrows hung at his back. "Don't worry," he told them. "I'll soon be back for another round of field archery and give you three another pasting."

After they had travelled for half a day, they saw a man with a mule approaching from the opposite direction. He was an old man with long grey hair, a grey beard, a stooped back and hunched shoulders. His clothes were tatty and well-worn, with patches on both elbows and on one of the knees, and he wore no shoes. Squire thought he must be poor as well as advanced in years. The mule, however, was probably only a year or two old and looked strong and healthy. His grey coat was glossy and well-groomed.

"Good afternoon," Vinny greeted the old man. "Where are you heading?"

JOURNEY TO TOBIN'S CASTLE

"Good afternoon to you," replied the old man. "I'm on my way to the market at Wellborough to sell my mule. I must sell him in order to get money to buy provisions. I have come upon hard times and this mule is all I have left."

"How much do you expect to get for him?" asked Helge.

He shrugged his shoulders "Maybe fifty shillings."

Helge felt compassion for the old man's plight. "We'll give you sixty shillings for the mule," she said.

The old man looked into her eyes and smiled. "Thank you, lady," he said.

"Does the mule have a name?" asked Squire.

"Yes, sir. I call him Faithful because that's what he has been to me."

The old man gave the mule a hug, and sobbed. "Goodbye Faithful," he said. "Thank you," he repeated as he accepted the money Helge offered him, and continued on his journey to Wellborough.

"The mule will prove invaluable to the success of our quest," said Helge as she watched the old man disappear. "He will carry our burdens across the most inhospitable terrain and into the most hazardous of places."

The walk to Tobin's castle took another two days and nights. The journey was uneventful except that it rained throughout the second day. Their progress became slow as they battled against the driving rain, and the dirt road turned to mud that sometimes reached up to their ankles.

At the end of the third day after leaving Wellborough, just after the sun had set, Squire saw before them the lights of a large building sitting high on a hill. In the valley to their left, he could just make out the outline of a narrow but swift-flowing river.

"What's the name of the river?" he asked.

HOPE

"It's the Moon River, the same one that flows through Wellborough," answered Vinny. He pointed towards the east. "There are the Air Mountains," he said. "The source of the river is high up in the ranges."

Though the sun had already disappeared over the nearest ridge, Squire could just make out the contours of the distant mountains. "Moon River is a very appropriate name," he observed, "since the full moon is now rising."

"There, on the hill, is Tobin's castle," said Helge. "We are almost there."

By the light of the moon, the travellers found their way up the winding path to the front entrance of the castle. As they approached, the gate swung open and the drawbridge was let down for them to pass over the moat and into the courtyard of the castle.

"We must be expected," Vinny surmised.

"Tobin has followed the progress of our journey and knew the time of our arrival," Helge replied. "Don't forget he's a wizard and has the power to see things that we cannot."

From the gloom a voice boomed out, "Greetings, Helge of Hanlin Forest. Greetings, Vineon D'Ur of Wellborough. Greetings, The Squire from another Land. I am Tobin. Welcome to my castle. Helge, it's a pleasure to meet you once again, and I am very pleased to make the acquaintance of your two companions. They have a vital part to play in the months ahead, freeing Thorland from evil and ensuring a future for humankind. Come now, I will show you to your rooms. You must be weary. We will talk tomorrow."

CHAPTER 3

BUTTERFLY AND SWAN

The next morning, all the companions slept late. Helge woke first, shortly before noon. She knocked on the door of the room shared by Squire and Vinny.

"Wake up you sleepyheads," she said. "Have a wash and meet me in the dining room for lunch."

An hour later, they met in the dining room where Tobin's servant, Digbee, served them lunch. Digbee was about sixty years of age, small in stature and very thin. His clean-shaven, wrinkled face had a gaunt look, and his ears stuck out.

After lunch he informed them, "My master wishes to meet with all of you in his study. Please follow me." He spoke with a low, deliberate, solemn voice. He led them through a series of courtyards and along narrow stone passages until they reached the foot of a stone spiral staircase.

"Two hundred. Are we nearly there?" asked Vinny. "I'm fair out of breath."

"Just a few more steps," Digbee replied.

"Two hundred and thirty six," panted Vinny as he climbed the last step and saw Digbee pause at a heavy timber door.

Digbee knocked. When a booming voice bade them, "Enter", he turned the huge brass knob and opened the door into the study.

"Thank you, Digbee," said the wizard. "That will be all." Digbee closed the door and they heard his footsteps descending the stairs. Tobin turned towards his guests. "Digbee has been my loyal servant for more than forty years," he said.

A large wooden desk dominated the wizard's study. Behind the desk, a wooden cabinet stood against the wall. To the right of the cabinet, light streamed in through a large bay window facing east and overlooking the courtyard below. Another smaller window faced towards the south.

Vinny had been unable to see the wizard clearly in the darkness the night before. When Tobin turned and the sunlight caught his face, Vinny recognised the wizard's close resemblance to his sister, Gordeve.

He was of a similar height, with the same thin face, pale complexion and long pointed nose. However, his attire differed from that of his sister. He wore a white cloak, and the white pointed hat on his head bore five silver stars arranged in the shape of a cross.

The wizard noticed the startled look on Vinny's face. "You look at me as if you recognise me, Vineon D'Ur. Yet we have never met before last night." Tobin's pointed, grey beard wagged when he spoke, and his eyes seemed to pierce deeply into Vinny's soul, as Gordeve's had done. Yet the wizard's kindly smile gave some comfort to the archer.

After a pause, Tobin continued, "Or have you met my sister? Surely that cannot be. I surmise you have a story to tell. Please sit down, all of you." He indicated four vacant seats arranged in front of a blazing log fire.

"Now, tell me your story, Vineon D'Ur," the wizard invited. The old man sat in silence as the tale unfolded, nodding from time to time, but not interrupting. The reactions of Helge and Squire, however, were less muted. Their occasional intake of breath, interspersed with frequent mumblings of "Wow!" and "Gosh!" showed their disbelief that anything so strange could have happened to their friend.

BUTTERFLY AND SWAN

When Vinny came to the part about the extra line to the prophecy, *'Gordeve will rule'*, the wizard could no longer contain his annoyance. "Stuff and nonsense!" he said, hitting the arm of the chair with his clenched fist. "The prophecy is incomplete, everyone knows that, but Gordeve has made up this last line to try to frighten us. However, what worries me more is the kind of magic she has used. She has mastered the magic needed to summon a person's soul. The use of a 'spell of summoning' is indeed a dangerous development."

"Why is the prophecy incomplete, and how will we know the real last line?" asked Squire.

"The words of the prophecy are those of Sohan, daughter of The Squire. Sohan was the first Quexitoxeri. She wrote the words on a papyrus, which she passed to the wizard Festas, my great-grandfather, for safekeeping. The papyrus remained sealed and forgotten for many decades, until my father, Gordin, discovered it by chance in this very room."

"The discovery proved to be both fortunate and unfortunate," he said. "One day Gordin noticed a file of termites disappearing through a crack in the floorboards." Tobin pointed to one corner of the room. "When he lifted the floorboards, he found the papyrus, partly eaten by the termites. Fortunately, the termite nest was new and most of the words of the prophecy were preserved, but the termites had consumed the last line. The words of that last line remain a mystery, but you can be sure they were not *'Gordeve will rule'*.

"Now, to business. I have four things to show you." The old man rose from his seat, using his white staff made from yew to assist him. He shuffled to the cabinet behind his desk. He reached inside and removed the first item.

HOPE

Squire noticed that the wizard struggled to carry the heavy object to his desk. "Let me help you," he said.

"No, I can manage. It's too valuable to risk being dropped."

Squire's eyebrows lifted a fraction. *How can gold be damaged?* he thought.

The object was bound with a long strip of white calico, similar to a bandage, which the wizard took his time to unwrap. When he had almost finished, the visitors gasped as beams of light streaming in through the window caught the object and reflected a bright gleam of gold.

"This is the golden skull," he said, although such an explanation was unnecessary. "The skull, as you will observe, has no teeth. Complete with teeth, it has magical powers. Whichever side possesses the skull intact shall have the advantage in the battles ahead. Many years ago, to prevent Gordeve's precursor, the wicked wizard Eve, from getting her hands on the skull and using it for evil, the teeth were removed and hidden in different locations throughout the lands of the west. Now Squire has returned to Thorland, it's time for the skull to be made whole again, so that its powers can be released. It's your mission to retrieve the teeth.

"When you leave this place tomorrow, you will be beginning the first quest, 'The Quest for the Teeth of the Upper Jaw'. When you have found them all, then you must return with them to me. After that, I will brief you on the second quest, 'The Quest for the Teeth of the Lower Jaw'." He left the skull on his desk, intending to replace it later, and turned back to the cabinet.

Next, he removed a piece of folded paper. "On this piece of paper," Tobin explained, "are instructions for locating the first tooth. When you have successfully located the first, you will also receive instructions on how to find the second tooth, and so on." He handed the piece of paper to Helge.

BUTTERFLY AND SWAN

"Take this," he told her. "As leader of the group, you are responsible for its guidance at each step of the journey." Squire glanced at the yellowed, dog-eared paper and thought it must be very old.

The next item Tobin removed from the cabinet was a shield. "This is the Shield of Squire," he explained and handed it to Squire.

Squire accepted the shield with some trepidation. It had a leather strap attached to its back, which he grasped with his left hand. He discovered that it was not heavy to hold, but sat comfortably in his hand. Indeed, he felt a strong bond with the shield as if he had held it before. Nearly circular in shape, its diameter was the length of his forearm. It was made from a glass-like substance, almost colourless and only a little tinged with gold, but strong and slightly flexible. The front surface appeared transparent and bore the five silver stars in the shape of a cross, just like the ones on Tobin's hat. The back surface, in contrast, had the appearance of a mirror.

"The shield will help to protect you in times of great danger," said Tobin. "Apart from you, Squire, the shield's magical powers can only be released by another from your own world, or by those tutored in the arts of wizardry. However, I warn you that whenever you use it, you will also get a glimpse of your own world as if you are looking through a window, and this may not be a pleasant experience for you. So do not use the shield unless the need is great. Now, are there any questions?"

"Sir, you said you were going to show us four objects," said Vinny. "You've only shown us three."

"Oh, yes, how forgetful of me!" Tobin reached into the cabinet a fourth time and removed a small cloth pouch with a cord attached. This he also handed to Squire. "You must keep this pouch at all times hung around your neck. Make sure it remains hidden from view inside your shirt. When you find the teeth, each one of them must be carefully stored inside the pouch."

"Sir, one more question," Vinny asked. "Who are the twins mentioned in the prophecy?"

As if on cue, the door to the wizard's study opened and two young men came in. Identical in appearance, they were short of stature, and had roundish faces with flat noses. Their hair was brown and cut short and they had no beards apart from a small wisp of hair each in the middle of their chins. Like the older wizard, they wore white cloaks and were barefooted, but they had no hats or staffs.

"These are my apprentices, Sim and Wim," said Tobin. "They will be accompanying you on your mission."

Helge frowned. "But won't you be coming with us?" she asked.

"No, it's too dangerous. I must stay here where I can keep watch and control events from the safety of my castle. Sim and Wim will communicate with me regularly, and through them I will be able to assist you."

Tobin used his staff to help himself to his feet. "Come, all of you," he said. "Stand before me. It's time for you to leave me now, and make preparations for your departure in the morning."

He raised his staff and placed it on Helge's right shoulder. He only tapped her lightly, but Helge's face appeared grim when she felt the power of the staff and the weight of responsibility its touch carried. "Farewell, Helge of Hanlin Forest. I charge you to lead this quest. Be courageous and wise in the decisions you make."

Tobin turned to Vinny. "Farewell, Vineon D'Ur of Wellborough. I charge you with the protection of the company and its provision of meat. Be bold and skilful in the use of your weapon." Vinny clenched his teeth.

BUTTERFLY AND SWAN

Next, it was Squire's turn. "Farewell, Squire from another Land. Be brave and use the shield prudently. You have a crucial part to play in the future of the Land. You are The Squire of the prophecy. " Squire winced as he felt power surge from the wizard's staff..

The wizard placed his staff on the right shoulder of each of the twins in turn. "Farewell, Wim and Sim, my dear apprentices," he said. "Be discerning in your use of magic, and remember that Gordeve has greater powers than you have." Squire saw a glow on each of their faces, as if the staff transferred some of its power to them.

"At a later date, three others will join you on this quest. When you meet the first of the three, you will know him. He will choose the other two. Until we meet again, I bid you all farewell. I look forward to the time when your mission is completed and you all return to my castle."

*   *   *   *   *

That evening the five companions met in the castle library to plan the first part of their journey.

"First of all, we need to look at that piece of paper," Squire said.

Helge removed the paper from her pocket, unfolded it and smoothed its edges.

"The writing looks very old," she said. "It must have been written by some ancient and unknown scribe. This is what it says:

Right central incisor – top jaw
Where Butterfly and Swan fly together
Seek out a place of learning.
Two must enrol.
Their goal?
Jaw and cranium of Mr. Durning."

HOPE

"Where can we find butterflies and swans flying together?" posed Vinny.

"How about the marshes near the mouth of the Tee River?" suggested Wim. "There are lots of butterflies there."

"But no swans," Sim said with a smirk.

"How about the Butterfly Lake?" Helge suggested. "I'm sure there are swans there."

"Wait," Squire interrupted. "The wording of the note does not say 'butterflies and swans'. It says 'Butterfly and Swan'. There's only one of each. There must be something significant in that."

"Of course," Vinny interjected. "Well done, Squire! It's referring to Rivermeet. That's where the Swan River and the Butterfly River merge. The words 'fly together' must mean 'where they meet'. Yes, it's Rivermeet all right."

* * * * *

The next day the five companions set off for Rivermeet. After a hearty breakfast, they loaded up the mule Faithful with everything they would require for the journey – clothes, food and water, tents and bedding. They expected the walk to Rivermeet to take about five days. In fact, it took much longer.

The first day passed free of problems, and they made good progress. That evening they found a place to pitch their tents in a small spinney close to the road. Nearby, a narrow stream gurgled down from the mountains. They savoured the cool fresh water and washed the dust from their grimy bodies. Vinny shot three rabbits that soon crackled and spat over a fire of brushwood.

After they had washed and feasted, they were ready for a good night's sleep. Vinny and Squire shared one tent, Wim and Sim another, and Helge slept alone in a third. Stars twinkled from a clear sky, and nothing stirred in the wood. The only sounds that disturbed the silence were crickets chirping in the grass close-by, and the occasional distant hoot of an owl. The five companions felt secure, and soon slept soundly.

In the middle of the calm night, Squire woke up feeling the need to relieve himself. Without waking Vinny, and not thinking to take the shield with him, he left the security of the tent and walked a few metres into the bush. As he returned to the tent, he saw a pair of green eyes staring at him from the gloom of the bush. He started to retreat to the safety of the camp, but saw another pair of eyes to his left, then another to the right. Panicking, he turned on his heels, but a fourth pair blocked the way forward.

"There is no escape," hissed one of the cougars. "You must come with us. Gordeve wishes to meet you."

"You can talk!" exclaimed Squire.

"Yes, Gordeve has very powerful magic."

Squire tried to call out to his friends, but found that he could not raise his voice above a whisper.

"More magic," the cougar said with a chuckle. "It's no use, they cannot hear you. Now, come with us."

Squire had no choice but to follow the instructions of his captors. One of the cougars prodded him in the back with its paw, forcing him to move in the direction indicated.

*   *   *   *   *

The next morning when Vinny awoke, he found Squire's bed empty. He went outside and called, "Squire, where are you?"

He searched for a few minutes around the camp area and called out again, but when no one replied, he shouted, "Helge, Wim, Sim, come quickly, Squire has gone."

HOPE

Helge found the tracks first. "Cougars!" she gasped. "The tracks show there were four of them."

"That's impossible!" exclaimed Vinny. "There's only one cougar."

"It is as we had feared," interrupted Wim.

"Yes," agreed Sim. "We heard rumours that Gordeve had learned how to breed copies of the cougar. Now we know the stories are true. Goodness knows how many of them there are now, but I bet there are more than four."

"We must follow," said Helge, "and quickly. But one of us must stay with the mule to look after the things."

"I will stay," volunteered Sim. "Wim can go with you and Vinny."

"If the cougars were on their own, we would have no hope of catching them," said Helge. "They already have several hours' start. However, with Squire to slow them down, they won't be able to move fast, which gives us some chance of catching them."

For the next day and a half, the three companions followed the tracks and pursued their enemies and their friend.

Near the end of the second day, as she bent to inspect the tracks once more, Helge observed, "They don't seem to be stopping to rest much, but we are still gaining on them. We should catch up with them by sunset."

Shortly after the sun had gone down, the three companions found them sheltering under the cover of a small clump of trees. The moon had risen, but was not at its fullest. Yet it gave enough light for them to make out four forms lying on the ground.

"There's one guard," whispered Helge, "but the other three and Squire seem to be sleeping."

Vinny readied his longbow, and took aim in the direction of the guard. He was just about to shoot when Wim pushed his bow aside.

"No," he whispered. "If he screams he will awaken the others, and they will escape. I have a better idea."

"But I can fell all four of them within a matter of seconds. There's no chance of them escaping. And Helge's ... "

However, Wim hadn't heard. Before the archer had finished speaking, he had stood up, blocking Vinny's line of sight. He spread out his arms and, whispering, invoked some magic words.

The next moment, the air around Squire and the cougars began to rotate in a vortex of swirling air and debris, producing a shrill whistling sound. The whistling soon gave way to a roar as the rotating mass increased in speed, and Squire found himself whisked up into the air, his body intertwined with the flailing limbs of the cougars.

This continued for several minutes until Squire, battered and bruised by flying rocks and sticks and cut by sharp claws, found the noise and pain unbearable. He had given up hope of escape when something plucked him from the vortex and lifted him into the air. The roaring sound stopped abruptly, and he floated down towards the ground. Seconds later, the vortex had disappeared along with the four cougars who had been swallowed into its swirling depths.

Squire looked up and saw a giant eagle. He recognised it as the one that had rescued him from the wolves several weeks earlier. Happy to see their friend safe, Vinny and Helge rushed to his side. Wim knew he had made a bad decision. Ashamed, he backed away to find a place to hide.

"Squire, are you all right?" Helge asked.

Squire took a cursory look at his bruised hands and cut forearms. "I, I think so," he replied.

The eagle landed, stood erect, spread its wings and in an instant transformed itself into the shape of a man. He wore a white cloak and a white pointed hat, bearing five silver stars. It took Squire only a moment to recognise the thin face, long pointed nose, piercing eyes and grey hair and beard.

"Tobin!" exclaimed Vinny and Squire simultaneously.

"Yes, it's me," confirmed the wizard. "I told you that I would not accompany you on this journey but unfortunately, because of Wim's foolishness, I have been obliged to come to your rescue."

Tobin glowered as he addressed the apprentice wizard, who still hid behind a tree. "Wim, come out of there," he commanded. "Let this be a warning to you, my boy. In future, do not invoke magic that you cannot control. Use only the magic you have mastered. Better still, do not use magic at all unless there is no other choice. In this case, your two friends could have easily dealt with this situation without your inter … er, help. Instead, you put Squire's life in danger. It was a very foolish thing to do."

A tear dropped from Wim's eye, on to the tip of his nose, then onto his shirt. "I … I'm sorry, Tobin," he said. "It won't happen again, I promise."

"Now I must return swiftly to the safety of my castle," concluded Tobin. With that, the wizard once again assumed the shape of an eagle. Squire watched as the giant bird launched itself into the air. It had a dark brown plumage with white at the base of the tail and gold feathers on its nape. Although it had a wingspan of nearly three-metres, it took to the air gracefully, and soon soared westwards towards the wizard's castle.

"Now I know who saved me from the wolves," he said. "Helge, you already knew this, didn't you?"

"Yes," she replied. "It was Tobin who brought you to my cottage."

As Helge tended Squire's wounds with some herbs and balms that she always carried with her, he began his story. "On the two previous occasions," he told them, "I couldn't see the cougars clearly, only their green eyes. However, while we travelled together, I got a good look at them. They are large animals, but have small heads, short faces, and long necks. Their fur is short and reddish-brown with white on the underside, and their ears and tails are tipped with black. They pushed me and prodded me in the direction they wanted me to go – they have very sharp claws and teeth. I suppose they wanted to take me to Gordeve's castle. We kept moving most of the time, with only occasional short rests for a drink at a stream, and we only stopped for about three hours during the first night. They weren't that rough, but very scary, and their growls and snarls were deep and fearsome … and," he added, "they have learned how to speak."

The others gasped.

"Tell us about the vortex," said Vinny. "What was it like?"

"It was like a mighty wind, so powerful that it swept me off my feet. The rotating mass of air seemed to go round and round in an ever-increasing circular motion, trapping the cougars and me. The noise from the rushing wind was deafening. In the turmoil, I felt myself bumping into one or more of the cougars and into branches and stones that the vortex had sucked in, and my face and body got scratched all over. This battering continued for ages until my body could take no more. I feared the vortex was going to suck me inside of itself into an unknown void never to return, just as the force of gravity sucks water down a plughole."

"That's exactly what did happen to the cougars," said Vinny. Addressing the apprentice wizard, he added, "Were they destroyed, Wim?"

"Not destroyed," the wizard replied. "They're dead, but their skin and bones still exist. If we dug, we would find their bodies somewhere under the ground. Tobin and I do not have the power to destroy. Only the Creator can destroy."

HOPE

They rested for the remainder of the night with Helge, Vinny and Wim taking turns to keep guard. From that day onwards, they made it a rule that they should always take turns to keep guard.

*   *   *   *   *

The next morning they started to retrace their footsteps back to the place where they had left Sim and the mule. After another day and a half, the fellowship reunited and they resumed their journey to Rivermeet. There were no further attacks and, eight days after leaving Tobin's castle, they reached their destination.

Rivermeet, a town of some nine thousand individuals, had a population consisting mainly of humans like Helge and Vinny. However, a small enclave of another race, Luchorpans, occupied the southern part of the town. Luchorpans were only about a metre tall, but they were not dwarves since their various dimensions bore the same proportions to each other as those of humans. They were hard-working people. Many of them were cobblers and renowned for the quality of the shoes they made. Their other main trade was banking, and Luchorpans had a reputation for thriftiness. One legend said that all Luchorpans possessed a hidden pot of gold. Usually solitary, anti-social people, when not working, they often hid alone behind bushes or trees smoking their pipes. The main population of Luchorpans still dwelt in Luchor, a country far to the west on the other side of the Air Mountains, but a small group had settled in Rivermeet several decades earlier.

When the travellers arrived on the outskirts of the town, the first person they encountered was one of the Luchorpans, sitting behind a tree smoking his pipe.

"Good day to you, friend," said Vinny. "Can you tell us where we can find an inn?"

BUTTERFLY AND SWAN

The startled Luchorpan did not answer, but got to his feet and prepared to run away. However, he stopped in his tracks when Vinny, who seemed familiar with the habits of these creatures, called after him, "Friend, we are looking for a piece of gold. I think you may be able to help us."

The Luchorpan turned and his eyes lit up mischievously. "In that case I may be able to assist you," he said. "Let me introduce myself. My name is Alvin Shoemaker, and I'm a cobbler by trade. I will take you to an inn, and then we can talk more about your ... gold." Alvin, a middle-aged Luchorpan, clean-shaven and with brown hair, was dressed in garish old-fashioned clothes – green trousers with braces, checked shirt, an apron, a red cap and brown buckled shoes.

Vinny introduced his four companions. Then Alvin led them into the town centre where they booked into the Rover's Retreat inn. As they sat together enjoying glasses of ale and, in Alvin's case another pipe-full of tobacco, Squire, Helge and Vinny related their story to the tiny Luchorpan. His eyes widened slightly when they reached the part of the story about the golden teeth and the golden skull.

As they talked, Sim accidentally knocked his glass with his elbow. He reached out to catch it, but missed. The glass fell to the floor and smashed into many pieces.

"Oh dear!" exclaimed Alvin. "That's very bad luck, you know. Take care. There might be an accident."

"I don't believe in such superstitious nonsense," declared Sim, glowering.

Helge removed the dog-eared paper from her tunic pocket and glanced at the instructions for finding the first tooth. "Alvin," she said, without showing the paper to the Luchorpan, "is there a school or a college in Rivermeet? Our instructions are to find a place of learning."

HOPE

"There's only one such place," he explained. "That's the Rivermeet Academy. All children in Rivermeet, young and old, human and Luchorpan alike, attend the academy. I'll take you there tomorrow if you like."

"Two must enrol," said Vinny. "But which two?" he asked.

"The two twins, of course," replied Alvin. "They look young enough to be senior schoolchildren, but they must shave the hairs from their chins."

The next day Sim and Wim enrolled in the Rivermeet Academy. After they had shaved and put on the academy uniform, they easily passed for students in their final year at school. They determined to settle into the academy for at least a week before trying to find out more about Mr. Durning. They were very anxious to locate the teacher as soon as possible, but knew that they should not draw too much attention to themselves.

After a week they approached one of their fellow students, a pimply youth called Bucklethwaite. "Do you know a teacher by the name of Mr. Durning?" asked Wim.

Bucklethwaite laughed. "Mr. Durning's not a teacher," he sniggered. "Mr. Durning is the name we give to the skeleton in the biology lab."

The twins had to wait another two days before their next biology lesson. During the lesson, they took the opportunity to ask the teacher some questions about the skeleton so that they could scrutinise it more closely. They noticed that the skeleton had a full set of teeth, but none of them seemed to be made of gold. The twins tried to hide their disappointment, but resolved to return later in the day, when all the students had left, to try to find the golden tooth.

When they returned to the laboratory after school, they discovered that the caretaker had locked the door. However, with a few magic words, Wim unlocked the door, and they passed unhindered inside. This time they could examine the teeth more closely.

BUTTERFLY AND SWAN

"Which one is the 'right central incisor'?" asked Sim.

"We'd better look it up in one of these biology books," suggested Wim. He looked up 'teeth' in the index, turned to the correct page, and then declared, "See here, Sim. It's one of the two teeth in the middle at the front. The one on the right."

Sim examined the tooth in the top jaw of the skeleton and discovered that someone had painted it white. As he scraped the tooth, some of the white paint came away. "Look," he said with a grin, "there's gold underneath!"

Sim pulled on the tooth. At first it wouldn't budge, so he tugged a little harder, then harder still until finally he managed to extract the tooth. However, he had exerted so much force that it threw him backwards to land painfully on one of the laboratory stools, and Mr. Durning crashed to the floor. "Ow!" he screamed. He sat up on the floor with a triumphant look on his face, and opened his hand to reveal the shiny prize. "I have it!" he said. "The first golden tooth."

"Sh," said his brother. "With the clatter of the skeleton falling and your noise, it's surprising no one's come by now. We must hurry. Let's look for the paper with the instructions on how to find the second tooth. I'll look inside Mr. Durning's cranium."

Wim reached inside with the tips of his fingers. Sure enough, there, taped to the underside of the top jaw, he felt a piece of paper. "Here it is," he said with a broad smile. "Goodness knows how many years this has been here." Wasting no further time, he stashed the piece of paper and the tooth in his jacket pocket.

"Let's go," he said to Sim.

As he said this, the door to the laboratory opened. The silhouette of a large figure blocked their exit.

51

CHAPTER 4

THE ISLAND

"What are you doing here?" The deep voice belonged to the biology teacher.

"Sir, we … er … we were so interested in what you told us about the skeleton that we wanted to take another look," replied Sim.

"And how did you get in here?" snapped the teacher.

"The door was already unlocked," Wim protested.

"That careless caretaker!" exclaimed the teacher. "He's always making mistakes and leaving rooms unlocked. He deserves the sack. Now run along, you two, before I change my mind and report you to the Principal."

He didn't need to tell them twice. As the twins departed, Sim tripped on the doorstep and found himself sprawling on the floor outside the laboratory.

"Are you all right?" asked Wim.

Sim grabbed the door handle and hauled himself to his feet. "I think so," he said, "but my arm's very sore and I've grazed my knee."

"Do you remember the glass you broke the other day? Alvin said it would bring you bad luck."

"Bah!" exclaimed Sim. "I don't believe in that nonsense."

*   *   *   *   *

THE ISLAND

That evening, the five companions met in Helge's room at the Rover's Retreat. Wim handed over the first golden tooth to Squire, who took it and placed it inside the pouch around his neck. Wim passed the piece of paper to Helge. She opened it, and read:

"Right lateral incisor – top jaw
On the island you will find
Steps cut in the crater's wall.
Go down thirty-five steps to a hall.
Turn left, then right, and right once more
Look on the floor,
Then you will know what to unbind."

"Any ideas which island?" she asked.

"It could be Gull Island," suggested Vinny. "If I remember my geography correctly, it's in the Southern Ocean near the mouth of the Moon River."

Helge shook her head. "It mentions a crater, so we're looking for a volcanic island, not one with high cliffs. The only other islands I know about are far away – Terrapo, Veraco and Tauto in the east and, of course, Atmos – my island, – and Tomos in the west." She sighed. "What do you think Wim … Sim?"

Sim scratched his head. After a moment, his eyes lit up. "There's a large island in the middle of Butterfly Lake," he said. "I can't remember its name."

"It's called Peak Island," said Wim, "and it's volcanic. That's where we should go."

HOPE

"It sounds favourable," agreed Squire. "That might be one mystery solved, but … one other thing, the prophecy lists those who will accompany me on the quest: 'woman tall, twins, archer, three others and a mule'. Who do you think the 'three others' could be?"

"I've been thinking about that too," said Helge, "I think they might be Luchorpans."

"Yes," agreed Vinny. "They have a taste for gold. They can even *smell* it! They will help us find the teeth."

At that moment, they heard a loud knock. Vinny opened the door and Alvin entered.

"Good evening, Alvin," said Helge. "We've just been discussing 'the three' mentioned in the prophecy, and we agree they must be Luchorpans. I hope you will consent to accompany us on our quest, my friend, and that you will choose two others."

Alvin's eyes sparkled with anticipation. "Certainly I will," he said. "I've been a cobbler too long. It's time I had a bit of excitement in my life, and what better adventure than to be looking for gold! But who else … ?" He thought for a moment before replying to his own question. "Why don't you come along to the midsummer festival tomorrow," he suggested. "I will introduce you to the two who I think should join us on our quest."

* * * * *

The following day, early in the morning before sunrise, Alvin led his guests a few kilometres to the west of the town.

As they walked, he spoke. "Back in our homeland, Luchor, our ancestors have observed this ancient festival since time immemorial, and those of us who migrated to Rivermeet have continued to keep this tradition. On this day every year, we put aside our tools and close up our banks to meet together for a time of celebration and enjoyment. There will be more than three hundred of us there."

On the way, they met other Luchorpans making their way to the meeting place. These included old Luchorpans walking slowly, some with the aid of sticks, young teenagers laughing and playing on the way, and families with children.

"There it is," said Alvin, pointing to a grassy embankment between the two rivers. Several Luchorpans had already found a good vantage point and sat in groups on the grass. Others were still arriving. An ancient stone circle surrounded the embankment, its most prominent monolith facing towards the east.

"It's the longest day of the year and the time for us to celebrate the midsummer solstice. See that big stone. At sunrise, only on the morning of the midsummer solstice, the sun's first rays stream in a perfect straight line through a hole in its centre. That's the signal for the start of the celebrations, which continue until well after sunset."

"What kind of celebrations?" Vinny asked.

"After welcoming the sun's arrival, the rest of the day is devoted to singing, dancing, eating, drinking and, of course, smoking of pipes. We are usually solitary people but at the time of midsummer, we forget about that. Although some of us drink heavily on these occasions, things never get out of hand. There's no fighting, or drunken revelry, or any kind of debauchery. We lust laugh and have fun. Our favourite activity is dancing, and this continues throughout the day."

"What kind of dancing," Helge asked.

"We have our own traditional and well-loved reels and square dances. We never tire of them. Where there's dancing, of course, there's also music – provided by a band. You see the young woman playing the violin? That's my little sister, Vylin."

"So Vylin plays the violin," joked Vinny.

Alvin laughed. "Yes," he replied. "She's not an expert, but she knows all the favourite traditional tunes, and the dancers like her playing."

Vylin had long auburn curls, blue eyes and an engaging smile. She was gaily attired in a green dress embroidered with brightly coloured flowers, and wore thongs on her feet.

Alvin continued, "And you see that fellow dancing, the one with the red jacket and hat. That's my best friend, Perkin Goldmaster. He's a banker. He's the best dancer here today. Perkin knows all the moves, and is so graceful that all the girls want to dance with him."

Older than Alvin, Perkin kept himself fit with his dancing, and he looked younger than his years. He had much darker brown hair than his friend had, and he sported a beard. Although he threw himself into the celebrations on this day, he was usually a much more sober-minded individual. His work as a banker called for a cool head and sound judgement.

"I think these are the two who should accompany us," asserted Alvin.

*   *   *   *   *

The following afternoon, Helge and Squire met again with Alvin. "Oh, my head," he said as he removed his red cap and placed it on Helge's bed. "It feels like it was put on my lapstone and hit with my cobbler's hammer."

Helge looked stern. "Too much beer," she said. "Now tell us why you think your sister Vylin and your best friend Perkin are the right ones to accompany us."

THE ISLAND

"Vylin can keep us entertained with her violin during the long evenings before we retire, and Perkin shall amuse us with his fine dancing," replied Alvin. "Besides, Perkin also has the Seeround Glass. Yes, they are the ones – if they agree."

"What's the Seeround Glass?" asked Squire.

"It's a magic glass that can see around corners. Many years ago the wizard Gordin, the father of Tobin and Gordeve, gave it to Perkin's grandfather. His grandfather commanded the Guards of Luchor in helping to defend the western lands from attack by the Kobalos. After he died, the glass passed to Perkin's father, and now it's Perkin's. The glass will be very useful whenever we want to check what is lurking around a dark corner, or what is hiding behind a rock or a tree. It even works in the dark!"

"Who are the Kobalos?" asked Squire.

"So far you have only come across two of Gordeve's evil creatures," explained Helge, "the wolves and the cougar – or should I now say *cougars*? The Kobalos, however, are a much greater threat. They are the evil creatures who have long supported the wicked wizards of the east and now make up the majority of Gordeve's army. War with the Kobalos is inevitable. You will know who they are soon enough."

"I'm sure Perkin and my sister will agree to accompany us," said Alvin. "I'll go and see them straight away. Now, where did I put my cap?"

"It's on the bed," said Helge.

"Oh, dear!" exclaimed the Luchorpan. "It's awfully bad luck to put a hat on a bed, you know?"

Vylin and Perkin did not take much persuading to join in the adventure. They too were bored with their routine lives in Rivermeet. "It is indeed an honour that three Luchorpans should be chosen to accompany you," professed Perkin. "We will also take my pony, Conny, to carry our things. She's strong and sure-footed and your mule can't carry everything."

"Where my brother goes, I go," declared Vylin. "Besides, I can cook and sew as well as play the violin. You need another woman to help look after you."

The three Luchorpans needed a few days to close up their businesses and prepare for the journey. A week later, the company of ten – three humans, two apprentice wizards, three Luchorpans, a mule and a pony – prepared to set off on the next leg of the quest. Their journey would take them along the main Rivermeet to Bunbury highway for about two hundred kilometres, and then on the narrow road north to the shores of the Butterfly Lake.

* * * * *

They had been travelling along the highway for two days when they saw a group of people approaching from the opposite direction. The group consisted of about twenty men on horseback who flanked, and appeared to guard, two horse-drawn carriages. The leading rider was carrying a standard bearing the picture of a leopard on a pale blue background.

"Whose standard is that?" asked Vinny. "It must be somebody important."

"Very important," said Helge. "That's the standard of the King of Manchor." She went on to explain, mainly for the benefit of Squire, "Manchor is a kingdom to the west of the Air Mountains, and south of Luchor. The king must have been to Bunbury for some important event."

"For the wedding of Prince Tycho, I believe," said Vinny. "Didn't you hear that he was to be married to the young daughter of a nobleman from Jackville? I think the wedding was last week."

THE ISLAND

When the royal cavalcade and the company met, the Captain of the King's Guard ordered his men to stop. The king looked out from the door of the first carriage to see what was going on. On seeing the king, Helge bowed, and the other seven followed her example.

"Good morning travellers," said the Captain of the Guard. Squire noted that he spoke with a strange accent. "Where are you heading?" he asked.

"We're on our way to Bunbury," Helge lied.

"But … " said Squire, his words cut short by a kick on the shin.

"We shouldn't tell them where we're really going," she whispered. "Manchor is a friendly nation, but we can't be sure whether all of the guards can be trusted."

"You are indeed a strange company," observed the Captain. "I wonder, what is your business in Bunbury?"

"We're going to a music festival," Helge lied again. "Our Luchorpan friends here are excellent musicians and dancers."

"Indeed. Perhaps they could be prevailed upon to entertain His Majesty and Her Royal Highness," suggested the Captain. "They are sorely in need of a rest. Come, we will go under the shade of those trees yonder, and your Luchorpans can play and dance for the king and princess."

The king and princess alighted from their carriages and with their attendants formed a circle under the trees. As Vylin played some of the same familiar tunes that had entertained the crowds at the midsummer festival a few days earlier, Perkin and Alvin began to dance.

They danced for several minutes before a deep voice interrupted them. "Bravo!" said the king as he rose to his feet and began to clap. "Thank you so much my little friends. Now we must be on our way. Good luck to you all at the festival in Bunbury."

HOPE

The king began to make his way back to his carriage, followed by the princess. As a mark of respect towards the royal travellers, Helge, Vinny, Squire and the twins had already risen to their feet. As the princess passed by, she glanced towards them and her eyes met those of Squire.

For several seconds their eyes remained locked together. *Those eyes are searching, longing for something*, Squire thought. Then the princess moved on and climbed once more, assisted by her lady-in-waiting, into her carriage. A few moments later the guards were all mounted, the Captain of the Guard saluted, and the entourage proceeded on its way towards the west.

The company remained motionless for some time before Squire broke the silence. "The princess is very beautiful," he observed.

* * * * *

After a further day's walking along the main highway, they reached a crossroads. The company took the narrow road leading off towards the left signposted: 'Lot's Landing, 40 kilometres'. Soon afterwards, they found a suitable place to spend the night underneath a small outcrop of rock close to a stream.

Since they had departed from Rivermeet, every time they stopped for a rest or for the night, Perkin had made it his habit to use the Seeround Glass to check for any hidden dangers. The circular glass, which sat comfortably in the palm of his hand, was transparent and a pale leaf-green in colour. Whenever he travelled, he always kept it in a small case for safety.

He took the glass out from its case.

"Look, it's beginning to glow, but it's not very bright," said Vylin.

"It'll get brighter in a minute," said Perkin. "When it's bright enough, I can see though the glass, just like looking through a lens." Perkin held the glass in front of his face, pointed it towards the outcrop of rock, and looked through.

THE ISLAND

"Can you see anything?" asked Vylin.

"There's an animal behind the rock," he whispered. "It looks like a wolf," he added with dismay.

Vinny prepared his bow. He and Helge crept around to the far side of the rock.

"It's just a wild dog," said Vinny with relief.

Helge threw a stone at the animal, which ran away yelping into the undergrowth.

After one more day's walk, they arrived at Lot's Landing, a small village consisting of about a dozen houses, situated on the western shore of Butterfly Lake. The villagers had constructed a wooden jetty to allow small craft to moor in the deeper waters about fifty metres from the shore.

That afternoon, they found only two vessels berthed at the jetty – a small fishing boat named *Pelican*, and a passenger boat bearing the name *Peak Island Ferry*. At the shore end of the jetty, they saw a sign that read: 'Ferry sails daily, Mondays to Fridays only. Departs mid-morning and returns late afternoon.' They would have to wait for the next day to travel to the island.

Lot's Landing was too small to boast an inn, so the weary travellers slept in their tents, which they pitched near the shore of the lake. However, the friendly villagers provided them with fresh water and sold them fish, caught that day, at a very reasonable price.

The next day they purchased their tickets, and boarded the ferry, ready to sail by the middle of the morning.

The ferryman smiled. "You are my only passengers today," he said, "and it's not often I have such a large party. However, I'm a bit worried about taking *them* on the ferry." He indicated the mule and pony.

Helge looked into the ferryman's ruddy face. "Don't worry," she replied. "They are very docile, and will give you no trouble."

The old man pulled a beret from his pocket and placed it on his balding head.

"This will help protect me from the cold wind," he said.

"How was this lake formed?" Squire asked the ferryman during the crossing.

"Nobody really knows," he replied, "but the legends of my people say the volcano first erupted hundreds of thousands of years ago. The eruption was so violent, and threw out such large amounts of material, that the ground surface collapsed forming a big hole. They call it a caldera, the hole. After that, the waters of the Butterfly River filled the caldera, and that's how the lake got here. Then in the much more recent past, there was a smaller eruption on the bed of the lake and Peak Island was created."

The wind blew strongly that day, making the waters very choppy. Wim and Sim both suffered from seasickness on the two-hour crossing.

The company bade farewell to the ferryman and took the only exit from the jetty – a small track that zigzagged its way up the sloping sides of the volcanic island. They spent the rest of the day ascending the long, winding track. Just before sunset, they pitched their tents two or three hundred metres from the peak.

Perkin once again employed his Seeround Glass, to check whether anything might be hiding over the rim of the crater. The glass revealed five sleeping animals.

"I'm pretty sure they're cougars this time," he asserted.

"Cougars!" exclaimed Helge. "They can swim, but don't much like the water and couldn't have swum all the way from the mainland. How could they have got on to this island?" she asked. "They can't fly!"

THE ISLAND

"That's a mystery," said Vinny.

Vinny and Helge once again prepared their weapons. "We'll manage without the help of your magic this time, Wim," Vinny teased.

After they had returned to the camp, Squire asked, "What happened?"

"We crawled up to the rim of the crater," Vinny replied. "When we looked over the edge, we could see the cougars concealed amongst some rocks a few metres below. They must have been resting as they waited for the chance to attack us after dark. They obviously weren't expecting us and proved an easy prey. I fired three arrows that found their targets in the necks of three of them. At the same time, Helge let fly two stones from her sling that embedded in the foreheads of the other two. Now, how about some food? I'm starving."

The ground where they pitched their tents was soft and warm. All around them, they could see small mounds of sand and rotting vegetation.

"What are those mounds?" asked Squire.

Vinny looked excited. "Why, they're megapode burrows!" he exclaimed. "Megapodes are chicken-like birds that often live close to volcanoes. They are unique because they incubate their eggs using the heat from hot sand and rotting vegetation. They dig burrows in the warm, soft ground, then pile up large mounds of vegetable matter, earth, and sand on top and leave the eggs to be incubated. Their eggs are easy to dig up, Shall we try some?"

"Yes, let's. We haven't had eggs for some time," replied Squire.

Vinny used a stick to dig at the mounds and soon had collected more than a dozen eggs. Alvin, whose turn it was to cook that day, wrapped the eggs in leaves and placed them on a hot stone oven to cook.

HOPE

That evening they feasted on megapode eggs with bread. "Wow, what enormous eggs!" exclaimed Squire. "They must be three or four times as big as chickens', and they are almost all yolk."

"Yes, and they're also very nutritious," explained Alvin.

*　　*　　*　　*　　*

The next day, the company set off in search of the tooth. When they reached the rim of the crater, they couldn't find any steps. In fact, they saw no features of note except a pile of large rocks, formed from solidified magma where the bodies of the five slain cougars lay. They encircled the rim of the crater, which took almost an hour, but still failed to find the steps.

"Maybe we've come to the wrong island," said Perkin. "Or perhaps the instructions are wrong."

"Or maybe there's been another eruption since the message was written," added Alvin.

"Impossible," said Vinny. "This mountain hasn't erupted for hundreds of years." He pointed to the depths of the crater. "Look, there aren't even any gases coming from down there. There's more hot air coming out of your mouth," he said with a grin.

"We'll have to make a more thorough search before we give up on this island," said Helge. "We'll split into two groups. Vinny, Squire, Vylin, and Sim – you take the mule and go that way." She indicated the anticlockwise route around the crater. "Move very slowly and stop every few metres to look for any sign of the steps. Wim, Perkin and Alvin – you three come with me and the pony. We'll go that way."

The two groups had almost met up again on the far side of the crater, when Sim startled Squire with a shout. "Look there," he said pointing over the rim of the crater, "a small step cut in the rock."

THE ISLAND

"It's hardly wide enough for a Luchorpan," remarked Vinny, "and the dense vegetation makes it impossible to see whether there are any more steps further down."

By this time, Helge and the others had joined them.

"Can you see anything with the glass, Perkin?" she asked.

"I can't see much through the vegetation," he replied. "It looks like the steps disappear into a hole."

She turned and addressed Alvin. "It looks as if you three will have to go down on your own," she said. "The rest of us are too big – by the size of them, it looks like those steps must have been cut by Luchorpans."

"Don't worry," said Perkin. "We're not afraid. It would take more than a dark underground passage to frighten a Luchorpan."

"Oh, Perkin, you're so brave!" exclaimed Vylin.

Armed with Alvin's machete, the three Luchorpans made their way down the steps. They had to cut away the undergrowth as they went, which made their progress slow. Squire watched the tiny people, brightly attired in greens, reds and checks, slowly making their way down a narrow, overgrown stairway into the unknown depths below. "What a strange sight they are," he said.

After they had descended about twenty steps, the staircase entered a hole in the rock and the Luchorpans disappeared from his view.

*   *   *   *   *

When the Luchorpans prepared to enter the hole, Vylin stopped to light a torch. They continued to descend, not knowing what dangers might be awaiting them. Abruptly the steps ended, and they found themselves in a cool, dry cave - or 'hall' as the instructions had described it. At the far end of the cave, passages led both left and right. They took the left-hand passage, which continued to slope steadily downwards. At the next fork, they chose the right, and right again at the next. At each turn, Perkin used the glass to check for any hidden perils, but he could see nothing dangerous hiding in the caves and passages. Only a group of bats, disturbed by the unwelcome visitors, screeched past, and disappeared towards the exit.

The final passage took the three Luchorpans to another small cave where they discovered, lying on the dusty floor, an object covered in cloth and bound with hemp. Alvin slashed the hemp with his knife, and removed the cloth to reveal a clay pot with a tight-fitting lid.

"That's a Luchorpan pot!' exclaimed Vylin.

Alvin prised the lid off, and there inside found a single gold tooth and a folded piece of paper.

"This really is a pot of gold," Perkin joked.

The Luchorpans hastened out of the series of caves and tunnels, and climbed back up the steps to where their companions waited.

Helge greeted them. "Do you have the tooth?" she asked.

"Yes indeed," replied Alvin, handing the tooth to Squire and the piece of paper to Helge. Squire put the tooth in the pouch around his neck.

Helge unfolded the piece of paper that bore the instructions for finding the third tooth, and read:

"Right canine – top jaw

In the ancient city of Ar
Go to the ruined amphitheatre.
On the fifth row, near the left
Find a narrow cleft.
Small hand inside will provide
What you seek inside a jar."

THE ISLAND

"Does anyone know about a city called Ar?" she asked.

"I believe it's somewhere in the Northern Desert," Vinny replied. "It is, if I am correct, the ancient city of the Telekai, the desert nomads. They weren't always nomads, but once occupied a magnificent city, and I believe its name was Ar."

"I think you're correct," agreed Alvin. "The Luchorpans have a song about an ancient city in the Northern Desert. We call it A'ar. But I'm sure it must be the same place."

"That may be very fortuitous," said Helge. "I know of someone who lives in the desert who may be able to help us to find Ar. He often stays at Fort Holt, which is not far from here at the southern edge the desert. We must leave for there at once."

The day was already far advanced and, when they had descended to the jetty where the ferry always moored, they found that it had already departed. Since it was not Friday, they knew the ferry would return the next morning, so they set up camp close to the shore of the lake.

The wind had died down and, as Squire lay with Vinny in their tent that evening, they could hear the waves gently lapping against the shore. "What a peaceful place," he said.

The following morning, while they waited for the ferryman to arrive, Sim, Perkin and Squire took a short walk along the beach. As they rounded a bend in the shoreline, they caught sight of an object lying on the sand.

"What's that?" Squire asked.

"It looks like a pile of rubbish that the waves had washed up onto the beach," said Perkin. "Let's take a closer look."

As they drew nearer, their curiosity turned to horror.

"It's a body!" exclaimed Squire.

The body of a man lay face downwards on the sand.

CHAPTER 5

THE NORTHERN DESERT

"There's no sign of any blood," said Squire. "Do you think he drowned?"

Sim turned the body over in the hope that the man might still be alive. "Look," he said. "The man hasn't drowned. Look at those marks on his neck."

"They look like bite marks," said Perkin.

"Cougars!" said Squire. "It must have been the cougars."

"It looks like the cougars must have forced him to bring them to the island," said Sim. "Then they must have killed him."

"I think you're right," agreed Perkin.

They returned to their friends and waited for the ferryman. Few words passed between them as they sat waiting in the hot sun. Though the ferryman arrived a few minutes before noon, it seemed like several hours had passed. He lowered the sail and used a pole to manoeuvre the last few metres to the jetty. He hailed them, but the worried look on his craggy face showed that all was not well. Attached to the ferry by a towrope was the fishing boat, *Pelican*.

They told the ferryman about the body. The man looked sad and a tear rolled down his cheek. "It must be Flitcher," he said. He pointed towards *Pelican*. "I found his boat drifting a kilometre or two from the shore, but there was no sign of him, so I feared something bad had happened. Let's go and have a look at the body." Squire, Sim and Perkin went with him.

THE NORTHERN DESERT

The ferryman groaned as he recognised that the body was indeed that of Flitcher.

"It looks like he came ashore and was attacked by a wild animal," said the ferryman. "It seems he didn't even have time to secure his boat and it must have drifted back out onto the lake. What kind of animal could have inflicted this fatal bite mark to his neck? I've been visiting this island all my life, but I've never seen any animal capable of doing this."

After burying the unfortunate Flitcher, the four rejoined the rest of the company. In the middle of the afternoon they boarded the ferry for the return voyage to Lot's Landing. On this occasion, the ferryman did not prove to be as loquacious as he had been during the outward journey. *He must be thinking about Flitcher's death*, thought Squire. *It must be preying on his mind.*

When they arrived at the tiny village, the news of Flitcher's death spread quickly among the small population. Instead of offering the visitors water and fish, this time the villagers ignored them.

"The people don't seem to be quite as welcoming towards us as they were last time," remarked Squire.

"There's no reason for them to connect our visit with Flitcher's death," said Helge, "but they must think it's a bit of a coincidence. We must leave the village this evening, and set off at once on the road north to Fort Holt."

* * * * *

The journey to Fort Holt took them another four days and nights. The only difficult part of the journey was the crossing of the Butterfly River, which they had to ford because there was no bridge. Recently a lot of rain had fallen in the foothills of the Air Mountains, and the river ran high. The water was about a metre deep in places, which meant that Helge had to carry

HOPE

the Luchorpans across on her back one at a time. The pony remained calm and allowed Squire to lead her across, but Vinny had to drag the reluctant mule. After a few minutes, they all reached the safety of the far bank and the remainder of the journey to Fort Holt passed without incident.

*   *   *   *   *

The man Helge hoped to meet at Fort Holt was named Yohan. Like Helge, he had been born on the large island of Atmos, which lay far to the west, beyond the Air Mountains and the Kingdom of Manchor. The two were distant cousins, though they had never met. Like Helge, Yohan had chosen to leave his native island to live a life of exile in Thorland. She had settled in a remote cottage in Hanlin Forest. He had chosen a quite different environment – the Northern Desert.

Yohan had first arrived in the capital city of Bunbury more than thirty years earlier as the Ambassador of Atmos to Thorland. During his term, he had held counsel with the paramount chief of the Telekai, the nomadic tribesmen of the desert, and had later accepted the chief's hospitality. He had been so impressed with the lifestyle that, after he had served out his five-year term as ambassador, he had decided to make his home amongst the people of the desert and had never returned to Atmos. He preferred to live a life of solitude.

After the company arrived at Fort Holt, word spread that a tall woman, of appearance similar to Yohan, was among the travellers. When this news reached Yohan, who lay recuperating in the fort hospital, he sent for Helge and the two of them met for the first time. Helge, accompanied by Squire, went to her compatriot's bedside to introduce herself and seek his help.

As soon as Squire saw Yohan, he recognised the similarities in appearance to Helge, though the man seemed much older. Yohan also had a thin face, a sharp nose, and thick eyebrows. He had blue eyes, and blond, shoulder-length hair. Although he sat up in the bed, Squire could see that he was very tall and slim. He didn't wear the usual attire characteristic of the Telekai, but wore instead a white hospital gown and his head was uncovered.

The two Atmosians greeted each other in their native tongue, but reverted to the common language for the benefit of Squire. Helge introduced him. "Yohan, this is The Squire, spoken of in the ancient prophecy." She went on to explain to him the purpose of their mission, and to seek his help to find the third tooth in the ancient ruined city of Ar.

"You are the only one who can help us," she implored. "You know the desert, how to survive in it, and you're familiar with its people. We need you to lead us to the city and help to protect us from the Telekai. They are allies of our people, but of very unpredictable nature, and we really need your knowledge to negotiate with them."

Yohan's jaw dropped. "But I fear I am out of favour with Ben Wai, the paramount chief," he said.

"Why, what's happened?" she enquired.

"The Telekai breed some of their camels just for racing. They usually hold race meets during the winter months when it's cooler. Three months ago, it was the last camel race meeting of the winter. I was here with Ben Wai and some other chiefs. For two days, we pitted our fastest steeds one against the other. During these meets, a fierce, but friendly, rivalry exists between us and big stakes are either lost or gained by those who cast their bets.

"But this time, on the second day of the meet, our friendship was severely tested. In the main race of the day, I entered my best camel, Sammy, against Ben Wai's best, The Bull. Sammy won that day, but a bitter argument erupted when the chief complained that Sammy's rider had jostled and nearly knocked The Bull's rider from its back. In the argument that followed, knives were drawn and I was badly cut here, and here." Yohan indicated his right forearm and an area on his left side, not far away from the ribs protecting his heart.

"Ben Wai left the fort the next day, still angry. I have been recovering in this hospital ever since. I am willing to help you, but we would be very unwise to travel to Ar without Ben Wai's blessing, and I fear he will distrust all outsiders at the moment."

"Then the first thing you must do is regain his trust," asserted Helge.

"He could be anywhere in the desert by now. It will be hard to find him," he protested. "But, as soon as I'm fit enough, we'll hire a group of Telekai riders and go in search of him. I'll need money to buy him gifts, though. Only the bearing of gifts will help to assuage his anger."

"We will provide money for those gifts, and also to engage the services of the riders and to hire camels for ourselves," she promised.

*　　*　　*　　*　　*

During the next two weeks, while they waited for Yohan to complete his convalescence, the others prepared for the journey to search for Ben Wai and the city of Ar. They purchased the gifts for the chief and supplies for themselves and their guides. Since none of them had ridden before, they also took lessons in camel riding.

"We depart tomorrow at first light," Yohan said to Helge one evening. "I'm now recovered enough to make the journey. However, your Luchorpan friends are not strong enough for the harsh conditions of the desert. They must stay behind. I have a friend I can trust who will look after them, also the mule and pony."

Perkin bristled. "I'm as strong and brave as any of you," he protested. "Besides I have the Seeround Glass."

THE NORTHERN DESERT

"We'll have little use for the glass in the desert", said Vinny. "There are no corners to see round there!" He laughed.

"What about Ar?" said Perkin.

"Ar is deserted," replied Yohan. "We'll have no need for your glass there. It's best you and your two friends remain behind. The desert is a very inhospitable place."

"But ... "

"Sorry, Perkin, Yohan is right," Helge gave him a reassuring smile. "You three bravely entered the caves on Peak Island. This time it's our turn. You must stay behind."

At first light the next day, Helge, Yohan, Squire, Vinny and the twins, accompanied by six Telekai, set off on twelve fully-laden camels. Each of the company was attired in the manner of the Telekai - a white cotton robe, belted at the waist, a white cotton headwear kept in place with a headrope tied around the forehead, and thongs on the feet.

The Telekai were a fearsome and hardy race who inhabited the desert regions from Fort Holt in the west to Dunton in the East. They had no permanent home, but wandered the desert as will and circumstance took them, moving from one oasis to another. Their beast of burden was the camel, which had the unique capacity for endurance in the sandy wastes and could survive for up to a week in the harsh desert environment without water. Winding camel caravans, often carrying goods for hundreds of kilometres, were a familiar feature of this desert landscape.

Following only a hunch, the group made a beeline for the Oasis of Yedi, seventy kilometres away in a north-easterly direction, a journey that they expected would take two days. The Telekai riders told them that the oasis was a favourite watering hole for Ben Wai and his tribe. Two hours after they set off, the sun had risen high into the sky, and the strangers to the desert began to feel the effects of the sun's relentless rays and the unbearable heat reflected from the desert sands. By late morning, they were forced to take a rest for three hours, and the Telekai pitched a tent for the visitors to get some respite from the merciless heat.

Soon after they had resumed their journey, they noticed a change in the weather and detected a strong dry wind coming from the north. The Telekai began to show signs of restlessness. They stopped frequently, their heads bobbing in all directions, their discussion animated.

"What's the problem?" Vinny asked Yohan.

"They're sensing a change in the wind. We may be in for a sandstorm," he warned. "They're also searching for a suitable place to shelter if one comes."

Squire looked in all directions, but all he could see from one horizon to the other was an endless landscape of rolling sand. One of the Telekai pointed towards the east. Another nodded. The six tribesmen lowered their heads and moved silently in the direction indicated. The group of travellers followed. Another quarter of an hour passed before they saw what the Telekai had seen earlier – a group of hard sandstone rocks up to ten metres high, rounded at the top like huge boulders.

As they headed for the shelter of the rocks, towards the north they observed thick clouds of sand raised up by the wind, approaching at a frightening speed. The twelve riders raced to reach the safety of the rocks before the storm arrived, but it took them a further twenty minutes to get there. Arriving only moments before the storm, the Telekai slid down from their camels. The others scrambled from theirs. Following the example of their guides, they squatted down on the lee side of the rock, facing towards the south, and covered their faces with cloth.

THE NORTHERN DESERT

Although the visitors had braced themselves, the arrival of the huge wall of sand and dust, a kilometre high, still caused them alarm. It hit with such force that they were almost swept away despite being shielded by the rocks. The noise of the swirling mass was deafening, and the dense clouds of sand obscured the sun and reduced visibility almost to zero.

The Telekai and Yohan had experienced such a sandstorm before and exhibited no sign of fear, but the five travellers were petrified by the clouds of sand swirling around them that made it difficult for them to breathe. For more than two hours, the choking sand did not relent until, as suddenly as it had begun, the storm subsided, and once again silence prevailed.

After waiting a few more minutes for the sand to settle, they removed the cloths from their faces. The air no longer suffocated them, yet a stifling heat pervaded, and they were very thirsty. Each of them drank freely from the leather water pouches. The Telekai began to murmur among themselves.

"What are they saying?" Helge asked Yohan.

"They say we must pitch our tents and stay here for the night," he replied.

The company dined on dry pita bread and salted beef, washed down with hot sweet coffee - not a very nutritious meal, but very welcome in the circumstances.

During the night, in stark contrast to the unbearable heat of the day, the temperature plummeted. The travellers were very grateful that their Telekai hosts were well prepared, with plenty of quilts and blankets to protect against the cold.

After a good night's sleep, they resumed their journey. The second day passed without incident, and they arrived at the Oasis of Yedi just as the last rays of the setting sun disappeared over the western horizon. They found

HOPE

about twenty Telekai tents at the oasis, but Ben Wai and his followers were not there. The Telekai who had travelled with the visitors enquired whether the chief had been there recently. Yohan translated the answer:

"Ben Wai was here for a few days, but early this morning he and his men set off for Dunton."

"Where's Dunton?" asked Squire.

Helge replied. "It's a small town on the edge of the desert, far away to the east. It's six days' ride from here."

"How can we catch up with him?" Squire remonstrated. "Surely they will be travelling much more quickly than we are able to."

Yohan consulted with the Telekai. After a few minutes, he came back to Squire and the others with a proposition. "There's a man here by the name of Ben Hoi," he said. "He's a cousin of Ben Wai and an expert horse rider. I'll give him money and send him ahead of us on his horse. Since horses can move faster than camels for short distances, they should catch up with Ben Wai within a half day. Ben Hoi will bear this gift for the chief and entreat him to wait for us. We'll follow on the camels and bring the rest of the gifts." The gift that he had indicated was a gold ring.

Vinny looked doubtful. "Can we trust Ben Hoi?" he asked. "What if he just takes the money and the gold ring, and disappears?"

"The Telekai may be fearsome and aloof, but they are honourable people. This man can be trusted," Yohan reassured him.

Ben Hoi and the chestnut-coloured Windracer set off at first light the following morning, and caught up with Ben Wai and his men in the middle of the afternoon. The chief was very pleased with the gold ring. The smile on his face showed that he anticipated receiving the other gifts that Yohan would be bringing. He decided to make camp there and then.

THE NORTHERN DESERT

The rest of the party set off on their camels soon after Ben Hoi had departed. In the middle of the second morning, they caught up with Ben Wai and the other Telekai.

The chief sat on a rug near the entrance to a green tent, which shaded him from the merciless sun. Above the tent, his standard – a green camel on an orange background – swayed in a light breeze.

"What's the significance of the standard?" Helge asked.

"The camel is coloured green because green is the colour of the grass and the trees that are not found in the desert," replied Yohan. "It signifies that the Telekai are dependent on the camel for all their needs, just as other men depend on the grass and the trees. Apart from being a useful pack animal, the camel also provides the Telekai with milk, meat, wool, skin and dung. They use the dried skins for water bottles, belts or sandals and the dung for fuel. The background of the standard is orange to represent the colour of the desert sun."

Yohan greeted Ben Wai in the traditional manner. He bowed, and then knelt, placing his forehead on the ground to show his respect towards the tribal chief. After this, Ben Wai clicked his fingers as a sign that he might stand

Yohan turned to his companions and signalled them to bring the gifts for the chief. Following Yohan's example, they also bowed and knelt, before laying the gifts on the ground at the feet of Ben Wai. The gifts comprised several intricately woven mats, blankets and bags, a basket of fresh fruit, bottles of wine, and sticks of tobacco. Ben Wai plucked an apple from the basket and took a bite. He licked his lips and invited Yohan to talk.

"First of all, your eminence," he began, "please accept my sincere apologies for the incident at the camel race a few weeks ago."

HOPE

The chief waved his hand dismissively. "Apology accepted," he affirmed before taking another bite from the apple.

Seeing the chief had nothing further to say, Yohan continued, "I also have a request on behalf of my companions." He turned and indicated them with a sweep of his arm. "Please let me introduce them to you. Helge, my compatriot who lives in Hanlin Forest, Vineon D'Ur, an archer from Wellborough, the twins Wim and Sim, apprentices to the wizard Tobin, and The Squire who is from another Land. They're on an important mission on behalf of Tobin, and seek your permission to visit the ruins at Ar. If you agree, I will accompany them on their quest and act as their guarantor."

"This is an unusual request," said the chief. He paused before continuing. "But in view of these wonderful gifts, I will give my permission … on one condition. Ben Hoi shall also accompany you to make sure your ... er … friends don't do any damage. He also speaks the common language, so can act as your guide."

"Your eminence is truly generous, and very wise," Yohan replied.

The companions remained at the chief's camp for the remainder of that day and the night. That evening Ben Wai's chefs prepared a banquet for his guests at which the wine flowed and there was much smoking and telling of stories.

* * * * *

The next morning, Ben Wai and his entourage continued on their way eastwards towards Dunton. Helge paid off the six Telekai who had acted as their guides, and watched them set off to return to the fort. The five members of the company, with Yohan and Ben Hoi began their journey south-eastwards towards Ar.

Three days later, they entered the city from the north.

THE NORTHERN DESERT

"As you can see, Ar is now a city of ruins," said Ben Hoi. "More than two thousand years ago it was resplendent, rich and fertile, but now it's lost its former splendour, and everything is covered with sand and dust.

"At that time the desert was much smaller, and the Bun River flowed through the city. Then the great earthquake struck and the course of the river changed. It formerly flowed from Fire Mountain, through Bo's Chasm and northwards to the city, before turning back towards the south. Now it bows towards the west rather than the north. The grand city of Ar lost its lifeblood, and soon its wealth and power disappeared also. After the earthquake, people continued to live here for several decades but, as the desert encroached further towards the south, there was a gradual exodus. Those remaining were powerless to do anything to stop the advance, and life gradually became more and more difficult, until finally they also abandoned the city."

Soon the seven companions found themselves in the city centre riding along a street paved with marble.

"There, on the west side of the street, are the ruins of the Ar Library," said Ben Hoi. He continued to indicate landmarks as they proceeded through the city centre. "And there to the right of the library is where the commercial district used to be. That gate, which connects the commercial district to the Library Square, is the Gate of Telemann, named after our great former leader. There, heading towards the east, is Ben Tui Street. That's where we're heading."

As they passed along Ben Tui Street, Ben Hoi resumed his commentary. "This was once a thriving metropolis. There were beautiful footpaths paved with mosaics where the pedestrians used to walk, and there on the right hand side you can still see some of the narrow little streets that led up to private hill houses, homes of the rich. There on, the left, are the ruins of the Temple of Patumann and other interesting buildings such as the baths, the brothel and the public toilets."

They continued up Ben Tui Street until they found themselves in a large rectangular esplanade. "This was the city square," explained Ben Hoi. "During ancient times, the square would have been full of life, with little shops and people everywhere. Around the square are the ruins of what once were the most important buildings of the city – the city hall, fountains, temples, baths, and over there is the amphitheatre. It used to seat up to 20,000 people."

Yohan and Ben Hoi, with Windracer and the camels tethered nearby, sat under the shade of one of the columns still standing just outside the amphitheatre and shared a pipe of tobacco, while the others went inside to try to find the tooth.

The former inhabitants of Ar had arranged the seating of the amphitheatre on a natural hillside using marble slabs joined together in semicircular arcs. After years of neglect, the amphitheatre had decayed and now partly lay in ruins. However, much of the original structure still stood intact. Three wide staircases led up to a columned gallery around the top of the theatre. Most of the stairs and the columns remained undamaged. At the front, facing the seating, a stage three metres above the ground and richly decorated behind with columns and statues, was still in one piece. The stage had formerly been used by the performers, whether actors, dancers, musicians or fighters.

Helge, Vinny, Squire and the twins busied themselves searching the left side of the fifth row of the amphitheatre seating. After a few minutes' searching, Wim called out, "Here, I think I've found the cleft. It's a small opening between these two marble slabs. I'll try to get my hand down inside, but it's very narrow."

THE NORTHERN DESERT

"You and Sim are the smallest, so if you can't then none of us can," said Helge. "It's a pity we haven't got the Luchorpans with us."

After a struggle, Wim located a small clay jar lodged in the cleft. His hand just passed through the narrow neck of the jar. He felt around inside. There he found the next tooth wrapped in a piece of calico and a piece of paper bearing the instructions for the next part of their mission.

"I've got it!" he announced with glee. He pulled out the tooth and paper but, just as he handed them to Squire and Helge, they heard a yell coming from the other side of the wall.

"It's Yohan," said Helge, starting to her feet. "Something's up."

As the five companions rushed outside and rounded the corner approaching the spot where they had left the others, a gory sight met their eyes.

The body of Ben Hoi lay on the ground covered in blood.

CHAPTER 6

BUNBURY

Horror was etched on Ben Hoi's face. Teeth marks and deep scratches covered his body. Blood oozed from his neck, and entrails welled out from a deep gash to the abdomen. Scarlet patches splattered the sand surrounding the body, and a trail of bloody paw prints led off towards the east.

The older man stooped over the body with his head in his hands.

Vinny found it difficult to speak. "Wh ... what happened?" he asked.

Yohan looked up and brushed his hands through his blond hair. "It was a wild cat," he said with a quavering voice. "It came from nowhere and attacked before we had a chance to draw our weapons. I was the lucky one." He wiped the sweat from his face, and looked up once more. "Before it could attack again, I raised the alarm. If you hadn't arrived so quickly and scared it away, I would have been its next victim."

Helge looked down at her countryman with a sympathetic smile, "Can you describe it?" she asked.

"It was a big cat, with long legs and large paws, and a long tail with a black tip. It had staring green eyes and it growled and snarled in a most fearsome manner with its tail twitching and its ears upright. It had short reddish-brown fur, I think."

"It sounds like a cougar," said Squire.

"Yes," Yohan replied, "it was big like a lion, but it wasn't a lion. And there's one other thing ... "

"Yes?" invited Squire.

"I could have sworn it spoke to us, but that's ridiculous."

"Can you remember what it said?" asked Helge.

"It sounded like it said, 'Gordeve will rule'," he replied.

"We must get out of here at once," urged Helge. "The cougar, or whatever it was, may strike again."

"There will be trouble when Ben Wai hears about this," said Yohan. "He will think you people have brought bad luck to the Telekai. You must go at once, south to the safety of Bunbury. I will return on the horse to Fort Holt to get your Luchorpan friends. We will meet you in Bunbury in … about ten days from now. If you get there first, wait for us at The Green Dragon inn in the city centre."

The travellers waited only long enough to give Ben Hoi a decent burial, and for Yohan to fill up his water bottles.

"I'll ride directly to Fort Holt," he said, "and only stop for short rests."

"Good luck," said Helge, as they prepared to part. "Watch out for the cougars. We'll meet you in Bunbury."

* * * * *

Helge, Squire, Vinny and the twins hastened to get away from the city environs as soon as possible. The ruins offered too many places where the cougar, or cougars, could hide.

"Maybe we were wrong to leave Perkin and the glass behind," said Vinny.

"You're right," conceded Helge. "Nevertheless, we'll be safer from attack once we reach the open desert."

They had one full day's journey in the desert before the landscape slowly began to change, and vegetation started to spring up. Firstly, they came across small patches of hardy grass, then the occasional scrawny bush, and later some small trees and other plants. In the middle of the afternoon of the second day, they reached the top of a low ridge and were relieved to see the shining ribbon that was the Bun River in the distance below. A patchwork of fields of different hues straddled the river.

"This area is very fertile," said Vinny. "The farmers of the Bunbury region are famous for their variety of crops."

This feeling of relief was short-lived. When they looked upstream, they saw thick black clouds gathering in the east. "I hope it's not another sandstorm," said Sim. "I wouldn't want to go through that again."

"I don't think so," said Squire. "We've left the desert behind."

The storm clouds were black and forbidding and were accompanied by a noise that resembled that of heavy rain. Yet the extraordinary speed with which it approached ruled out an ordinary storm.

Thirty minutes later, the storm was almost upon them. "They don't look like rain clouds to me," said Squire. A few moments later, a look of recognition came over his face. "It's a swarm of flying insects."

"Locusts!" exclaimed Vinny. "I've heard that they are able to devastate entire fields of crops in just a few minutes. If the locusts strip those fields bare, it could be disastrous for the city."

"But look," interrupted Helge, "they're not heading for the fields. They're coming straight for us! This must be Gordeve's work."

"You're right," agreed Vinny. "Even though the wet, mild conditions may have been ideal for them to swarm, the evil wizard has used magic to send them at high speed in our direction. They're not bent on devouring crops. They're more interested in destroying us. Let's get out of here!"

They turned their camels towards the west and tried to outrun the locusts, but this proved fruitless. As Squire glanced back over his shoulder, he saw the leading group of insects swoop down. They were getting closer and would soon overtake them. He had visions of the locusts stripping their skeletons bare of flesh in a matter of seconds.

"Can't you do something?" Helge shouted to Sim and Wim, her voice hoarse in desperation. "Can't you invoke some spell to counteract the magic of Gordeve?"

The twins stopped and turned their camels to face the swarm. They lifted up their arms in a gesture towards the clouds of insects. "Locusts go back," they commanded.

At first, this seemed to work and some of the early arrivals turned back, but the pressure of locusts was too great to repel them all.

"Stop them! They're getting through!" shouted Helge.

"We're doing all we can. There are too many of them!" yelled Wim.

Soon a cloud of hungry, man-eating locusts surrounded them and they felt the crazed look in their compound eyes boring into them.

"We're not strong enough," said Sim, casting his eyes to the ground. "We're only apprentices. We can't invoke a powerful enough incantation. We need Tobin's help."

"There's one more hope," said Squire. "I have the shield. Tobin said it would protect us in times of great danger. Now is the time to put it to use and test its power."

Squire held up the shield, training it towards the group of approaching locusts. Almost immediately, the five stars on the face of the shield began to glow, increasing in intensity until beams of light shot forth from the stars, directed at the approaching locusts. The force emanating from the shield frazzled many of them, and repelled others, just as a mirror reflects light, to collide with great force into the next group arriving. Stunned, they fell to the ground, only for Helge, Vinny and the twins to stamp on them before they could recover their strength.

Squire sustained this onslaught for several seconds, by which time many thousands of locusts had been fried or stunned and killed. However, as his eyes focused on the back of the shield, he himself became victim to its power. The force knocked him backwards off his camel and onto the ground. He screamed as his back arched in pain. Squire's friends, who crowded around him, saw his face had turned pale, and his eyes stared vacantly upwards.

Squire continued to look into the back of the shield and became aware of a picture forming, as if he were looking through a window. The picture was hazy at first, but slowly cleared, and he could visualise a scene. Though his eyes remained open, they lost touch with the new world and focused on the picture that drew him into itself. He was not Squire any more, but once again his real self in the world from which he had come.

He saw himself with a young girl, fishing on the bank of a river. Where the river bent sharply on a flat piece of land, there was an area of still water where he and the girl hoped to catch a few minnows or even a trout if they were lucky. Downstream, he saw rapids where the river passed through a narrow ravine.

The girl sat, reading a letter. Its envelope lay on the ground near to where she sat. In his dream, Squire looked closely and saw that it was addressed to Mr. Grant Cowie.

So, that's my real name, Squire thought, *Grant Cowie. Who is the girl? She must be my daughter, or maybe a niece.*

A few minutes later, Grant felt the tug of a bigger fish on the line. He jumped to his feet, gritted his teeth and reeled furiously when he saw it was a large rainbow trout. Then a breath of wind drew his attention to the envelope blowing into the water. He looked to his right and saw that Theresa no longer sat on the bank beside him. He called out in desperation, but there was no reply. He abandoned his rod and the trout and started to run along the bank calling the girl's name, "Theresa, Theresa."

Theresa, her name is Theresa, *Squire thought.*

Grant began to sweat. As he ran, he could feel the small scar on the left side of his top lip throbbing. "Theresa," he shouted. "Theresa, where are you? Please answer me."

Then he saw her, downstream, struggling to attract his attention. Her arms flailed wildly, and she could barely keep her head above the water. He knew she could swim a little. Nevertheless, she was approaching the rapids, and he was certain that the swirling waters would sweep her under.

Grant ran along the bank in a frantic attempt to reach the rapids. Then he tripped on the root of a tree and fell. He felt his head hit something hard. Amid the pain, darkness descended.

Squire awoke from his vision to find Helge and Vinny bending over him. Helge held his arms and shook gently.

Her face was drawn and pallid. "Squire, are you all right?" she asked.

Chest heaving, his breathing laboured, Squire wheezed his answer. "Yes, I think so," he said. "What happened to the locusts?"

"Many of them were killed. Those we didn't kill saw their efforts were to no avail, turned and retreated towards the east. But, what happened to you?"

HOPE

"The shield has a hidden power, just as Tobin told me. When I had finished using it to ward off the locusts and fell backwards off the camel, I looked in the back of the shield and had a glimpse of the world from which I come. It was like a 'Window on my World'."

Vinny looked at him with concern. "What did you see?" he asked.

Squire strained to sit up. "That's the strange thing," he replied. "I don't remember much about what I saw or what happened! All I can recollect are a river in flood, rushing waters, cries for help, and falling and banging my head, just as I remember dreaming on my first morning in the forest. As Tobin warned me, the experience was not pleasant. What can this mean? Who am I, really? Am I ever going to be able to return to my own world?"

"I don't know," said Vinny, "but the good news is that the shield has shown that it holds magic to fight against the evil of Gordeve."

But, at what price? thought Squire. *With the aid of the shield, I might be able to overcome further attacks from Gordeve, but I fear using it because of the agony and distress it causes me.*

The five made camp for the night on the banks of the Bun River.

"We let everyone down earlier," Sim said to Wim. "We had to leave it to Squire to use the shield against the locusts. Do you think they will forgive us if I use magic to catch some fish for supper?"

"It might help make amends," Wim agreed, "but have you forgotten Tobin's warning about not using magic unless it's really necessary?"

"It can't do any harm," his brother said. "After all, Gordeve already knows where we are."

"I suppose you're right," conceded Wim.

*   *   *   *   *

The next day they looked for a place to cross the river.

BUNBURY

Vinny cast his eyes upstream and downstream. "There doesn't seem to be a bridge anywhere near here," he said, "and the river looks too deep to ford."

"We'll have to swim across," said Helge. "Can camels swim?"

"I think they can," replied Squire.

Sim sniggered. "How can camels swim?" he said. "They live in the desert and the only water they ever get to see at the oases only comes up to their knees."

"I don't see why we have to cross the river at all," said Wim. "Bunbury straddles this river. Surely, we could follow the eastern bank of the river until we reach a bridge nearer to the city? After all, the farmers must have some means of getting across."

"You're right," said Helge. "That's what we'll do."

It took them a further two days' riding before they arrived at Bunbury.

* * * * *

Meanwhile Yohan and Windracer had made their way back to Fort Holt, a distance of two hundred and fifty kilometres. Under normal conditions, this would have been an easy ride, but these were not normal conditions. The horse had to endure the extreme temperatures of the desert, and Yohan gave him little rest as he was determined to get back to the fort in the least possible time. With only short breaks for food and water, they continued their journey throughout the day and the night.

Bedraggled and exhausted, they arrived back at the fort in the middle of the following morning. A hostile crowd of Telekai quickly surrounded him and Windracer.

"Where's Ben Hoi?" demanded one. "That's his horse!"

"Ben Hoi has been attacked and killed by a wild cat," replied Yohan.

HOPE

"You're lying," said the man. "There are no wild cats in the desert. They wouldn't be able to survive without adequate food and water."

"Seize him!" said another man. "He has killed Ben Hoi and stolen his horse. And get those small friends of his. They've brought nothing but bad luck to the Telekai. Throw them all in prison."

Two burly Telekai grabbed Yohan and dragged him away. They took him to the fort prison and locked him in a cell. A few minutes later, the three screaming Luchorpans joined him. As they sat dazed and confused on the cold concrete floor, he related all that had happened to their companions since they had separated.

"How are we going to get out of here?" wailed Vylin. "Our only friends are far away from us, and they don't even know that we're in trouble." She began to cry.

"I don't know," replied Yohan, "but I think we must be prepared for a long stay in prison. If I'm found guilty of horse theft, they may even kill me."

"It's the cap," said Alvin.

"What cap?" asked Perkin.

"When I visited Helge and the others at the Rover's Retreat on the day following the midsummer festival, I took my cap off and put it on the bed. It's really bad luck, you know. That must be why we're in this predicament. I've been waiting for something bad to happen."

The four of them languished in prison for three days and nights. Their guards gave them only a little bread to eat and water to drink.

*   *   *   *   *

Three days after Yohan and the Luchorpans had been imprisoned was also the day of the locust attack. That same afternoon, far away on the eastern edge of the Air Mountains, the giant eagle prepared himself once more to fly to help those of the company in need. He flew first to the Bun River. Circling high above the shining waters, he glided and looked down with satisfaction. *Good, Squire and the shield have successfully dealt with the plague of locusts sent by my sister*, he thought. Then he noticed Sim and Wim once again using magic when they didn't need to. *Oh no! When will they ever learn?*

The eagle did not land, but after completing his glide, he flapped his wings and set off towards the north-west to fly to the aid of the four prisoners at Fort Holt.

With a final beat of his wings, the eagle landed outside the prison gate, and transformed himself once more into the wizard Tobin. He stole up behind the guard at the gate and put him to sleep with a gentle touch to the back of his neck. Then, with a spell quickly muttered under his breath, he had the gates unlocked, and passed unnoticed inside.

He overcame another guard in the same way, and entered the cell that held the prisoners.

The four prisoners were startled as he flung open the door to their cell.

"Who ... who are you?" asked Perkin. He was in awe at the sight of the wizard, and more than a little frightened, but despite his fear, he tried to show bravado.

"I am Tobin." Even as he spoke, the wizard didn't stop, but proceeded further into the cell.

"Tobin!" Relief showed on their faces as they all chimed in unison. None of them had met the wizard before.

"Hush!" warned Tobin. "You must be quiet, and prepare to leave this place without delay. Here are some provisions for your journey." With a sweep of his staff and a few words of magic, the wizard produced a pack full

HOPE

of food and a water bottle. Then he issued a shrill whistle. A few seconds later the mule, Faithful, and the pony, Conny, came trotting into the cell. "They seem to be very happy to see you again," said the wizard. "Now listen carefully. From here, you must travel south-eastwards to Bunbury. The journey will take you about five days. There you will meet up with your companions. Go now, and don't look back."

With a flurry of his robe, the wizard turned, and left as silently as he had come. The four friends followed him out of the gate, but they could see no sign of him. All they saw was a large eagle flying off towards the west.

By that time, it was almost dark. Eager to obey the wizard's words, the four companions set off at once towards Bunbury.

It wasn't until the next morning that the prison guards awoke and raised the alarm, by which time Yohan and the Luchorpans had travelled several kilometres. The Telekai set off in hot pursuit, but their former prisoners had too much of a lead on them and by noon the Telekai made the decision not to pursue them further. They feared the use of further magic and were glad to see the back of the troublemakers.

* * * * *

Yohan, the three Luchorpans, the mule and the pony arrived at Bunbury four days after Helge and the others had. As agreed with Yohan before they had separated at Ar, their five friends waited for them at the Green Dragon Inn.

Bunbury, the capital and largest city in West Thorland, lay in the central eastern part of the country and straddled the Bun River. The river, which had been pivotal to the development and growth of the city, was the hub around which it revolved, being the means of communication, water supply and drainage. The waters also supported a thriving fish population.

BUNBURY

Bunbury was the seat of government for West Thorland, over which King Jovanius II and his queen, Vinabelle, had ruled for more than thirty years. Prince Tycho, who had recently married, was their son and heir. The chief minister, How Tree, led the government from the parliamentary building close to the banks of the river in the centre of the city, not far from the royal palace.

Three bridges crossed the river. Yohan, who knew the city well, led his three companions past the king's palace and the parliamentary building, across the central of the three bridges, and onto the opposite embankment where they found the Green Dragon Inn.

When the three Luchorpans and Yohan were reunited with their friends, there was much rejoicing and relating of stories. The ale flowed that evening, pipes were smoked, and Vylin played the violin whilst the two male Luchorpans danced joyfully for the entertainment of the others.

The following morning, Yohan bade his friends farewell.

"I must return to the desert," he said. "That's where I've lived for many years, and there I must return."

Squire looked directly at Yohan and raised an eyebrow. "But won't you be in danger?" he asked. "They'll just put you in prison again."

"I'm not returning to the fort," he replied. "Instead, I'll ride to Dunton where I hope to meet with Ben Wai. I'll explain everything to him. I need to warn him about the cougars and other dangers, and offer my services to assist him. We've known each other a long time. Despite our disagreement a few weeks ago, he trusts me and I'm sure he will believe my story. I'm prepared to take that chance."

Yohan purchased a horse from the innkeeper. The mare was nothing as fine and graceful as Windracer, but nonetheless she was swift and strong.

HOPE

Yohan set off eastwards to Bo's Bridge where he would join the road going north to Dunton.

After his departure, the eight companions met to look for the first time at the piece of paper with the instructions for finding the fourth tooth.

Helge read:

"First right premolar – top jaw
Go to the River City and enquire
About the tunnels that can be found
Underground,
Beneath the Palace Royal.
Seek out a narrow tunnel dug from soil,
That toward the Bun does run.
A rodent's nest is the test
To find what you desire."

"The River City must be Bunbury," said Vylin. "And here we are already!"

"But what are the tunnels referred to, and how are we going to find our way around them?" asked Alvin. "I don't much like tunnels – the ones on Peak Island were bad enough – and I certainly don't like rodents."

"I'll ask the innkeeper if he knows anything about these tunnels," suggested Helge.

"I don't know anything about tunnels," said the innkeeper, "but I know someone who might. You must go to see Jippers, the royal rat-catcher. I'm sure he'll be able to help you. I'll take you to him this afternoon."

They found Jippers in a small cottage in the grounds of the royal palace. He was an old man, and looked even older than his seventy years. If he could have stood up straight, he would have been of average height, but his bent back made his body permanently stooped. His wore ragged clothes and had long, dishevelled grey hair. A tangle of grey beard almost completely concealed his flat nose and large flaring nostrils.

Jippers looked after six cats, which were his only family, his constant companions, and fellow workers in his job as rat-catcher to the king. When the visitors arrived, he had just finished work for the day. As he opened the door, an odour, a mixture of smells of excrement and stale tobacco, greeted them. He indulged in the unsavoury habit of chewing tobacco and spitting the juices every few minutes.

Jippers squinted and looked at the strangers. The brown colour of his irises was difficult to see in his deep-set, hollow eyes. "Who have we here?" he asked the innkeeper. While he spoke, he chewed and then spat.

"These people need your help … " the innkeeper began.

Jippers interrupted. "People, people? What manner of people are these three little ones?" he asked, pointing to the Luchorpans. "They look like pixies, or dwarves to me, not people." He spat again.

Perkin puffed his chest and looked into the old man's eyes. "We are Luchorpans," he replied. "Our people come from Luchor beyond the Air Mountains, but we live in Rivermeet. We may be small, but we are not afraid."

At that moment, a black cat came crawling out from under one of the chairs, stretching its legs and arching its back.

"A black cat!" exclaimed Alvin. "Did you know that black cats are demons in disguise and very bad luck? If one of them crosses your path, it will create a barrier of evil, cutting you off from the Creator."

"Nonsense," replied the old man. "I've had Sooty for seven years and he has never brought me bad luck."

HOPE

Sim curled his lip. "Take no notice of him," he said. "He's always carrying on about superstitions and bad luck."

"Who is the leader of your group?" the old man asked.

"I am," replied Helge.

Jippers turned to face the tall woman and glared. "And how can I help *you*?" he asked.

"We need to explore some tunnels under the palace," she explained.

"There are no tunnels except the sewers, and they're full of rats."

"Then that's where we must go," she conceded.

"What's in it for me?" asked the rat-catcher.

"Fifty shillings," Vinny interrupted before Helge could answer.

"One hundred," said Jippers.

"Sixty."

"Eighty," insisted Jippers, spitting again.

"Done," confirmed Vinny.

"Meet me here at first light tomorrow morning," said the old man. "Bring the money, and wear boots." He indicated his own pair of dung-crusted, leather boots placed near the door. "And some old clothes. And you'll need torches," he added.

They decided that they wouldn't all need to accompany Jippers the following day.

"I'll go," volunteered Squire, "since I have the shield. Perkin must accompany me with the glass, and either Vinny or Helge to help protect us; and one of the twins must go in case there's a need to use magic. Four of us should be enough."

They decided that Vinny should be the fourth. Helge would be too tall for the tunnels, and it would be impossible for her to use her sling in the confined spaces. Vinny carried a small catapult that he had made during the night, and a selection of pebbles. As well as being an expert with the bow, he also considered himself a fine shot with the catapult.

Squire, Perkin, Vinny and Sim bought some boots, donned their oldest clothes, made torches, and met Jippers as arranged at sunrise. Alvin complained that the boots were a very cheap type, and that he could have made them some very fine leather ones if he had had the time.

"What's that in your pocket?" Jippers asked Perkin.

"That's the Seeround Glass," Perkin explained. "With it I can see around corners."

"Very interesting," Jippers remarked. Then, addressing Squire, he added. "And what is that thing you're carrying?"

"It's the Shield of Squire," he explained. "It was given to me by the wizard Tobin to help protect me in times of great danger. But I only use it when really necessary for, when I do it also gives me very unpleasant glimpses of my own world."

On hearing these words, Jippers became very alert, his ears pricked up, and he almost stood straight. "So you are not from this world?" he said with a smile. "This is my Hope, the shield."

"What did you say?" asked Squire.

Jippers hesitated before replying: "Er, I said I hope you will let me hold the shield."

"No!" said Squire with alarm. "No one touches the shield except me."

"Very well, let's get going," said Jippers, spitting as he spoke. "But, first of all, where's my money?"

Vinny handed over forty shillings. "You can have the rest when you've finished the job," he said.

Jippers scowled and spat again. "If you insist," he said. "Follow me."

HOPE

Jippers carried with him a bag of tools and a small basket. He led them towards the royal palace. When they were a few metres away from the wall separating them from the royal kitchens and bathrooms, he stopped. Beneath his feet, they could see a manhole cover. He removed a crowbar from the bag of tools he carried, and, with the experience of much practice, in only a few seconds he had prised the lid from the manhole. A waft of foul-smelling gases coming up from below almost knocked over the four friends. Jippers, who was used to the smells, seemed unconcerned. Nevertheless, he pulled five pieces of rag and a small phial from his bag. He poured a few drops of liquid onto each piece of cloth.

"This cheap perfume will help to disguise the more unpleasant smells," he said. "We must also tie ourselves together for safety, and so that none of you gets lost."

He removed a length of rope from his bag, tied one end around his own waist, and then passed it to the others so they could do the same. Hesitating only long enough to spit once again, he then hauled himself over the side of the manhole and placed his feet on the top rung of a metal ladder.

"Follow me," he ordered. "But don't light your torches yet. There's methane in these gases, and methane can explode. I'll tell you when it's safe to light them."

Slowly the five individuals made their way down the ladder – Jippers first, followed by Perkin, Squire, Sim, and finally Vinny. After a few minutes, they found themselves standing on a flat, muddy surface.

Their ears detected the sound of running water or effluent of some kind, the atmosphere was damp and clammy, and the perfume did little to disguise the unbearable stench. With only a thin shaft of light seeping down from far above, the darkness, the confined space and the unpleasant smells were daunting enough. Nevertheless, when they heard shrill squeaks and squeals coming from distant parts of the labyrinth of tunnels, they became even more alarmed.

Sim grabbed Jippers by the arm. "What's that?" he asked.

"It's only the sewer rats," replied Jippers. In the dim light, Squire thought he detected a thin smile on the old man's face.

"Follow me," said Jippers. "This is the way to the tunnel that opens into the Bun River."

He sure-footedly led the way, frequently stepping from one side of the stream of effluent to the other, and turning corners with the knowledge of experience. The others, partly because of the darkness, but more because of their inexperience in these unpleasant conditions, frequently slipped and fell into the stream of effluent flowing past. Only Perkin, who used the glass to help him find his way around the corners, didn't suffer as many falls as his friends. Many a curse was uttered during those few minutes. *I'm sure he must be smiling and silently laughing at us*, Squire thought.

After several minutes, Jippers stopped. "Here's the tunnel that leads to the river," he said. "This tunnel was cut from the soil, not rock, so the walls and roof are made from bricks and mortar. There's also an underground stream that joins here with the effluent from the palace. Above us is a shaft that takes away most of the gases." The four looked upwards and could detect a distant gleam of light. "The air is much purer from now onwards, so you can safely light your torches," he added.

"This colony," Jippers explained, "feeds on waste that the cooks from the royal kitchen toss down the airshaft twice a day. Therefore, the rats have made their home in the tunnels close to the bottom of the shaft. I'm quite confident that I will be able to find the nest mentioned in the instructions.

HOPE

"As long as I can remember, and that goes back nearly thirty years, there's always been a nest in that particular hole." He indicated an opening in the brick wall just ten metres from the bottom of the shaft.

"But won't there be rats hiding inside?" asked Sim with concern.

"Undoubtedly," replied Jippers. "That's why I've brought Sooty along." He opened his basket and there, snuggled inside, lay the black cat. "He'll flush the rats out."

Jippers picked up the cat and placed it by the entrance to the rats' burrow. Seconds later, they heard a sound of squealing as the female rat, followed by her young, raced out of another exit from the burrow and scurried past in an effort to get away from the cat. When one of the fleeing rats brushed past Sim's leg, closely followed by the cat, he lost control of himself. In an effort to evade the rodent, he moved back a pace, his feet slipped from under him and he found himself sprawling in the stream of effluent. *Curse Alvin and his unlucky black cat,* he thought to himself.

Vinny let fly some pebbles from the catapult, and succeeded in hitting two of the rodents. Meanwhile Sim had regained some of his composure. *I will not be made a fool of,* he thought. *I'll deal with those rats.* Still sitting in a pool of effluent, he pointed the index finger of his right hand towards a retreating rat and uttered a few magic words under his breath. A beam of energy emanated from the tip of his finger and the rat collapsed in a heap. Seconds later, he had zapped another two rats.

"That's not necessary," said Jippers. "Although they can be very ferocious when cornered, sewer rats are really quite cowardly, and will usually run. They will never normally attack people. You shouldn't be afraid of them."

The old man turned his attention to the nest. "Now all you have to do is put your hand inside to find what you're looking for," he said with a smirk.

"How about you, son?" he said looking at Sim, at the same time turning his head to spit on the ground. The poor light offered by the torches did much to conceal the angry glare on Sim's face.

"I've a better idea," said Vinny. "Open up that tool bag of yours and find us something to dig with."

Jippers opened the bag and handed a small trowel to Vinny, who began to dig. The ground inside the hole was quite soft. After about five minutes digging, the trowel hit something hard. Vinny pulled it from the dirt.

"It's a small airtight tin," he said. He opened the tin and inside found the tooth and the instructions for finding the next one.

The return journey to the top of the manhole, though unpleasant, seemed to pass much more quickly than the downwards journey. On reaching the surface, the four friends gratefully breathed in the cool, fresh air once again.

Vinny handed over the remaining forty shillings to the old man.

Once they were out of earshot, he said, "I hope that's the last we will see of him."

CHAPTER 7

BO'S CHASM

The four who had searched for the tooth in the sewers beneath the royal palace were happy to see their companions again, but the others who had stayed behind didn't seem quite so enthusiastic.

"You stink," Wim said to his brother. Sim glowered.

"You're filthy," Vylin said to Perkin, who looked embarrassed.

Once the four of them had taken hot baths and put on fresh clothes, they were much more welcome.

They shared a good hot meal, then met in Vinny's room where he related to the others what had happened in the tunnels beneath the grounds of the royal palace. Helge then opened the piece of paper with instructions for finding the next tooth. She read:

"Second right premolar – top jaw

Go to the river where the water runs black.
Under the bridge, at shoulder height,
Find a brick that is white.
Behind the brick, further back,
A rubber ball will reveal all."

"Which river has water that runs black?" asked Vinny.

BO'S CHASM

Nobody spoke for a few moments. Helge interrupted the silence. "We have a volcanic mountain on Atmos," she said. "The waters of the Blacksilt River carry black volcanic ash. Maybe that's what it's referring to."

Alvin shook his head and rubbed his chin. "I don't think so. I think we should be looking for something a bit closer." He paced the room then stopped. "Let's try asking the innkeeper."

They made their way downstairs where they found the innkeeper washing some glasses. Helge asked him if he had heard of a river that could be referred to as 'black' and if it had any bridges.

He scratched his head for a moment before replying. "Why, it must be the Blackwater River," he said. "It carries black volcanic ash from Fire Mountain. And the bridge referred to is surely Daly's Bridge. It's the only bridge over the Blackwater River."

"Well you were almost right, Helge," teased Vinny. "Thank you, sir," he said to the innkeeper.

The companions stayed two more nights at the inn to recover from their previous ordeals, and to buy fresh provisions. Then they settled their bill, thanked the innkeeper for his hospitality and help, loaded the mule and pony, and set off on the road from Bunbury leading towards the east.

At the end of the first day, they set up camp close to the roadside where a group of rocky outcrops afforded them some shelter. After they had enjoyed a tasty meal of roasted pheasant, Squire decided to go in search of some fruit. It was still half an hour before sunset and he carried his shield with him, so he felt quite safe. However, when he hadn't returned by sunset, the others began to worry, recalling the time the cougars had abducted him on the way to Rivermeet. Their concern increased as darkness descended.

In the distance, an owl hooted.

HOPE

Alvin grabbed Vylin's arm. "Did you hear that?" he said. "The owl hooted three times. It's a sign of bad luck. Something bad has happened to Squire. I know it has."

"Don't be silly, Alvin," said his sister. "We'll find him."

They decided to split into two groups. Perkin, Alvin, Vinny and Sim went to search for Squire, while the others stayed at the campsite in case he should return. Using the glass, Perkin looked behind every rock and every tree within five hundred metres of the camp, but to no avail. They were ready to give up when the light of Sim's torch revealed a pair of legs sticking out from behind a rock. Vinny drew his bow and they edged closer.

Then Vinny recognised the boots. "It's Squire," he said.

"But he's not moving. Is he dead?" asked Perkin, stepping back a pace.

At that moment, Squire grunted and turned on his side. Vinny laughed. "No, he's only sleeping." He prodded Squire's leg. "Wake up."

"Squire, are you all right?" asked Alvin. "We thought something bad must have happened to you again, especially when we heard the … "

Sim raised the torch in the direction of Alvin. "Shut up, Alvin," he said. "Take no notice of him, Squire. Are you hurt?"

"No, I'm fine. I was very tired after the journey. I sat down to eat an apple and must have dozed off."

"Thank goodness you're all right," said Perkin, drawing closer again. "But I'm puzzled. Why couldn't I find you with the Seeround Glass?"

"Maybe you just missed him," suggested Vinny. "Why don't you go around the other side of this rock and try again."

Perkin did as Vinny proposed. "I don't get it," he said. "I still can't see Squire with the glass, but I can see the rest of you without any trouble."

When they returned to the camp, the whole group discussed this strange phenomenon. After some of them had mooted some less plausible ideas, Helge suggested, "There can only be one explanation. The glass cannot see Squire because he's from another Land."

Perkin frowned. "If you're right, how can we trust the reliability of the glass from now onwards?" he asked.

"I think we can," she replied. "As far as we know, Squire is the only person who has been brought here from another Land. But we must be cautious." She stiffened and turned towards Squire. "This is the third time this has happened. Don't you know the dangers by now? Don't ever go wandering off alone like that again."

Squire's head dropped. "I'm sorry," he said. "I only wanted to find some fruit to eat, but I dozed off."

The next day dawned to a low cloud cover and incessant rain, which made travel impossible. Fortunately, the rain stopped in the evening and they managed make a fire to dry their sodden clothes.

The following day, the weather was fine, and they resumed their journey towards Daly's Bridge. As they silently trudged along the muddy road, trying to avoid the potholes, out of the corner of her eye Vylin thought she saw a shadow, something following them in the cover of the trees. She turned her head and listened intently to the sounds all around her, waiting for the snap of a branch or the sound of a voice, but she heard nothing.

"Come here, everyone," she said. She spoke softly, but the urgency of her tone broke their concentration and mechanical stride. "Don't look back now, but I think we're being followed. I'm sure I've seen a shadowy figure two or three times since we left the campsite this morning. I don't know whether it's a person or an animal, but every time I look in its direction, it quickly disappears behind a rock or a tree."

"Could it be another cougar?" Vinny surmised.

"I'll try to check up with the glass," suggested Perkin. He searched behind every rock and tree within sight, but the glass revealed no animal or person. "There's nothing there," he concluded.

Sim looked at Vylin with a smirk. "You must be imagining things, Vylin," he said.

"I did see something." Vylin struggled to hold back her tears. "Really, I did. You believe me, don't you Perkin?"

"Of course, I do." He placed a reassuring arm around her shoulder.

Vylin didn't catch sight of the shadowy figure again that day. By evening, she began to think that Sim must be right.

That night passed without incident, and they expected to arrive at Daly's Bridge by the evening of the next day.

The new day dawned to clear blue skies, and they were all in high spirits. However, when they were just twenty kilometres from their destination, they heard a horse approaching from the northerly direction. They quickly dived for cover behind some bushes.

When the horseman came in sight, his long blond locks billowing in the wind, Helge let out a low hiss of breath. "Yohan," she called out. "We didn't expect to see you again so soon. Is there something wrong?"

Yohan's mount came to a standstill in front of the travellers. The mare shook her head and whinnied, steam issuing from her open mouth and nostrils. Yohan dismounted and patted the mare's flank. "Well done girl," he said. "Now you can rest." While he spoke, he tied her reins to the branch of a tree. Still breathing heavily, he sat down on a log to talk with his friends.

"I never made it to Dunton," he said. "Before I reached the fork where the road to Dunton and the main highway separate, I noticed a lot of activity in Dun Wood. The animals that live in the wood were behaving strangely, and running away towards the south. I decided to investigate and continued travelling north until I was in sight of Telemann's Wall."

"Whose wall?" interrupted Alvin.

"Telemann's Wall. The Emperor Telemann, the former ruler of Ar, built the wall more than two thousand years ago. The Telekai are his direct descendents."

"What's the wall for?"

"Telemann had the wall built to separate West Thorland from East Thorland, to keep his enemies at bay."

"Wow! It must be a big wall."

"Enormous. It's the height of ten men and stretches from the Air Mountains near Swanborough in the west to the Southern Ocean far to the south of here. From the western mountains, it passes to the north of the desert and at Dun Wood bends towards the south and around Fire Mountain, and then continues to the sea east of Ash Wood."

Vinny interrupted, "I believe I've seen this wall," he said. "When Gordeve summoned my soul on the day after the fire at Wellborough, I flew over what I thought was a long winding road. It must have been the wall."

"The wall is wide enough to be mistaken for a road when viewed from above," agreed Yohan. "As far as we know, there are only two ways through the wall. The first is a gate near Dun Wood. This has remained closed for more than two centuries. Further south, to the south-east of Fire Mountain, there's a tunnel under the wall. The tunnel has remained open, but is always guarded on both sides of the wall. No one can travel through the tunnel unless they have a valid pass."

"So, what did you see happening at the wall?" Squire asked.

Yohan got up to stretch his legs, before answering. "When I got within sight of the gate in the wall, I noticed that it had been opened. I hid behind a rock and waited to see what would happen. Then I saw why the animals were running away. A group of about twenty cougars passed through the gate, but they were not alone. They had riders. After they had passed through, someone closed the gate again."

"What kind of riders?" asked Helge.

"They were Kobalos."

"This is bad news indeed," she said. "Gordeve must have used some kind of magic to tame the cougars so that they will allow the Kobalos to ride them. The Kobalos will be able to travel much more quickly now. Twenty is not many, but this is just the beginning. She might have a whole army of these creatures. In which direction did they go, Yohan?"

"I followed them, but with difficulty because they could travel much more swiftly than my horse. Nevertheless, I managed to keep them in sight until I saw them turn towards Dunton. Gordeve's spies must have thought that your party was on its way to Dunton."

Vinny shook his head. "No, that cannot be," he said. "Remember she sent the locusts when we were already well south of the desert. She knows where we are. There must be some other reason why they were going to Dunton."

"Anyway," continued Yohan, "whatever the reason, they've gone to Dunton, and I believe it's only a matter of time before they come south to try to find you."

Squire paced backwards and forwards. "What are we to do?"

"Well," said Helge, "we have the advantage because they're not aware that we know they're coming. We must prepare an ambush."

Yohan thought for a moment. "I know just the place," he said. "It's called Bo's Chasm. It's north of here, on the way to Dunton, but it will probably take you a day to walk there."

BO'S CHASM

"Then we'd better get started at once, so that we get there before the cougars and Kobalos," said Helge.

* * * * *

As the companions spoke, the cougars and their riders attacked Dunton. Dunton, a small township, had a permanent population of only about two hundred citizens, but at certain times of the year, its population was swelled by an influx of visitors, nomadic Telekai from the desert. At this time, there were some three hundred nomads housed in their tents, and these included Ben Wai, paramount chief of the Telekai.

The cougars struck without warning. With their sharp claws and teeth, they easily ripped open and destroyed the tents. They ran rampant throughout the camp, killing and devouring as they went. Five of the cougars and seven Kobalos were killed, but that was a small price for them to pay compared with the carnage they inflicted on the Telekai. Not one of the nomadic Telekai survived the onslaught, including Ben Wai himself. The Dunton people, better protected in their permanent buildings, fared rather better. Nevertheless, the axes of the Kobalos killed some fifty of their number. The men finally succeeded in driving them away. The remaining cougars and Kobalos regrouped in Dun Wood and rested before racing southwards towards Bo's Bridge.

* * * * *

At the same time the companions marched northwards with greater urgency than ever before, while Yohan rode on ahead to scout for the enemy.

By noon the following day, the rest of the company arrived at Bo's Bridge, which spanned the Bun River just a few kilometres south of the chasm. Since Yohan had not rejoined them by that time, they were optimistic that they would get to Bo's Chasm before the enemy.

HOPE

They crossed the bridge, not stopping for a rest, and continued on their way towards the chasm, a narrow cleft in the deep red-coloured sandstone characteristic of the area. In the early afternoon, when they rounded a bend in the road, a breathtaking display met them, as light streaming down from above created images of stark form and rich hues of reds and yellows on the high cliff walls.

Soon afterwards, they heard the sound of hooves again. Yohan arrived with another rider whose clothes appeared dishevelled and spotted with blood.

"This is Heremann," said Yohan. "He's just arrived from Dunton."

Heremann dismounted and sat on a rock by the roadside. With his head in his hands, he tried to restrain his grief but couldn't hold it in any more.

Helge laid a reassuring hand on his shoulder. "Can you tell us about it?" she asked.

Tears ran down his face. "It was awful," he sobbed. "The carnage was such that you couldn't have imagined in your worst dreams. Bodies and bits of bodies, partly devoured, litter the desert around Dunton. My family, my friends, camels and horses … The sand is stained red with blood. We started burying the dead, but before we could complete the job, some of the bodies had begun to decay in the heat of the desert sun, and there was such a stench as to make even the strongest of stomachs retch.

"Many are dead from the attack of the enemy, including Ben Wai himself. The chiefs have chosen Ben Wai's son, Ben Lei, to succeed his father as paramount chief. Even now he is calling up all able-bodied Telekai men to form an army."

Heremann turned towards Yohan. "We now know that you spoke the truth about the circumstances of Ben Hoi's death. Ben Lei seeks your counsel, my Lord. He dispatched riders to search for you, three into the desert – to Fort Holt, to Yedi and one by way of Ar to Bunbury. I was sent south on the road. Ben Lei requests that you accompany me and return at once to Dunton. First, we must deal with the enemy. They're coming this way."

"Are they far behind?" asked Helge.

"They can only be a couple of hours away," said Heremann.

Vinny turned to Yohan. "What's your plan?" he asked.

"We must trap them in the chasm," replied Yohan. "As you can see it's very narrow. The floor was once the riverbed of the Bun River, before it changed its course about two thousand years ago. Look, at the top its cliff walls nearly touch each other and it's so narrow that light only reaches the base for a couple of hours around noon each day."

Squire repeated Vinny's question. "But what's your plan, Yohan," he asked.

"When I passed through here earlier in the day, I did a bit of scouting around," he replied. "In particular I climbed to the top of those cliffs." He pointed high to the right at the northern end of the chasm. "I discovered that there's a large boulder very close to the edge. Some of us must wait near the boulder until the cougars and Kobalos have passed through the northern entrance to the chasm. Then I reckon, with the help of the mule, the three horses and some ropes, we should be able to topple the rock so that it will block their line of retreat. Meanwhile, Vinny, Helge and the twins will defend the southern exit to the chasm. Once the enemy are trapped the rest of us will rain down rocks on them from above."

There wasn't much time left, so everyone moved quickly to get ready and into position. Vinny prepared his bow, and made sure his quiver was full of arrows. Helge went in search of stones of the correct size to use with her

HOPE

sling. Then they searched for the perfect vantage points from which to surprise the enemy. Vinny found a rock, about his own height, with a small fissure through which he could fire his arrows. Helge needed more space to propel the stones from her sling. She chose a large rock close to the road behind which she could hide, but from which she could easily move to one side in order to take aim and shoot. The twins hid behind another rock on the opposite side of the road.

Yohan led Squire, Heremann, the three Luchorpans, Faithful and the horses up a winding path to the top of the right-hand cliff above the chasm. He decided to entrust the job of toppling the boulder to the three Luchorpans, while the three men stationed themselves a bit further to the south and prepared to throw down smaller rocks onto the heads of the trapped enemy.

A few minutes after everyone had taken up their positions, the cougars and Kobalos arrived. The Kobalos sat imperiously upright on the cougars, with reins in hand. Some unfamiliar guttural sounds wafted up to the Luchorpans' ears.

"Look," said Alvin. "They're charging into the chasm without even bothering to stop. They can't be expecting an ambush."

"They must be expecting to find us further south," said Perkin. "There must be about thirty of them altogether."

As soon as the enemy had all passed through the northern entrance to the chasm, Alvin began to coax the mule and the horses to pull on the rope that Yohan had earlier secured to the large boulder, while Perkin and Vylin assisted by pushing the rock. When it just teetered on the edge, Alvin cut the rope.

"Give it one last heave," he said. "Push." The heavy rock rolled over the edge and crashed down to the base of the gorge.

BO'S CHASM

"Perfect," said Perkin with a smile. "The boulder's blocked the road, and they have no way to retreat."

The Kobalos must have heard the sound of the rock falling. They stopped the cougars in their tracks and looked back to see what had happened. For several seconds they remained motionless, and became sitting targets for the archer and the sling-wielder.

Yohan, Heremann and Squire looked down from their vantage point. They saw Helge and Vinny kill five Kobalos and three cougars. The twins stunned four other cougars with their magic.

"There are too many of them for Helge and Vinny to deal with," said Yohan.

"Look," said Squire. "The Kobalos are dismounting and looking for places to hide."

"The cougars are not so intelligent," said Heremann. As he spoke, a series of arrows pierced the hearts of four cougars and pebbles from Helge's sling felled three others.

By this time, the three Luchorpans had joined Yohan and the others.

"They don't know we're here," said Yohan. "Let them have it."

The six of them launched a bombardment of small rocks. They felled some of the Kobalos with direct hits, and flushed others out from their hiding places so that Vinny, Helge and the twins could deal with them. After only twenty minutes from the time of their arrival, every one of the enemy was dead, injured, or stunned senseless by the twins' magic. As soon as Yohan saw that the rout was complete, he descended and had no qualms in putting his sword through those who still lived.

As Yohan kicked one of the bodies onto its back, Squire noted it had large pointed ears, a small flat nose, and a pair of fang-like teeth sticking up from its lower jaw giving it a fearsome appearance. He turned up his nose.

113

HOPE

"So this is what Kobalos look like," he said. A bronze helmet rolled from its head, revealing a mop of dark grey curly hair.

They were similar in height to the Luchorpans but much stockier in build. Their disproportionately large feet were unshod. They wore brown, studded leather jerkins and brown leather breeches that reached just below the knees, and a thin layer of grey hair covered most parts of their bodies. Each of them also carried a short, wide sword made from bronze.

Squire watched Vinny as he searched through the bodies. "What are you doing?" he asked.

"I'm looking for some jerkins and breeches that are not damaged or covered in blood. We'll take them, and their swords and helmets."

"What for?"

"You never know when they might come in handy," he said. After a few minutes, he had recovered the belongings from four Kobalos.

"Evening is approaching," said Yohan. "We must retreat to Bo's Bridge to make camp for the night. Leave the bodies where they've fallen. I for one have no desire to bury them. Leave them to the vultures and the jackals. Look."

They followed Yohan's gaze and saw vultures wheeling overhead. Others stood erect like sentinels on the top of the cliffs of the chasm, waiting to gorge themselves.

High above the vultures, another bird circled. The giant eagle looked down with satisfaction at the scene below him before flying off towards the west.

The next morning the company returned to the chasm to remove the boulder that blocked the road, and discovered that the scavengers had already stripped the carcases of the dead clean of all flesh.

BO'S CHASM

When they had finished hauling the boulder to one side of the road, Yohan spoke. "Heremann and I must leave now," he said. "Ben Lei seeks my counsel and I have no choice but to go."

The companions bade farewell to Yohan once again, and wished him and Heremann good luck. Without delaying further, the two of them mounted their horses, wheeled them around once more, saluted and galloped off towards the north leaving a cloud of red dust in their wake.

The rest of the company braced themselves for the return walk towards the south. It took them two days and nights to cover the distance from Bo's Chasm, south to rejoin the main east-west highway, then on eastwards to Daly's Bridge.

When they arrived at the bridge, they went at once underneath to try to find the white brick referred to in the instructions. They were baffled to find several white bricks.

"The instructions say 'at shoulder height'," Helge asserted.

She stood close to the brick wall on one side of the river. "This must be the one," she said, indicating a brick near to her left shoulder.

Using a chisel and hammer, she removed the brick. "No rubber ball here," she said with a frown.

Meanwhile Vinny had gone to the other side of the bridge and located a brick on a level with his shoulder. He removed the brick, but also found nothing.

Vinny and Helge were still pondering this dilemma when Squire interrupted. "You're both wrong," he told them. "Do you recall that only the Luchorpans were able to descend the tiny steps to find the tooth on Peak Island? Moreover, they found the tooth in a Luchorpan pot. I believe that a Luchorpan, or a group of Luchorpans, must have hidden all of the teeth and instructions. I suggest, therefore, that we look for a white brick at the shoulder height of a Luchorpan, or about this much above the ground." He indicated about eighty centimetres.

"You are probably right," conceded Helge.

It didn't take them long to discover that there was only one brick at the required height. With the aid of the chisel and hammer, Vinny easily removed the brick. Behind it, he found a rubber ball. He cut the ball open to reveal the next golden tooth, which he handed to Squire, and a piece of paper with the next set of instructions.

Helge quickly read the instructions, silently to herself. As she did so, a look of horror came over her face.

CHAPTER 8

MELIAE AND NEREIDS

"What's wrong? Why are you looking so worried?" Vinny asked Helge.

"Is it something to do with the instructions?" asked Squire.

"Yes," she replied. "I think you had better all listen to this." Helge hesitated before she read the instructions aloud:

"First right molar – top jaw
Over the wall you must go,
To Trow.
In the cobbler's shop
Find a boot high on top.
The heel will reveal
That which you seek, and where next to go."

Vylin looked perplexed. "What does it mean, '*Over the wall you must go*'," she asked.

"It means we must go into enemy territory."

"But didn't Yohan say the wall is very high, and there are only two ways through to the other side?"

"That's right," said Vinny. "We have no choice. We must go through Patumann's Tunnel."

HOPE

* * * * *

They took three days to cover the distance to the tunnel. On the morning of the second day, Vylin told them that she had again seen a shadowy figure following them. As before, Perkin used the Seeround Glass, but detected nothing.

"You Luchorpans are always imagining things, or fearful about something," sneered Sim.

Vylin's eyes welled with tears. "I know I'm not imagining things," she said.

Helge spoke with a gentler tone. "Let's assume that you are not," she said. "It can't be one of the enemy, or they would have attacked us by now. No, this person or animal has a more sinister reason for following us, as if they are after something – maybe the Seeround Glass itself. We must split up and make a thorough search of the area. Vylin, you come with me – we will look back the way we have just come. Squire, you go with Sim – you two search towards the north. Alvin, you go with Vinny, and search towards the south. Perkin and Wim – you two explore the road ahead to the east. We will all meet back here in an hour. Are there any questions?"

"What do you want us to do if we find them?" asked Alvin.

"Try to capture them," said Helge. "We need to find out what they want."

When they met together again, Squire could hardly contain his excitement. "We saw a man," he said, "or at least we think it was a man because it looked like he had a beard. He ran away towards the north."

"I'm sorry, Vylin, there really was somebody there," confessed Sim. "He was very scruffy, and seemed so old and bent that he had difficulty running. Nevertheless, he managed to elude us and disappeared into the cover of the trees."

MELIAE AND NEREIDS

"Jippers!" exclaimed Vinny. "That sounds like Jippers. But, why would he be following us? What do we have that would interest him?"

"When we were preparing to go down into the sewers, he seemed to be very curious about my glass," said Perkin.

"And the glass cannot see him," added Vylin. "Maybe he's got some magic powers himself. He obviously wants the glass for his own use."

"We must be more alert from now onwards," warned Helge. "Not only do we need to keep watch for the enemy, but Jippers is an added threat. At night we must double our guard."

There were no more incidents during the remainder of the journey to the tunnel. However, with each hour that they progressed eastwards towards their destination, the more weary and anxious they became. When they finally arrived at the border patrol point at the western end of the tunnel, a sign greeted them. It read, 'Border closed until further notice'.

Squire looked downcast. "What are we to do now?" he asked.

"We must set up camp for the night and discuss our next move," said Helge.

They found a couple of huts near the western end of the tunnel used to house the border guards, men of King Jovanius' army sent from Bunbury. Vinny and Squire decided to go to question the guards.

"Why is the border closed?" asked Vinny.

"The king's orders," replied the guard. "The armies of Gordeve are on the move. He interprets this as a sign of her intention to declare war. There have even been reports that the enemy breached the gate near Dun Wood, and a raiding party has attacked the Telekai at Dunton. The King has sent a platoon of his soldiers north to assist the Telekai to defend the gate."

"So how can we get into East Thorland?" asked Vinny.

HOPE

The guard laughed. "That's impossible, unless you want to climb the wall," he said. "You couldn't go there anyway without a pass," he added.

Vinny and Squire reported the information that the guard had given them to the rest of the company.

"Can we really scale the wall?" asked Alvin. Turning to Wim, he added, "Can't you and Sim perform some magic to get us over the wall? Perhaps you could turn into eagles, like Tobin did, and fly us over."

Wim shook his head. "We're only apprentices," he replied. "We've not mastered the magic of 'changing' yet."

"So why doesn't Tobin come to our aid?" persisted Alvin.

"He will not leave the safety of his castle for more than a few minutes at a time," replied Sim. "Besides, he wouldn't risk flying into Gordeve's territory. This could make him very vulnerable."

Helge's face brightened. "I have an idea," she said. "There might be another way. If we can't go under the wall and we can't go over the wall, then we must go *round* the wall. We will travel south to the point where the wall meets the ocean, and find a way around it."

"That's a good idea, Helge," said Vinny, "but it won't be easy. The road south lies several kilometres to the west of the wall. To reach the southern extremity of the wall, we will need to pass through Ash Wood. I've heard that there are strange spirits lurking in the wood."

"I've heard those rumours too," confirmed Helge. "However, I've also heard that travellers may pass unhindered through the wood as long as they don't harm the trees in any way."

The journey to the coast required them to retrace their steps westwards for half a day, before taking the road south towards Ash Wood. After four days' walking, they arrived at the northern edge of the wood.

MELIAE AND NEREIDS

None of them had travelled this way before, and the wood was a mystery to them all. They approached it with caution.

Helge was wide-eyed as she looked around. "These trees are magnificent," she said. "Living in Hanlin Forest, I'm used to the conical-shapes of the pines and firs. But these trees are not only tall, they have huge girths as well. Some of them look really old."

She touched the smooth, ash-grey bark of the nearest tree and looked up at the expansive canopy. "They're colossal," she said. "Look at the large boughs growing from the main trunk. They divide into hundreds of branches. And look, the fruits are beginning to ripen."

"We must find a clear space in amongst the trees to pitch our tents," said Vinny. "We cannot risk offending the trees by carelessly allowing a fire to spread."

"There's a good place," said Perkin, pointing to an open space near the banks of a shallow stream. "We can pitch our tents under the shade of the trees and make our fire down near the stream."

As Alvin tried to hammer in the tent pegs, his face turned red, and sweat ran down his chin. "What kind of soil is this?" he asked.

"It seems to be some kind of loam," replied Vinny. "It's very rich and moist."

"So why's it so difficult for me to hammer in these pegs? Ow!"

"It's all these roots. They're only growing just beneath the surface and seem to have spread out horizontally from these trees." Vinny indicated two large ash trees.

"I'll go to collect some firewood," said Vylin.

"No!" said Helge. "We cannot use wood from the ash trees, not even dead wood. We must use only firewood that we have brought with us."

HOPE

They spent their first night under the trees of Ash Wood with both a sense of awe, and an apprehension of the secrets it held.

Squire slept restlessly. In the middle of the night, the sound of a female voice awakened him, a voice he did not recognise. It came to him as a whisper and sounded distant and hollow.

"Squire from another Land," the voice whispered, "what brings you and your friends into our wood, and what do you require of us?"

"Who are you?" he asked. "How do you know my name?"

"My name is Melia," the voice replied. "I am one of the Meliae of Ash Wood. We heard whispers of your arrival in Thorland from the trees in Hanlin Forest. I have answered your questions. It would please me greatly if you would now answer mine."

"We are travelling to the Southern Ocean to try to find a way around Telemann's Wall," he replied. "But what kind of people are the Meliae?" he enquired.

"The Meliae are not people. We are hamadryads, descendants of the great mother Rhea. We are ethereal beings that dwell in the ash trees. Some call us 'tree spirits'."

"Are you immortal?"

"No, but we live a very long time," replied Melia. "Each one of us is bonded to one tree, over which we constantly watch. If the tree dies, we also will die."

"Can you help us find a way around the wall?"

"We can grant you safe passage through the wood. Beyond that, we cannot help you."

The next morning, Squire related his strange experience to the rest of the company.

MELIAE AND NEREIDS

Vinny looked surprised. "But we were on guard and heard nothing, eh Perkin?"

"Not a thing," Perkin affirmed.

"I've heard tales of these Meliae," said Helge. "But there are no such spirits in Hanlin Forest. Since Melia said that we would be granted safe passage through the wood, we must continue to make our way southwards. Progress through the trees will be slow, so it's likely to take us another two days. However, be warned, we must not harm the trees in any way. I've heard tell that the hamadryads will punish any thoughtless person who should somehow injure the trees."

They spent the next night also among the trees, but the hamadryads remained silent and Squire did not receive any further messages.

Towards the end of the second day, they reached the sea and set up camp for the night at the southern edge of Ash Wood where it embraced the ocean. Waves crashed onto the rocky seashore, throwing up mists of spray.

The next morning they considered their options.

"We must make our way to the wall and see if it's possible to wade or swim around its extremity," said Vinny.

"The beach is very rocky, and the rocks look slippery and full of potholes," said Helge. "I don't think Faithful and Conny will find it easy going. Besides which, they won't be able to make it through the water. At least two of us must stay behind with them and the supplies."

"But who?" said Vinny.

"If we do succeed in finding a way, then the three Luchorpans must go," said Squire. "If properly disguised, they are the ones most likely to pass off as Kobalos."

Helge interrupted. "I'll stay with one of the twins," she said, hiding the fact that she was afraid of deep water. "My unusual height will make me

HOPE

conspicuous and may jeopardise the mission. Vinny, in my absence you will be leader."

Helge was happy when Sim chose to accompany the others. She found his manner irritating, especially the way he teased Alvin, and preferred the company of the more considerate Wim.

A few minutes later, Helge and Wim said farewell to their companions who set off towards the east.

Later in the day, as Wim was grooming the pony and mule, Helge sat on the beach watching the progress of her friends. In the distance towards the east, she could see Telemann's Wall where it met the seashore. There was no cliff there, so the wall continued to snake its way towards the ocean, and into the water. *It must finally end some fifty metres or so from the shore,* she thought. *But, the sea looks very rough and it's hard to see any way around all those rocks.*

A few minutes later, she saw Vinny and the others turn and start back towards the wood. *They're coming back. There is no way. Now what are we going to do?* She was still deep in thought when a cry coming from the wood disturbed her. She quickly picked up her sling, crept closer to the source of the noise, and took cover behind a nearby rock.

She saw a group of four Kobalos. Two of them kept watch. She gasped when she saw the other two wielding heavy, long-handled axes. They were trying to chop down one of the largest and oldest ash trees in the wood. As each blow of the axe struck, blood gushed from the cuts in the bark. Helge heard a voice coming from inside the injured tree. "Please stop. You are hurting my tree, and you are murdering me," wailed the hamadryad.

Helge looked around, but could see no sign of Wim. *He couldn't have heard the noise,* she thought. *Should I go back to find him? No there's no time. I must help the tree.* She picked up a handful of pebbles and rushed

MELIAE AND NEREIDS

to its aid. With swiftness and deadly accuracy, she felled the two guards with pebbles to their foreheads. The other two Kobalos stopped chopping the tree and turned their axes on Helge who was now too close to wield her sling. As they rushed headlong towards her, the ground beneath their feet began to give way, roots came to the surface and a large hole appeared. They tripped on the roots, fell headfirst into the hole and disappeared from view. As quickly as the hole had opened, it closed again and trapped them in an underground dungeon of earth and roots. Helge heard their muffled screams for several seconds. Then the roots tightened around their throats, and death silenced them.

"Thank you, Helge of Hanlin Forest," whispered the hamadryad who inhabited the injured tree. "My name is Pitys. Those evil creatures stole up on me unexpectedly and, once they started to chop, they were too close for my roots to entrap them. Only when they saw you and started to run away from me, were my roots able to reach up and pull them down. This I could not have done without your help. How can I repay you?"

"Can you help me and my companions find a way around the wall?"

"You have shown great courage and resolve today, and I will always be indebted to you. I will talk to my sisters to see if there is a way."

"Are you badly hurt?"

"My wounds are not serious and will quickly heal. The sap that you now see seeping from the wounds is a healing sap, called méli. It helps my blood to clot. Take some of the sap and keep it. The méli is strong medicine for any of your companions who should in the future suffer a deep gash or even a mortal wound. However, this is a small repayment for what you have done."

Helge took two empty flasks from her pack and filled them with the sap from the bleeding tree.

HOPE

Pitys continued. "However, I have another request. Although my wounds will quickly heal, my tree is old and will soon die. I will also die unless I can find a new home. Remember me, Helge, when you pass this way again. I do not wish to die and would welcome a new home close to yours in your forest. You will forever be my friend."

"I will remember you, Pitys," replied Helge. "If you can help us, I promise that I will help you find a new home. However, I cannot tell how many moons it will be before I pass this way again."

A yell from Wim interrupted her. "They're back," he shouted.

"Goodbye for now, Pitys," she said. "We will meet again soon."

"Goodbye, my friend," repeated the hamadryad.

"It's impossible," said a breathless Vinny. "There's no way across the wall except by entering the sea, and strong rip tides in this part of the ocean make that an almost impossible task without a powerful boat."

"We must wait for further instructions from the Meliae," said Helge. She told her friends about the attack on Pitys and her promise to talk with the other Meliae. "Pitys said they might be able to help us."

That night a soft voice once again woke Squire.

"I am Atlantia, hamadryad of Ash Wood," the voice whispered. "I have received word of your passage through the wood from my sister Melia and you and your companions have also respected our wood and not harmed any of our trees. Pitys has also told me of her deliverance from the Kobalos at the hands of the tall woman. We will help you with your quest. When you awake in the morning, you must enter the sea and wade until the water reaches up to your necks. Do not be afraid. Our cousins, the Nereids, will be watching. You must show them that you trust them by displaying no signs of fear. Once they are satisfied that you trust them, they will come to you with

MELIAE AND NEREIDS

their dolphins. The dolphins will take you on their backs and carry you to where you wish to go."

"What are Nereids?" asked Squire.

"They are sea-nymphs, the daughters of Doris," she replied. "They live in the ocean and are companions of the dolphins, just as we are the companions of the trees."

The next morning the eight friends considered everything that Atlantia had told Squire.

"I think we have no choice but to trust the Meliae and Nereids," said Helge.

Helge and Wim said farewell to their companions once again, and the other six waded into the sea as instructed. Squire and Sim didn't feel very brave but, when they witnessed the courage of the tiny Luchorpans and saw them climb onto the backs of their dolphins, they took heart and continued to wade in until their own dolphins were ready for them to mount.

With the riders safely on their backs and clinging with both arms around their necks, the dolphins swam off at great speed towards the east. As Squire rode, another voice came to him, a strange guttural sound that seemed to emanate from beneath the dolphin.

"I am Thetis the Nereid," the voice said. "Welcome Squire from another Land. My sisters and I, with our dolphins, will carry you safely to the beach south of Trow."

A few minutes later, the dolphins stopped close to the shore once again. "Here we must leave you," said Thetis. "It is unsafe for us to approach closer to Trow harbour. You and your companions must climb the cliffs you see in front of you. Then you will find the road that will take you to Trow. Do not fear. When you have completed your mission in Trow, we will be waiting here ready to take you back to your companions at Ash Wood."

HOPE

The six friends climbed down from the backs of the dolphins, bade them farewell, and waded to the shore. Two hundred metres from the shoreline they saw a high granite cliff strewn with boulders. There seemed to be no proper path, and they had a difficult climb to reach the top of the cliff. Where the ground levelled out close to the top, they found a small clump of trees where they could hide and discuss what to do next.

"We have a problem," said Vinny. "How are we going to pass off as citizens of Trow when none of us can speak the language?"

"I can speak the language," said Sim. "As part of our training to be wizards, we are required to learn the tongue of East Thorland."

Vinny looked relieved. "That is indeed fortunate," he said.

After a few moments in thought, Vinny spoke again. "I have a plan. Perkin and Alvin must disguise themselves as Kobalos and you, Sim, must accompany them dressed like a man of Trow. Since Squire and I don't know the language, it would be too risky for us to go with you to Trow, and Vylin will not easily pass off as a male Kobalos. No, it's going to be up to you three to find the tooth. Luckily we took the trouble to remove and keep those jerkins and breeches after the battle at Bo's Chasm."

Perkin glared. "But we don't look like Kobalos, even if we wear their filthy clothes," he said. "They're covered with hair, have big ears, flat noses and large feet. And what about those teeth?"

"We can't do much about the noses and feet," Vinny conceded. "But I think we can improvise as far as the hair, ears and teeth are concerned. We will just have to hope that no one takes much notice of the other parts. The helmets will help the disguise, and you must stay in the shadows when you reach Trow."

The look on Alvin's face showed that he was less than enthusiastic. "What if someone speaks to us? We won't understand."

MELIAE AND NEREIDS

"Sim must introduce you and Alvin as mutes. That will also help to draw attention away from the false teeth. We will find ourselves a couple of young wild boars for our supper. They will provide us with the teeth and the ears we require."

"But what about the hair?" protested Alvin.

"There's your answer," Vinny replied, pointing towards a stone wall a few metres away. The wall enclosed a paddock where sheep grazed.

"You see where the sheep have brushed against the stones, the sharp edges have caught and torn some wisps of moulted wool from their coats. We'll use that wool and dye it dark grey by boiling it up with some charcoal. Then we'll get some sap from the pine tree to use as glue."

"How do you know all this?" asked Squire.

"Remember that I am an archer," replied Vinny. "We use pine pitch to set the arrow heads into the arrow shafts. So all we need to do now is find a pine tree, and the wild boars."

They found the perfect place just a couple of kilometres away – a small wood that had a number of pine trees, and by chance a group of wild boars lived there. Even before they had gone fifty metres into the wood, Vinny had expertly shot two of the smaller boars with his bow. With a sharp knife, he gutted them, cut off and cleaned the ears, and removed the canine teeth. The two boars were soon roasting on a spit over a roaring fire, and the ears were drying in the heat of the fire.

While the boars roasted, Vinny sought out a suitable pine tree for the sap. "This one will do," he said, grabbing hold of a young pine tree. "This should be full of sap. There are no hamadryads in this wood, so it's safe to cut it. I'll just cut a notch here in the trunk and wait a while for the sap to drip down into this cup."

HOPE

Next, he took some charcoal from the charred firewood, mixed it with some water and boiled the sheep's wool in the mixture in a pot over the fire. Vinny also took the opportunity to melt some of the sap and mixed it with charcoal to make some pine pitch to prepare for himself a new set of arrows.

The six friends slept that night in the safety of the wood, well satisfied with their meal, but very apprehensive about the day ahead. That night they took turns, two at a time, to be on guard.

The following morning, they rose early and immediately set to work on the disguises for the two Luchorpans. They rubbed charcoal into the hair on their heads to make it dark grey in colour, and Perkin did the same with his beard. Then the others helped them plaster the sheep's wool, dyed dark grey, over the other exposed parts of their bodies – face, arms and legs – and glued it on with warm melted sap. They stuck the boars' ears, also with the help of some of the glue, over the top of the Luchorpans' own ears.

"Now for the hard part," said Vinny. "How can we attach the boars' canines into the Luchorpans' lower jaws?"

"That's easy," said Sim. "Since they will not be talking, they also don't need to open their mouths. We can secure the teeth to a short stick. When the time comes for Alvin and Perkin to wear the canines they will have to grip the stick with their own teeth."

Preparing Sim proved to be much less of a problem. The men of East Thorland wore much the same clothes as those of the west. To make him fit the part, all they had to do was to shave his head in the manner of the men of the East. Squire did this with the razor he always carried with him.

Trow was a small town of about three thousand inhabitants, men and Kobalos living in harmony, but all served Gordeve. The main street of the town consisted of one continuous line of shops and other businesses. There were few shoppers about at that early hour, and nobody took much notice of the strangers or spoke to them as they passed unobtrusively along the street. It was with little difficulty that Sim located the Cobbler's Shop, the only one in the town.

"There it is," he said, pointing across the street. "See the sign above that shop, written in Kobalos language. It says 'Puck's Cobblers'."

Leaning against the front wall of the shop, they noticed a ladder.

"Don't walk under the ladder ... " cautioned Alvin.

Before he could finish his sentence, Sim interrupted with a jeer. "I know," he said. "Walking under the ladder is bad luck."

Having skirted around the ladder, they stood in front of the shop. "What does that notice in the window say?" asked Alvin.

Sim translated. "It says 'Cobbler's assistant required. Enquire within'."

"That's a stroke of good luck," whispered Alvin. "I'm a skilled cobbler, and surely will get the job."

"But we must be very careful," said Sim. "Remember you cannot understand the language. With my help, you may pass off as a mute today. But, once you are on your own, how will you understand what Mr. Puck is saying to you?"

"I don't need to," replied Alvin. "Applying for the job is only a means for us to gain access to his workshop. Once we're inside, we must overpower him, find the tooth and be on our way."

They delayed while Alvin and Perkin removed the sticks with boars' teeth attached from their pockets and gripped the sticks with their own teeth. Sim nodded when he was satisfied that they were correctly aligned. Then the three friends entered the cobbler's shop. As they passed through the door, the tinkle of a bell announced their arrival.

HOPE

Sim spoke on behalf of Alvin. "Good morning, Mr. Puck," he said. "My name is Simson. I would like to introduce to you my good friends here, Mr. Blobins and his assistant Mr. Brags. The army has recently discharged them because, being deaf mutes, they were unable to perform their duties properly. They are now looking for work. Mr. Blobins is a highly skilled cobbler and is interested in the job advertised in your window. I have come along to assist him with sign language."

Mr Puck smiled. "Please come in," he said. "Come along into my workshop at the back, so that Mr. Blobins can show me his work." The cobbler's shop was quite dark inside, so Mr. Puck did not detect the disguises. "Here, Mr. Blobins, some leather and tools," he continued. "Will you please cut the leather to make a shoe to fit my foot and start to sew the pieces together, so that I can see the quality of your workmanship?" Sim made some signs, directed at Alvin, although he didn't really know sign language at all.

Alvin set to work and, with the sure skill of a trained cobbler, he had measured and cut the leather in no time at all, and started to sew the pieces together. Mr. Puck bent over to inspect the work, and was just about to compliment Alvin, when Sim grabbed him from behind and held him tight while Perkin gagged him with a piece of cloth which he tied at the back of his neck. Sim wrestled to hold Mr. Puck's hands and tied them at the back behind his chair as Alvin bent down and bound the shopkeeper's legs. After that, Sim moved quickly to the front of the shop, turned the key in the lock and reversed the sign on the door to say 'Closed'.

Alvin removed his false canines. "Now all we have to do is find a boot up high on top," he said. "It can't mean up high on a shelf because the boot we are looking for must have been here for a very long time."

MELIAE AND NEREIDS

"I think it means up high in the attic of the roof," suggested Perkin. "There's a trapdoor there. Help me move that ladder, so that I can have a look inside." He pointed to a stepladder leaning against the wall.

Perkin and Alvin positioned the ladder under the trapdoor while Sim kept watch in case Mr. Puck should attempt to free himself. Perkin climbed cautiously until he reached the top of the ladder, and threw open the trapdoor. Still standing on one of the top steps, he used the Seeround Glass to scan the dark interior of the attic.

"There are lots of things up here," he said, "including several pairs of shoes and boots." He scanned again before looking down at Alvin and displaying a wide grin. "I see it," he said. "A single boot, in the corner. It must have been forgotten a long time ago."

Perkin hauled himself up onto the floor of the attic, stood, and gingerly walked across the beams until he reached the boot. He prised open the heel of the boot and pulled out a pouch. Inside the pouch, he found the tooth and the inevitable piece of paper. He carefully placed these inside his pocket and made his way back to the trap door, and down the ladder.

The three friends made a hurried exit from the shop. They had forgotten about the ladder leaning against the front wall and, in their haste to get away, carelessly walked under it. *What have we done?* Alvin thought to himself.

Whilst trying not to draw attention to themselves, they walked urgently along the length of the main street and out of the town. Once they were clear of the town, they started to run for fear that Mr. Puck would free himself and raise the alarm. Perkin, who had gained a level of fitness through his dancing, ran ahead, followed closely by Sim. Alvin, who smoked too much, lagged behind.

* * * * *

HOPE

Another yell from Wim disturbed Helge. "They're back," he shouted.

Helge rushed to the seashore, anxious to see her friends again. She watched as Vinny and Squire dismounted from their dolphins first, then Sim, followed by Perkin, and finally Vylin.

However, she could see no sign of Alvin.

CHAPTER 9

HOMAR'S FOREST

The attack came without warning. As Helge and Wim rushed towards the water's edge to greet their friends who had just set foot on the sandy beach, a group of cougars appeared from the cover of the trees near the shoreline.

The cougars followed Helge as she ran down the beach. "Did you get the tooth?" she asked. "Is everything all right? Where's Al … ?"

"Cougars," Squire warned. "Behind you."

Helge turned and instinctively bent to pick up pebbles from the beach. "I never knew cougars hunted in packs."

"They don't," said Vinny, "but these are not normal cougars. Gordeve sent them." He raised his bow and drew the first arrow from the quiver at his back.

"That's useless," Squire shouted. "There must be at least twenty of them. Your sling and bow won't save us this time. I must use the shield."

Before he had finished speaking, the cougars surrounded the company and there seemed no way to escape. However, they did not attack immediately, but slowly encircled the group, their green eyes flashing and their black-tipped tails swishing.

As Squire removed the shield from his back and prepared to use it, the fearsome cougars bared their teeth, ready to rip their prey to pieces.

"Keep clear everyone," he said. "Remember the shield is very powerful, but I know the consequences. Just leave it to me."

HOPE

When Squire raised the shield ready to ward off the first cougar preparing to pounce on him, he noticed Wim and Sim rush together to embrace each other.

"What are you two doing?" he yelled. "I know you've been apart for a day or so, but this is not the time to hug each other! Get out of the way."

As he spoke, the five silver stars on the front of the shield began to glow, dully at first, and then more brightly, making a low humming sound. The sound increased in intensity until, reaching a crescendo, he heard an enormous crash of thunder and saw a great flash of lightning emanate from the shield itself. Beams of light from the stars reached out towards the twins and energy passed from the shield to them, empowering them as never before.

Until that time, apart from Wim's disastrous creation of the vortex, the twins' powers had been restricted to opening locked doors, catching fish, or zapping a few rats or cougars. However, they now seemed to grow in stature. Light from the shield engulfed them and Squire saw ripples of energy pass up their bodies from the tips of their toes to the tops of their heads.

The release of energy was so powerful that the force of it threw Squire backwards While his body arched, he just had time to look into the back of the shield and became aware once again of a picture forming, as though through a window. Like the first time, when he had used the shield against the swarm of locusts, he felt himself drawn into the picture. When his head hit the ground, blackness engulfed him and he landed flat on his back, oblivious to the events that followed. He was not Squire any more, but Grant Cowie trying to save his drowning daughter.

Grant returned to consciousness, his head aching, and sat up. He slowly rose to his feet. He felt dizzy, and blood poured from the wound to his head. At that moment, he heard Theresa yelling to him, pleading him to save her. Then he remembered what had happened. He quickly removed his canvas shoes, his jeans, the thin cotton jacket and his shirt. He dived into the icy water, but as he did so, he saw Theresa's head go under.

He took a deep breath and started swimming underwater towards his daughter's limp body. However, as quickly as he swam, the current took Theresa away from him. He used all his strength to propel himself forward, but every muscle in his arms and legs ached. He rose to the surface to take a breath, filled his lungs and went under again. He gained on her now, but it would take one last effort to reach her. He rose again to the surface to draw breath. In the same instant, a floating log hit him in the midriff. He lost his balance, was momentarily dragged under, and lost all hope of reaching Theresa before it would be too late.

Squire awoke from his nightmare to find Helge, Vinny, Vylin and Perkin looking skywards, mesmerised.

"What happened?" he asked, sitting up and rubbing his eyes. His gaze followed theirs upwards. "I had another unpleasant glimpse of my world. Is anyone listening? What can it mean?" When no one answered his questions, he raised his voice and almost shouted as he asked, "Can any of you please tell me what it all means? I don't remember what happened and I don't understand, but I do know it was very distressful."

After a pause when no one answered, his expression relaxed and he glanced around. He asked more gently, "What happened to the cougars?"

Helge replied. "After you lost consciousness, the twins raised their arms and faced the enemy. They still glowed full of energy. However, this time they did not zap the cougars, but just stared at them and with one voice commanded, 'Go, cougars, back to the one who created you. Tell her to prepare to do battle with the wizard twins. Come back here at your peril, for you shall surely die.' The cougars turned obediently and disappeared back into the bush."

Squire was wide-eyed. "But, where are the twins now?"

"No sooner had the cougars vanished, than we saw the twins transform themselves into hawks. They flapped their wings and launched themselves into flight. Seconds later, we saw them wheeling overhead as they made their way westwards. We think Tobin must have summoned them to his castle."

When she had finished explaining this, she remembered she had a question of her own. "Where's Alvin?" she asked.

Perkin cast his eyes towards the ground. "The Kobalos have him."

"How? Tell me what happened."

Perkin looked up, but a tear slowly oozed from one eye and ran down his nose. "After Alvin, Sim and I had found the tooth, we made our way out of the town to rejoin the others in the wood. We tried to be inconspicuous, but once we were clear of the town, we started to run. I don't know how, but somehow Mr. Puck – he's the cobbler – Mr. Puck must have freed himself. We'd tied him up, you see. He must have freed himself and raised the alarm. Before we knew it, there were about twenty Kobalos behind us. We could hear their heavy footsteps closing in on us, and could almost feel their hot breath on our necks."

"You're so brave!" interjected Vylin.

Perkin blushed. "Well, Alvin's not as fit as me, on account of him not really being a dancer," he continued. "He smokes too much too. So, he lagged behind Sim and me. When we reached the safety of the trees and rejoined the others, we realised that Alvin was not with us." Perkin paused for breath. "It must have been the ladder."

"What ladder?" Helge asked.

"The ladder outside the cobbler's shop. We walked underneath it, and it must have brought us bad luck. Sim said it was a load of nonsense, but look what happened."

Vinny put his hand on Perkin's shoulder to reassure him. "It's not your fault, Perkin. We were all to blame. We all abandoned Alvin."

"Why didn't you stand and fight?" asked Helge.

"There were too many of them, and probably others close behind, so we knew we had no chance of rescuing Alvin. Our only option was to leave him and make good our own escape. There was no time to be lost. The Kobalos were almost upon us. Regardless of our own safety, we ran down the cliff with such urgency that we tripped and rolled, and almost lost our footing completely. Battered and bruised, we waded into the sea where the dolphins waited for us. Where Alvin is now, we can only guess. He could be a prisoner in Trow, or he may already be on his way to Gordeve's castle, or he could even be dead for all we know."

Helge waited a moment to take in all she had heard. She looked grim as she said, "I don't think they will have killed him. Undoubtedly, they'll be taking him to Gordeve so she can question him to try to find out about our plans. We must find some way to rescue him."

By that time, evening had arrived and the five remaining members of the company prepared to spend a very unsettled night on the edge of Ash Wood. They didn't fear the cougars would return since there was no doubting the assertiveness of the twins' command, but the absence of three of their friends made them feel ill at ease.

HOPE

Vinny and Vylin took the first watch. All remained silent in the wood except for a few insects chirping and the occasional hoot of an owl. They had been on duty for about an hour when the rustling of leaves and the flapping of wings disturbed the silence, heralding the arrival of two hawks and an eagle. The kafuffle awakened the other three who came out from their tents to investigate.

"Good evening," said the booming voice of Tobin. "Behold, Wim and Sim, wizards. Today my two apprentices have come of age. Just as a caterpillar metamorphoses into a butterfly, so have they changed from useless worms feeding on the leaves of indecision and doubt into fully mature beings of beauty and grace that can flutter above the troubles of this world, effortlessly flapping their wings when they move from one bright flower of hope to another. Today they have grown to become adult wizards. After the shield empowered them, and they gained ascendancy over the wicked cougars, I summoned them to my castle. This afternoon I have performed the initiation ceremony that confers on them the title of 'wizard'. From now onwards, they will have much greater discernment and increased magical powers. Your company will be all the safer because of that."

"Tell us about the initiation," said Helge.

"The ceremony is secret," replied Tobin. "All I can tell you is that I performed the initiation according to ancient tradition, and no one else was present."

"What new powers do the twins have?" asked Vinny.

"As you have seen, they now have the ability to transform. They can also perform many of the ancient rites such as spells of changing, spells of binding and spells of naming. You will witness these powers yourselves when you continue on your quest. Enough talk. Now, I must return to my castle, and I bid you all good night."

HOMAR'S FOREST

Before anyone had time to speak further, the old wizard transformed himself once again into an eagle and flew away westwards. However, the two younger wizards remained and shared more of their experiences of that day with the rest of the company, who noticed another change in the twins. They now carried staffs and wore hats similar to that of Tobin, each bearing the five silver stars arranged in the shape of a cross.

"The hats and staffs will remain concealed in our packs most of the time," explained Sim. "We'll only get them out and use them when the need arises."

* * * * *

The new day dawned with a bright autumn sun. The company felt more high-spirited, but the uncertainty about the fate of Alvin preyed on their minds.

"I'm going to rescue him," announced Helge during breakfast.

Vylin's face brightened. "I'll go with you," she said.

"We'll all go," said Perkin.

"No, the quest is too important. Now the twins have greater powers, you don't have to rely so much on my skills with the sling. I intend to seek help from Yohan and the Telekai. One of the twins can accompany me, but the rest of you must move on and search for the next tooth."

"I will accompany you," said Wim without hesitation. Helge was relieved when Wim volunteered. She preferred his even-temperedness to that of his more bumptious twin.

"Take this," said Helge, handing one of the flasks of sap to Vinny who once again assumed the mantle of leadership. "The hamadryad Pitys gave me this healing sap. She called it 'méli' and told me that it could heal a deep gash or even a mortal wound. You never know when you might need it."

HOPE

"Before we separate, I suggest we look at the instructions for finding the next tooth," said Squire.

Perkin handed the piece of paper, which he still carried from the previous day, to Helge. She read:

"Second right molar – top jaw
Homar's Forest conceals a bridge
That swings with the wind
High above the river.
At the northern end
Find a ring under a plank.
Give the ring a yank,
The plank will bend.
Then, with a snap,
Tooth and paper will deliver."

"I've heard tell of Homar's Forest," said Vinny with a shudder. "It has a reputation as a dark and forbidding place. People say there's an ancient road passing through it."

"Where does the road lead?" asked Squire.

"Nowhere really. It's another way to travel from Rye to the main southern highway, but nobody travels that road any more. It passes over the Hom Mountains, through the forest and back over the mountains again before rejoining the main highway halfway between Ash Wood and Winterton. People say the forest has evil spirits and that Homar controls them. Nobody has seen Homar for many years, but the legends say he is half man and half beast."

HOMAR'S FOREST

"But the instructions are clear, we must enter the forest and find a bridge, a suspension bridge by the sounds of it," said Squire. "We don't need to worry about this Homar. We've got Sim to protect us now, and the shield."

"Yes," agreed Helge. "Squire is right. You have no choice but to enter the forest and find the bridge. We will all travel together from here, following the coast until we reach the town of Rye. This should take us about a day. At Rye, Wim and I can buy two horses. We'll leave you then, and travel north to find Yohan. The rest of you must take the road to Homar's Forest. We must depart at once. If we are to rescue Alvin, there's no time to lose."

The next morning, Helge and Wim said their emotional farewells and parted from the rest of the company, riding northwards to seek help from the Telekai.

*　　*　　*　　*　　*

Alvin had tried desperately to keep up with Sim and Perkin, but he lacked fitness. As he breathlessly endeavoured to keep pace with the others, a group of six Kobalos had caught up with him just outside Trow. They tied his hands together and, pushing him roughly in front of them, took him back to Mr Puck's Shop.

"Do you recognise this impostor?" one of the Kobalos asked Mr. Puck. *He looks like he's the leader of the group*, thought Alvin, *but I don't understand a word he's saying.*

"Surely he's one of them," replied Puck. "Look at his hair. It doesn't even look real. He's the one who pretended to be a cobbler."

"Let's find out," said the other. With that, he grabbed hold of the hair on Alvin's face, and yanked it. Alvin winced with pain as the glue pulled away from his flesh. "What have we here? It looks like wool," said the leader of the Kobalos. "How do you like that, cobbler?"

HOPE

Alvin looked perplexed. He didn't understand their language, so didn't answer.

"Who speaks the language of West Thorland?" asked the leader.

"I do … a little," replied one of the others.

"Then ask him what he was doing here," said the leader.

The Kobalos who could speak Alvin's language spoke. "What are you doing in Trow? Are you a spy?" He kicked Alvin on the shin.

"Ow!" Alvin held his leg and felt frightened, but didn't speak.

"Don't want to answer, eh? Gordeve will get it out of you."

"Still pretending to be a mute, are we?" asked Puck, swiping Alvin across the face with the back of his hand. "What manner of being is he?"

"He's a Luchorpan," replied the leader. "They come from Luchor far away to the west, but there's an enclave of them living at Rivermeet. I would wager this one is from Rivermeet, since he and his friend travelled with one of Tobin's apprentices. We'll take him to Gordeve. She'll torture him until he talks."

*   *   *   *   *

The rest of the company – Squire, Vinny, Perkin, Vylin and Sim – left Rye on the same day as Helge and Wim, travelling by foot westwards. As usual, the mule and pony carried their supplies, replenished at Rye. They had a four-day walk to reach the edge of Homar's Forest.

During the second night, under the brilliance of a full moon, Vylin and Perkin kept guard while the others slept. However, they became careless and both had dozed off for a few moments. As Squire slept in the tent he shared with Vinny, the shield at his side, the sound of a man's voice awakened him. It was only a whisper, but he could hear clearly in the silence of the night.

"Give it to me, my Hope," the voice hissed. "I need my Hope to find my way home. Give it to me, or I will take it."

The next instant Squire saw a hand creeping through the tent entrance, a very old and wrinkled hand. The hand crept nearer to the shield. However, before it could grab the shield, Perkin woke up and uttered a startled cry. "Who's there?" he asked. In the light of the full moon, he recognised the outline of the stooped figure that followed the hand through the entrance. "Jippers, is that you?" Perkin started towards the intruder.

Jippers backed out of the entrance, glanced in Perkin's direction and rushed off towards the cover of some trees. Despite his advanced age, he was still very agile from years of catching rats in the sewers beneath the king's palace. He was too quick for Perkin and soon disappeared into the darkness. As Jippers ran away, Squire heard him utter, "My Hope, I need my Hope to find my way home."

After Jippers had disappeared, the five friends discussed what had happened.

"So it's not the glass he's trying to steal after all," said Perkin. "It's the shield he wants."

"But why should he want the shield?" asked Squire. "Unless he thinks it can empower him as it did the twins."

"No, I don't think so," said Vinny. "He's just an ordinary man like you and me, Squire. He must have some other reason to covet the shield."

"We may never know, unless he actually gets his hands on it," said Squire, "and I don't intend to let that happen."

*　　*　　*　　*　　*

On the second day of the journey, they made slow progress, since they had a steep climb to cross the Hom Mountains. The top of the pass afforded them with magnificent views of the Southern Ocean to the south and

HOPE

Homar's Forest to the west where, in the far distance, they could see a mist-shrouded coastline of rugged fjords, storm-battered islands and magnificent valleys.

At the end of the fourth day after leaving Rye, they arrived at the outskirts of the forest. It seemed very different from both Hanlin Forest, with its smaller conifers, and Ash Wood's spreading deciduous giants. Homar's Forest was a temperate rainforest of towering evergreens – cedars, redwoods, spruces and Douglas firs – only eight thousand years old. Some of these huge trees grew to heights of eighty metres or more with vast girths at the base, and foliage that started high above the ground.

"We should camp here for the night and enter the forest tomorrow," suggested Vinny.

During the night, it started to rain. Their tents were not protection enough against the heavy downpour, and the company awoke to find the canvas sodden and many of their clothes and possessions damp. When the rain eased for a time, they made a fire out of dry wood they had brought with them. They managed to dry out some of their clothes, and also cooked breakfast.

"It looks like we'll have to endure several days of this kind of weather," said Vinny, "but we don't have much dry firewood."

The first thing they noticed as they entered the forest was the denseness of the vegetation, including sword ferns, rhododendrons, huckleberry, and other shrubs. The second thing they noticed was a sudden drop in temperature. At this season of early autumn, they found it uncomfortably cold and damp.

They had been walking throughout the day. Just before dusk, Perkin, who led, suddenly howled in pain and fell to the ground nursing his right leg. He had inadvertently stepped on a porcupine. The porcupine had just emerged from a hollow log where it had slept during the day, and was now foraging for some leaves to feed on. The angry animal spun around into a position of defence, its deadly quills facing towards Perkin. At the same instant, it lashed out its tail towards the Luchorpan, causing many of the sharp quills to detach and embed themselves into the skin of his shins above boot level. It then shuffled away into the bush.

Perkin was writhing in agony when the others gathered around him. Vinny bent down beside him and started to remove the quills using a pair of tweezers that they usually used for extracting small stones from the hooves of Faithful and Conny. It took several minutes to remove all the quills, and Perkin cried out as Vinny withdrew each one.

"Don't be such a baby," Vylin said.

"Try pick on someone your own size next time, Perkin," Vinny teased.

When Vinny had completed the task, he applied some ointment, and bandaged the injury. The soothing coolness of the balm eased Perkin's discomfort.

They made camp soon afterwards and prepared to spend their first night in the forest without yet having seen any sign of the legendary Homar. Darkness came early and before long, the rain started to fall again. As Squire took the first watch that night with Sim, the dark silhouettes of the tall trees and the familiar sounds of the forest reminded him of his first night in Thorland several months earlier. Though no snow fell here, the cold from the rain gushing down from the foliage above seemed equally unpleasant and chilling to the bones.

In the early hours of the morning before the sun was yet up, Vinny and Vylin kept watch. The rain had ceased and the clouds parted to reveal the bright orb of the moon overhead. By its light, they made out the silhouette of what appeared to be a very tall man with long, powerful legs and thick, muscular arms. His head, topped with horns, was that of a bull. His human body was clothed in the skin of a brown bear, and he wore leather thongs on his feet. His gigantic, hideous appearance sent shockwaves of fear through Vylin and Vinny.

"Vinny," screamed Vylin. "Who's that? He's huge, and look at his fangs! He's going to make a meal of us."

Homar spoke with a deep, booming voice. "Why are you in my forest?"

CHAPTER 10

THE FORD AND THE BRIDGE

Vinny reached for his bow, but his hands shook so much that he couldn't control them. His eyes darted up towards the face of the creature called Homar. "His teeth are as long as my fingers," he whispered to Vylin. "It looks like they could rip me in half."

Saliva glistened on Homar's fangs. "Why are you in my forest?" he repeated.

"W…we're on a mission for the wizard Tobin," replied Vinny. "We're searching for the golden teeth that belong to the g…golden skull. We think one of them is hidden in your forest at the suspension bridge over the River Hom."

"Tobin. Who is Tobin?" Homar asked. "I only have knowledge of the wizard Gordin. Gordin is my friend. I know of no Tobin."

"Tobin is the son of G…Gordin. Gordin died many years ago."

Homar's tone mellowed. "Ah! That's very sad, but how do I know you are telling the truth?"

A voice called out from the gloom. "I am Sim, apprentice to Tobin. I'm of the same line as Gordin."

"Come closer."

Homar squinted at the young wizard. "Ah, I see it's true. Your face bears a resemblance to Gordin's. Anyone from Gordin's line must also be my friend." He turned towards Vinny. "Then you and your companions must also be friends, and I welcome you to my forest."

HOPE

The muscles in Vinny's throat relaxed. "So, you're not the ogre that the legends speak of," he said. "They say you control evil spirits. But what manner of creature are you?"

Homar sighed. "I am a minotaur," he replied, "and there are no evil spirits in my forest. These rumours must have been spread by those who themselves control evil."

"Probably by the evil wizard Gordeve, Tobin's sister." said Vinny. "Gordeve controls the Kobalos and cougars, and is trying her best to thwart our mission."

"That's very disturbing, that a daughter of Gordin should be a source of evil. Now, will you waken your companions? I invite you all to my home where you can join me for breakfast and wash yourselves. I will be glad of the company. It's many years since I had visitors. I will also help your little friend with his injuries. It's lucky for you that you only ran into a porcupine, and not one of the brown bears."

Homar's cottage was situated just a short distance away. It had stone walls and a slate roof. A roaring log fire in a stone hearth greeted them. After the cold and dampness of the forest, it seemed very warm and cosy inside the tiny cottage.

"Even in the hottest months, the forest is cool and moist," he explained. "Now, make yourselves comfortable in front of the fire while I prepare some breakfast."

A few moments later, they heard the sounds of bacon spitting in the frying pan and soon the salty aroma reached their nostrils and their mouths began to water.

Homar served them a fine breakfast of bacon, eggs and toasted bread.

THE FORD AND THE BRIDGE

"I cure the bacon myself from wild pigs I catch in the forest," he explained, "and I bake the bread myself."

After breakfast, he prepared baths for each of them in turn, then cleaned and dressed Perkin's wounds, applying some kind of balm to the sore spots. The kindness shown by the minotaur convinced them that he was no beast who hunted like a wild animal, but a civilised person.

They stayed three days and nights at Homar's cottage, by which time Perkin's wounds had completely healed and he could again walk without pain. He even managed some dancing on the third evening, accompanied by Vylin on the violin. When it was time for a rest, the friends exchanged stories with the minotaur. Some of Homar's stories, which told of a time long before they were born, fascinated them.

"You must be very old," said Squire.

"Once I lived in the outside world," he told them. "My mother did a very evil thing by uniting herself with a bull, and I was the unfortunate result of that union. This was a shameful burden to bear so, when I was still quite young, I left home and came to live alone in this forest and to hide from the world."

"Do you still live alone?" Squire asked.

"Yes, I've always preferred it that way. I have few friends and many of them, like Gordin, will be dead by now. Only Sacumed comes to visit me, and that is not often."

"Who is Sacumed?" enquired Vinny.

"He's an old friend," replied the minotaur. "He does not shy away from me because of my appearance. He respects me for who I am. If you have not already met him on your journeys, you surely will. Gordin always told me that Sacumed will have an important part to play in the future of Thorland."

HOPE

He turned to Squire. "Now tell me where you came from. You are Squire, and yet you are not the Squire I knew. You have the scar, but somehow you are different. Are you a reincarnation?"

"No," replied Squire. "I am a different man from the one you knew. I was summoned here from another Land by Tobin, to fulfil the ancient prophecy."

"I am familiar with the prophecy," said the minotaur. "But what is this other Land to which you refer? I have heard of such a place once before. When Sacumed last visited me, maybe thirty years ago, he brought me news of a man who came from another Land. What was his name ... ? It was Jeffers, or Jiffers, or some such name."

"Not Jippers?" suggested Squire.

"Yes, that's the name."

"Now it all makes sense to me," said Squire. "Jippers has been following us. At first we thought that he was after Perkin's Seeround Glass, but when he tried to steal the shield from me the other night, we realised that's what he really wanted. 'My Hope' he called it. 'I need my Hope to find my way home,' he said. Jippers must also be from my world, and he's looking for a way home."

Perkin could hardly contain his excitement as he interrupted, "That would also explain why the glass couldn't see him when we were on our way to Daly's Bridge. Do you remember, the time when Vylin thought she saw someone following us, but the glass revealed nothing? It couldn't see him, just as it can't see you, Squire."

"But what is the significance of the shield?" asked Homar. "How can the shield help him to find his way home?"

"The shield is very powerful and was given to me by Tobin to help protect me in times of great danger. However, when its powers are released,

THE FORD AND THE BRIDGE

something strange happens. I don't really understand it, but when I look into the back of the shield, I see images – like looking through a window. They give me a glimpse of my own world."

"What do you see?"

"I don't remember anything, but I do know the experiences aren't pleasant. Jippers obviously wants to get such a glimpse, or maybe he thinks the shield will provide a means of returning to our world. I called these images 'Windows on my World', but now I know I am not alone, I will call them 'Windows on Our World'."

* * * * *

When Helge and Wim arrived at Dunton after a journey of four days, they discovered it was the centre of a great deal of activity. Stretching in all directions, as far as their eyes could see, tents of many colours covered the sands surrounding the town.

"Ben Lei must have called up every able-bodied man from all parts of the desert," said Helge. "There must be at least two thousand tents, housing something like ten thousand Telekai."

When Helge and Wim reached the entrance to the camp, a group of guards confronted them. Most of them were young men, but their leader was a mature Telekai warrior.

"Halt! Please state your names and your business in Dunton," he ordered.

"My name is Helge from the island of Atmos, otherwise known as Helge of Hanlin Forest. This is the wizard Wim, apprentice to Tobin. We seek counsel with my countryman, Yohan."

The guard recognised the name of Atmos, Yohan's place of origin, and the woman's features seemed familiar. He also knew of the wizard Tobin.

HOPE

He turned to one of the younger men. "Go to Yohan's tent. Tell him that friends are here seeking his counsel. Beg his indulgence to join us here, so that he can confirm their identity." Turning to Helge, he added, "Formalities, please forgive my caution."

A few moments later, Yohan arrived. He did not seem surprised to see them. "Welcome cousin," he said. "And welcome to you once again Sim, or is it Wim?"

"I am Wim," the wizard replied.

"Follow me. We will find somewhere private where we can talk."

They passed a large green tent, instantly recognisable as the chief's by its standard – a green camel on an orange background.

Yohan led them to another tent close by where he indicated a seating rug for them to sit on. "As you can see, since we parted at Bo's Chasm three weeks ago, I have been busy helping Ben Lei prepare for war. But, what brings you here, and why are you separated from the rest of your company?"

"Alvin has been captured by the Kobalos," said Helge. "He and some others were on a mission to Trow to find one of the teeth."

"Trow! How did they get to Trow?"

Helge explained to him all that had happened from the time they had parted at Bo's Chasm until now.

"We fear that even now they are taking him to Gordeve's castle," she said. "If Gordeve gets her hands on him, she will make him talk and the future of our whole quest will be in jeopardy. We need your help and the help of the Telekai to rescue him."

When she had finished speaking, he said, "You must rest a while. Later you can tell your story to Ben Lei. Please lay down for an hour or two on those sleeping rugs." He indicated a pile of rugs in a different section of the tent.

THE FORD AND THE BRIDGE

When Helge and Wim had travelled with the others in the desert on the way to Ar, they had witnessed the ornate beauty of the Telekai's sleeping rugs. Now, in Yohan's tent, they saw many other kinds of rug, each one embroidered with a unique intricate pattern.

"Can you explain to us the uses of all these different types of rug?" Helge asked.

"These, of course, are seating rugs. The Telekai do not use chairs, so instead they pile several layers of these one on top of the other to make a comfortable place to sit. Over there, in the corner, are the dining rugs. When the Telekai share their meals, they place the serving dishes on them to help keep the seating rugs clean. Over there, in the other section of the tent, you can see some sleeping rugs, ones that have an extra long pile that provides a softer sleeping surface. The Telekai sleep on them on the floor and wrap themselves in quilts and blankets. The heavy ones on the door are, of course, door rugs. They prevent dust from entering the tents."

After they had rested for a while, the chief summoned them to his tent. Ben Lei sat on a brightly coloured seating rug of reds, yellows and blues. His tanned, handsome face was clean-shaven apart from a small black moustache. He wore the traditional desert clothes of the Telekai.

Helge and Wim greeted the young chief in the same way that they had witnessed Yohan greet Ben Wai in the desert several weeks earlier. After the chief had clicked his fingers as a sign for them to stand up, he indicated another seating rug for his guests.

"You can begin now," said Yohan. "Ben Lei understands much of your language. Nevertheless, I shall translate for him."

The chief sat in silence as they told their story. It wasn't until they had finished that he finally spoke. "If you had come to me with such a story a few weeks ago, I would not have believed you and would have had you thrown in jail for wasting my time. However, I have witnessed the massacre that occurred here at Dunton, and the death of my beloved father. I know the things you speak of are true. I will therefore sanction a group of fifty Telekai to accompany Yohan and yourselves on this mission to rescue your friend. All necessary preparations will be made for your departure at first light tomorrow."

That evening Wim prepared to transform himself once again into the shape of a hawk to fly eastwards to try to locate the current position of Alvin and his captors. It would be a dangerous incursion into enemy territory, but essential if they were to be successful with their mission.

"Can't you rescue him yourself and fly back with him?" asked Yohan as Wim prepared to leave.

"As a hawk, I don't have the strength to carry him," replied Wim. "When Tobin transforms, he takes on the form of a giant eagle, which is much stronger. Even so, he can only carry people for short distances."

Yohan watched in fascination as the wizard transformed himself. The red-tailed hawk, with a broad band of dark streaking across its white belly, flew off towards the east.

Wim returned later in the evening with the news that he had spotted Alvin and his captors travelling on the road from Wichtlein to Gordeve's castle, already a day out from Wichtlein.

Yohan unrolled a map of East Thorland and pored over it for several seconds before he spoke. "We have no time to lose," he said. "Within three days they will be at Gordeve's castle."

Wim also reported that he had seen very few Kobalos on the road they would be travelling, except for a garrison of fifty or so guarding the gate on the far side of the wall. "It seems that Gordeve has underestimated the resilience of the Telekai," he said. "Most of her troops are stationed near to

THE FORD AND THE BRIDGE

the tunnel. It looks like she's expecting the king's army to launch an attack from Bunbury."

*　　*　　*　　*　　*

At daybreak the next morning the fifty Telekai, together with Yohan, Helge and Wim, departed. Each individual had a horse, but heading the cavalcade, Yohan sat tall on his magnificent mount.

"It's Windracer," said Helge.

"After I returned to Dunton and gained favour with Ben Lei, he gifted me the horse," said Yohan. "The other horse I purchased in Bunbury was hardworking and true, but for stamina and speed, Windracer is in a league of his own. I treat him as if he's one of my family. Windracer, in return, remains loyal."

Before they departed, Ben Lei addressed his men. "This is a very dangerous mission," he said, "but it is essential that there should be a successful conclusion. Therefore, I am giving all authority to Yohan, and instructing you to take your orders from him. Good luck."

From Dunton they travelled to the gate in the wall near Dun Wood.

"This is our first obstacle," said Yohan. "We really have no alternative. Apart from the group of cougars and their Kobalos riders who passed through the gate four weeks ago, it's remained closed for more than two centuries. Now it seems to be locked once again. How can we open it?"

"I will open the gate," replied Wim. "You and your men must be ready to engage with the enemy as soon as it is opened."

Wim raised his staff towards the gate, closed his eyes, and concentrated his mind on the task. With the confidence of a mature wizard, he commanded, "Gate, be open." When he uttered these words, a flash of light passed from the tip of his staff towards the gate.

HOPE

At first there was silence, then after a few seconds, Helge heard a creaking sound as the gate began to move. Slowly it swung on its hinges, and before long it had opened wide enough for the riders to pass through.

They caught the Kobalos by surprise. Most of them still slept, and the guards were ill-disciplined and lazy. Before they knew what happened, the Telekai riders charged into the camp, with swords flashing. The next moment, Kobalos heads rolled in the dirt. The others who had been sleeping were roused from their slumber, but too late. Telekai swords ripped through the canvas of their tents and, amid muffled cries, slew some of them in their beds. They hacked others down from behind as they tried to flee, screaming for mercy. Within twenty minutes, all the Kobalos were dead. On the other side, however, there were few casualties. With their short swords, the Kobalos succeeded in killing two Telekai, and severely injured five others.

Yohan immediately despatched a messenger to Ben Lei with a request to send reinforcements to guard the gate, and medical treatment for the injured. Then he gave instructions for a small contingent to remain to bury the dead and to guard the gate until the reinforcements arrived. The remainder, about thirty-five Telekai, and the three friends set off on the road towards Gordeve's castle.

After a hard day's ride, during which they encountered no further resistance, they made camp by the bridge over the Trow River.

Before settling down to sleep, in anticipation of an attack from the enemy during the night, the Telekai warriors encircled their camp with several piles of dry grass and twigs, with flints and tinder on hand ready to light them.

Soon after midnight, the expected assault came from a pack of thirty cougars, but the Telekai were ready. When the cougars launched their first wave of attack, Telekai soldiers simultaneously lit all the fires. As soon as

THE FORD AND THE BRIDGE

the cougars saw the flames and the smoke reached their nostrils, they were filled with such confusion and dread that they started to retreat. As they raced away, their howling echoed through the night air. Caught with their defences down, they were like sitting ducks for the Telekai archers.

"Why did the cougars come again when you and Sim ordered them to return to Gordeve?" Helge asked Wim.

"Gordeve has greater powers than we have," confessed Wim. "Though the group of cougars that we commanded at the beach will not come again, she has bred new ones to take their place. I'm afraid we will never get rid of all of them, unless we can first defeat Gordeve."

Early the following morning, Wim once again transformed himself into a hawk and flew eastwards to determine the progress of Alvin and his captors. When he returned, he reported that they were only about a day and a half's travelling time away from Gordeve's castle. "Our best chance is to cut them off at the ford across the Phooka River," he said. "We must be there waiting for them by the middle of the afternoon."

Meanwhile, these developments had not gone unnoticed at the wizard's castle. Gordeve had sent out the group of thirty cougars with the expectation that they would defeat the Telekai. Now she hatched another plan. She despatched a battalion of Kobalos from the castle, and at the same time gave orders that another battalion should travel northwards from Wichtlein to cut off the Telekai's line of retreat.

In the middle of the afternoon the Telekai and friends arrived at the ford, a wide shallow crossing of the Phooka River, silent except for the gentle trickle of water passing over the stones that littered the riverbed. They took up positions ready to ambush the carriage carrying Alvin. Some of the Telekai warriors, together with Helge, stationed themselves on the southern side of the river and hid behind rocks. Others hid amongst the trees on the northern side. Yet another group, with Wim, scouted ahead along the road leading to Gordeve's castle, anticipating that reinforcements were on their way. A fourth group, with Yohan, doubled back to the rear of the approaching carriage.

As the carriage slowed down to enter the bubbling water, the group of Telekai hiding behind the rocks stole out from their hiding place. Two of them jumped aboard next to the unsuspecting driver. While one snatched the reins from him, the other overpowered the driver and slit his throat quickly and with precision. A third Telekai jumped onto the footboard of the carriage, reached through the open door and grabbed hold of the guard by the neck. The two of them fell backwards into the water and rolled. A fourth Telekai went to the assistance of his friend and throttled the guard.

Alvin was both surprised and overjoyed to see Helge.

"Are you all right, Alvin?" she asked.

"I've been treated very roughly and they gave me only a little food and water ... and my shirt is torn," he replied. "But it's so good to see you. I'll be fine now."

"Come, let me see if I'll be able to mend your shirt."

"Oh, no! It's extremely unlucky to mend a garment while you're still wearing it."

She laughed. "It's also very lucky for you that Sim's not here to make fun of you. Anyway, we don't have time now to stop to mend shirts."

A few moments later, a Telekai scout arrived with news that a Kobalos battalion approached from the north. "Most of them are on foot," he said, "but some are riding cougars."

Soon after, a second scout arrived from the south. He had a similar story about the approaching battalion from Wichtlein. "Some of them are

THE FORD AND THE BRIDGE

rapidly approaching the ford," he said. "Another group has branched off towards the west to cut off our line of retreat."

By that time, Yohan had joined the others. He looked grim. "Gordeve knows we're here and what we're trying to do. They have us trapped. All our lines of retreat are cut off."

"That's where you're wrong," said Wim who had just rejoined the group. "There's one road left unguarded."

"That's not possible," said Yohan. "Which road?"

"The road eastwards to Spriggan," said Wim.

Yohan's face dropped. "Spriggan! That's on the coast of East Thorland, still in enemy territory, and far away in the opposite direction from where we want to go."

"We have no choice," said Wim. "From Spriggan we can commandeer a ship to take us to Terrapo. The people of Terrapo are our allies. Once we are on the island, we can look for a way to return home."

"But first of all we have to get to Spriggan," Yohan pointed out. "It's several hours' journey away, even if we can get there without encountering any further problems. Gordeve's armies will be sure to pursue us, and we don't know if she might have more troops stationed at Spriggan. I don't like this idea at all, but I don't think we have any choice. Is there some kind of spell you could conjure up?" he asked Wim.

"If we can reach the bridge over the Brag River first, then I can put a spell of binding on the bridge," replied the wizard. "However, the spell will only last a few hours, less if Gordeve can destroy it."

"That's the best chance we've got," Yohan conceded. "How far is it to Spriggan?"

"It's about two hundred kilometres," Wim replied.

"And how far to the bridge?"

"About sixty."

"We must depart at once," he said. "If we don't stop, we should reach the bridge in about two hours. However, the cougars can outrun our horses, so I fear they may overtake us before we get there." He turned to address Alvin, "We have no pony for you, so you must ride with me on Windracer's back. He's more than strong enough to carry us both."

Yohan called his men together and they made haste towards the bridge. Luck was with them. After ninety minutes hard riding, they arrived at the bridge over the Brag River just as darkness set in. The riders at the rear reported that they sensed the cougars followed not far behind.

Wim, Helge, Alvin and Yohan dismounted in the centre of the bridge, while the Telekai riders crossed and waited on the eastern side. As the other three stood behind the wizard, they watched him raise his staff and saw a bright flash of light emanate from it that almost blinded them. Then he moved the staff from one side of the bridge to the other, and as he did so commanded, "Bridge, I bind you not to allow anyone or anything to pass until the new day dawns."

Wim had hardly completed issuing the spell of binding before the pack of cougars, some with Kobalos riders, arrived at the far end of the bridge. The first wave of cougars charged forward encouraged by the sight of the enemy standing, apparently vulnerable, halfway across. They hit the spell of binding with such force that it threw them backwards and knocked many of them unconscious. The next few cougars approached the centre of the bridge more warily and discovered an invisible wall through which they could not pass. The Telekai riders waiting on the eastern bank of the river, cheered when they heard howls of anger and despair coming from the other side.

THE FORD AND THE BRIDGE

The four mounted their horses once again and the party resumed its journey towards Spriggan. As they prepared to leave, the unmistakable hissing voice of one of the cougars came to them from across the bridge, "Gordeve will rule!"

"We must keep riding through the night," said Yohan. "However, we can now slacken our pace a little so as not to overstrain the horses."

They arrived on the outskirts of Spriggan just when the first rays of sunlight appeared over the eastern horizon.

* * * * *

At about this time, the rest of the company departed from Homar's cottage. Homar, who accompanied them, offered to be their guide as far as the suspension bridge. The day was cool, but the rain had stopped and the smell of decaying vegetation filled the air. With Homar's assistance, they made good progress and the walk through the forest to the bridge took them just over four hours.

Soon after the sound of rushing waters reached their ears, the track opened out into a clearing just before the bridge over the Hom River. There they shared lunch with Homar before saying goodbye to the minotaur.

They blindfolded the mule and the pony to prevent them from panicking, in case they should look down at the rocks and rapids far below. Vylin crossed first, leading Faithful. Perkin followed with Conny. Squire, Vinny and Sim, fearful that the bridge might not bear all the weight at once, waited until the others had crossed safely before following.

When they stepped onto the swaying planks, pulses began to quicken. The bridge, which stretched one hundred and fifty metres, swayed up and down as they made their way across. It also moved from side to side if they inadvertently transferred too much of their weight to one side of the bridge or the other. As they looked down at the mists drifting around the

HOPE

swirling waters of the canyon eighty metres below, their heads began to swim. The vertigo and the aroma of the sweet smelling, cedar-scented rainforest air, gave their senses an experience that was both frightening and awe-inspiring.

When these three had reached about halfway across, a shout from Homar alerted them. They looked back to see a familiar figure had just stepped onto the bridge brandishing a large knife.

"Jippers!" exclaimed Squire. "He's obviously been following us through the forest, and must be after the shield. Quick, this time he's armed. We must get to the other side and hide from him."

Despite the violent swaying, the three friends rushed ahead to try to get off the bridge as soon as possible and to hide from Jippers. However, when they reached just a few metres from the far end, they heard another shout from Homar.

A brown bear followed Jippers onto the bridge.

CHAPTER 11

HEADING FOR WINTERTON

The bear had caught the strong scent of Jippers, and was hungry.

When Jippers heard Homar's call, he was about halfway across. He looked back and saw the bear stepping onto the southern end of bridge. It took the old man only an instant to note that he was a large, heavy male with a black coat, grizzled with grey at the tips of the hairs. His shoulders were humped with muscles, his claws long and sharp.

The other three looked back and saw a look of terror on the old man's face.

"I thought brown bears were herbivores," said Squire.

"Not this one," said Vinny. "Look at the way he's sniffing after Jippers. Sometimes they become predators and hunt large animals such as moose, or even people. Quick, let's get out of here! But don't run or the bridge will … "

At that moment, Jippers panicked and started to run towards the northern end, showing an agility that belied his years. As he did so, the bear started bounding after him on all fours, causing the planks of the bridge to swing wildly. All on the bridge found it difficult to keep their balance.

Homar knew from experience that it would be foolish for him to pursue the bear since he would become even more aggressive if trapped. The minotaur put too high a value on his own life. He could see there was only one way to save Jippers.

HOPE

"Wait. Listen," he called to the four on the bridge. "I'm going to have to cut the ropes that hold the bridge. You must hang on to the planks under your feet."

Homar used his machete to cut the ropes. His broad, muscular arm effortlessly wielded the enormous blade, and it took him just a few seconds to cut through the first of the thick ropes. Nevertheless, he noticed that the bear was closing on Jippers and would soon catch him. When the first rope snapped free from its moorings, the bridge tipped precariously to one side and began to swing up and down uncontrollably. The three companions and Jippers tenaciously clung to the planks of the bridge. As he did so, Jippers dropped the knife he had been carrying.

The bear, however, had not had the benefit of Homar's warning, and his efforts to hang on to the planks with his sharp claws proved fruitless. He lost his balance, and with it his footing. With a wail, he succumbed to the force of gravity and fell to his death on the rocks far below.

When Homar had almost cut through the last of the ropes, there was a creaking sound as the bridge began to move, then a crash when the end nearest to Homar broke free and began to swing in a pendulum arc towards the opposite side of the gorge. Jippers and the others grimly clung on, and waited for the bridge to collide with the opposite cliff face with a jarring jolt.

The three, who had been very near to the far end of the bridge, scrambled up to safety using the planks like the rungs of a ladder. They hauled themselves up onto the rocky platform where the others waited. The five companions looked down from the safety of the rocks at the north end of the bridge. They could see Jippers several metres below them clinging for dear life to the planks, a strained look on his face.

"He's finding it difficult to keep holding on," said Vinny. "Hang on Jippers," he shouted. "I'm coming to get you."

HEADING FOR WINTERTON

"No!" cried Homar. "It's too dangerous. Let down a rope so that Jippers can tie it round his waist. Then you can help to haul him up."

Vinny did as Homar suggested. Jippers tied the rope around his waist and began to ascend the 'ladder'. Vinny hauled on the rope to give assistance and reassurance, but the old man climbed very slowly. All of a sudden, Vinny felt the rope slacken. From where he and the others stood, the angle of the ledge made it impossible to see what had become of Jippers.

Vinny expected to hear a cry and a crash as the old man fell and smashed into the rocks, but he heard nothing except the roar of the rushing river far below.

"Perkin, search for him with the glass," he said.

"The glass can't see him."

"Of course, I'd forgotten." Looking for another way, he shouted across to Homar, "What's happened? Has he fallen?"

Homar replied, "No, he untied the rope from his waist and jumped onto a ledge lower down. It looks like there might be a cave there. Yes, he's disappeared. Did you hear that?"

"What?" asked Vinny.

"It's difficult to hear above the roar of water, but it sounded like he said, 'My Hope. Where is my Hope?'"

Vinny looked at the strained faces of the other four. "We might as well forget about Jippers for the moment," he said. "Either he'll perish there in that cave, or he'll find some way out and we'll see him again. But I think that's the last we'll see of him today."

"I agree," said Squire. "Let's search for the tooth and be on our way. I hope it wasn't dislodged from its hiding place when the bridge crashed into the cliff."

HOPE

They examined the first few planks nearest their end, the end by which the damaged bridge now dangled from the ledge at the northern edge of the gorge. After a few minutes, they located a metal ring embedded in the wood on what had been the underside of one of the planks. Vinny cut away the plank and placed it upside down on the rocky platform. Squire pulled sharply on the ring until the plank bent and then snapped. As it broke into two, he saw a hollow space in the wood.

"Here's the tooth," he said with a smile, "and the next set of instructions."

Perkin was anxious to get going. "What does it say?" he asked.

Squire read the words:

"Right Wisdom tooth – top jaw
To the University City you must proceed.
Seek out the College where the bells are pealed.
Climb the bell tower, indeed
Two hundred steps you must ascend, so that
Inside the clapper for B flat,
Tooth and instructions will be revealed."

"The University City can only be Winterton," asserted Perkin. "That's where we must go next."

Vylin nodded. "You're quite right, Perkin. Winterton is famous for its ancient university."

The five companions picked up their belongings and prepared to continue their journey. They looked back to wave to Homar, but saw that he had already left. If they could have seen him at that moment, they would have witnessed the tears in his eyes as he set off to return to his lonely cottage. He had to resign himself once again to a life of solitude, and the realisation that he would never rid himself of the curse of his unnatural birth.

*   *   *   *   *

The riders approached Spriggan with caution, unsure whether they would find any of Gordeve's army there, but were relieved to discover that the entrance to the town remained unguarded. They passed unhindered, and unobserved at that early hour, through the town and on towards the docks.

The Telekai hid with the horses behind the wharf warehouse while Yohan, Helge, Wim and Alvin searched for a ship from Terrapo.

"There's a ship," said Wim, pointing to a large schooner with two masts. "I wonder if she's from Terrapo."

"She is indeed," said a strange voice behind them. It was barely above a whisper. "I am First Mate of *Bethia*. What business do you have with us? You are very unwise to use the language of the west here in Spriggan. Though we speak your language, we always use the eastern tongue when we are here."

"We require passage to Pixar," explained Yohan, also lowering his voice. "Can you take us to your captain?"

"I'm on my way to the town on business, but go to the ship and ask for Redbeard," the man replied. "But take care that no one else hears you speaking the western tongue."

When they reached hailing distance of *Bethia,* Yohan looked around in all directions before calling out, "Good morning. I would like to speak to Redbeard."

A short, stout, dark-skinned man with a crop of ginger-red hair and a beard of the same colour came to the railing on the main deck. He leaned over and called back, barely above a whisper, "I am, Redbeard, the captain. What business do you have with me, and why are you using the western language here in Spriggan?" A scar on the captain's left cheek, which stretched from his ear almost to his chin, glistened in the morning sun. Large circular earrings adorned his ears, adding to his fearsome appearance.

"May we come on board so that we can discuss our business with you in private? I don't want to draw attention from the local people by using our language," said Yohan.

Redbeard glowered. "Come aboard," he replied. "You'll get me into trouble too if you're heard."

Yohan led the way. He was about to board *Bethia* when Alvin called to him. "Don't step onto the ship with your left foot first," he cautioned. "It's very unlucky." His companions didn't really believe him. Nevertheless, they all made sure they boarded the ship with their right foot first.

Redbeard invited the strangers into his cabin where they could speak more freely. They relaxed when they saw that he now had a more conciliatory look on his face.

"Would you care for some tea?" he asked.

"Yes, thank you," said Yohan. "We are very dry after our ride." The others nodded in agreement.

Yohan introduced himself and his three companions, and went on to explain to the captain everything that had happened over the last few months, and the events that had led to their present predicament.

"I've heard rumours of a build-up of troops near the border," the captain informed them. "But I hadn't realised the seriousness of the situation until now. Spriggan is remote from the border with the West and so far has been untouched by the war. Although people and Kobalos loyal to Gordeve populate the town, they are not fighting people and still go about their business peacefully and life goes on as normal. The people of Terrapo

HEADING FOR WINTERTON

continue to trade with the inhabitants of Spriggan. Now tell me, how is it that I can help you?"

"We need passage to Pixar," explained Helge.

"But I have a schedule to keep to and cargo to transport. Last evening we finished unloading our cargo of copper and tin ore. We've just woken up and my crew are having breakfast in preparation for the day's work of loading the vessel with flour, rice and maize for the return trip to Pixar. If I don't keep to my schedule, I'll lose money and my customers."

"We'll make it well worth your while, captain," said Helge. "We'll give you double what you would expect to make in profit from the sale of your cargo."

Redbeard stroked his beard as he considered the offer. "That will be one thousand guineas," he said.

"Agreed," she confirmed.

"Then you and your men and horses must embark without delay. We must sail on the high tide in the mid morning. But I don't know how you are going to get them all on board without drawing attention to yourselves."

"I'll deal with that," said Wim with a mischievous look in his eye.

An hour later, all the riders and horses had boarded. They put the horses below decks and provided them with plenty of water and hay. The Telekai and others had to make the best of the space available on deck for the crossing to Pixar. Redbeard told them that he expected the voyage to take about eight hours, providing the weather remained fine.

Courtesy of a little magic from Wim, the workers in the docks and warehouse had an unexpected sleep that morning.

*   *   *   *   *

At about the same time the other five companions, with the mule and the pony, left the suspension bridge behind and resumed their journey

HOPE

through the northern part of Homar's Forest. The rain had eased and their spirits were raised somewhat, but they knew that they would still need to spend one last night in the dark forest. They worried about a further attempt by Jippers to steal the shield, but feared even more another attack from a bear.

They walked for another three or fours hours before sunset. The going got tougher as they started to ascend the pass over the Hom Mountains. The final night in the forest passed without incident, but none of them slept very much.

They left the forest the next morning with a sense of relief. Although they had accomplished their task, and despite their worst fears, Homar had proved to be a welcoming host, yet they had not enjoyed their time in the forest.

They continued to climb until about midday. Having reached the highest point of the pass over the mountains, they then followed the winding track northwards back down to where it joined the main east-west highway. Here they made camp for the second night.

They spent the third night at the bridge over the Bun River. Here they could refresh themselves at last after their ordeal in the forest. As Squire took a bath in the cool waters of the river, his nostrils detected the delicious smell of rabbit roasting. *Well done, Vinny*, he thought. He gave a satisfied grunt as he glanced downstream and saw Vylin haul in a salmon. They feasted well that night.

It had been a very warm late autumn's day and, after the coolness of the forest, they felt suffocated by the higher temperatures and for comfort slept outside. At times like these, they let their guard down and the next attack of the enemy took them by surprise.

HEADING FOR WINTERTON

In the middle of the night, Perkin and Squire kept watch, but they were too busy telling stories and lost concentration. There was not a lot of noise, just a last-minute rustling of wings, as a colony of vampire bats homed in on their prey using smell and echolocation. These bats, corrupted by Gordeve, had a craving for human and Luchorpan blood.

Before the two guards realised what was happening, the bats settled down to feast on the blood of their sleeping friends. Using special heat sensors located in their noses, the bats sought out the veins of their prey close to the surface of the skin around the neck and the top of the back, and used their sharp teeth to make tiny incisions in the skin. Blood oozed from the wounds, and the bats lapped it up.

Finally, Squire and Perkin came to their senses. Squire snatched up his shield, and Perkin grabbed an axe that they usually used for cutting wood. Perkin charged towards the bats that already feasted, kicked them from the bodies of the three victims, and dealt some deathly blows with the axe.

When Squire lifted the shield up in front of his face to ward off the attack of the bats still arriving, he once again experienced the strange phenomenon that he had witnessed twice before. The energy emanating from the five stars started as a glow and gradually increased until beams of light shot out aimed at the bats, repelling some and stunning others, knocking them to the ground. At the same time, Squire saw an image begin to appear in the back of the shield. The power of the shield threw him backwards onto the ground. Darkness engulfed him, and the 'Window on Our World', as he had called it, opened once again and he became drawn into the image as his alter ego, Grant Cowie, fighting for the life of his daughter.

He had lost all hope of reaching Theresa before it would be too late. However, fortune came from an unexpected quarter. The same log that had struck Grant and made him lose his balance, hit a rock that just jutted up above the surface of the water. The log lost some of its forward momentum and the current forced its upstream end into a circular motion towards the drowning girl. With one last effort, Theresa managed to grab hold of the log before it continued its wild journey downstream. Grant saw what had happened and felt some relief that his daughter had something to hang onto. However, his relief was only momentary as he observed the log heading towards what could only be the top of a waterfall.

By this time, the noise and the disturbance from Perkin hacking at the bats with the axe had awakened Vinny, Sim and Vylin. When the wizard came to his senses, despite his weakness from loss of blood, he quickly put an end to the attack. Sim raised his staff and swept it in an arc, directed at the bats. With authority, he ordered them to be gone. As quickly and silently as they had arrived, they flew away eastwards back to the wicked wizard who had sent them.

While the others preoccupied themselves with the bats and Squire still lay unconscious, an unwelcome visitor crept unobserved towards him. Although Squire still held onto the leather strap with a powerful grip of his fist, the intruder managed to wrench the shield away from him. Amid the commotion, no one heard the words issue from the thief's lips, "My Hope. I've got my Hope". Before anyone realised what happened, Jippers had run away into the cover of the trees clutching the Shield of Squire.

Squire woke from his dream. "Where's the shield?" he cried. "It's gone! Someone has stolen the shield. Jippers, it must be Jippers! He must have found a way out of that cave near the bridge."

HEADING FOR WINTERTON

"This is serious," said Vinny. "However, our first priority is to see to our wounds before we bleed to death. We need to staunch the flow of blood. I remember learning at school that the saliva from the bats' mouths contains two chemicals. One of them numbs the victim's skin so that they won't wake up. The other prevents their blood from clotting. What can we use to stop the bleeding?"

"How about the healing sap that the hamadryad Pitys gave Helge?" suggested Perkin. "That should do the trick."

"Of course!" exclaimed Vinny. "You're quite right Perkin. I'd forgotten about it. Go and find the flask in Conny's saddlebag."

Squire and Perkin used cloths to apply some of the healing sap to the wounds of their three friends. There was an immediate effect, and it wasn't long before the blood stopped flowing and they could bandage the wounds.

"It's a very strong medicine," said Perkin. "Why didn't anyone think to use it for my porcupine wounds?"

"It slipped my mind," admitted Vinny. "Besides we have only a limited supply of the sap, and must use it sparingly."

"Now, what are we going to do about the shield?" asked Squire. "I don't like using it, but there's no doubting its power. We must find Jippers and recover the shield for our own protection."

"Maybe he's on his way back to Bunbury," suggested Sim. "A few kilometres from here there's a road going towards the west which leads to Foxtown, then on to Bunbury. I'll go to look for him as soon as it's light enough."

When the first rays of daylight beamed from a red sky on the eastern horizon, Sim transformed himself once again into the hawk. He was soon swooping over hill and dale searching for any sign of Jippers. Despite the pinpoint eyesight of the hawk, his search proved unsuccessful, and he returned to his friends an hour later.

"He must be lying low somewhere," said Sim. "Maybe in a small wood, or in a cave. We must try to follow his tracks."

Vinny found some footprints that probably belonged to Jippers, but they had only been following the tracks for a short time when the rain began to fall. The light rain soon became a storm, and a few minutes later they encountered a deluge. The ground quickly turned to mud that obliterated the tracks, and soon there seemed no hope they might follow them any further. In fact, there was little point in them trying to go anywhere, and for the rest of the day they were forced to stay in their tents to shelter from the battering storm. Dampness pervaded the air and lowered their spirits.

The next day dawned to clear skies, and it was time for the company to make a decision.

"We have to forget about the shield for the moment," said Vinny. "With the increased powers that Sim now has, we don't need to rely on it so much for protection. I think we should go on to Winterton to locate the next tooth. The continuation of the quest is more important than chasing after Jippers, who is harmless. As long as we are travelling westwards, we are moving further away from the real threat – that's the enemy, not Jippers. We can try to find him later. I'm sure Tobin will know where to look."

Squire's lower lip quivered. "I don't agree," he said. "Now Jippers has the shield, he might indeed be a threat. Besides, for Jippers and me, the shield might be the only means of returning to our own world. We must get it back."

"I don't think we have any choice," said Vinny. "We must put our trust in Tobin. He sent us on the quest."

"Very well," said Squire, "but I don't like it."

HEADING FOR WINTERTON

Thus they decided, and the company set off once again towards Winterton. The journey would take them another three days.

* * * * *

The crossing to Pixar had been a smooth one and *Bethia* docked at the wharf of the small town in the early evening. The visitors disembarked at once to give their horses a chance to stretch their legs and recover from the voyage. The officials at the wharf murmured among themselves when they saw Redbeard's strange cargo, but willingly accepted a small payment from Helge to permit the visitors to gain access to the island unhindered.

"You're unfamiliar with the island and its people," said Redbeard. "If you wish, I can arrange for someone to go with you to Hamil to act as your guide."

"That's very kind of you," Helge replied. "We would gladly accept your offer."

"Then my niece, Seline, shall accompany you. She's a fine rider and knows the country well. I'll go at once to her parents' house here in Pixar and ask her to go with you."

Seline, a tall, slim, dusky beauty, joined the group of riders the following morning. They bade farewell to Redbeard and his crew, and began their journey overland to Hamil. No sooner had they started than Seline manoeuvred to ride alongside Helge.

"Do you like our island?" she asked.

"It's very beautiful," Helge replied. "Tell me more about it."

"There are only two towns of any size, Pixar and Hamil," she said. "They are connected by the only main road on the island. Most of the people of Terrapo live in small coastal villages, and eke out a subsistence living, growing their own vegetables, keeping a few animals for meat, and fishing. About halfway between the two towns are the tin and copper mines that provide wealth for the elite of the island. The mines are also the chief source of work on Terrapo."

Later, as they approached the mines, Helge stood on her stirrups when she saw several grand, ancient buildings with tall, grey chimneys silhouetted against the western skyline.

"What are those strange tall building?" she asked, pointing.

"Those are the engine houses," explained Seline. "There are twenty or more of them straddled across the landscape around West Central Terrapo and the Karce peninsular. They serve the tin and copper mines. Many years ago, the people of the Karce region constructed them from enormous blocks of granite, with roofs of slate. Most of them remain in good working order. The mineworkers use the engines to pump water from the workings, to raise the mined rock to the surface, and to crush the rock to extract the ore."

"What are those long, narrow wooden buildings?" Helge asked.

"Those are the dormitories where the mineworkers live."

The ride from Pixar to Hamil was uneventful. The road, which was poorly constructed and full of potholes, mainly followed the coastline and passed through numerous small villages. The villages, which looked all quite similar, typically had twenty or thirty houses, simply constructed from bush timber with sago palm walls and roofs. Whenever the riders stopped at one of these villages, inquisitive brown-skinned children would gather around asking questions and giggling.

The party arrived at Hamil, the capital and largest town on Terrapo, towards evening two days after leaving Pixar.

"Hamil is not large compared with the cities on the mainland," Seline explained to Helge as they approached the town. "However, it has a sizeable commercial area, and several government buildings are scattered around the town centre."

HEADING FOR WINTERTON

"What's that large building up there on the hill?" asked Helge, pointing to a building overlooking the harbour and dominating the eastern skyline.

"That's the bronze foundry," Seline replied. "It's two-hundred years old. At the foundry the tin and copper that are extracted from the ores from the mines are smelted together to make the alloy bronze. The foundry workers cast the bronze to make many different kinds of objects. These include parts for all sorts of machines and weapons, not forgetting the bells for the carillon in Beck's College at Winterton."

"Also up there on the hill, can you see that huge house?" Seline pointed to a palatial building just to the south of the foundry. "It's the home of the ruler of Terrapo, Earl Philippo. It has ten bedrooms and has magnificent views of the harbour. He also owns the foundry. He's very rich."

"Your uncle advised us that we should pay a call on the earl as a matter of courtesy," said Helge.

"I'll you take you to meet him tomorrow," promised Seline.

CHAPTER 12

REUNION

"Just a few more hours to Winterton," said Perkin as they passed a road sign. The next moment he heard a ringing sound coming from behind. "What's that noise?" he said.

Squire looked back and saw a strange object approaching them, travelling also towards the city. As it came closer, he observed that the object consisted of two wheels, a large one at the front and a small one behind. Moreover, a man rode on top of it! He sat high up on a small seat, and his legs seemed to rotate on tiny platforms.

"What on earth…?" asked Squire. "It looks very cumbersome."

"I've never seen anything like it before," said Perkin. The others nodded in agreement.

"It's only got two wheels," said Vylin. "How come it doesn't topple over?"

"It seems to be balanced," replied Vinny, "and it's approaching us quickly, almost at running pace."

As the object began to slow down, the man on top pressed something that again made the ringing sound like a bell. At the same moment, he yelled, "Good morning."

When the contraption had almost stopped, the man threw his left leg back and placed it on a small step just above the smaller of the two wheels. Next, he moved his body off the seat and lowered his right leg to the ground whilst bending his left leg. Once the thing had completely stopped, the

REUNION

stranger took his left leg off the step and placed it on the ground. He performed all of these movements fluently with the expertise of much practice.

"Good morning," the man said once again. "My name is Trumper. I'm the Professor of Science at the University of Winterton."

"I'm Vinny," said the archer. "These are my friends – Squire, Sim, Perkin and Vylin." He indicated each of them in turn.

Trumper was a short man of about fifty years. His roundish face was topped with a crop of unruly hair that had already turned grey, but his thick bushy eyebrows and his moustache were still coloured black. The skin under his brown eyes was slightly wrinkled and his nose was flat and wider than the normal. He wore a pair of baggy trousers and a tweed jacket, both dark blue in colour. On his feet, he wore black laced boots.

"What's that … thing you were riding on?" asked Perkin.

Trumper's chest swelled as he breathed in before replying, "It's my latest invention. I call it the 'iron mule' because it's made of iron, and rides like a mule." He laughed.

"But how does it work?" asked Perkin. "What makes it move, and how do you keep it going straight?"

"Look at the big wheel," said the professor. "I place my feet on these two platforms, pedals I call them. As I make my legs go up and down, this forces the wheel to rotate. See." He lifted the wheel up from the ground and rotated the pedals using his hands. "As for going straight," he continued, "that's just a question of balance. It's easy when you know how."

"Can I have a try?" asked Vinny.

"Sure," replied the professor. "But don't be surprised if you can't do it at first. This is what you have to do. First stand behind the iron mule and hold onto those two bars – I call them handlebars – and put your left leg on the small step. That's right. Now, look straight ahead, don't look down, and push off with your right foot so the iron mule begins to move. Now it's moving at a steady pace, stand up on the step. Now slide your body onto the seat and at the same time throw your right leg forward to catch the pedal."

Vinny's right leg missed the pedal, and he came crashing to the ground with the iron mule landing on top of him. Vylin and Perkin exploded with laughter.

"Try again," suggested Trumper.

He tried again several times, so did Squire and Sim. However, none of them could succeed in mounting the iron mule. Vylin and Perkin were too small even to try, so they could afford to laugh.

"This is how you do it. Watch me," said Trumper. "It's easy." In just a few seconds, he had remounted his iron mule and rode around showing off his invention to his new friends. "You have to remember to always keep looking in front, not down to the ground," he said, "and always look out for any obstacles on the road ahead."

Trumper dismounted once again. "Where are you heading?" he asked.

"We're on our way to Winterton," replied Squire.

"Then you must be my guests," he said. "We will travel together to Winterton. My iron mule can travel faster than your legs can carry you. I will double back every so often so that I don't get too far ahead. It will be easier than getting on and off."

* * * * *

Earl Philippo was a rotund man, made fat on the profits from the sale of the iron and copper ores to both West and East Thorland, as well as finished bronze products from the foundry. His head was completely bald and his face clean-shaven. His clothes, which must have been made

REUNION

especially for him, consisted of a loose-fitting colourful shirt and huge baggy trousers. As his servant showed the visitors into the lounge, he struggled to rise from his chair.

Seline introduced each of her companions.

The earl smiled. "You are very welcome," he said. His teeth were stained red, the result of his habit of chewing betel nut mixed with lime. As he spoke, some of the juices from the mixture drooled down his chin.

Seline went on to explain the sequence of events that had brought the party to his house.

The earl scowled. "I'm not happy about the prospect of war. It is likely to curtail my source of income from the East. On the other hand," he said, smiling, "should there be war, my plentiful ores might significantly increase their value in the West."

The audience with the earl lasted just over an hour, at the end of which time he promised them safe passage back to the West. There would be a ship sailing in two days' time for Winterton, he told them.

"Unlike *Bethia*, this ship is equipped to take passengers and has enough cabins to accommodate you and all your companions," he informed them. "However, there is one small problem," he added. "The ship will also be carrying ore to Winterton, destined for King Jovanius II himself. I cannot possibly allow the shipment to be delayed. I must ask, therefore, that you leave your horses behind. I will accept them as payment for your passage."

Helge and Yohan conferred together before the latter replied. "We accept your offer, earl," he said. "However, I must insist on taking my own horse, Windracer, with me. The paramount chief of the Telekai, Ben Lei, entrusted this horse to me. He is very valuable, and Ben Lei would not be pleased if I should return to Dunton without him."

HOPE

"I understand," said the earl. "Very well, I give my permission for you to take this one horse ... Windracer."

*   *   *   *   *

Far away in her castle at the foot of the Central Kobold Mountain, Gordeve paced the floor of her study as she waited for her chief spy to arrive from the west.

The man entered Gordeve's study with a very worried look on his gaunt face. His sticking-out ears were red from embarrassment and his clean-shaven face showed signs of the wrinkles characteristic of a sixty-year-old man.

"About time," she yelled. "What took you so long?" The man felt her eyes piercing deeply into his own, asserting her authority over him.

"I ... "

Before the man had a chance to say more, she ranted, "Can you explain to me how the enemy was able to escape? In particular, how was the apprentice Wim able to put a spell of binding on the bridge over the Brag River?"

"He is no longer an apprentice, my Lady," replied the small, thin man.

"How can that be?" demanded the wizard.

"After we captured the Luchorpan Alvin at Trow, the rest of Tobin's company were reunited close to Ash Wood," he replied. "You sent a large group of cougars to attack the enemy near the shoreline."

"Yes, yes, I know all that," said Gordeve. "Get to the point, man."

"The man called Squire used his shield against the cougars. Somehow, the energy released from the shield empowered the twins as never before. I cannot explain how this happened. They commanded the cougars to return to you. You must surely know this. After that Tobin summoned the twins to return to his castle in the form of a pair of hawks, and he performed the initiation ceremony that conferred on them the title of 'wizard'."

"Wizards! Couldn't you do something to stop him? We now have three wizards to contend with. This makes the enemy stronger than us."

Stop him, how could I stop him? Doesn't she realise the foolishness of her question? "I realise that, my Lady," he replied, "but I didn't want to blow my cover. Remember that I am Tobin's trusted servant. If I had tried to interfere with the initiation ceremony of the twins, then I would have lost the trust your brother has in me. Which is more important, that I continue to feed you with vital information, or that we risk all?"

"You're right, Digbee," Gordeve conceded as her anger subsided. "What other information can you give me about the enemy?"

"The woman Helge with her compatriot, Yohan, the wizard Wim, Alvin the Luchorpan and thirty four Telekai riders are now on the island of Terrapo. They have gained the favour of Earl Philippo and are awaiting passage aboard a ship to Winterton, a schooner by the name of *Milton*, where they hope to be reunited with their friends."

Gordeve's face brightened. "Good, we will arrange a little storm to help them on their way," she said. "That will test the new wizard's powers. He still hasn't gained the strength to compete with me. That should finish them off! And, what of the others?"

"They have recently succeeded in finding one of the golden teeth at the suspension bridge over the Hom River. That minotaur, Homar, assisted them. They are now on their way to Winterton with some lunatic professor called Trumper."

"Trumper! He's not a lunatic. He's a very dangerous genius. He has devised all sorts of destructive weapons that the enemy can use with effect against us. What other news have you to tell me, Digbee?"

HOPE

"My Lady, the Shield of Squire has been stolen by a man called Jippers." At the mention of Jippers' name, Gordeve's eyebrows lifted a fraction, but Digbee didn't seem to notice. *Jippers*, she thought, *I wonder what he's up to. I won't tell Digbee that I know Jippers.*

Digbee went on: "He was lately the rat-catcher for the king. I have yet to determine why this man stole the shield, but Tobin doesn't seem concerned. He's of the opinion that Squire will regain the shield within a few days in Hanlin Forest."

"This seems to be of some significance," said the wizard. "As soon as you find out more about this man Jippers, you must let me know. Keep me informed of further progress, Digbee. I value your service highly. Now you must return to my brother before he realises you are missing." Raising her staff towards Digbee, Gordeve transformed him into the form of a bat and he flew off towards the west.

* * * * *

The five friends and Trumper entered the city of Winterton in the middle of the afternoon, and Trumper led them down a succession of narrow, cobbled streets, and drew up outside a stone building. "This is where I live, Capel College," he announced. "Please come inside. I will ask the porter to find you rooms for a few nights as my guests."

A red face with a crop of curly, fair hair appeared at the hatch. "Professor, can I help you?"

"Good afternoon, Spooner. Please escort my friends to the guest rooms. They will be staying for a few nights at my expense. Can you bring them to my room when it's time for supper?"

"Of course, professor," replied the porter.

"And could you please check if there is room in the college stables for their mule and pony. Oh yes … and can you find somewhere to store my

REUNION

iron mule? There's a good chap." Trumper left the five friends with the porter.

After several weeks on the road, they were very happy to find themselves in such luxurious accommodation. Each of them bathed and changed into clean clothes before meeting again at the porter's lodge. The porter then led them to Trumper's room, and knocked on the door.

"Come in," the professor called out.

The five companions entered to find themselves in a large room that served as both sleeping accommodation and study for Trumper. The dull, old-fashioned furniture reflected both the antiquity of the college and the staid character of the professor. The room had three windows, all on different walls, one looking out onto the street, and the other two overlooking the college quadrangle. They were large, but the small diamond-shaped panes of glass divided by strips of lead gave the room a gloomy feeling. However, an open fireplace and grate, with logs flickering, added a dimension of warmth.

"Please sit down," the professor said, indicating the sofa and armchairs near the fire. "Welcome to Capel College, Vineon D'Ur of Wellborough, Sim – apprentice to the wizard Tobin, Squire from another Land, and Perkin and Vylin from Rivermeet."

"You know exactly who we are!" exclaimed Vinny.

"Naturally, and I know your mission. My old friend, Tobin, paid me a visit yesterday. He flew in through that window to be precise." Trumper indicated the window facing towards the west. "It was open at the time, of course," he joked. "He told me all about you. He also told me that the enemy is building up its troops on the far side of Telemann's Wall, and that war is inevitable. He brought news of your other friends too."

"Where are they? How are they?" Vylin asked, a glimmer of hope replacing her worried frown.

HOPE

"They are at Hamil on the island of Terrapo," he replied. "They have the Luchorpan, Alvin, with them."

"Thank goodness my brother is safe," said Vylin with tears in her eyes. "But what are they doing on Terrapo?"

Trumper explained to them the events that had befallen their friends and how they came to be on the island.

"They are waiting for a ship that will give them passage either to Winterton, or to Jackville. They hope to be reunited with you at one of these two places," continued Trumper. "And one last piece of news from Tobin – he says you can expect to meet up with the man called Jippers at a later date in Hanlin Forest."

"Thank you, professor, for all the good news," said Squire. "Now, could you please advise us about how to find the next tooth?" He handed the piece of paper with the instructions to Trumper.

"The College where the bells are pealed is undoubtedly Beck's College," said Trumper. "Beck's College is the only one in Winterton that has a bell tower and a carillon. I will take you there tomorrow and introduce you to the carillonneur, Helena Bosca. Now, would you care for some supper?"

Trumper escorted his guests to the college hall where they dined at high table with the dons and other tutors. White-coated waiters served them with roast beef, roast potatoes, peas, and broccoli with a cheese sauce, followed by steamed treacle pudding and custard.

After he had finished, Vinny patted his tummy. "Superb," he said. "I haven't dined so well since leaving my home several weeks ago."

"Yes," agreed Perkin, "and look at the students. They enjoy the same food as the staff. What a life! I'm sure I could warm to this."

REUNION

The next day, after a similarly splendid breakfast, the six of them walked to Beck's College, a ten-minute stroll away. As they approached the college, they could see the magnificent bell tower, forty metres tall. Shortly afterwards the bells of the carillon sounded.

"There's a total of sixty bells hanging in the open tower," said the professor. "They're cup-shaped and made from cast bronze."

They passed through the college gate, Trumper exchanged a 'Good morning' with the college porter, and they proceeded to the bell tower on the far side of the quadrangle. As they did so, they passed several groups of students, on the way to their first lecture of the day.

They found the carillonneur inside the building, in a room at the base of the tower. She sat at the keyboard of the carillon.

"Good morning, Helena," said Trumper.

"Good morning, Trumper," she replied.

Helena Bosca was a plump, middle-aged woman. Her round face didn't yet show the signs of aging, and her long, neatly-brushed blonde hair added to her youthfulness. She smiled as she spoke.

"Have you finished playing for the moment?" asked Trumper. "These friends of mine would like to seek your help."

"Yes," she replied. "I've just completed the daily tune calling the students to begin their studies. From now onwards, until suppertime, my work is over. During the daytime, and again during the night, we ring the same bells every half hour, using a programmable drum. One of your inventions, I believe, Trumper."

"Quite correct."

She turned to the five companions. "Now what can I do for you?" she asked.

Squire explained to her in as few words as possible.

HOPE

"Since the bells in the tower cover a range of five chromatic octaves, there are in fact five B flat bells," she explained, "but only one of them will be located two hundred steps up the tower. Come this way."

They followed her through a low-arched, thick wooden door that led to the foot of a stone spiral staircase that wound its way up the bell tower. They counted exactly two hundred steps before Helena stopped. "Here is the B flat bell," she said. "But I don't know how anything can be inside the clapper. When they forged the bells at the foundry in Hamil, they made each bell to exactly the correct size and weight for its note and tuned each one precisely for harmonious effect."

Vinny reached out and grabbed hold of the clapper. "Look, near the top there's a small hole, and there's a thin piece of string hanging from it. You can hardly see it." He gently pulled on the string, and out popped a tiny pouch containing the next tooth and instructions.

"Well, I never!" exclaimed Helena. "Who would have believed …? I've been working in this bell tower for more than twenty years, and I never knew this was here. I suppose such a small change in the weight of the clapper will not perceptibly alter the tone of the note."

Half an hour had passed since they had entered the college gate and, just as Helena Bosca finished speaking, the programmable drum had completed its rotation, and the bells played the melody.

*　　*　　*　　*　　*

"You are all welcome to stay here as long as you wish," said Trumper the following morning, "but shouldn't you think about resuming your quest?"

"We all need a few days more rest," replied Vinny. "Besides we heard that a ship from Hamil is due to arrive at Winterton port in three days time, and we hope to be reunited with our friends."

REUNION

Trumper proved to be a very accommodating host. They felt like university dons as they continued to enjoy the comfortable accommodation and the sumptuous cuisine.

When he was not busy with his lecturing or research, Trumper spent many hours with his guests. Apart from telling them all about his latest inventions, he also delighted in entertaining them with stories about his early life and his first scientific experiments.

"I was born in the small hill town of Veca which lies in the shadow of the Air Mountains," he told them, "the son of the local policeman. At that time, Veca comprised about twenty stone houses all clustered together around a central marketplace, and was surrounded by fertile farmland. I remember small streams ran down from the mountains above to the valley of the Butterfly River below, and grapevines, fruit trees and olive groves adorned the hillsides around Veca. The Air Mountains towered high above the village, and as a young man, I used to enjoy hiking in their foothills, observing the flora and fauna. For a curious boy who loved nature, the area around Veca proved to be a wonderful place in which to grow up. One of the things that I remember observing was the appearance of patterns in many natural things, which convinced me that the laws of nature are universal."

"What do you mean?" said Vinny.

"Let me give you an example – have you noticed that the rings in a tree trunk and the ripples made by a stone dropped in water show similar patterns?"

"I never thought about it before, but I can see you're right," said Vinny.

"When I was about 13 years old, my father gained promotion and we moved to Wellborough. There I began to get interested in how machines work and first formed the idea of inventing various new ones myself. In particular, I was fascinated with flight, and tried to discover the secret of how birds fly. I even attempted to design a human-powered flying machine.

"By the time I was eighteen years old, they told me I showed signs of genius, and I gained a scholarship to study mathematics and science at the University of Winterton. However, it soon became evident that the tutors at the University had little they could teach me. By the time I reached twenty-one, I was myself appointed a lecturer at the University, and two years later filled the vacant position of Professor of Science."

"Tell us about some more of your inventions, professor," said Perkin.

"Well, let me see," replied Trumper. "First of all there was the giant rounded mirror which I used to make a reflecting telescope with which to study the moon and stars. I also invented a sophisticated water lift that uses the screw of Archimedes. Don't forget the programmable drum for the carillon at Beck's College. My most recent invention is the iron mule. I have also designed machines for use in war – a machine gun, a large mechanical catapult and a rotating mechanical crossbow, amongst others.

"Prince Tycho has heard about the war machines I have designed and has brought them to the attention of his father, King Jovanius. In about a week's time I'm expecting a visit from one of the king's aides to determine whether my war machines might prove useful against Gordeve's armies."

* * * * *

At the end of the first day of the voyage from Hamil to Winterton, shortly after sunset, *Milton* sailed past the coast of East Thorland, near to the mouth of the Phooka River. The passengers could just make out the dim lights of the port of Phooka far away to the north. Without warning, the sails began to billow as a squall came from the north. Events then happened so quickly that, before the crew had time to lower the sails, the squall had turned into a storm and the sea began to throw giant waves against the sides of the

REUNION

ship. The crew had to work hard in the driving rain and the heaving waters to lower the sails. This accomplished, the captain ordered them to lower the anchor, and the ship hove to in order to weather the storm. The crew battened down the hatches, and both crew and passengers sheltered below-decks.

The gale continued unabated throughout the night.

As day dawned, they opened the hatches, but could only see a ghost of the sun through the thick covering of cloud. Huge waves continued to batter the ship, and the captain feared that she might not be able to withstand the constant pounding much longer.

Recognising the cause of the situation, Wim summoned Helge and Yohan, and the three of them left the safety of their cabins to see if they could do anything to counter the magic. To climb the steps up onto the deck, they had to fight against the elements. The powerful sea threw waves at them with such ferocity that it nearly bowled them over, and the icy, salty water stung their skins. Once they stood on the deck, they had to cling resolutely to the railings at the ship's side in order to prevent the hurricane winds from blowing them into the raging waters.

"This is the doing of Gordeve," Helge asserted. "Wim, is there nothing you can do to put an end to this magic?" she asked.

"I'm still new to the art of wizardry," Wim replied, "and Gordeve is much more powerful than me. I'm not sure what I can do."

He had hardly finished speaking when they discerned the sound of flapping wings. They only heard the sound above the noise of the storm at the very last moment. The giant eagle alighted onto the deck and clung with his talons to the anchor chain.

"That was a bumpy ride," said Tobin as the shape of the eagle transformed into that of the wizard. "My sister has certainly stirred things up a bit today! How, Wim, can't you put up a good fight against her yet?"

HOPE

"I'm still learning, Tobin," Wim replied. "I'm very glad to see you though, because I really don't know what to do."

"Well," said Tobin. "You're the one who is going to do something. I will direct you through it. I don't want Gordeve to know that I am here, so she must perceive that you are the one who calms the storm. It will be good practice for you, and will make Gordeve aware that you now have greater powers. She won't treat you so lightly again. Now, this is what I want you to do … "

Tobin quickly talked Wim through what needed to be done. Then the young wizard raised his staff towards the north, the direction from which the storm was coming, concentrated his mind, uttered the words that Tobin had told him, and commanded, "Storm, be still!" Almost at once, the storm began to abate and the seas became calmer. Then, without warning, the clouds raced away towards Gordeve's castle and the ship found herself sitting on a calm sea under clear skies and a radiant sun. A light wind from the east signalled their way to Winterton.

No sooner had this happened than the old wizard transformed himself back into the form of the eagle. "Well done, Wim," he said as he prepared to fly. "I must go now, before the captain and crew come back on deck. Now, farewell until we meet again." He flapped his wings, took to the air, and flew away towards the north-west. Moments later, the captain and his crew came up from below-decks. They expressed surprise that the storm had subsided so quickly, but knew nothing of its cause or its undoing.

The remainder of the voyage to Winterton proved uneventful. The sea stayed calm throughout the rest of the trip, and the ship made good headway. By the end of the second day after leaving Hamil, they sailed off the coast near to Telemann's wall, and could see Trow away to the north.

REUNION

Alvin reflected over the events of the last few days. *I wonder what happened to the others after we were separated outside Trow.*

As the ship passed Ash Wood, Helge couldn't help thinking about the hamadryad Pitys. *I hope she can survive until I'm able to return and take her to a new home in Hanlin Forest.*

By the end of the third day, the ship had reached Homar's Point. After rounding the point, the next morning the ship changed direction and sailed northwards towards the mouth of the Butterfly River and the port of Winterton. Homar's Forest lay to starboard. Looking towards the land, Wim thought, *I wonder if Sim and the others are still in the forest.*

Late in the afternoon of the fourth day after leaving Hamil, *Milton* berthed at Winterton wharf. As the ship edged its way towards its mooring, Helge and the others shouted for joy when they saw their companions there waiting for them at the wharf's edge. The crew had hardly had time to secure the ships ropes before Vinny, Sim, Perkin and Vylin had jumped aboard. Only Squire showed more restraint, and remained standing on the wharf with Professor Trumper at his side. Sim and Wim embraced each other. Vylin, Perkin and Alvin threw themselves into each other's arms and did a dance on the deck of the ship. Vinny shook hands with Yohan and Helge.

After saying their goodbyes to the captain and crew of *Milton*, the companions walked the short distance to Capel College where Trumper had arranged accommodation for all nine of them, including Yohan. Windracer joined Conny and Faithful in the college stables. The Telekai were billeted at the local army barracks.

That evening at Capel College there was much drinking of ale, smoking of pipes and dancing, especially by the Luchorpans. Trumper was very impressed by Vylin's playing and Perkin's dancing. They exchanged

HOPE

stories of their adventures into the early hours of the morning, and none of them slept much that night.

The next morning, they prepared to resume the quest. Helge asked Squire for the instructions to find the next golden tooth. He handed her the paper and she unfolded it carefully before reading:

"Left central incisor – top jaw
By winding path you must descend
The tall cliffs of limestone.
Walk westwards until, around sharp bend,
Behind a rocky beach, a large cave you will see.
Deep inside the cave,
Untouched by the sea,
Find a whale bone.
It conceals that for which you crave."

CHAPTER 13

TINLIN

That afternoon the company bade farewell to Yohan and the Telekai who set off on the road north towards Foxtown on new horses they had bought at the local stud farm. Their journey would take them through Bunbury, then on to Bo's Bridge and back northwards through Bo's Chasm to Dunton.

The company spent one final day in Winterton as the guests of the professor, buying provisions and preparing for the next adventure that lay ahead of them.

The next morning they said goodbye to Trumper and set off on the road westwards which would take them to the Limestone Cliffs and eventually on to Jackville. Their mood was animated once again and they spent their time on the road talking, laughing and even singing. The walk to the cliffs passed without incident.

The Limestone Cliffs, which stood for the most part more than two hundred and fifty metres high, stretched for over a hundred and fifty kilometres from west to east, but the road only followed the top of the cliffs for a short distance. They arrived at that point two and a half days after leaving Winterton.

"Look," said Vinny. "There's a winding path cut into the cliff face going down to the beach."

Sim wrinkled his nose. "It looks a bit precarious to me," he said. "Look at those rocks below. I wouldn't want to fall down there."

HOPE

The company left the road and started their descent. It took them most of the rest of the afternoon to reach the base of the cliffs, but the task proved to be less arduous than they had expected. They pitched their tents well above the high water mark, collected, cooked and ate a tasty meal of mussels, and then settled down for the night.

The next day they set off walking along the beach towards the west in search of the cave. The beach was mainly sandy, strewn with rocks, some quite small. Others, which had more recently broken away from the cliff due to erosion, appeared much larger. In some parts, there was no sand at all. The slippery, seaweed-covered rocks made their progress slow.

They had been walking along the beach for about two hours when they came to a sharp bend as the coastline pushed out towards the sea in a small promontory, decked with another very rocky patch of beach. As an extension of the promontory, out to sea, they could see several large rocks that the powerful waves had partly eroded, but which still stood like proud sentinels guarding the coastline. The craggy walls of these rocks provided a home for thousands of gulls and other seabirds.

As the friends turned the corner, they were met by the sounds of the squawking birds, the crashing of the waves on the rocks and a strong spray-laden wind coming from the south-westerly direction that nearly bowled over the tiny Luchorpans. After turning the bend, the mouth of a large cave loomed up before their salt-stung eyes.

Perkin pointed. "Look, there's a cave," he said. "Do you think it's the right one?"

"Well, we've turned a sharp bend, the beach is rocky, and it's a large cave all right," said Helge. "I should think it's the one."

TINLIN

They were relieved to reach the mouth of the cave where they could shelter from the biting wind. Here they snatched a quick lunch before venturing inside.

Helge gave her instructions. "Alvin, Vinny, Vylin and Wim, you four stay here to look after the mule and the pony, and keep watch in case the enemy should attempt something. Perkin, Squire and Sim, you three come with me. It's very dark in there. Light your torches, but take care. We don't know what might be inside, or what hazards there might be."

The cave had a high entrance, so that even Helge could pass through without having to stoop.

"I wonder what made the entrance so big," said Perkin.

"I think it was the action of powerful ocean waves carving into the cliff face," replied Squire.

A few metres from the cave entrance the roof lowered to less than two metres. As they proceeded further inside, the roof of the cave gradually sloped upwards again, but the low point caused the cave to be very dark towards the back.

"I don't think the sea reaches this far into the cave," said Helge, "though perhaps it did in the past."

"This cave is quite different from the ones on the island in Butterfly Lake," said Perkin. "They were like solid tubes of lava. This one is irregularly shaped and much wetter. See there's rainwater seeping down from the cliff top above."

The light from their torches revealed some parts of the wall where a constant trickle of water ran down, but elsewhere there was just a tiny monotonous drip from the ceiling as stalactite reached down through the centuries to try to unite with stalagmite.

HOPE

"I think it's more likely this formation was caused by rainwater from above that ran into cracks in the limestone," said Squire. "The rainwater probably ate away at the rock until the cracks had widened, to form the inner part of the cave."

"Be careful, the floor is quite slippery here," said Helge as they moved towards the back of the cave. She raised her torch to illuminate further towards the back. "Look, there's a small ledge." Her voice became more excited as she approached further inside. "And it looks like there's a large bone on the ledge. It's quite dry over here."

Squire pushed past her and was the first to reach the bone. "It's a whale vertebra and there's a shallow indentation in the pedicle. Look, someone's hidden a small jar inside the hole. It must be airtight." He opened the jar, removed the tooth and instructions, and secured them in the pouch hidden inside his shirt. "Let's go," he said.

Their mission accomplished, the four prepared to leave. Perkin, Squire and Sim went ahead, and Helge brought up the rear. As she scrambled to keep up with the others, her foot slipped on the wet rocks, she lost her balance, landed on her posterior, and found herself sliding down an incline. She didn't have time to call out. *What's happening?* she thought to herself. *I can't stop myself. I'm sliding into some sort of hole. Maybe it's an abyss. I'm going to crash to my death on the rocks far below.*

At that moment, her body collided with, and then bounced on, some springy material that arrested her fall, much like a trapeze artist falling onto her safety net.

Helge froze when she felt four pairs of legs wrap themselves around her body. She tried to shout to her friends, but such terror gripped her that the muscles in her neck clamped, and she was unable to make more than a

200

muffled sound, which they did not hear. In the darkness, she couldn't see her aggressor, but just the feeling of the enormous hairy legs terrified her.

The animal that had captured her was a giant spider that had constructed its funnel-shaped web in a deep crevice in the rock. It was the web, with fibres as strong as rope but elastic in texture, which had broken Helge's fall. With its hardened fangs, sharp as knives, the aggravated spider lunged at her and inflicted multiple lacerations to her arms and legs, at the same time injecting the deadly venom, atraxotoxin, into her veins.

Perkin, Squire and Sim had almost reached the low part of the cave before they noticed their friend was missing.

"Where's Helge?" said Perkin. "She was right behind us."

"Helge," Sim called, "are you there?"

Receiving no reply, they turned back and searched the cave, but could see no sign of her.

"Quickly, Perkin, get out the Seeround Glass," urged Squire.

Using the glass, Perkin soon located their unfortunate friend in the crevice lying on the web with the spider's arms still around her. Sim raised his staff towards the giant arachnid and issued an order: "Spider, free your prey." Alarmed by the sudden flash of light from the staff, the spider instantly released its grip on Helge, laboriously climbed out of the crevice, and scuttled away into a tunnel leading off from the main cave.

Retrieving their friend's unconscious body proved very difficult.

"She's too heavy for any of us to carry," said Squire. "Can you use magic, Sim?"

"No," the wizard replied. "I haven't studied the magic of levitation. The only other way, would be to transform Helge into some kind of bird so that she could fly up, but that's impossible if she remains unconscious."

HOPE

"I have an idea," said Squire, "One of us will have to descend on a rope to join Helge on the web. Then he will have to tie ropes to its four corners before cutting the fibres that anchor it. The rest of us should then be able to haul the two of them up to safety."

"It might work," said Sim. "Who's going down?"

"I'm the lightest," said Perkin. "I'll do it."

They tied one end of a rope to a large stalagmite projecting from the floor of the cave and secured the other end around Perkin's waist. Then he began the perilous descent, abseiling down five metres until he reached his unconscious friend. He gingerly transferred his weight onto the fibres of the web, making sure it was strong enough to hold both of them. He cast a cursory glance at Helge, but knew there was nothing he alone could do.

Perkin called up to his friends to lower four more ropes, which he tied to the corners of the web. After the others had secured the top ends of the ropes, he drew a knife from the sheath at his waist and cut the several fibres that had anchored the web. Squire and Sim braced themselves at the top of the shaft, hauled on the ropes and gradually hoisted the two of them to the top.

As soon as they had laid Helge's body on the rock floor, Squire moved to her side. She was barely breathing and sweating profusely. Saliva drooled from her open mouth. As he bent to wipe her brow and mouth, she convulsed and her tongue began to move in spasms. A fit of vomiting followed.

"Helge, can you hear me?" he asked. Observing her vacant expression and dilated pupils, he shook her gently.

At first she made no reply, but after a few seconds she began to groan. "Where am I?" she asked. "Mum, I feel so sick. I have so much pain in my belly, and my mouth feels numb. Mum, can you give me some water?"

"She's delirious," said Sim.

"I'm here, Helge," said Squire, playing the part of Helge's mum. "Drink." He poured a few drops of water from his flask into her mouth. After that, she convulsed again, and lapsed into a coma.

"What can we do?" he pleaded with Sim. "Can you find some magic to help bring her back?"

"I'm sorry, Squire, but this is beyond my powers. I doubt even Tobin could save our friend now. The toxin has spread throughout her body. It's only a matter of time before it reaches her heart."

"I have an idea," interrupted Perkin. "What about the healing sap that Pitys gave Helge? Don't we still have some of that? It worked when the others were bitten by the vampire bats."

"But that time it was used to help the blood clot," said Sim. "Do you really think it could help Helge now? Her wounds are quite different, and her body is racked with poison."

"Wait," said Squire. "Didn't she say Pitys said something about it being a strong medicine that could help heal even a mortal wound?"

"Of course," said Perkin. "Where is it?"

"It's in Faithful's saddle bag," said Squire. "Perkin, go to the others quickly and find the bottle. But, watch your step – we don't want another casualty."

Perkin returned shortly with the bottle of sap, accompanied by a very worried Vylin. With cloths, they gently applied the sap to the wounds on Helge's arms and legs. The effect was not as immediate as it had been with the bat bites, but she soon began to breathe more easily and her temperature slowly began to return to normal.

After about half an hour, Helge opened her eyes and spoke again. Unlike the first time, she was not now delirious and she recognised her

HOPE

friends. "Perkin, Vylin," she said. "What happened? I remember feeling very sick like my veins were on fire, but then it seemed like a cool liquid quenched the flames." Then she turned over onto her side and went back to sleep. This time it was not the sleep of death, but the normal sleep of an exhausted woman.

* * * * *

Meanwhile Yohan and the Telekai riders had arrived at Bunbury. Yohan planned to seek an audience with the king to brief him on all that had happened, advise him to prepare for the war, which now seemed imminent and, on behalf of Ben Lei, to make plans for an alliance with the Telekai.

The king's guards knew the man from Atmos, famous as his country's former ambassador, and King Jovanius II granted him an audience the day after their arrival.

"Tell me all the news," said the King. "What are Gordeve and her armies up to in East Thorland?"

After Yohan had finished briefing him, the king spoke. "The war is my concern. The progress of the company doesn't interest me so much – I leave those matters to Tobin. However, one piece of news surprises me greatly. Jippers has been in my employ for nearly thirty years and I was concerned when he disappeared. He's always seemed to me a very simple man, a recluse, who enjoys only the company of his cats. He has proved a very efficient rat-catcher and will be difficult to replace. Now you tell me he has turned into some kind of criminal and is pursuing this man they call Squire. Why do you think he has an interest in this shield?"

"I don't know, Your Majesty," replied Yohan. "But they say he refers to it as his 'Hope'. No doubt, all will be revealed when my friends catch up with him in Hanlin Forest. Now, to more important matters. Your

Majesty, may I ask if you have given any further thought to my earlier suggestion for an alliance?"

The king nodded. "I agree that such an arrangement would be beneficial to ourselves and the Telekai. However, I envision a broader alliance. I have already decided to convene a council of all our potential allies as soon as possible. I charge you with the task of taking the news to Ben Lei. With the chief's permission, I am scheduling the council to take place in one month's time at Fort Holt."

Yohan smiled. "I'm sure he will agree," he said.

The king continued, "I will arrange for messengers to be sent to King Litimas of Manchor, Trevin the High Lord of the Luchorpans, Queen Sofee of Atmos and Earl Philippo of Terrapo, with invitations to each to send a delegation to the council. I also intend to send an invitation to the man I have chosen to chair the meeting and a special invitation to Trumper as an advisor. My envoy has recently returned from Winterton with encouraging news about the professor's war machines."

* * * * *

The company spent two more days and nights in the cave. Helge needed that time to regain her strength and the cave seemed a safe place to wait out of sight of the enemy. The only danger they feared was that the spider might return, or that there might be others. However, Sim felt confident that the spider that had attacked Helge would not return, and said he and Wim could deal with others in the same way.

No further attacks ensued, and after two days, the company resumed its journey. Before they left, Helge read the words of the next set of instructions:

HOPE

> **"Left lateral incisor – top jaw**
> *Take the highway north*
> *To enter the forest of firs and pines.*
> *In village small, seek out*
> *The place where they make fine wines.*
> *From oldest bottle will come forth*
> *Tooth within cork, and instructions without."*

"I've heard about this place," she said. "There's a village in the eastern part of Hanlin Forest called Tinlin, reputed for the excellence of its wines. It's located on the Butterfly River in a beautiful spot, surrounded by lakes and rolling hills. The people who live there have felled some of the trees and replaced them with grape vines."

They set off from the cave and began their journey by retracing their steps eastwards along the beach and up the winding path to the top of the cliffs to rejoin the highway. From there they travelled on the western road towards Jackville for about eighty kilometres before turning north. After travelling the northward road for more than a hundred kilometres, they entered Hanlin Forest and proceeded on to Tinlin. Throughout the journey, they encountered no problems and experienced no further attacks from the enemy, although occasionally during the twilight hours a lone bat was seen circling overhead.

They arrived at Tinlin late in the afternoon of the sixth day. The unique beauty of the place made an immediate and lasting impression on Squire. The landscape around the village was an unspoiled haven of lakes, forests, gently rolling hills, deep gorges and panoramic heights surrounded by vineyards and sunflower fields. The terrain, soil characteristics and the near-perfect climate made Tinlin an ideal location for the cultivation of grapes. As they approached the village, on the nearby hillsides Squire could see row upon row of vines laden with ripened grapes of different hues, reflecting a myriad of colours in the rays of the setting autumn sun. It was time for harvest.

Although it was backbreaking work, the time of the grape harvest at Tinlin was such a popular event in West Thorland that people came from all over the Land to participate. The only remuneration they asked was wine, food and fellowship. The eight friends decided that they would join the volunteers. Instead of booking into the local inn, they pitched their tents near the riverbank, joining the hundreds of others already erected along the banks of the Butterfly River and around the shores of the Blue Lake.

The next day, the weather changed. They woke to discover a freezing and wet early morning.

Squire took one look outside and shivered. "It's awful," he said.

"The Tinlin vineyard won't stop work just because of the weather," said Vinny. "In fact, when the weather is bad, work must proceed more quickly in case the crop is damaged."

"I'm looking forward to this," said Perkin. "After all our adventures, I relish the idea of working, meeting new people and enjoying myself."

Squire took another look at the teeming rain. "I'm not interested. I'll stay behind to look after Conny and Faithful."

"And I'll stay with you," said Sim. "If the enemy should choose to attack, you will need my protection."

The other six set off to work. In the village square, they teamed up with about twenty other volunteers and boarded a series of horse-drawn carts to take them to the vineyard. As they bounced along the rough, pot-holed track, sitting on the dilapidated old carts in the rain, they sang and laughed.

HOPE

When they reached the vineyard, the supervisor handed each of them a bucket and a pair of clippers. After she had allocated them with several rows to pick, they set to work. With bent backs they started cutting bunches of grapes. Some were large and easy to reach, but others hid behind leaves and the pickers found it difficult to separate every bunch from the vine. As the workers filled the buckets, they emptied them into large woven baskets used to transport the grapes to the winery.

By midday, they had finished the last of the allocated rows, and stopped for lunch. They celebrated their accomplishment by sharing a couple of bottles of wine, the product of the previous year's harvest. This finished, they loaded the baskets and their juice-stained buckets and clippers back onto the wagons, and then headed back to the village.

When they reached the winery, they unloaded their produce and decided to stay to watch the pressing, the work of a different group of volunteers. These workers deposited the grapes in the pressing machine that was used to squeeze out the light pink juice. The juice flowed directly from the vat by means of a long rubber tube to large wooden barrels in the cellar below, where it would ferment.

"We'll work one more day," said Helge that evening.

Vylin's face dropped. "Can't we stay until the harvest is finished?" she said. "I was talking to a girl from Foxtown this morning. She told me that there will be a huge party for those who stay to the end of the harvest – a final shared meal and lots of wine, followed by the harvest ball in the village hall."

"I'd so love to join the dance," said Perkin.

"I'm sorry," said Helge. "We need to find the next tooth and instructions and continue with our quest." Vylin looked at Perkin, then down at her feet.

"There'll be other times to dance," he said.

During the second day, while the six friends picked grapes, Squire and Sim met up with a familiar acquaintance. The weather had improved and they decided to take a stroll along the shore of the Blue Lake. As they rounded a bend, they noticed a shadowy figure lurking in the trees watching their every move. The man muttered to himself. They couldn't hear every word he said, but they heard 'Hope' repeated several times.

"Jippers!" Squire whispered. "It sounded like he said 'I need help with my Hope.' So, that's why he's looking for me. He thinks I can help him find a way to use the shield to return to our world."

"Yes," said Sim, also keeping his voice low. "We've caught up with the rogue at last. Now we must get the shield back."

A shout interrupted their conversation. They looked again in the direction of Jippers and saw a group of about twelve Kobalos running from different directions to surround the old man. They caught Jippers by surprise and he had no time to run, even if his old legs had enabled him. In an attempt to protect himself, he stood facing the enemy and raised the shield in front of his face. He turned his head to one side and spat tobacco juice on the ground.

"The Kobalos are trying to steal the shield from Jippers," whispered Sim. "No doubt Gordeve has her eyes on it."

As the enemy moved in to attack, the five silver stars on the face of the shield began to glow, increasing in intensity until they shone brightly. Jippers laughed and wielded the shield to direct its beams towards one of the Kobalos. He turned his face and spat again disdainfully. He focused once more on the back of the shield and saw an image beginning to form. At the same time, the power of the shield tossed him backwards, and all was blackness as he felt himself drawn into the image to become a part of it.

HOPE

In an instant, Sim joined in the fray. He stood his ground before the Kobalos who were already mesmerised by the power emanating from the shield, raised his staff and, using the language of the East, commanded, "Kobalos go home."

The Kobalos obeyed quickly, but events moved on at such a pace that it is difficult to record accurately the order of them. While Sim issued his command, Squire ran to intercept Jippers and struggled to wrest the shield from him. Although unconscious, the old man held on tightly to the shield and seemed determined not to give it up. Sim moved to assist Squire. When the latter felt himself losing consciousness and sensed the power of the shield drawing him in also, he noticed Sim disappear.

As Grant helplessly watched his daughter heading towards the top of the waterfall, he sensed a second person in the water beside him. He had never seen the man before. He had a roundish face and a flat nose, his brown hair was cut short, and he had no beard apart from a small wisp of hair in the middle of his chin. The man possessed a strange aura, as if he were not human, but some kind of being from the spirit world.

The stranger stood erect in the water as if he were standing on the riverbed, though the river was quite deep at that point and his feet could not possibly have reached the bottom. Having assumed this posture, he began to wade through the water, slowly at first, then quickly, more quickly than any normal man could wade through the viscous medium. When he was almost out of sight near the top of the waterfall, he reached down and plucked something out of the water. Grant couldn't see at first what it was. Then he recognised the limp form of his daughter in the stranger's arms. The man waded with his burden to the edge of the river, bent and gently laid the motionless figure on the grass. The next moment the stranger had vanished.

As this happened, Grant's sister, Jacqueline, and her husband Ron, together with Grant's young son, Anthony, had met an old man on the walking track. He must have been about seventy years of age. His bent body had a permanent stoop, and his grey hair and beard were long and unkempt. A posse of flea-riddled cats surrounded him. The three of them knew instinctively that he must be some kind of recluse, for his clothes were rags, he smelt dreadfully and he engaged in the disgusting habit of spitting every so often. When he approached them, Ron and Anthony stepped to one side of the path, but Jacqueline stopped in her tracks as she recognised something familiar about the deep-set eyes. Jacqueline and the old man stared at each other for a few seconds before the man turned and, despite his years, quickly disappeared into the bush.

Sim reappeared as Squire and Jippers simultaneously awoke from their experiences in their own world. When Jippers relaxed his grip on the shield, Squire snatched it and held it in his arms like a baby.

"Wh … what happened?" stammered Jippers. "For a brief moment I achieved my Hope and returned to my own world, but I don't remember anything."

"So you also experienced a 'Window on Our World'!" exclaimed Squire. "This has happened to me four times now. When I wake up, I also can't remember a thing, but I do know the experiences have not been pleasant. Yet, strangely, this one seemed less harrowing than on previous occasions."

HOPE

"I don't understand any of this," wailed a distraught Jippers. "I thought the shield was my Hope. I'll never get back to my own world now." As he spoke, he jumped up and ran off into the trees. From a distance, Squire and Sim could hear him sobbing while he cried, "My Hope, all my hope is gone."

"I wonder if we'll ever see him again," said Sim.

*   *   *   *   *

When the other six returned late in the day, Squire and Sim shared their story with them, at least as much as they could remember. No one could explain the strange events, but they congratulated Squire for regaining the shield and rejoiced that Jippers had walked out of their lives.

"Now we must search for the tooth," said Helge. "What did the instructions say we should look for?"

"The oldest bottle of wine," said Alvin. "We must go to the winery and find the oldest bottle."

That evening Alvin, Perkin and Vylin crept into the winery. The winemakers still worked, but were so engrossed and more than a little bit tipsy that they didn't see the three tiny Luchorpans creep past. Alvin opened the door that led to the cellar and the three tiptoed down the stairs. In the gloom, they found it difficult to see, but Vylin had taken the precaution of bringing a torch with her. At the bottom, they lit the torch and began their search. The cellar had two rooms. The first contained the barrels of fermenting wine, so they quickly moved on into the second room, where they found row upon row of bottled wines, housed in special racks.

The oldest wines all seemed to be stored on one side of the room, so it wasn't difficult for them to know where to begin their search. However, finding the oldest wine of all proved to be a laborious task. They had to examine more than three hundred bottles before they found it – a dry white, bottled three hundred and forty years ago. Alvin carefully drew the cork and, embedded inside it, found the tooth. Before they began the difficult task of trying to remove the label, they decided that they couldn't allow such a good wine to go to waste, so they shared it amongst the three of them. When they had finished drinking, they soaked the empty bottle in a sink full of water. After a few minutes, the label floated away to reveal on its reverse the instructions for the next step of their journey.

"What does it say?" asked Perkin. "Hic … "

Alvin replied, "It … hic … says:

"Left canine – top jaw
Find a ledge of rock behind the veil.
Upon the ledge
Near water's edge,
Look for a hole shaped like a bowl.
Those which you seek, it will avail.
Within a glass box they are confined."

The three Luchorpans hid in the cellar for two more hours until all was quiet in the winery above, which was just as well since they were themselves now too tipsy to expect to creep past the winery workers undetected. It was late in the evening before they rejoined their friends at the campsite. For the first time in several weeks they were all together, and secure in the knowledge that the shield was safely back in the possession of Squire. By the light of a full moon, the company shared a few more bottles of wine.

CHAPTER 14

HANLIN MONASTERY

The first messenger to arrive at his destination was the one sent to Earl Philippo of Terrapo. His journey took just six days – two days of hard riding to Winterton and a further four days aboard a ship to Hamil.

The earl's face turned grave as he read the message. "To call such a council must mean the situation is much worse than we had feared," he said to the messenger. "The importance of this council cannot be underestimated. I will attend in person. Please return here in the morning, after you have rested, and I will give you my written reply to King Jovanius."

During the next few days, other messengers arrived at the palace of King Litimas of Manchor, the headquarters of Trevin, High Lord of the Luchorpans and the palace of Queen Sofee of Atmos. All the leaders came to the same conclusion and decided that they would personally head their country's delegation to the meeting at Fort Holt, and each prepared to depart without delay. The messengers went on ahead and delivered their replies to King Jovanius.

*　　*　　*　　*　　*

Yohan and the Telekai riders returned to the camp at Dunton, welcomed as heroes. Ben Lei was overjoyed to learn of the success of their mission, and was encouraged by the news Yohan brought of the proposed alliance and the meeting at Fort Holt.

HANLIN MONASTERY

"Dispatch a messenger to King Jovanius at once," he said. "I accept the proposal, and please inform him that I will personally supervise all necessary preparations for the council."

Within a week, Ben Lei had handed over command at Dunton to Yohan and had set off for Fort Holt. Being familiar with the harsh conditions in the desert, the crossing took him and his entourage just four days.

On arrival at the fort, the chief gave his orders. One group of men began preparing the living and sleeping quarters for each of the distinguished guests and their entourages within the fort itself. Another group set about erecting two large marquees – one to serve as a banqueting hall, and the other to be used as a conference room. A third group trained in preparation for the added security needed for the protection of the important guests.

*   *   *   *   *

The company left Tinlin on the day after the Luchorpans had recovered the latest gold tooth and instructions. Their journey would take them to the Veil Falls, a walk of five days through the forest by way of Hanlin Monastery and Helge's Cottage.

On the fourth evening, the company set up camp in a small clearing in the forest. Sim flew off towards the west in the shape of a hawk for a meeting with Tobin. Each of the others set about their tasks. The three Luchorpans busied themselves collecting firewood and preparing the fire to cook the food, Wim attended to the needs of the mule and the pony and Vinny went with his bow in search of food for their supper. Helge and Squire kept guard.

Despite their vigilance, the pack of seven wolves caught them by surprise. Not a whelp issued from their throats, not a stick was broken, as they crept in, concealed by the trees, and formed a circle to encompass the company. The wolves appeared intelligent and knew that the greatest threat would be from Wim, so they concentrated their first attack on him. He was busy brushing the coat of Conny when he noticed the pony, sensing the danger, become very restless. As the wizard held onto the pony's bridle to comfort her, she reared up onto her hind legs and tried to wrest herself from his grasp.

Wim bent to reach for his staff. However, as he stooped to pick it up, two of the wolves attacked without warning. Leaping with teeth bared, each of them grasped an arm and threw the powerless wizard to the ground, where he knocked his head against a stone and lay motionless.

Simultaneously, another four wolves attacked Helge and Squire in a similar way. The attack was so unexpected and planned with such precision that, although Helge had prepared her sling, she had no time to use it. The force of the attack knocked the shield from Squire's grasp and it lay innocuously out of his reach on the ground. The remaining wolf stood guard over the three cowering Luchorpans, tongue slavering and saliva drooling from his mouth.

They didn't expect Sim to return for several hours, so the only hope for the captured friends remained with Vinny. The wolves had planned their attack so well and with so little noise, that he remained unaware of the predicament of his friends until he heard the frightened whinny of Conny, followed by braying from Faithful and then the shouts of the Luchorpans. Vinny abandoned his search for food and, with bow at the ready, crept closer to the camp to see what caused all the commotion.

This was the wolves' only mistake for, when the archer saw what had happened to his friends, so much rage consumed him that he felt he could deal with fifty wolves all on his own. He primed the first arrow, raised his bow, aimed and with precision felled the first wolf. Four other arrows followed in quick succession, felling the wolves that had attacked Squire and

HANLIN MONASTERY

Helge and the one who kept guard over the Luchorpans. However, before Vinny could prepare his bow again, the two wolves holding Wim had dragged him away into the bush. With teeth sunk deeply into the flesh on the arms of the unconscious wizard, they pulled him without mercy over rocks and tree stumps, through gorse and briar. They didn't stop for rest until they had moved well out of range of the archer's arrows.

Vinny was torn between attending to the needs of his injured friends, and trying to save the wizard. *There might be more wolves,* he thought, *so it would be foolish to abandon my friends. Besides, Wim is capable of looking after himself and should be able to conjure up some magic once he regains consciousness. As soon as the others have recovered, we'll follow the wolves' tracks to rescue Wim.*

Vinny's first task was to calm down the mule and the pony, while maintaining his vigil with the bow and keeping an eye open for any further attacks. The three Luchorpans, still jittery but aware of the need to do something to help, set their minds to the task of attending to Squire and Helge. Although the sharp jaws of the wolves had clamped tight around their arms, the bites sustained by these two didn't seem too deep, thanks to the quick work of the archer. Vylin retrieved the flask of méli from Faithful's saddlebag, and the three Luchorpans carefully applied the sap to the wounds of their two friends. They soon felt its healing coolness.

Once they had regained their composure and their weapons, which still lay on the ground where they had fallen, they prepared themselves in case of another attack. Several minutes passed before Helge relaxed her vigilance and sighed. "There don't seem to be any more wolves," she said.

"Quickly, we must pack up and follow," said Vinny, starting to load things onto Faithful's back. "It shouldn't take us long to catch up with them.

HOPE

The wolves won't be able to move quickly, dragging Wim through the undergrowth."

"It's too late tonight," said Helge. "Darkness comes early in the forest. Look, the sun is about to set." The others followed her gaze upwards and saw the last of the sun's rays bathing the treetops.

Vinny cursed and unpacked the things again. They waited for the dawn.

The clearing where they had camped was more open towards the east, and the sun reached them early. As its first rays peered over the eastern horizon, they were relieved to hear the flapping of wings as Sim came in to land. He quickly assessed that something was wrong and, even as he transformed himself from hawk to man, gasped, "What's happened, what's wrong, and where's Wim?"

After Vinny had related the events of the previous evening, Sim lost no time in making plans to help his twin.

"Leave it to me to rescue him," he said.

Vinny felt less hopeful. "They might have killed him by now," he said.

"I don't think so," replied Sim. "If they wanted him dead, they would have killed him instantly. The fact that they dragged him away, suggests that they're taking him to Gordeve. I must leave at once. The rest of you continue on the journey, all of you except Conny," he insisted. "I'll transform myself into the shape of the hawk, and go in search of my brother, and I'll instruct Conny to follow the trail left by the wolves, so that she can aid me when required. We'll meet the rest of you at Hanlin Monastery. Take heart and don't fear. I'll find him."

Sim issued a low whistle and Conny trotted to his side. Sim spoke softly into the pony's ear, words that the others could not hear. The pony appeared to nod her head as if she understood, then turned and set off at a gallop towards the north-east following the tracks left by the wolves. Within moments, the wizard had made the transformation, and had flown away in the same direction.

The hawk flew up above the treetops, but kept as low as possible in order to keep following the tracks. He soon overtook the galloping pony, and within an hour had located the wolves that had captured Wim, still dragging their hapless prey through the undergrowth. Sim swooped down to alight on the ground a few hundred metres in front of their anticipated path. He transformed, concealed himself behind a tree, prepared his staff and waited.

When the wolves were just thirty metres away, he came out from his cover and, standing tall, directed his staff towards the snarling beasts. He commanded, "Wolves, release your prey." When the wolves had freed the unfortunate Wim, Sim raised his staff once again. Showing no mercy, he discharged a ray of energy from its tip aimed first at one wolf, then the other. They had no time to escape the deadly rays, and in an instant, the energy had reduced each of them to a heap of smouldering ashes.

Sim ran to his brother's side. "Wim, Wim," he cried, "are you all right?"

His anxiety turned to hope, and then to joy, when he heard his brother murmur, "Sim, is that you?"

Wim still lived, though his injuries looked severe. The tooth marks in his arms were deep and festering, but he also had multiple injuries to other parts of his body, the result of the predators dragging him through the undergrowth, and he had a large bump on his forehead. *Oh, my dear brother*, Sim thought. *I wish I had the power to heal you.*

He again issued a soft whistle. A few moments later, he heard a whinny as the pony crashed through the undergrowth to join him. He removed the flask of healing sap from Conny's saddlebag and gently applied some to Wim's wounds. Then he wrapped bandages around parts of Wim's arms where the incisions from the wolves' teeth seemed deepest.

That will have to do for now, he thought. *However, I must get him to a safe and comfortable place where we can tend his wounds properly. I know – Hanlin Monastery. He will get the right care and attention there. It's not far from here, but it will take us the rest of the day to get there. How can I transport Wim there? We can't fly. Maybe, I'll construct a travois, and Conny can pull him.*

By this time, it was mid-morning. He spent the next hour constructing the temporary travois. He used straight branches lashed together with strips of leather, and secured the tips of the two longest branches that converged at the horse's shoulders to her harness.

Wim was barely conscious. Nevertheless, Sim whispered in his ear, "Wim, I'm going to use a spell to put you into a deep sleep to make it easier for you to endure the journey. He then carried his brother to the travois, gently lowered him onto the branches and lashed him securely with more strips of leather.

They arrived at Hanlin Monastery just as the sun set. The rest of the company waited at the gate to meet them, together with a stranger. The man was short and plump. His oval face was clean-shaven and the hair on his head was cut very short. He wore a simple orange robe tied at the waist with a rope. On his feet, he wore sandals.

"I am Brother Beghlin," said the monk. "I'm one of the brothers of Hanlin Monastery, but I have also studied the art of medicine." He turned to Vinny. "Please carry the young man to my surgery so that I may examine him."

HANLIN MONASTERY

Vinny lifted the wizard from the travois and carried him the few metres to Beghlin's surgery. Sim and the rest of the company, together with the monk, followed. As Beghlin removed the bandages from Wim's forearms and saw that the wounds had already started to heal, he looked up at Sim with a puzzled frown.

"How can this be?" he asked. "The wounds were clearly very deep and the indications are that infection had set in, yet the healing process has already begun."

"It's the sap," replied Sim.

"Sap? What sap?" asked the monk.

Helge explained to him about the healing sap that the hamadryad Pitys had given her. "It's called méli," she said.

"I've never heard of that name," he said. "Can I see it?"

"Of course," she replied. "Alvin, could you please get the flask of sap from Conny's saddlebag?"

Alvin returned after a couple of minutes and handed the flask to Beghlin. The monk opened the bottle and brought it up close to his nostrils.

He wrinkled his nose as the sweet aroma made him light-headed. "I've studied the art of medicine and have a wide knowledge of healing plants, herbs and gourds, but I don't recognise this medicine," he remarked. "Nevertheless, I'll put it to the test."

Beghlin removed a scalpel from the shelf behind him and proceeded to make a small incision on the tip of his left index finger. He then applied some of the sap to the cut with a cloth. In an instant, the wound was healed.

"Remarkable! How can I get some of this ... méli?" he asked.

Helge replied. "When the time is right I'll be returning to Ash Wood to bring Pitys back here to a new home in Hanlin Forest. You may accompany me if you wish."

HOPE

"That would please me very much," replied the monk. "I'd like to know more about this sap and its properties."

Brother Beghlin applied some more of the méli to the wounds on Wim's body, and dressed them again with gauze and bandages. Then he instructed Vinny to carry the patient to the next room where a soft bed awaited him. Shortly afterwards Wim woke up.

"Where am I?" he asked. "What happened?"

Sim related all that had happened. When he had finished, Wim said, "I'm tired now. Please leave me, all of you, so that I may rest."

They stayed at the monastery for two weeks until Wim had made a full recovery. During that time, Brother Beghlin watched over him constantly and monitored the healing process. The potency of the healing sap never ceased to amaze the monk.

The monks provided the rest of the company with rooms in the monastery. Very small and modest, each room had a hard single bed, a wooden table and chair, and a tiny cupboard. The visitors didn't see much of the other monks who were preoccupied with keeping to their daily routine of work, two sparse meals a day, and constant prayer.

On the evening before they departed, Brother Beghlin prepared them a simple, but generous meal as a farewell party.

After the meal, Squire took the monk's arm and led him to a corner of the room. "May I speak privately with you?" he asked.

"Of course, my son," said Beghlin. "What is troubling you?"

"Tell me," he said. "This is the first time since my arrival in Thorland that I've been aware that there is a religion here, apart from the obvious supernatural powers of the wizards, that is. Tell me about your religion, the God you worship, and your beliefs. How many of you are there?"

HANLIN MONASTERY

"It's true that there are not many of us who practise the faith," replied the monk. "In this monastery there are sixty-four monks. There are four other monasteries similar to this one, and three convents of nuns. However, there are also many believers scattered throughout Thorland, Terrapo and the Western lands. We believe that there is but one God, the Creator, who watches over us and constantly provides us with every good thing that we need. We also believe in the Evil One, and that the Creator and the Evil One are in a constant battle for supremacy in the world. However, ultimately good will triumph over evil and the Evil One will be defeated."

"How do the wizards fit in with your religion?" asked Squire.

"Gordeve serves the Evil One. Tobin serves the Creator, as do Wim and Sim. They have an important part to play in the war against evil. However, they use magic not only for good, but also as a means of aggression against the servants of the Evil One. We also have a part to play in the war, but ours is a peaceful battle against the Evil One, through prayer. We do not serve Tobin, or any wizard. We serve only the Creator. Our inspiration comes from the teachings found in The Book of Squire and from the words of Quexitoxeri."

"Who is Quexitoxeri? I heard that name before, when I first arrived in the Land. Helge told me she is the living prophet of the Creator."

"That's true. Her name means 'Enlightened One' in the ancient tongue. We believe Quexitoxeri has a special relationship with the Creator and the words she speaks are His. She is our spiritual leader. Only Quexitoxeri has the power to heal and bring the dead back to life. She dwells at the Thymas Convent in the northern part of Manchor called Kand-e-Har, and has continued to serve the Creator for hundreds of years through spiritual descent. When one Quexitoxeri dies, one who is born in the same hour of her death replaces her. The line is never broken."

HOPE

Later in the evening, Squire spoke to Sim. "You're a wizard," he said. "Why is it that you don't have the power to heal? Brother Beghlin told me about Quexitoxeri who has the power to heal people, and even bring them back to life."

"Quexitoxeri is not a wizard," replied Sim. "She is the prophet of the Creator and His representative in our world. Let me try to explain. This world is controlled by the Creator and the Evil One. Only the Creator has the power to create or destroy. He creates everything in this world and, when He does so, it is perfect. The Evil One cannot create or destroy. He can only corrupt what already exists, or generate illusions. Gordeve is the servant of the Evil One and he has given her the power to corrupt the work of the Creator, and to imitate His work with illusions."

"What do you mean?"

"When she sends wolves or locusts against us, they are already evil because her wicked magic has corrupted them. When she learned how to modify the cougars, this was a corruption of the natural order of things. Even the Kobalos were once good people like ourselves, but became depraved through the influence of evil wizards of whom Gordeve is the most recent.

"On the other hand, servants of the Creator, like Tobin and ourselves, use magic only for good purposes. We cannot create, destroy or even heal, but we do have the power to undo the evil instigated by the servants of the Evil One. Don't misunderstand me. We can kill, just as Vinny can kill with his arrows."

"Isn't killing the same thing as destroying?"

"No. To destroy means the person or animal no longer exists, which is the same thing as saying that they never existed at all in the first place. This we cannot do. Thus, I was able to kill the wolves that attacked my

HANLIN MONASTERY

brother, but I couldn't destroy them. Though they were burned to ashes by my power, their existence continues as a pile of ashes."

"But I still don't quite understand. Healing is not the same thing as creating. Why couldn't you heal Wim?"

"Healing by natural means takes time. The body cannot be healed in an instant. I can heal, just as any man who has knowledge of medicine can, but this may take many days if the wounds are severe like those of Wim. I don't possess the power to heal instantly, neither does any man, or wizard; only by illusion, and illusion cannot be sustained. Among men and women, only Quexitoxeri has the power to heal."

"Now I think I understand," said Squire. "But I have one more question. If you, Wim and Tobin are servants of the Creator, do you also pray like the monks?"

"In our own way we do," replied the wizard, "but we are different from the monks. They have dedicated themselves to serve the Creator by living a life of poverty, chastity and abstinence. They pray constantly to the Creator. We serve the Creator by performing magic for the good of the Land. When we speak the words to invoke magic, it is like prayer, though we do not call it so. The monks and ourselves both have a function to serve the Creator, but in very different ways."

Helge joined them at that moment. "I must go now," Sim told her. "Tobin has need of me once again. He instructed me to return to his castle after two weeks. This time I may be away for several days. We'll meet at the location of the next tooth – not the one at Veil Falls, but the one after that, wherever it may be. I will find you. Farewell."

He transformed himself into the shape of a hawk once again, and flew off towards the west.

* * * * *

HOPE

The next day the company resumed its journey. They had to walk just one day to reach Helge's Cottage, where they spent the night, although the cottage seemed rather small for seven people. The following day they walked to the Veil Falls, retracing Squire's footsteps from that day eight months previously when he had ignored Helge's advice and left the safety of her cottage.

The scene was every bit as beautiful and awe-inspiring as Squire remembered – the foam of cascading water descending 120 metres from top to bottom, the clouds of white vapour, the fresh, moist air, the rainbow of myriad colours and the swirling waters at the base of the falls. He saw the rapids worming their way between rocks and boulders of all shapes and sizes, the trout playing in the calmer waters downstream and the precipitous ledge from which he had fallen on his first day in Thorland and from which Tobin, in the shape of the giant eagle, had saved him.

However, this time it was not an eagle that launched itself from the ledge, but instead they saw a brown owl swoop down in pursuit of some prey.

"Look," squealed Vylin, "an owl."

"It is indeed a misfortune to see an owl during the daylight hours," said Alvin.

Vinny glowered. "Are you still harping on about things that bring bad luck?" he asked. "Our quest is full of dangers and perilous situations. Not every misfortune that befalls us can be ascribed to some so-called 'bad luck event'."

Alvin sounded hurt as he replied. "All right, wait and see whether or not I'm telling the truth."

They sat down on rocks to admire the beauty of the place. *This could be the same small rock I sat on all those months ago*, thought Squire.

"Now to business," said Vinny. He turned to Helge, and asked, "What did the instructions say again?"

"They said we should look for a ledge behind the waterfall," she replied. "Not that ledge on the far side of the gorge, but one behind the waterfall itself. On the ledge, near to the water, we should find a small bowl-shaped hole, and in the hole we should find a glass box."

"So one of us must risk his or her life by climbing up behind that waterfall," declared Vinny. "Which of us should it be? Any volunteers?"

"I'll go," said Perkin without hesitation. "I got used to climbing when I had to rescue Helge from the spider's web."

Vylin cast a glance at the little man. "You're so brave, Perkin," she said. "Be careful."

They all clambered across the rocks until they reached a point close to the waterfall where the others could safely wait. They tied a rope around Perkin's waist and secured the other end to the stump of a tree. He waved goodbye and started to scramble across the slippery rocks towards the waterfall. On his left, he passed a beech tree that seemed to cling to the rock face and grow almost horizontally, but which otherwise looked strong and healthy. The bowl of the tree sat very close to the water's edge. *I wonder how it manages to cling on at such a precarious angle*, he thought.

As he got closer and closer to the rushing waters and the rocks became increasingly slimy, he found the going more and more difficult. Three times he lost his footing and almost fell, but each time managed to hold fast to the rocks above with his hands. He was grateful to have the Seeround Glass with him. When he reached a place where he could safely hold on with one hand, he used the glass to search behind the falls for the ledge mentioned in the instructions. Once he had located the position of the ledge, he found it much easier to negotiate the shortest route to it. As he edged his way behind the falls, all he heard was the thunderous noise of the water plummeting interminably downwards. Here it became quite dark, with only a thin shaft of light reaching him from around the two edges of the waterfall.

His progress became very slow. Eventually he found his way to the top of the ledge, which sloped at quite a sharp angle down towards the rushing water. Moss and lichen grew on it, and it became difficult for his boots to grip. He doubted that he would ever be able to make his way to the front of the ledge, close to the water's edge. However, where necessity demands, there is always a way. Sensing a shadow, Perkin looked up, and near his left shoulder saw a thick root belonging to a tree. Somehow, the root had found enough soil in cracks in the rock to grow and snake its way across several metres. *It must be one of the roots of that beech tree*, he thought.

Perkin held on to the root, which felt thick and strong, and made sure that he had a good purchase on the rocks with his feet. Then he untied the rope from around his waist, tied several knots each about thirty centimetres apart in the first six metres or so of rope, and tied the end securely to the tree root. He got down on all fours, and inched his way backwards towards the edge of the ledge by holding onto the knots he had tied in the rope. After he had descended in this way for about four metres, he moved from side to side to try to locate the hole. At first it eluded him, but after he had eased himself down another metre, he found it. He groped inside and felt the small glass box. This he stuffed into the inside pocket of his jacket.

Having completed the task, Perkin was about to leave when a log came over the waterfall. It almost hit him as it fell, causing him to lose concentration for a second. His feet lost their grip and, with his right hand still inside his jacket pocket, he found himself clinging to the rope with just his left hand. As his feet slid away from him, he lost his hold on the rope and slithered down towards the rushing waters.

CHAPTER 15

THE COUNCIL AT FORT HOLT

Perkin squeezed his eyes shut to keep out the spray. He had lost all sense of where he was and in which direction he was sliding. He could sense the icy coolness of the cascading water, the wall that threatened to suck him down into the depths below.

He bumped down the smooth rock face that had no cracks or protrusions for him to grasp. Desperately he scrabbled at the surface to try to find something to cling onto, but to no avail. *My feet are almost touching the water*, he thought. *There's no hope. I'm going to die.*

At the last moment, his clawed free hand encountered something hard. With a last desperate effort, he grabbed hold of it. It was the final knot he had tied in the rope. Using his left hand, he clung to the rope with all his strength, his shoulder burning as the strain of his whole body's weight began to tell. He struggled for several seconds trying to free his other hand from his jacket pocket, though the time seemed much longer. Having freed it, he grabbed hold of the knot with both hands. He shook uncontrollably, and knew he was still not safe. He willed himself to haul on the rope. One knot at a time, he used the rope to pull himself up until he could again find a purchase for his boots. Knot by knot he forced himself up the sloping ledge until he reached the top of the rope. He lunged and grabbed hold of the root of the tree. He turned and eased himself to sit beneath the root, in the crack where the ledge joined the vertical cliff face, breathing heavily.

THE COUNCIL AT FORT HOLT

Perkin remained there for several minutes, regaining his strength and his composure. After these exertions, the traverse back to his companions seemed an easy task.

Alvin looked aghast at the dishevelled appearance of his friend. "Are you all right, Perkin? Have you got the tooth?" he asked.

"Yes indeed, but not without some difficulty," Perkin replied, trying to smooth his hair with his hand.

"Somewhat of an understatement by the look of you," said Alvin.

Perkin laughed. "It was easy really," he said.

He removed the glass box from his jacket pocket. The box had a hinged top, but appeared to be watertight. He opened the lid and removed the tooth and instructions. These he handed to Squire and Helge respectively. Then he noticed something unexpected.

"Look!" he exclaimed. "The Seeround Glass and the glass box are made from the same kind of material."

Alvin peered over Perkin's shoulder, his eyes widening. "Gosh! It must be some kind of magic glass," he said.

Perkin replaced them both in his jacket pocket and tapped them as if to make sure that they were still there. "From now onwards I will always keep them together," he said.

*　　*　　*　　*　　*

The month of waiting was over, and Ben Lei's staff had completed all necessary preparations for the council at Fort Holt. A group of them had furnished and equipped the accommodation suites. Others had erected the dining and conference marquees. The chief ordered that guards be posted at all entrances to the fort, and outside each of the rooms being occupied or used during the council.

HOPE

Inside the conference marquee, the staff had arranged tables along three sides, and placed a nameplate at the front of each group of tables, one for each of the delegations – West Thorland, the Telekai, Manchor, Luchor, Atmos and Terrapo. On the fourth side, a single table for the chairman stood in front of a blackboard. Although it would soon be winter, the temperature inside the marquee was already high as the guests began to arrive.

The Telekai delegation headed by Ben Lei took their seats first.

The next contingent to arrive was the one from Manchor. King Litimas, a small, mouse-like man in his fifties, with a pointed nose and large ears, marched in with his group of five advisors.

A few minutes later, the representatives from Luchor, headed by Trevin, High Lord of the Luchorpans, arrived. Trevin was about forty years of age, had curly, light-brown hair and an equally curly full-faced beard, and like all Luchorpans, was very short in stature.

They had hardly settled in their seats when there was a commotion as the fat Earl Philippo and his delegation from Terrapo arrived. Sweating in the heat, his black face contorted with effort and consternation, he struggled to his seat near the back of the marquee.

The largest group, the one from West Thorland led by King Jovanius, was next. The burly, muscular king with short brown curly hair took his seat near the entrance. His group included Professor Trumper.

Heads turned at the arrival of the tall Queen Sofee and her delegation from Atmos. She wore garments befitting a queen, a red velvet gown with an ermine collar and a silver tiara on her head.

The last to arrive was the chairman. The giant eagle flew in through the open entrance of the conference marquee, landed on the chair and transformed himself into the familiar shape of the wizard Tobin. A ripple of surprise passed through the crowd of waiting delegates. As always, the

THE COUNCIL AT FORT HOLT

wizard wore the white cloak and the pointed hat bearing the five silver stars, and he clutched his staff in his right hand.

After their initial astonishment, the members of the council became silent, anticipating the wizard's words. Tobin stood, cleared his throat, and addressed them, "Your Majesties, Ladies and Gentlemen." As he spoke, he stroked his long grey beard and looked around the marquee, his piercing eyes studying each of the members of the council in turn. "I make it a rule that I never leave the safety of my castle for more than a few hours, but the present situation is of such grave importance that I have felt obliged to attend this council and have accepted the invitation to be its chairman. I have, therefore, charged my castle to the care of my apprentice, the wizard Sim."

Tobin paused before he continued. "We are facing a very serious situation in our lands. After years of inactivity, my sister has recently started unleashing evil once again on West Thorland. She has already sent wolves, bats, locusts and cougars into the west. Her scientists have succeeded in breeding the cougar, so that there are now many of them, and Gordeve has used some kind of magic to give these cougars the ability to talk. The Kobalos armies are on the move. Some of them have learned to ride and control the cougars. The purpose of this council is for us to find ways to work together, to develop strategies, and to mobilise our armies in preparation for war.

"The peoples of East Thorland, who seethe in resentment and oppression, are subject to the wicked ideologies of the tyrant Gordeve, who is my sister – ideologies that feed violence and excuse murder. The forces of hatred have driven them on to find new ways across the wall, across the borders into our free lands and have raised a new threat against all liberated and decent people. The defeat of the forces of evil that hold sway over the peoples of East Thorland can only be achieved by exercising the three greater forces. These are the *hope* of all decent and tolerant people, the *faith* of all who fear the Creator, and the *love* of freedom and equality.

"There have, however, been some positive developments. The words of the ancient prophecy are beginning to come to pass. The Squire has returned to the Land." At the mention of Squire, there was a sudden hush, followed by whispering, and then all the members of the council spontaneously broke into applause.

When all was quiet again, Tobin continued. "As I speak, a company of brave people and Luchorpans are risking their lives in a quest to recover the golden teeth that belong to the golden skull. Once all the teeth have been recovered and replaced in the skull, our power will be greatly increased and we will be better equipped to lead the fight against the Evil One."

High Lord Trevin spoke next. Trevin was not a common cobbler or a banker, but neither did he possess the bearing of a king or wear any special regal garments. On the contrary, as befits the thriftiness of his race, his garb was similar to other less distinguished Luchorpans. He wore green trousers with braces, a checked shirt and buckled shoes and a yellow cap. "It is indeed good news that The Squire has returned to the Land," he said with a gruff voice. "And I am very proud that some of my people are accompanying him in the quest to retrieve the golden teeth. However, there is one thing that puzzles me. How did the cougars, Kobalos and wolves gain access to Thorland? There are but two ways through the wall. The first has been closed for two centuries, the second has remained under constant guard."

"I'll answer that," said Ben Lei, speaking with a thick accent. "A few weeks ago, the gate near Dun Wood was opened from the other side allowing several cougars and Kobalos to enter."

Having had the leadership thrust upon him at an early age, the chief was by far the youngest leader present at the council. His tanned, handsome

THE COUNCIL AT FORT HOLT

face was clean-shaven apart from a small black moustache. Like all Telekai, he wore a white cotton robe, belted at the waist, a white cotton headwear kept in place with a headrope tied around his forehead, and thongs on the feet.

The chief continued, "The gate has been closed once again and is now also guarded. However, other cougars, Kobalos and wolves have also breached the wall. We don't yet know how, but there can be only one explanation. They must have found another way through, under or over the wall."

Queen Sofee rose to her feet, and everyone in the marquee fell silent. "Then one of our priorities must be to search every inch of the wall," she said. "My people are ill-equipped for war, but I will lead a group from Atmos. Our job will be to monitor the wall, find out how the enemy is getting through, and put a stop to it."

Queen Sofee, like all Atmosians, was very tall and slim. In many ways, she resembled Helge, but she was a few years older. She had a similar thin face and sharp nose, but her long, straight hair was blonde. The queen had never married, and still sought a companion fit to share her throne.

"Thank you for your offer, Your Majesty," said Tobin. "It is recognised that not all of you will be able to deploy armies," he continued. He turned to address the rotund figure from Terrapo. "Earl Philippo, I know that your people have no army, but I hope that you will also support our cause by providing us with the copper and tin we so vitally need for the construction of weapons."

"Yes, of course," replied the earl, baring his red stained teeth, sweat streaming down his face. "However, we will lose our trade with East Thorland, so we must be compensated with an increase in the price of both our ore and our forged bronze."

HOPE

"You will be compensated," agreed King Jovanius. "Now, with your permission Mr. Chairman, it's a good time for me to introduce my good friend, Trumper. Trumper is Professor of Science at the University of Winterton. Professor, please stand up."

Most people in the marquee had heard of Trumper by reputation, but had never met him before. However, introductions proved unnecessary, as the eccentric professor was recognisable by his crop of unruly grey hair, thick bushy black eyebrows and moustache, and the baggy trousers and tweed jacket he wore.

King Jovanius continued, "The professor has invented a number of weapons that could be used against the enemy. These include a machine gun, a large mechanical catapult and a rotating mechanical crossbow. Professor, would you like to explain how these weapons work and how they might be beneficial to the members of the council?"

"Of course," replied Trumper, moving to stand by the blackboard behind Tobin. "First the machine gun. This in fact consists of three sets of eight guns. Each set of eight is arranged on one face of a frame that has the shape of a triangular prism. The frame is attached to a rotating drum." As he was speaking, Trumper taped a picture of his invention onto the blackboard. He indicated the prism and drum on the picture, then continued, "When the first set of guns is fired the force of the explosion causes the drum to rotate and the next set of guns is then in position and ready to be fired, and so on…

"Next, the catapult. This consists of a wooden base, an arched wooden beam, gears and a release mechanism." He taped a new picture onto the blackboard and continued speaking as he pointed. "A stone will be placed on the top of the beam here, and this release mechanism will be tightened using this gear. When the release mechanism is triggered, the tension in the curved beam will produce a force that will hurl the stone into the air …

THE COUNCIL AT FORT HOLT

"Finally, the crossbow." Trumper taped a third picture onto the blackboard before continuing. "You will observe that this consists of a wheel, four crossbows and a shield on a stand. The wheel is turned by men walking on it, just like a treadmill. This shield protects them. An archer stands inside the wheel, here, and fires each of the crossbows in turn, as they come around.

"You will see, each of these weapons has certain advantages over conventional weapons, and has been designed with the intention of taking the enemy by surprise. Does anyone have any questions?"

"Yes," said Earl Philippo. "Does the construction of these weapons require bronze? Or are they made of timber?"

"Their construction requires both timber and bronze," replied Trumper. "Be assured, earl, your bronze will be in high demand."

King Litimas rose to his feet. "How long will it take to construct your weapons, professor? And how long will it be before we can go on the offensive?"

"The prototypes have already been constructed and tested. The rate at which others can be built will depend upon the supply of materials, but I anticipate a turnover of roughly one machine per day if the materials are plentiful."

"I'll answer the second question," interrupted Tobin. "Our priority is to be prepared for a defence if the enemy should attack first. It may take several weeks before we are ready to go on the offensive in strength, but small incursions into enemy territory can begin as soon as the armies and navy are mobilised – a matter of days, or one or two weeks at the most."

Tobin paused a few moments before he spoke again. "Now, if there are no more questions about the weapons, let's discuss our plans for war."

HOPE

The council meeting continued for the rest of that day and the whole of the following day, during which the members made several resolutions. Before closing the council meeting at the end of the second day, Tobin read out the resolutions.

"One. It is resolved that all members present will form an alliance in a declaration of war against the forces of East Thorland. West Thorland, the Telekai, Manchor and Luchor will provide the majority of the armed forces. Each country will have its own commander, but the commander-in-chief of the land forces will be Prince Tycho of West Thorland. Atmos and Terrapo will not be sending any combat troops. However, Atmos will send a group to patrol the wall and to try to close any new ways across the border. Terrapo will provide the tin and copper and forge the bronze for the construction of weapons at its foundry in Hamil.

"Two. It is resolved that all ships in the member countries of the alliance will be commandeered, to form a navy under the command of Prince Dernis of Manchor. The only ships that will be exempt are the personal flagships of the various leaders and the cargo ships of Terrapo. At the same time, shipbuilders in Manchor will set about constructing new warships at the shipyards in Tarmouth harbour using timber from Tar Forest.

"Three. It is resolved that Prince Tycho, Prince Dernis, and all the commanders are ultimately responsible to me, to whom they will report regularly.

"Four. It is resolved that Professor Trumper will personally supervise the construction of his weapons at Winterton. The cargo ships from Terrapo will transport the bronze parts forged in Hamil by sea to Winterton. The inhabitants of the eastern part of Hanlin Forest will fell the timber required, and transport it by cart to Winterton.

THE COUNCIL AT FORT HOLT

"Are these the resolutions that we agreed during the last two days? All those in favour, please say 'Aye'."

A loud "Aye" echoed around the marquee.

"All those against, say 'Nay'."

This time, the room remained silent.

"Thank you, Your Majesties, Ladies and Gentlemen, the council is now closed."

Tobin set off at once to return to his castle. Soon afterwards, the various delegations departed for their homelands in order to mobilise their armies and engage construction workers.

* * * * *

Meanwhile the company had left Veil Falls. Before leaving, they studied the next set of instructions, which Helge read:

"First left premolar – top jaw
The festival town awaits
Your entry through its northern gates.
Go to the gardens, and there you'll find
A monument from loved ones left behind.
Unscrew memorial plaque.
Behind find a crack
Where tooth and note have been confined."

"The festival town – that's Jackville," asserted Vylin. "Every year there's a music and dance festival held at Jackville in the late autumn. Perkin and I always go there. It should be around about this time, shouldn't it, Perkin?"

HOPE

Perkin smiled. "Yes indeed," he replied. "Maybe we will be in time to join in."

The walk to Jackville by way of Helge's Cottage and the Hanlin Monastery took just three days, and they entered the town through the ancient stone gates at its north end.

When Vylin saw a large poster pasted on a board alongside the gates announcing the 'Jackville Autumn Festival of Music and Dance' starting in a week's time, she pulled at Helge's cloak and adopted a child-like tone. "Can we please wait for the festival to start? We would love to join in the music and dance, but we will also meet some of our friends from Rivermeet. Please, Helge."

"I think we could stay a few days," affirmed Helge. "Besides, we need to wait for Sim to rejoin us."

Since most of the accommodation in Jackville was fully booked for the festival, the company were fortunate to find a suitable place to stay at the Rose Inn, quite close to the gardens where the festival would be held.

The following day they decided to waste no time and went immediately to visit the gardens and to seek out the next tooth and set of instructions.

Perkin, who had visited Jackville several times before, told the others, "In the gardens there's a memorial to the soldiers of Jackville who were killed in the last war between east and west more than fifty years ago. Thousands were killed on both sides, but the people of Jackville have erected this memorial to remember their own loved ones who were lost. That must be the meaning of the phrase '*A monument from loved ones left behind*' in the instructions. I think we should pay a visit to the memorial and see if there is a crack behind the plaque."

THE COUNCIL AT FORT HOLT

The gardens were situated adjacent to the mouth of the Moon River and the open sea facing Gull Island. The Jackville Gardens Trust had begun the development of the gardens more than forty years previously and ten years later had added the Jack Rose Garden, but most development had occurred during the last ten years. By this time, the Jackville Gardens had become the most popular visitor attraction in West Thorland with nearly half a million visitors each year.

The unique theme of the Jackville Gardens was 'Gardens through the ages', which exhibited gardens from four different eras and cultures. The Luchor Garden Collection featured early Luchorpan methods of gardening using peat, rich in nutrients and moisture. The Ar Garden Collection reproduced a luxuriant garden from the time when the Bun River passed through the city of Ar. The Terrapo Garden Collection illustrated how the native people of Terrapo use subsistence methods to grow their own vegetables and fruits. The Manchor Garden Collection featured the story of how the Princess of Manchor had inspired the cultivation of the area around her father's palace with exotic plants.

Also incorporated within the gardens were a visitor information centre, a café, and greenhouses displaying plants for sale. Prominent in the centre of the gardens stood the festival canopy facing a large grassed area that was used for the annual Festival of Music and Dance, as well as other events throughout the year. The memorial stood on the opposite edge of the grassed area.

The company had no difficulty in finding it. On its front surface, a bronze plaque bore the words: 'In memory of the men and women of Jackville who gave their lives in the war against East Thorland', followed by a list of names of the fallen, arranged in alphabetical order and by date.

HOPE

"This must be it," said Helge. "It's got four screws, one at each corner, securing the plaque to the concrete. They should be easy enough to undo."

Squire frowned. "The only problem is it's in a very public place," he said.

Vinny nodded. "Yes, if we set about unscrewing the plaque, others might construe this as an act of vandalism," he said. "How are we going to remove the plaque without anyone seeing us?"

"We must return after dark," said Wim. "Under the cover of darkness, and with a little magic, there should be no problem."

They returned that evening after the sun had set. They saw few people in the gardens. A drunk lay asleep on the grass. A short distance away, on a bench facing the river, a young couple sat giggling, too preoccupied to notice the intruders.

While the others watched, Wim raised his staff and said a few words. At once, a thin beam of light shone from the staff and illuminated the plaque. When he pointed his staff towards one of the screws and turned it slowly in an anticlockwise sense, the rest of the company watched with amazement as the screw turned in the same way. When he had removed one screw by this method, Wim repeated the action for each of the other three screws. The plaque fell to the ground with a clang, and Vinny ran forward to inspect what lay behind it. As expected, the concrete behind the plaque had cracked, and inside the crack, wrapped in a piece of cloth, he found the tooth and the next set of instructions. Vinny handed these to Squire and Helge.

Vinny held the plaque in place while the wizard used magic to screw it back onto the memorial, and the company returned at once to the inn.

In the privacy of Helge's room, she read the next set of instructions:

THE COUNCIL AT FORT HOLT

"**Second left premolar – top jaw**
Climb to the summit on the island of birds.
There find a hut.
Inside the hut, find some words.
The letter 'V' conceals a key
And the box can be opened or shut."

"The island of birds must refer to Gull Island," said Vinny. "I visited it once before many years ago. As I recall, it is surrounded by high cliffs and is populated by thousands of seabirds of many different species, not just gulls. Only a few people live there, scattered throughout the island. I remember the land rises gradually to a high point at its centre, from which there are magnificent views on all sides. The island's quite close to here, so I believe it must be our next destination."

"It sounds very much as if you're right," agreed Helge. "After the Luchorpans have enjoyed a couple of days of their festival, and once Sim rejoins us, we'll find a way to cross over to Gull Island."

*   *   *   *   *

On the evening of the day his friends approached Jackville, which was also the evening of the first day of the council at Fort Holt, Sim sat in Tobin's study reading the old wizard's book on spells of binding. Before leaving for the council, Tobin had charged his apprentice with the care of his castle until his return. As Sim read, a gentle knock on the door disturbed his concentration. Following Sim's invitation to enter, Digbee opened the door and passed inside.

"Excuse me, sir," said the servant. "I have received a message that my aunt is ill and I wish to go to visit her. With your permission, I will return in the morning."

HOPE

"Of course, Digbee," replied Sim.

A few minutes later a bat circled high above the castle, on his way to the other castle in the foothills of the Central Kobold Mountain, summoned there by Gordeve.

"Well, Digbee," said the wizard after he had arrived. "What news do you have for me?"

"Madam," replied Digbee, "your brother is away from his castle attending a meeting at Fort Holt with the leaders of all your enemies. I understand they are making an alliance against you and that they are making plans for war."

"It is good," asserted Gordeve. "I expected that this would happen, and it shows that they are not yet ready. We are ready, and we will catch them by surprise. But does this mean that my brother has left his castle unattended?"

"No, madam," replied the spy. "The wizard Sim is looking after the castle in Tobin's absence."

"Sim!" exclaimed Gordeve, her eyes lighting up. "Then I must pay him a visit. We will leave at once."

An hour later, a bat and a giant eagle soared away towards the west.

In the early hours of the next morning, just as the sun rose, the sound of the beating of wings awoke Sim from a deep sleep. The giant eagle came in through the open window and landed at the foot of his bed.

"Tobin!" gasped Sim. "I didn't expect you to return so soon. Is the meeting over?"

As the giant eagle transformed into the shape of a wizard, Sim's eyes widened.

"I am not Tobin," said Gordeve.

"Wh … what are you doing here?" stammered Sim.

THE COUNCIL AT FORT HOLT

"Don't worry, my dear son," replied the old wizard. "I wish you no harm."

"Why do you call me 'son'?" he asked.

"For that is what you are," she replied. "Twenty eight years ago I bore you and your twin. While I remained weak from the exertion of your births, my brother stole you both away from me. From that time until now he has kept you here as his apprentices, misleading you and teaching you his devious ways. Did you not realise that he is the evil one, not I?"

"How do I know you are telling the truth?" he asked. "Tobin has always been good to us and treated us like sons. Why did he not tell us that you are our mother? And, who is our father?"

Gordeve glowered. "Your father! Don't talk to me about him. He's a lazy, useless man. Nevertheless, what I have told you is the truth. Look."

Gordeve raised her staff and pointed it towards the bare wall at the far end of the room creating an image, a series of pictures. The images were an illusion, but looked very real. The first pictures showed Gordeve herself, many years younger, and pregnant. The next depicted her in the strains of labour as two babies, identical in all respects, were born one after the other. Then Sim saw the mother, cradling the two babies in her arms, smiling yet exhausted. The next pictures showed her asleep. The two babies also slept, in cots, one on each side of her bed. While they slept, the unmistakable figure of Tobin entered the room. He raised his staff. At the same time his lips moved, a sign that he had issued the words of a spell to make the weakened mother unaware of what happened. Then he stole the babies away while the mother slept.

"So, it's true," conceded Sim.

The next moment, while Sim was still off-guard, Gordeve raised her staff once more, and spoke to her son.

HOPE

"Go to sleep," she commanded. "Now you know the truth, my son – that Tobin is wicked, and I am good. Remember that it is written, 'Gordeve will rule'. When you awaken, I will be gone, and you will remember nothing of my visit. When you return to your companions in a few days from now, they will not notice a change in you. They will not know that your allegiance has changed. However, from now onwards you will fight for what is right. Sometime in the future when I call you, you must obey."

With that, Gordeve transformed herself back into the shape of the giant eagle. As she prepared to alight from the window, she issued the final command, "Now, wake up my dear son. We will meet again soon."

He awoke to find brilliant sunshine filtering through the open window of the room. He felt relaxed, and eagerly awaited the return of Tobin.

CHAPTER 16

THE KEEPER OF SECRETS

As the company waited for the Festival of Music and Dance to begin, they occupied their time visiting many interesting places in and around Jackville. Apart from the gardens, Jackville was also famous for its modern opera house, its museums and art gallery, the quality of its restaurants, and of course, cruises on the Moon River.

Three days before the start of the festival, those taking part began to arrive. Among the early arrivals was a group of Luchorpans from Rivermeet, which included one of Alvin's best friends, Daykin.

After the four Luchorpans had greeted each other, they retired for the evening to the comfort of the Rose Inn lounge to share a pipe and tankards of ale. The three members of the company related all that had happened to them since they had left Rivermeet some five months earlier.

"This is a good drop of ale," said Daykin, drawing on his pipe. "Now, Alvin, tell me more about the story of your capture in East Thorland and the rescue."

As Alvin related the story, Daykin interrupted him frequently with gasps of surprise and many questions.

When Alvin had finished, Daykin said, "You three really have had some adventures. But I think I would rather stay at home making shoes and enjoying myself dancing."

"I, too, have some exciting news," he continued. "High Lord Trevin passed through Rivermeet a few days ago on his way to a very important

HOPE

meeting with other leaders at Fort Holt. It was his first time to visit Rivermeet. Do you know what? They call him 'High Lord', but he's just an ordinary Luchorpan like us. He stayed two nights and we put on a big party for him, with music and dancing, of course. I think he was very impressed with our dancing. It's a pity you weren't there, Perkin."

"Tell us more about this meeting," said Perkin.

"Well, I heard that the King of Manchor was going to be there, and Queen Sofee of Atmos, and King Jovanius, of course, and ... who's that fellow who is now paramount chief of the Telekai?"

"That's Ben Lei," answered Vylin.

"Oh, yes," continued Daykin. "And the earl of Terrapo – I forget his name too – and I also heard that the wizard Tobin was invited, and some professor chap from Winterton University."

"That will be Trumper," said Alvin. The other two nodded.

"Trevin told us the meeting was to discuss plans for an alliance against East Thorland, and to plan for war," explained Daykin.

*   *   *   *   *

Three days later, the Festival of Music and Dance began in the Jackville Gardens, using the canopy for the musicians to shelter from the sun or rain, and the grassed area in front for the dancing. Of course, Vylin joined with the musicians and Perkin and Alvin enjoyed the dance. Apart from the group of Luchorpans, groups of people from Bunbury, Winterton, Wellborough, Southport and Jackville also attended. There was even a small group from Tarmouth in Manchor. The festival lasted four days, and everyone had a good time.

On the second day of the festival, Sim rejoined them. He had spent several days with Tobin after the latter's return to the castle, learning more magic from the older wizard. Tobin had told Sim all about the result of the meeting at Fort Holt, and Sim passed on the news to the rest of the company. The forming of the alliance and the plans for war gave them more confidence and assurance that they should now be better protected from attacks by the enemy.

However, they didn't know about Gordeve's visit during Tobin's absence, and the spell she had placed on Sim. The spell was such a powerful one that Sim didn't remember a thing about her visit, and nobody could detect any change in the apprentice's behaviour, not even Tobin.

*   *   *   *   *

Once the festival was over and they had said their goodbyes to Daykin and other friends they had made in the last few days, the company resumed its quest.

"I've found a fisherman who is willing to take us to the island," said Vinny.

"How long is the crossing?" asked Helge.

"According to the fisherman, it should take us four hours or so," Vinny replied.

Helge frowned. "I don't much like sailing in boats since the storm near Phooka – especially small boats. I'll stay behind to look after the mule and the pony."

"And I'll stay with you," said Wim.

The crossing to Oxe, a tiny settlement at the north of the island, took nearly five hours. Once they had disembarked from the vessel, although it was still only mid-afternoon, they decided to make camp, get a good night's sleep, and wait for the new day before attempting the ascent.

The following day Vylin rose early, and Squire awoke a little later to the delicious smell of ham and eggs that she was preparing for their breakfast. After enjoying a generous meal, they started their climb.

HOPE

From the mouth of the River Oxe, the land rose gently from sea level to the highest point on the island at about five hundred metres. They followed a well-marked path which wound its way up gentle hills, along ridges, sometimes downhill again for a short distance, then up again.

The island had few trees, but the hills and valleys were covered with grass, clover, and patches of wild autumn flowers, such as the bright pink flowers of wild foxglove, the small bell-shaped purple-dotted white flowers of gypsywort and pale purple flowers of marjoram. There being no wild animals, the island was also a sanctuary for sheep, which fed on the grass and clover.

The walk to the top took most of the day. It was not a difficult climb, but the company made frequent stops to take in the marvellous views and revel in the beautiful autumn scenery. They arrived at the summit in the early evening. There they found a small hut that had been built for trampers and equipped with the bare essentials – ten bunk beds, a rough wooden table and chairs, and a stock of medicines and tools to be used in an emergency.

Vylin turned up her nose. "It smells very musty in here," she said.

"It looks like it hasn't been occupied recently," said Vinny. "By the look of things, it's been empty for a number of weeks."

A thin layer of dust covered the table and silky cobwebs stretched across the door and window frames. The inside had bare timber walls, three small windows and just the one door, facing eastwards.

Vinny reached for his bow and raced outside where he saw a brace of pigeons circling overhead. A few minutes later, Vylin and Alvin had lit a roaring fire close to the hut and the pigeons roasted on a spit.

After they had feasted well, as darkness descended, they decided to retire for the night. They could only find a small kerosene lamp inside the

THE KEEPER OF SECRETS

hut. Since they had no kerosene, and they were very tired, all they could do was sleep.

When they awoke the next morning, they set about trying to decipher the words of the instructions. Since they had started their quest several months earlier, this set of instructions proved to be the most difficult to understand.

"What can be the meaning of *'Inside the hut, find some words.'?"* asked Alvin. "There are no books or documents of any sort."

"Is there anything pinned to the wall, like a list of rules or anything?" asked Vylin.

"There's a sign," said Perkin, "near the door."

Vylin looked excited. "What does it say?"

"It says, 'If you use something from this hut, please donate two other items as payment for future guests'."

"No letter 'V' there," said Squire. "We must search everywhere. Maybe there is something hidden under one of the beds, or the table. Perkin, can you use the glass?"

They searched all that day. They examined the walls, under the beds, around the door and windows, and even the outside of the hut, but their search proved fruitless.

Perkin sat on one of the bunks with his head in his hands. "What are we to do?" he asked. "If we can't find these 'words', then our quest is over. We can't return to Tobin with four teeth still to find."

Vinny put a hand on Perkin's shoulder. "We'll sleep on it," he said. "If we don't get any good ideas by the morning, then I suggest that Sim go to seek some help from Tobin."

The following morning, Perkin woke first and lay restless in his bunk, which was a top one, waiting for someone else to stir. From outside, he heard the squawking of gulls and the chirping of petrels. A puffin growled in the distance. As his eyes wandered across the ceiling, they caught sight of something carved on one of the wooden beams. This discovery so excited him that, as he sat up to get a closer look, he almost fell off the bunk.

"Wake up," he yelled to his friends. "I think I've found it. Look, someone has carved some words on the side of the beam."

"What does it say?" asked Vylin, jumping up beside him.

"It's not easy to see," he said. "We missed seeing the words altogether yesterday, but the angle of the early morning light makes them show out. Just a moment, I think I can see. It says … 'Trevin, High Lord of the Luchorpans'."

As the others were still stirring after their rude awakening, Perkin was already standing on his bunk and had a hold on the beam with one hand.

"It's a bit difficult to get at the V," he said, stretching his free arm towards it.

"Let me try," said Vinny. "I'm a bit taller than you."

Perkin made one last effort. "No, I've got it," he said. "The letters are quite deep." He reached inside the letter V and pulled something out. "It's a small key. It seems to be made of glass."

"Well done, Perkin," said Vinny. "But, what's the key for?"

"It's most interesting," observed Squire, "that the words were written by or on behalf of Trevin. Ever since we discovered that the staircase down into the caves on Peak Island was too narrow for the rest of us to pass, I have always suspected that Luchorpans must have planted the teeth and instructions. The discovery of the tooth at Daly's Bridge reinforced that suspicion. It seems to me that the Luchorpan race has had a very important part to play in the history of this Land, and I guess they will have a very important part to play again in the future."

THE KEEPER OF SECRETS

"You're probably right," agreed Vinny. "Well, that's half the mystery solved, but where's the box that the key fits?"

Before anyone could answer his question, they heard a loud knock on the door. Vylin rushed to the window closest to the door and peered out.

"There's a man outside," she whispered. "He's quite short, but not as short as us, and he's very thin and has a pale face. He's wearing a yellow robe and a yellow hat, a bit like Tobin's hat, but smaller. But, he doesn't seem to have a staff. Do you think he's a wizard?"

"I know of no wizards except Tobin, Gordeve, Wim and myself," answered Sim. "He may be a sorcerer. I have heard that there are such people in the Land. They can perform some magic, but their powers are limited."

There was another knock at the door, this time louder than the first. Vinny prepared his bow.

"Sim, open the door ... slowly," he said.

A rush of cold air entered the hut and the stranger, silhouetted against the rising sun, passed inside.

"Good morning," he said. His voice was quiet and soothing. "I am Percival, the Keeper of Secrets. I am a peaceful man and good friend of the wizard Tobin. Why do you greet me thus, with an arrow pointed at my heart?"

"Now I remember," said Sim, "Tobin told us about Percival once. I'd forgotten that he lives on this island. He really is a friend."

Vinny lowered the bow. "Welcome Percival, Keeper of Secrets," he said. "Please forgive us for this unmerited welcome. We have not heard of such a person as you before. Even the wizard Sim, here, didn't recognise you at first. Please come in."

"Ah, Sim," said Percival while he entered the hut. "You may have forgotten about me, but I know all about you, and I also know your secret."

HOPE

"What secret?" asked Sim. "I have no secret."

"Your secret was revealed to you once, and shall be again," continued Percival. "And your secret shall yet be revealed to all."

Sim's face turned red. "Are you a keeper of secrets, or a riddle-maker?" he asked. "I repeat, I have no secret."

"So be it," replied Percival. Then he turned to Perkin and said, "Now little man, I also know your secret, but I will not tell." Perkin glanced furtively at Vylin and tried to conceal a blush. "Your secret is safe with me, but do not tell another until the time is right, or the secret will not come to pass." Percival continued to address Perkin. "Where is the glass box that you found at the Veil Falls?" he asked.

Perkin removed the glass box and the Seeround Glass from his jacket pocket.

"Ah, I see you also have the Seeround Glass," observed the secret-keeper.

"How do you know all these things?" asked Perkin.

"I am a keeper of secrets, but I also have some powers to see things happening far away," replied Percival. "However, I can only see things that pertain to the secrets that I keep. The Luchorpan Trevin revealed to me the secret of the glass box and the Seeround Glass. Now turn the box upside down," he urged. "You will see there's a small hole in the base of the box."

Perkin let out a low whistle. "You're right!" he exclaimed. "I didn't notice this hole before."

"Now put the glass key inside the hole and turn it."

The key fitted the hole perfectly and, as Perkin turned it, he discovered another lid on the base of the box. As the lid opened, a tooth and a piece of paper fell out.

THE KEEPER OF SECRETS

"Oh!" he exclaimed. "But there was nothing inside the box before. Look, it's made of glass and you can see right through it. Why couldn't I see the tooth and paper?"

"It is of course made from magic glass, the same kind of glass from which the Seeround Glass is cast," replied Percival. "Do not be surprised by what you have seen. Now put the Seeround Glass inside the base of the box and lock it."

"Look, it's a perfect fit," said Perkin.

"Now I will tell one more secret before I leave," said Percival. He turned towards Squire. "This secret is for your ears only, Squire from another Land. Please follow me outside."

Outside the hut and out of earshot of the others, Percival addressed Squire. "You will be a great king, and Xanatia shall be your queen."

"Who is Xanatia?" he asked, his face turning red.

"You have seen her once and will know her when you see her again. Do not tell anyone of this secret yet, not even Tobin, or it will not come true. Now I must go. Farewell."

With that, Percival turned and started walking down the hill. Within seconds, he had disappeared out of sight.

Squire called after him, "Wait … who is she? I don't remember her." *Where did he go?* he thought. *King? Xanatia? I hope this hasn't been another one of those dreams.*

When he returned inside the hut, the others urged him to tell them his secret.

"I cannot tell you or it will not come true," he told them. "Now let's look at the instructions for finding the next tooth. Give me the paper Perkin." He read:

HOPE

"First left molar – top jaw

In southern port,
At the place where folk train for the navy,
Find a pole coloured white.
Near its base is a hole hidden from sight
By ivy."

"The port where sailors train, that will be Southport," asserted Vinny. "There's a big naval training academy there. By land, Southport's quite a distance from Jackville because of the river estuary being so wide. After we get back to Jackville, we'll have to return to Hanlin Monastery, before taking the road south again to Southport."

"That's a long way," said Sim. "I've a better idea. Why don't we take a boat directly from Oxe to Southport? However, before we do so, I'll fly to Helge and Wim to tell them to travel by foot to Southport by way of Hanlin Monastery. We can all meet up again at Southport. Even if they take a few more days to join us, it will save the rest of us time, and we can search for the next tooth while we're waiting for them."

"That's a good idea," agreed Vinny. "Does anyone know a good place for us to meet up with the others at Southport?"

"There's a tavern called The Black Dog," said Perkin. "I've heard they serve very good ale there."

"Tell Helge and Wim that they should meet us at The Black Dog tavern," Vinny instructed Sim.

The next moment, Sim transformed himself into the shape of the hawk once again and flew off northwards towards Jackville. The rest of the company began the descent down the winding path towards Oxe.

THE KEEPER OF SECRETS

About twenty minutes after Sim had departed, the birds attacked. From all directions, seabirds of every kind – gulls, terns, gannets, loons, petrels, razorbills, cormorants, guillemots, kittiwakes and puffins – homed in on the hapless friends, who only became aware of the attack just before it happened. The birds swooped in with a sudden cacophony of sounds, a flapping of wings and rushing of air.

"Quick, back to the hut," shouted Squire.

"It's too far," yelled Vinny. "Cover your eyes everybody. That's what they're going for."

They covered their eyes with their hands.

"Ouch!" said Vylin. "They're pecking at my face. Do something somebody."

The birds came at them one after another with beaks pecking and talons flaying, and they all received myriad cuts to their faces, necks and hands.

"It was foolish of me to let Sim go," moaned Vinny. "I didn't even think about the risk of being separated from both wizards, even for a short time. And, I can't even take my hands away from my face for long enough to reach my bow. It would be futile against all these birds anyway."

"It's not your fault," said Perkin. "None of us thought about the risk. We are all to blame. Ouch!"

"We still have the shield," said Squire.

As soon as he could, using his left hand to ward off the birds, Squire raised the shield with his right hand and held it in front of his face. Nevertheless, even when the shield was in place, the birds just arriving and ready to attack were not instantly repelled. As wave upon wave came at him, he could feel the full weight of the birds pushing against the shield, and it took all his strength to hold it in position.

HOPE

However, when the silver stars began to shine brightly, the release of power pushed the birds aside – some lay prostrate on the ground, others limped away, and those that just arrived turned and flew back where they had come from. The release of power pushed Squire backwards and darkness engulfed him once more.

Grant Cowie had swum as quickly as he could, and now approached the riverbank where the stranger had laid the limp body of his daughter, but saw no sign of the man who had saved her. Grant waded the last few metres towards the shore, and then began to run when his feet encountered dry ground. He rushed to Theresa's side, threw himself down on the ground beside her, and placed the side of his face close to her chest. He couldn't detect any heartbeat or any sign of breathing. He had no training in the use of CPR or the technique of mouth-to-mouth, but he'd seen it done on the movies. He tried to emulate what he had seen. First, he tilted Theresa's head back and pinched her nose. Next, covering her mouth with his own, he blew for about two seconds until he saw her chest rise. Then he began chest compressions. Using the heel of his right hand, he pushed down about three centimetres on the chest between the breasts, pumping at a rapid rate. He continued to give one breath and five chest compressions in this way several times in the hope that she would begin to breathe normally or cough, but to no avail. In desperation, he looked up. He saw another figure approaching – a stooped old man wearing ragged, stinking clothes.

"Let me help you," said the second stranger. "I know what to do."

THE KEEPER OF SECRETS

Grant felt nauseated by the thought of this disgusting old man performing mouth to mouth on his dear daughter. "No," *he said.*

"I have had training and was once a paramedic. Please let me try to revive the little girl."

Grant's will to see his beloved girl live was stronger than the repulsion he felt towards a vile creature who had offered to help them.

"All right," he said, "go ahead."

The man had told the truth, and knew exactly what to do. After a few moments, Grant saw his daughter's chest begin to heave. She took her first gasps of breath, and then breathed freely once again, though she remained unconscious.

"Thank goodness," he said. "How can I thank you enough, Mr...?"

"Jepsen," replied the old man. "The name is Jepsen."

Grant Cowie started at the mention of the name. He had heard it before, but struggled to recall when. Then he remembered. It was the name of his sister's first husband, who had mysteriously disappeared many years ago. Before he could confirm his suspicions, the stranger had disappeared into the bush.

Squire regained consciousness. He flinched when he saw that another man also held onto his shield.

"Jippers, what are you doing here?"

"The shield is my Hope," replied the old man. "After I ran away from you at Tinlin, I began to think, and now realise that the shield rightfully belongs to you. However, it is also my only hope to get back to the world from which I come – our world. Therefore, I decided that I must no longer try to fight you or take the shield away from you by force. Instead, I must join your company. Together, when the time is right, we can try to find the means to return to our world. I have followed you ever since you left Tinlin and have waited for the opportunity to reveal myself to you again."

"How do I know I can trust you?" asked Squire.

"I will answer that," said another voice. Percival, the Keeper of Secrets, had returned as suddenly as he had previously disappeared. "This man you know as Jippers came to this world more than thirty years ago. He has now told you his secret – that he is not of this world – just as you, Squire, are also not of this world."

He doesn't seem to know that Homar's already told me about Jippers, Squire thought to himself. *I wonder why. He claims to have powers to see things happening far away if they pertain to the secret. Moreover, what about this mysterious Sacumed? He also knew the secret, and he was the one who told Homar about Jippers. Maybe Percival's powers cannot penetrate inside the deeper secret that is Homar's Forest.*

Percival continued addressing Squire. "To reveal this secret means that he trusts you. You must also trust him. The only way you will both return to your own world is if you can learn to trust each other and work together towards that common goal. Did you not notice that your experience seemed less distressing than the previous occasions when you used the shield?"

"You're right. Maybe it was because we shared the experience, Jippers and me."

"However," Percival continued, "you, Squire, have a mission in this Land that is so far only partially completed. You, Jippers, therefore must join with the company on that mission. There is one more thing. Jippers, you have yet to reveal another secret. When the time is right, you must share your secret, but not yet. Now I will leave you. Farewell until we meet again."

THE KEEPER OF SECRETS

Vinny, Alvin, Vylin and Perkin were astonished at the events they had just witnessed.

Vinny explained to Squire what they had seen. "After you had fallen unconscious and the power of the shield had sent the birds away, Jippers returned unexpectedly. He appeared without warning from behind a tree and grabbed hold of the shield. However, this time he didn't seem to be trying to wrest it from your grip, but he also fell under its power and seemed to be sharing the experience with you. When you both regained consciousness at the same time we were ready to arrest Jippers but, before we could do so, Percival had appeared and revealed the future for Jippers, and for all of us."

Then they remembered that, apart from Jippers, they had all sustained scratches and bites from the attack of the birds, and they required the healing sap of Pitys.

Vinny continued to speak, addressing Jippers. "Can you please open the haversack on my back? Inside you will find a bottle containing a liquid, a healing sap given to Helge by the hamadryad Pitys. Please apply some of the sap to the wounds each of us has sustained."

After Jippers had applied the sap to the wounds of the five friends, they decided to make camp for the night. They found a sheltered spot close to a stream.

"By morning our wounds should be healed," said Vinny, "and we'll be sufficiently recovered to continue our journey."

"Yes," said Jippers. "I witnessed the wizard Sim and the monk Beghlin using this sap to heal the other wizard after his severe wounding by the wolves. It is indeed a very potent remedy."

After he had finished, Vylin looked up into the old man's eyes. "Thank you," she said. "We welcome you as one of our company, but there are just two things I need you to do."

HOPE

Jippers frowned. "What's that?" he asked.

"The first is to allow me to cut your hair and shave your beard. The second is for you to jump into that stream over there and have a good wash!"

The others laughed.

CHAPTER 17

MEETINGS AT SOUTHPORT

Sim returned to Gull Island the following morning and caught up with the others as they approached Oxe. When his hawk's features changed to those of the wizard, his face could not conceal his contempt. "What's *he* doing here?" he asked, pointing at Jippers.

"It's all right, he's our friend," Squire reassured him. He then went on to relate to Sim all that had happened the previous afternoon.

The glower was replaced by a thin smile. "You can trust him if you like," said the wizard. "I don't trust him. Only time will tell who's right."

"When my other secret is revealed, then we will see who is to be trusted," said Jippers, spitting tobacco juice.

"That's enough banter," interrupted Vinny. "In Helge's absence, I'm the leader. I've accepted Jippers, and that's the end of it. Now we must be on our way to Oxe. We have yet to find passage from there to Southport."

The company arrived in the small settlement later that afternoon, only to find no boats moored in the harbour. They decided to make camp for the night in the hope that a craft would arrive by the following morning. However, they were out of luck and three more days passed before another fishing boat arrived. As soon as the fisherman had stepped ashore, Vinny was negotiating with him.

"I'm not going to Southport," the man said. "I'm from Jackville and intend to return there tomorrow."

"We'll give you fifty shillings," said Vinny.

HOPE

"I'm a busy man. I'll lose a day's fishing if I take you to Southport. That's worth at least twice as much."

"Eighty shillings, and that's my final offer," said Vinny.

"Suit yourself," said the fisherman, turning to leave. "You might have to wait a week for another boat. Goodbye."

"Okay," said Vinny. "One hundred."

The man turned slowly and looked Vinny in the eye. "We will set off early in the morning," he said.

The crossing, a similar distance to the one from Jackville, took about four hours.

When they had paid the fisherman and said their goodbyes, they set off on foot to seek out The Black Dog tavern, which they found without trouble on the main street of the town. They discovered that Helge and Wim had arrived before them, but this did not surprise them after their long delay in Oxe.

Helge also had initial reservations about the trustworthiness of Jippers, but was reassured when she heard the story about Percival, the Keeper of Secrets.

"When I braved the rough seas and visited Gull Island many years ago, I too met Percival," she said. "He revealed to me the secret of who I really am, and what is my destiny. However, they remain a secret between Percival and me. Having once met Percival, I know that we must respect his judgement. If he says that Jippers can be trusted, that is good enough for me. Now tell me, Squire, what are the instructions for finding the next tooth?"

* * * * *

In the castle at the foot of the Central Kobold Mountain, the wizard Gordeve was holding her own war council with the Kobalos leaders and the traitor Digbee.

MEETINGS AT SOUTHPORT

"Inform us, Digbee, of the latest developments and news of my brother's involvement," she said.

"Well, madam," the spy replied, "after you left Sim the other morning, he seemed to remember nothing of your visit. He has now returned to his companions, but none of them suspects that he has changed his allegiance. However, he did leave them unprotected on Gull Island while he took a message to his brother and the woman Helge who remained at Jackville."

Gordeve smiled. "My spell was too powerful. Sim didn't realise it at the time, but the knowledge I'd instilled in him made him leave the others vulnerable. Then I sent the birds to attack them. They would have succeeded in destroying the company if it hadn't been for the shield."

"Then it's high time we captured the shield," interrupted one of the Kobalos leaders by the name of Bax. "What about Jippers? Can't we use him to recapture the shield for us?"

"He is lost to us," replied Gordeve. "He only ever wanted the shield for himself, to find a way back to his own world. He now realises that his only hope of doing so is to join forces with Squire."

"Thanks to the interference of Percival, he has now joined the company," added Digbee. "I think we should capture Squire and the shield. I suggest that you use Sim to kidnap him and bring him to us."

"That's an excellent idea, Digbee," she replied. "When the time is right I shall again reveal myself to my son, and will instruct him to do as you suggest. Now tell me of my brother, Digbee."

"Your brother, madam, has done little since he left the council at Fort Holt a couple of weeks ago. His only foray from the safety of his castle was to visit Trumper to ascertain his progress with the building of the war machines. So long as he stays in his castle, he doesn't pose a threat to us."

HOPE

On hearing these words, Gordeve slammed her fist on the table and rose to her feet, towering above Digbee. "Never underestimate my brother. He has been, and remains, the biggest threat to the successful completion of our plan to take over the Land. Remember, Digbee, you are not dealing with ordinary people. My brother and I are wizards. We can both invoke magical powers beyond anything you can imagine. Be assured that the final conflict will come down to which of us has the greater powers, Tobin or myself." She resumed her seat and, her voice took on a softer tone. "Of course it will be me, for doesn't the prophecy end with the words 'Gordeve will rule.'?"

Digbee replied with a quavering voice. "Yes indeed, madam. Please excuse my ignorance and the stupidity of my remark."

Ignoring Digbee's discomfort, Gordeve turned to address Bax. "Now, plans for war. General, can you brief us on the movement of your troops?"

"Madam, our land forces are concentrated in three areas and are ready for war. Firstly, we have a large contingent of Kobalos, cougars and men camped to the west of Wichtlein ready to storm the tunnel under the wall. A second similar contingent is amassed north of the gate in the wall near Dun Wood. I have dispatched a third contingent, which is on its way to Boggarton. However, I have given the commander of the troops strict instructions that they are to travel only by night and are to lie low during the daylight hours. The enemy must remain unaware of the secret route to the other side of the wall. These troops are expected to be in place within the week."

"And what of our navy?" enquired the wizard.

"Our ships are assembling in the ports of Spriggan, Brag and Phooka," explained the General. "The largest armada is at Phooka, under the command of Tenison, and ready to wage war against the ships of the enemy

MEETINGS AT SOUTHPORT

coming from Winterton and Tarmouth. However, our navy is very under-strength. We need to build more ships."

"Is there any threat from Terrapo?" she asked.

"No threat, madam," he replied, "but I suggest that we must take the island without delay. The ores of tin and copper are of vital importance to both sides in this conflict. Even now Earl Philippo's people are working around the clock forging the bronze parts needed for Trumper's weapons, and shipping them to Winterton."

"Dispatch some of the troops stationed at Wichtlein at once to Spriggan and Brag," she commanded. "The ships at these two ports, including cargo ships, must be filled with troops and sail as quickly as possible to Pixar and Hamil to storm the island."

"Yes, madam," replied General Bax. "But this will take some time to organise, maybe about ten days."

"Do it," she barked. "Then coerce the people of Terrapo to build us more ships."

* * * * *

At about the same time, another woman was making her own preparations for war. Queen Sofee, who had recently returned to Atmos, had assembled a group of two hundred volunteers to be responsible for the monitoring of Telemann's wall. The group prepared to depart from Atgaart, capital of Atmos, sailing by way of Tarmouth to Southport.

Queen Sofee was in all respects the opposite of Gordeve. The former was beautiful, graceful and kind-hearted, the latter ugly, inelegant and evil.

Sofee had decided to lead the delegation herself. For the purposes of this mission, she dispensed with her gown and tiara, and wore instead the common clothes of the people of Atmos – a shirt and slacks, and a plain

HOPE

cloak. The only concession to her royal standing was the golden brooch that secured the cloak clasped at the neck.

Nevertheless, she still maintained her regal bearing. As she stood majestically at the prow of the royal ship *Renown*, the ship's captain observed the tall, slim figure with long, blonde hair blowing in the wind. *The queen epitomises the symbol of hope and pride in the values of the lands of the free world,* he thought.

Renown docked at Tarmouth after a day and a half's sailing. Prince Dernis of Manchor met the queen at the wharf, and that evening he entertained her at his palace with a banquet and concert. Before she departed the following morning, the queen gave the prince some advice.

"Thank you very much for your shrewd counsel," said the prince. "You can be sure I will act on it."

When *Renown* docked at Southport two days later, a carriage stood by to take the queen to a temporary lodging at the Southport Naval Academy. Waiting to greet her at the academy was Prince Tycho himself, who had spent a few days there checking on the progress of the preparations for war, and another man whom she did not know. The man was mature, very slim and tall. His had a thin face, a sharp nose, and his shoulder-length hair was blond. The queen recognised at once that he came from Atmos.

"Your Majesty," said Prince Tycho. "Let me introduce you to your countryman and my friend, Yohan, formerly ambassador of Atmos to West Thorland, now adopted by the Telekai of the Northern Desert. Yohan has lived in the desert for many years and is a trusted advisor to Ben Lei, paramount chief of the Telekai. He will act as your escort to take you to Dunton where you and your group of volunteers will begin monitoring the wall."

MEETINGS AT SOUTHPORT

"I'm delighted to meet you, sir," said Queen Sofee, smiling and with her eyes sparkling. "Your reputation has gone before you, and I had often wished that we should meet some day."

Yohan bowed. "Your Majesty, it is an honour to meet you and a pleasure to serve you," he said.

"The honour is mine," replied the queen.

"Your Majesty, our need is great and urgent. Tomorrow we must depart for Dunton. With a day in Bunbury to meet with the king, it will take us five days to get to Dunton if we ride, longer if you travel by carriage. Do you ride, Your Majesty?"

"Of course. Have you forgotten the Plains of Klein, famous for its herds of horses, where every young Atmosian learns how to tame and ride?"

"Forgive me, Your Majesty. I didn't mean to insult you, but I assumed that royal children might have other interests and duties to perform. Now you should rest, for early tomorrow we must depart. However, before you do so, I would like to introduce you to some other friends of mine who are waiting outside."

"Please, bring them in," invited the queen.

"Your Majesty," Yohan began after the others had joined him, "please let me introduce to you – Squire from another Land, our countrywoman Helge of Hanlin Forest, Vineon D'Ur of Wellborough, the wizard twins Wim and Sim, my three Luchorpan friends Alvin and Vylin Shoemaker and Perkin Goldmaster, and finally Jippers, lately rat catcher to King Jovanius."

As he introduced each of them, they bowed and greeted the queen with "Your Majesty". She returned each greeting with a smile.

Yohan continued, "My friends are the ones who are on the mission for the wizard Tobin to find the golden teeth that belong to the golden skull.

HOPE

They have lately arrived in Southport in search of the fourteenth tooth. I had no idea they would be here and was surprised to meet them yesterday."

"Friends," she said, "I welcome this opportunity to meet you. I have heard from Tobin himself all about the perilous quest you are undertaking. In different times, I would invite you to talk more with me about your adventures, but we must depart at first light tomorrow, so please excuse me. I must sleep now."

*   *   *   *   *

The next morning Yohan, with six Telekai who had accompanied him on his journey from Dunton, Queen Sofee and the two hundred volunteers departed on their long journey to the Northern Desert outpost. The horses for the Atmosians were a gift from Prince Tycho.

The same morning, our nine friends approached the parade ground of the Southport Naval Academy. As they surveyed the parade ground from outside the perimeter fence, they could see a white flagpole at its centre. The flag of West Thorland, that billowed in the breeze at the top of the pole, consisted of three equally sized horizontal stripes. The top stripe, coloured yellow, signified the northern desert; the middle light-green stripe represented the lush arable areas around Central West Thorland; and the bottom dark-green stripe signified the expanses of forest in the south of the country. The flag of Atmos, heralding the visit of the Queen, flew from a similar green flagpole.

Vinny indicated the white flagpole. "That must be the one," he said. "Look, there's ivy growing near its base."

High fences surrounded the naval academy on all sides. To gain admission, they would have to enter through a gate guarded by sentries bearing muskets.

MEETINGS AT SOUTHPORT

As they approached the gate, they heard a commanding voice say, "Halt. What is your business here?" The voice belonged to an overzealous guard who stood with musket raised.

Vinny tried to explain to the guard the purpose of their visit.

"I don't know of such a mission," said the guard. "These are troubled times and any strangers to this academy must be viewed with suspicion." His eyes roved over the nine faces. "It seems to me that you have some very unusual members in your company. I'm afraid I'm going to have to ask you to accompany me to the commanding officer. Please follow me to his office."

"Can't you do something?" Vinny whispered to Wim. "Can't you use some magic to overpower the guard?"

"I think that would be unwise," said Wim. "We'd best go along with what the guard says."

The commanding officer, Vice Admiral Von Trip, was an imposing figure. He wore his full military uniform with many ribbons and two silver medals, and a huge, curled auburn moustache largely concealed his ruddy face. He also had no knowledge of their mission, and advised them that he couldn't allow them to enter the grounds of the academy until he had made some enquiries.

"Sir," said Vinny, "Prince Tycho himself is aware of our mission. If you speak to him, he will surely verify who we are."

"The prince departed this morning for Tarmouth," said the Vice Admiral. "He will not return for at least four days. Please try again then .Good day."

"But … "

"Good day to you, gentlemen, ladies. Please shut the door behind you as you leave."

*   *   *   *   *

HOPE

Later that evening, when everyone had settled down for the night in The Black Dog, a voice woke Sim from his slumber. It came from outside the window of the room he shared with Wim.

"Sim, it's me," said the voice.

"Mother?"

"Yes, Sim, it's your mother. My son I have a task for you, which may prove to be both difficult and dangerous. When the time is right, you must capture Squire and the shield. You must wait for the right opportunity to do this since you must execute the abduction and make good your escape before the others realise what's happening. Take him north to the Caves of Boggart. There you will find friends waiting who will show you the way through the caves to the other side of the wall. It's important that you don't permit any members of your company to follow you, or know of the route you take. The way through the caves is still unknown to the enemy and must be kept secret."

"Yes, mother, I understand."

"One more thing," said the wizard, "when I leave in a few minutes, you won't recall this conversation or remember that I am your mother. When the time is right, you will know what to do. Do you understand?"

"Yes, I understand."

"Good. Your brother still sleeps and will know nothing of my visit. You and I will meet again at my castle with the prize. Farewell."

The next moment, the giant eagle soared off towards the north-east.

*   *   *   *   *

Five days later Prince Tycho returned from Tarmouth and met with Vice Admiral Von Trip to brief him on the outcome of his visit there, and his meeting with Prince Dernis. At the conclusion of the briefing, the Vice Admiral said, "Your Royal Highness, there is just one more thing. A group of strangers turned up at the gate a few days ago. They claim to be on a special mission for the wizard Tobin and say that you will verify their story. They say they need to have access to the flagpole on the parade ground. Do you have knowledge of such a group?"

"Indeed I do," replied the prince. "They're on an important and urgent mission. They didn't say anything to me about needing to enter the parade ground, or I would have warned you. It's unfortunate that you didn't know. I commend you for your vigilance, Vice Admiral. However, unfortunately, it has caused them unnecessary delay. Please make arrangements for them to have access to the flagpole at once."

As soon as the prince had departed, Von Trip sent for the company. He rose as they entered his office. "I apologise profusely for the delay," he said. "I was only following orders. If I had allowed you access and you had subsequently proved to be impostors, then I would have been in danger of losing my job."

"We understand," Vinny reassured him.

The Vice Admiral took a pass from the top drawer of his desk and scribbled out a message allowing the company access to the parade ground. He signed the pass and handed it to Vinny.

"Thank you," said the archer.

They went at once to the parade ground and showed the pass to the guards. When they reached the flagpole, they quickly cut away some of the ivy around the base of the pole, and found the hole. Alvin reached inside and discovered a box with the tooth and instructions inside. He handed the tooth to Squire who put it in the pouch around his neck, and the instructions to Helge.

"Where are we going to next?" he asked.

Helge read:

HOPE

"Second left molar – top jaw

The estuary of the Tee
Is marshy and wet.
A strange folk live there;
They're called Ballybogs, and furthermore ... ,
There's another called Phynnodderee.
What you seek you will get
If you open the door,
The trapdoor at the top of the stair."

Alvin screwed up his nose. "Ballybogs! I've heard of those creatures. They've got small round bodies and a head, but no neck, and long spindly legs like a spider. They live in bogs and marshes and are covered with mud."

"They sound very unpleasant," said Squire. "But the instructions seem to suggest that we will need to meet with them. I hope they will not be aggressive towards us."

"And who is Phy … Phynnodderee?" asked Vinny, glancing at the paper.

"I heard tell of a creature by that name," said Perkin. "The story goes that there was once an elfin knight living on the Isle of Phynn who saw a human maiden sitting under the shade of a tree and instantly fell in love with her. That night, rather than attend the Royal Harvest Festival at the king's behest, the knight chose instead to spend the time dancing with the beautiful maiden. When the elfin king found out, he was very angry. He banished the knight to live forever alone in the Phynn Mountains and cursed him with a thick coat of red hair, and to be known as Phynnodderee, which means 'Hairy one'."

MEETINGS AT SOUTHPORT

"That's right," agreed Alvin. "However, it is said he wasn't an evil creature, but was very helpful towards the people of the island. Sometimes he drove their sheep home or helped in the harvesting if a storm was brewing and, in the swirling mists near the mountaintop, he would help a lost traveller find his way home. Once one of those he had helped offered to give him clothes, but he threw them from the mountaintop into the sea."

"If he was banished to live forever in the Phynn Mountains, I can't see how he can now be associated with the Ballybogs in the marshes," declared Vinny. "No doubt, we will find out. However, we do know where we are heading next. The Tee River estuary is due west of here. It will take us about five days to walk there."

They departed the following morning. It was a dull, overcast day that promised to bring rain before evening. The dullness of the day reflected their mood, as the prospect of spending time in the marshes with Ballybogs and the mysterious Phynnodderee bore an ominous premonition. Their journey took them eastwards towards Tee Crossing where the main highway connecting Southport to Tarmouth met the road coming south from Wellborough. The fourth road of the crossroads led south to the tiny settlement of Cambel on the northern edge of the marshes.

The journey to Tee Crossing proved uneventful, but unpleasant in view of the inclement weather. They arrived there in the middle of the fourth day and found accommodation at the local inn.

"You're in luck," said the innkeeper. "This is a very busy crossroads and the inn is usually full. However, with the preparations for war, the common people are not travelling as much as before. I have three rooms available."

The next day dawned more brightly, but did little to raise their spirits. When they arrived in Cambel that evening, they discovered that the village had no inn and they were obliged to use their own tents for the first time for several days. After a hearty meal of trout from the river, which at that point remained unpolluted, they settled down for the night, not relishing the prospects of the following day.

*   *   *   *   *

On their way to Dunton, Yohan and Queen Sofee stopped for one night at Bunbury. They arrived there in the late afternoon, and the king's aide scheduled them an audience for the following morning.

"So, Your Majesty, we have some time to kill," Yohan said to Sofee. "Will you do me the pleasure of dining with me tonight?"

"Thank you, sir. I will be honoured," the queen replied.

They dined that evening at a restaurant near to the royal palace where Yohan had dined many times in former years. During the meal, which had several courses, they exchanged stories of their experiences and were surprised at how much they had in common. By the end of the evening, they were sharing jokes and laughing together like old friends.

After the meal, that lasted nearly three hours, Yohan escorted the queen back to her chamber at the royal palace.

"Sir," said the queen as they parted, "it's been a pleasure to share the evening with you. I hope we will have the chance to do so again. I've never before met a man who will treat me as an equal, rather than act as if he's my servant. It has been most refreshing."

"Your Majesty, I will look forward to it," he replied, bowing and kissing the queen's hand.

The following day, they held counsel with King Jovanius. Queen Sofee briefed the king on her conversation with Prince Dernis of Manchor when she stopped over at Tarmouth a few days earlier.

MEETINGS AT SOUTHPORT

"Your Majesty is very perceptive," said the king. "If you are correct, and I believe you are, then I have nothing but praise for you. What do you think, Yohan?"

"I agree, Your Majesty. Not only is the queen very beautiful, but she is also wise."

They went on to talk about the forthcoming task for the queen and her volunteers. "I suggest," said the king, "that you divide your party into two groups. Forgive me, Your Majesty, if it seems that I am giving you orders. I'm merely suggesting to you what is, in my opinion, the best course of action."

"Of course, King Jovanius. Continue, please."

"From the gate near Dun Wood, one group should travel north-westwards, and the other group south-eastwards. You must thoroughly inspect every metre of the wall for any signs that it might have been scaled, any holes in the wall, or tunnels under it. If each group can inspect twenty kilometres a day, I estimate it will take three or four weeks for you to complete the task – unless you find the way through the wall earlier, of course."

"We will find it, Your Majesty. You can be sure of that," promised the queen.

*   *   *   *   *

The Kobalos army, under the command of General Bax, commandeered every civilian ship in port at both Spriggan and Brag. There were about twenty ships in all, including *Bethia*, which had recently docked at Spriggan. Owing to his own greed and foolishness, although he knew that the start of war was imminent, Redbeard had risked bringing one last cargo of precious ore to East Thorland. He already regretted his decision.

HOPE

Kobalos are not good sailors and their own navy was not large. About ten warships had recently arrived at the two ports from Phooka. Under the command of the Kobalos Admiral Tenison, their crews for the most part comprised men of East Thorland. A further two warships, whose job it was to patrol the southern seas, remained stationed at Phooka.

The improvised navy was now prepared for the invasion of Terrapo.

"We need to take control of the mines," said Bax. "Their capture is strategically the most important part of our mission. Whoever controls the mines, will probably win the war."

"Regrettably, General, there is no suitable place to make a landing around the Karce Peninsular," said Tenison. "You will need to approach the mines by land."

"Then we must first of all concentrate on the occupation of Hamil," said the General. "The earl has no navy and we have already commandeered most of his cargo ships. I do not anticipate that the undefended town will offer much resistance. After capturing Hamil, our troops will be able to march largely unhindered through the sparsely populated lands northwards to the mines. We will also take Pixar by land, later. When will you be ready to sail, Admiral?"

"The crossing from Spriggan to Hamil will take about fourteen hours. It will take rather less time for the other fleet to sail from Brag to Hamil, probably about ten hours. Therefore, the invasion of Hamil will take place early on the morning of the day after tomorrow. We sail in the morning."

"Very well," said Bax.

Redbeard was nominally in command of his ship and his crew of eighteen men from Terrapo, but a group of armed Kobalos soldiers closely watched their movements on deck. Another forty Kobalos were billeted

MEETINGS AT SOUTHPORT

below decks. The crew of *Bethia* had no choice but to obey the order to set sail in preparation for the invasion of their own homeland. In a similar way, Kobalos soldiers occupied other ships from Terrapo.

Late on the first evening, the small armada approached the island of Tauto, which lay to the south of the main island of Terrapo. The fleet hove to close to the north-western coast of Tauto, facing Hamil, and waited for the dawn. A few minutes later, General Bax joined Admiral Tenison on board the flagship *Invincible* to discuss their strategy.

"At first light we will move the ships closer to Hamil harbour," said Bax. "From there a select group of your men must row silently to shore in the small boats. Most of the population of the town will still be asleep and we will catch them unawares."

"Don't worry, General," said Tenison. "Their meagre force of guards will be no match for my men. Once we have overcome them, the ships can dock and your troops can disembark."

Just before dawn, Tenison's men prepared to take to their boats. The Admiral had just finished his breakfast and was wiping his mouth with a napkin when he heard a shout from a nearby vessel. As he jumped to his feet, he heard more shouts, this time from his own men. These were followed by the *boom* of cannon fire.

CHAPTER 18

STRANGE BEINGS

Redbeard trained his telescope towards the north-east from where the sound came, to be greeted by the sight of a foreign warship rounding the North Cape of Tauto. High above the deck of the ship, a flag billowed in the wind. It bore the picture of a leopard, the standard of the King of Manchor. Minutes later, another ship rounded the cape, then another, then two more.

The captain's eyes showed a glint of satisfaction. This quickly turned to fear as he realised that *Bethia* might come under attack. He watched as altogether more than twenty western warships – thirteen ships of the line, six frigates and some smaller craft – rounded the cape. The western warships, most of them from Manchor and under the command of Prince Dernis, had been hiding on the east side of Tauto ready to pounce on the vessels of the unsuspecting Kobalos.

Redbeard looked around and noted that the Kobalos fleet, about thirty craft in all, comprised just five ships of the line, three frigates and several smaller craft like *Bethia*. The Kobalos flagship, *Invincible,* lay anchored to the starboard of *Bethia,* and beyond *Invincible* he could see the frigate *Phooka. Invincible*, a huge three-decker warship carried more than ninety guns.

Redbeard watched as the western ships manoeuvred close to the Kobalos fleet. The Kobalos sailors on the larger ships were still racing to man their guns when the western flagship *King Litimas* delivered a broadside at a range of thirty metres, firing towards the sterns of the enemy craft.

STRANGE BEINGS

"Broadside!" shouted Redbeard. "Take cover everyone."

The crew and Kobalos guards all dived for cover, but Redbeard knew there would be little hope if *Bethia* should be hit. He sighed with relief when he realised that his ship was undamaged.

One of the Kobalos guards came up behind Redbeard and grabbed hold of his shoulder, forcing him to turn his head. The guard looked directly into the captain's eyes, his face twitching. "What's broadside?" he asked.

"They're firing their guns from one side of the ship directly at our sterns," replied Redbeard. "The intention is that the shots should travel the length of *Invincible* to wreak havoc and destruction. At the same time, *Invincible's* ability to return fire is very limited. She's facing the wrong way! Our ship's also in danger."

"I know which way I'm going," said the Kobalos. He jumped overboard and swam towards the shore.

As Redbeard's eyes followed the Kobalos, he saw wisps of dense smoke rising above the top deck of *Invincible*. "Look," he shouted to his first mate, Cassio, "*Invincible* is on fire."

"No," Cassio replied, "it's *Phooka*. The enemy ships are getting closer. They're using close fleet tactics. *Invincible* could be next, or it could be us."

"They're double-shotting, using grape shot on top of the iron balls," said Redbeard.

"She's listing. She's sinking fast," said the mate.

He had just finished speaking when a second broadside from *King Litimas* simultaneously struck *Invincible* and *Bethia*. The Kobalos who had been keeping guard over *Bethia's* crew, panicked and jumped overboard in an attempt to swim to *Invincible*.

HOPE

"They've fired chain-and-link shot at our rigging," said Redbeard. "But we're not on fire yet. Tell the men to abandon ship, Cassio. Man the boats."

"Aye, aye, captain. What about the Kobalos below decks?"

"Let them drown."

The ships on both sides also carried a variety of smaller weapons on the top deck and in the rigging. These included swivel guns firing grape shot or bags of musket balls, and hand-held muskets and pistols. As *King Litimas* approached *Invincible*, her crew fired at the enemy officers and sailors on deck.

Many of them suffered terrible injuries. Some had limbs ripped off by cannon balls, others were wounded by splinter fragments from the wooden decks and bulwarks, or crushed by falling masts and rigging. Sailors stationed aloft, fell from collapsing masts and rigging into the sea and drowned.

While his men set to rowing the lifeboats towards the shore, Redbeard sat facing the scene of the battle. He saw *King Litimas* and *Invincible* locked together and watched as troops from *King Litimas* boarded. Savage hand-to-hand fighting ensued.

The Kobalos, who had been so sure they would face no resistance from the people of Terrapo, couldn't themselves put up much of a struggle against the might of the navy from Manchor. The Battle of Tauto lasted little more than four hours, during which the western navy destroyed two enemy warships and three of the ships commandeered by General Bax. With his own life in danger, Bax, on *Phooka*, raised the white flag of surrender. Soon afterwards, Admiral Tenison also surrendered his warships.

As the day progressed, all the ships on both sides took turns to berth at the wharf in Hamil. Prince Dernis had forewarned Earl Philippo of the attempted invasion and of the planned ambush by the ships of Manchor. In anticipation of the victory, the earl had given his men orders to repair an old fort near the east side of the city and to secure it against the imminent arrival of the prisoners. The prisoners of war, nearly two thousand men and Kobalos, were marched off the ships and taken to the hastily improvised prison.

That evening, Earl Philippo entertained Prince Dernis at his residence to celebrate their victory. While they sank several glasses of rum, they discussed the successful thwarting of the plans for invasion and the capture of so many enemy craft and soldiers.

"Much credit for this victory must go to Queen Sofee of Atmos," declared the prince. "On her way from Atgaart to Southport a couple of weeks ago, she stopped over at Tarmouth and warned me that such an invasion might take place. She cautioned me that the mines of Terrapo would play a very important part in the war, and that the East would surely try to capture them. I followed her advice and within eight days had my navy prepared for this surprise ambush."

"How did you manage to outsmart them?" asked the earl, speaking through red-stained teeth.

The prince smiled. "We sailed well to the south of the land so that none, not even Gordeve, was aware that we were on the move. Two frigates of the Kobalos based in Phooka patrolled in the area. We could have easily destroyed them, but we didn't want word of our intentions to reach Gordeve's ears, so we used one of our own ships as a decoy. The ship approached from the south and sailed close to Phooka harbour before turning west, pursued by the two enemy craft. Whilst they busily occupied themselves with this pursuit, the rest of our navy slipped through undetected far to the south."

HOPE

"What was the fate of that ship?" asked Philippo.

Prince Dernis' expression turned grave. "She had a nominal crew of ten. We don't yet know whether she was apprehended and what was the fate of her crew, but those brave men have helped to avert a major coup for the enemy. They will be heroes back home in Manchor and forever remembered for the part they played in this victory."

"My people will always be grateful to them," said the earl. His nod revealed his voluminous double chin. "We thank you, your father King Litimas, and the people of Manchor for this great victory. We also acknowledge our thanks to the Queen of Atmos. Without her inspiration, my people would now be a captive race."

They raised their glasses and clinked them together. "The queen," they said in unison.

*   *   *   *   *

As soon as she heard the news of the defeat, Gordeve summoned Digbee to her castle. When he arrived, he found her pacing the floor, cursing loudly.

"Why didn't you forewarn me of this ambush?" she asked the trembling spy. "A significant part of my army and navy has been captured."

"I … I was unaware of this, my Lady," replied Digbee. "Not even Tobin knew about this plan, otherwise you can be sure I would also have known."

"Who was responsible for this atrocity?" demanded the wizard.

"My Lady, since the time of the defeat I have made some enquiries and have discovered that the ambush was led by Prince Dernis of Manchor himself. However, the idea for this assault was that of the Queen of Atmos."

"Sofee!" hissed Gordeve. "That woman has always been a thorn in my flesh, as her father was before her. Where is she now, Digbee?"

STRANGE BEINGS

"I understand she is leading a delegation from Atmos that is inspecting the wall, trying to find our secret way through."

"Aha! Then let's hope she finds it. For, if she does, we will have a welcoming party for her."

*   *   *   *   *

The new day dawned on Cambel.

"It's time for us to venture into the unfriendly marshes," said Helge. "But it's not necessary for all of us to go. Besides, the mule and pony won't be able to travel in the boggy terrain."

"I'll go," said Jippers. "I'm experienced at tracking down unpleasant creatures."

Wim, Vinny and Perkin volunteered to accompany him. The four of them left the relative safety of Cambel and set off with heavy hearts.

"Which direction should we take?" asked Vinny.

"Our exact destination is a mystery," said Jippers, "so any direction is as good as any other. All we know is that we have to enter the marshes and that we should eventually expect to encounter the Ballybogs. I suggest we set off in a southerly direction."

The beginning of their journey took them along a well-worn path that, though muddy in parts, was relatively dry. After they had walked for about three hours, the path became muddier and less distinct, and their walking slowly changed to wading when they entered an area of wet-meadow, saturated with water from the Tee River. The vegetation also showed signs of change. The grasses gave way to the triangular stems of sedges, the lance-shaped leaves of water pepper, and the large, heart-shaped, red-veined leaves of rose mallow. After another hour or so, cattail and bulrushes began to replace the sedges, some up to three metres high with flat sword-like leaves and swaying thick brown spikes.

HOPE

By this time, the path had vanished, and the four companions waded, sometimes up to their waists in putrid water, while they proceeded aimlessly southwards. The cold water made them shiver uncontrollably and the smell of marsh gases made them feel nauseous. Their only consolation was that it was not mid-summer; otherwise, they would have been a feast for a myriad of flying insects. There were, however, plenty of frogs and birds of many kinds including bitterns, red-winged blackbirds, swamp sparrows, yellow rails and ruddy ducks.

A few minutes later, they once again stumbled onto dry land, an island amongst the wetlands between two branches of the Tee River. They were thankful to rest for a few moments and for the opportunity to eat their lunch and drink some fresh water from their bottles.

Half an hour later, they continued their journey.

They had walked and waded for nearly five hours before they finally met the Ballybogs, but not quite in the way they had anticipated. Even Jippers, who led and had a keen sense of smell, did not perceive the danger until too late. He was walking along the dry island path, when unexpectedly he felt his feet giving way beneath him. As his feet lost their purchase, he fell with a bump onto his buttocks and then felt himself sliding down on the wet, slippery surface into a mud hole. The hole opened up and increased in size as he went deeper. He shouted a warning to the others, but it was too late. They also became victims to the mud hole and, seconds later, the four of them landed in a heap at its bottom.

They must have looked a sight covered from head to toe with greenish-brown, slimy mud. They tried to stand up, but the base of the hole was too slippery, and they could find no stone or root to hold onto. Before they had time to discuss their predicament, the Ballybogs came slowly crawling out from the mud, shaking the slime and muck from their bodies as they did so. There were about fifteen of them. Just as Alvin had described, they were quite small like crabs with round bodies, a head but no neck, and long spindly legs.

"Are … are you the Ballybogs?" asked Vinny, trying to back away.

The Ballybogs did not reply, but only made grunting, slobbering noises that may have been intelligible to each other, but meant nothing to Vinny and the others.

"I don't think they can hear us," said Perkin.

"They can hear you, but they cannot speak," said a deep, strange voice. The sound startled the four friends, for they could see no one except the grunting Ballybogs. Yet the afternoon sun streamed in from above, and bathed the hole in light.

"Who's there?" asked Vinny. When he got no reply, he said, "Perkin, use your glass to see if there is someone up there outside the hole."

Perkin removed the Seeround Glass from its box and trained it towards the top of the hole. He rotated a full three hundred and sixty degrees, but could see nothing.

"There is no one there," he said, "unless it's Squire, or someone else from his world."

"I'm certainly not from his world," said the strange voice.

Vinny looked towards the source of the sound and blinked. Standing at the bottom of the hole close to the Ballybogs, he saw a strange creature. He resembled a very small, old man. Coarse, thick, reddish-coloured hair covered his naked body, with bits of twigs and mud stuck to the hair. Vinny couldn't believe his eyes, for the stranger had not crawled out of the mud as the Ballybogs had done, but had simply materialised out of thin air. He blinked again and rubbed his eyes, but there was no mistaking the man was there. Besides, Vinny could smell him. An unpleasant odour reminded Vinny

HOPE

of the way Jippers used to smell before Vylin had cut his hair and persuaded him to have a bath.

"I am Phynnodderee," said the old man. "I dwell with the Ballybogs and have learned how to communicate with them. What is your business in their domain?"

"We're on an errand for the wizard Tobin," explained Vinny. "We're seeking a tooth that belongs to the golden skull. Our instructions told us to come to the marshes to find some stairs with a trapdoor at the top. The tooth must be somewhere on or near the trapdoor. Can you help us find it?"

Phynnodderee turned to the Ballybogs and issued a series of grunts. One of the Ballybogs, who seemed to be their leader, then replied with some more unrecognisable sounds.

"He says that, as friends of Tobin, you are welcome," translated Phynnodderee. "You are to follow them to their home. I'm coming too. See you there." With that, Phynnodderee promptly vanished again.

One at a time, the Ballybogs dived towards the side of the mud hole and disappeared into the mud. The last Ballybog to exit gestured with a spindly arm, indicating to the four friends that they should follow. Once again, Jippers took the lead. Shutting his eyes and holding his nose, he dived headfirst into the mud where he had seen the Ballybogs disappear. With no other option open to them, the other three followed suit. After sliding headfirst downwards for a few seconds, they found themselves disgorged from the muddy tunnel into a large dry cavern. A thin shaft of light reached down from far above.

Vinny looked around. "It looks like limestone," he said. "This small island in the middle of the marshes must be a relic of an extension of the limestone cliffs where we found the whalebone, and the cliffs on Gull Island."

STRANGE BEINGS

Finally, they managed to scramble to their feet, and tried to remove the sticky mud from their faces and hands.

The Ballybogs already waited. However, with no way of communicating with each other, the two sides found themselves at an impasse.

"What do we do next?" whispered Perkin.

"We can try looking for the stairs," suggested Vinny. "The instructions tell us to find a trapdoor at the top of some stairs." However, when he tried to move in search of the stairs, he found that a group of Ballybogs blocked his way. They issued a series of grunts. "It looks like they don't want us to go anywhere," he said. "Perhaps we'd better wait for that Phynnodderee fellow to turn up again."

The archer had no sooner finished speaking when the little, red-haired man reappeared. "Phynnodderee at your service," he said. "Now, what was it you were looking for? Stairs? Oh, yes. There are some stairs somewhere around here. Some people, who used to occupy these caverns many years ago, cut them into the rock. However, the Ballybogs have no use for stairs, and I ... well I just appear and disappear whenever I want to go somewhere."

"Tell me," enquired Vinny, "how did you come to live amongst the Ballybogs? The stories say that you were banished to a life of eternal exile in the mountains on the Isle of Phynn."

"It's true," replied Phynnodderee. "However, the spell that bound me was broken a few years ago when Percival visited the island and revealed my secret to the people. It was then that I learned that my dear love had passed away many years earlier, so I had no reason to remain any longer on Phynn Island. Percival offered to take me to the mainland before returning to Gull Island. I didn't want to go to Southport, or any other town, so he took me in his little ketch and delivered me safely to the estuary of the Tee River. It was there that I met the Ballybogs. They adopted me and taught me their language, and I have lived with them ever since."

He turned to the leader of the Ballybogs and made some grunting sounds. After the Ballybog had replied, Phynnodderee translated once again: "He tells me the stairs are in the next cavern, but to get there we need to cross the bridge over the underground river, and that is guarded by the Water Woman."

"Who is the Water Woman?" asked Vinny.

"She is an evil sprite who lives under the water. The legends say that she will reach up and drag down any who try to cross the bridge, and pull them under the water so they will drown. The Ballybogs do not fear her for she only covets larger beings like the three of you." Phynnodderee indicated Jippers, Wim and Vinny. "Your Luchorpan friend may be too small to interest her, and she doesn't scare me since I can make myself invisible. However, you three will be in danger if you try to cross the bridge."

"Is there no other way to get to the next cavern?" asked Wim.

"Only through the exit which you will take when you reach the top of the stairs," replied Phynnodderee. "But nobody knows where that exit is on the outside. It hasn't been opened for many years."

"Then we have no choice," declared Wim. "I'll have to fight the Water Woman with magic. Tell the Ballybogs to lead me to the bridge."

Phynnodderee once again made some grunting noises. Then the leader of the Ballybogs raised an arm and indicated for Wim to follow him. They entered a narrow, unlit tunnel. *They seem to be used to the dark and know their way around*, thought Wim.

After they had walked for about a hundred metres, the tunnel turned a corner and Wim could see a brightly lit pathway in front of him leading to a bridge spanning an underground river, a width of about twenty metres. Looking upwards, he could see a gigantic hole high above through which the sunlight streamed. Its sides looked precipitous and covered with mud. *There's no way I could climb up there*, he thought.

The only way forward was the bridge, so the wizard followed the Ballybog's lead. The other three remained behind, with Phynnodderee and the rest of the Ballybogs, keeping a safe distance in case the Water Woman should make an appearance.

The bridge was narrow – little more than a metre wide – and had no barriers. As Wim approached the middle, there was a swirling from the depths below. He saw a large white hand thrust itself out of the water. In an instant, the hand had grabbed him by the left ankle with an iron-grip. Wim felt the powerful hand trying to pull his leg towards one edge. He almost lost his balance, but braced himself and raised his staff.

Although he couldn't see the Water Woman's face in the murky depths, he guessed where she would be from the position of the hand and pointed the staff in that direction. As he aimed the staff, he uttered the words of command, "Water Woman, release me."

A beam of energy flashed from the staff and sizzled into the water towards the evil sprite. Hearing Wim's command, and reeling under the impact of the force from the staff, she let go of his ankle. As she did so, she issued a shrill, unnatural shriek, and the wizard almost lost his balance once again. Then he commanded, "Water Woman, go home. Go back to the depths from where you came, and don't bother me or my friends again." There was another swirling of water, followed by a deep groan, and then silence and stillness prevailed.

"It's safe now," the wizard called to his friends. "Come on."

HOPE

The other three and Phynnodderee followed Wim and the Ballybogs onto the bridge and, within a couple of minutes, they all safely reached the far side. The Ballybogs led them into another dark tunnel which soon opened out into a second cavern, similar to the first, but much larger. At the far end of the cavern in the gloom, they could make out the silhouette of a set of stairs cut into the rock and leading upwards. However, the top of the stairs remained in darkness.

Phynnodderee pointed. "There's the staircase," he said. "The trapdoor bars the exit at the top of the stairs. We will leave you now. The leader of the Ballybogs wishes you well as you continue your mission for the wizard Tobin. I bid you farewell, until we meet again." In an instant Phynnodderee had vanished once more and the Ballybogs had melted away into another mud-hole.

"What now?" asked Perkin.

"First we must eat, and then sleep," said Vinny. "We've had no food since lunchtime many hours ago, and it would be better for us sleep here in the relative safety of the cavern. I don't think we would sleep much up there surrounded by the marshes."

"You're right," agreed Perkin. "But there may yet be some unknown dangers here in the cavern."

"I'm not worried about anything following us across that bridge," said Vinny. "The Water Woman would deal with them. However, I am concerned about the staircase. It's very dark up there. Can you use your glass, Perkin, to see if there's anything unpleasant lurking on the stairs?"

Perkin raised the glass once again and searched the stairs from bottom to top. "Nothing, except a few rats," he said.

"I'll deal with them," said Jippers. He issued a shrill whistle, causing the rats to scurry harmlessly away.

STRANGE BEINGS

After they had eaten, they settled down to try to rest for a few hours. They took turns to keep watch, though they could see nothing in the darkness of the cavern. Perkin and Wim took the first turn, using the glass to see if anything unpleasant should materialise. Vinny and Jippers took the second watch, relying on Jippers' acute senses of hearing and smell to warn them of any danger. After a restless few hours, they decided to move on.

Jippers led the way up the stairs. He removed a rope from his pack, tied one end around his own waist, and then passed it to the others so they could do the same. His experience in the dark sewers of Bunbury gave him the advantage of sure-footedness even on these slippery steps. The others followed cautiously. More than once one of them lost his footing and began to slide backwards, but Jippers was strong enough to take the weight until they had regained their balance, before pressing on. The stairs had thirty-four steps altogether – not many, but it took them several minutes as they edged towards the top.

When he got there, Jippers reached up to touch the base of the trapdoor. He discovered that it was wooden, hinged on one edge, and secured on the opposite edge by two iron bolts. Rust had corroded the bolts and they proved very difficult to move. Nevertheless, after a few minutes of struggling to free them, he managed to slide them back and pushed up the heavy trapdoor. Light streaming down from above dazzled the four friends.

Once their eyes had adjusted to the unfamiliar light, they hauled themselves up through the trapdoor and onto a dry grassy area. As they lay on the grass to catch their breath, they heard a *clunk* as the trapdoor shut itself.

When they stood up, they noticed that the trapdoor was set below ground level and partially covered with overgrown vegetation that concealed it from the view of any passer-by. Vinny knelt down to search for any sign of

HOPE

the tooth. He saw no handle on the outside of the door, so couldn't open it again. However, a small groove in the wood, into which his fingers could just pass, caught his eye. He pulled, and a thin piece of wood detached itself from the rest of the trapdoor. Hidden in a hole on its reverse side, he found the tooth and the next set of instructions.

He jumped up. "Here they are," he said.

"What do the instructions say?" asked Perkin.

Vinny read:

"Left wisdom tooth – top jaw
In Air's shadow stands a town,
Surrounded by fertile land,
With rills dancing down,
And hills planted with fruit, olives and grapes.
Nearby you will find a place of prayer,
A cloistered courtyard with a fountain.
Inside the mouth, gushing from the mountain
Find the last of the teeth there"

Just as Vinny read the final line, Jippers let out a cry. "My Hope!" he said. "My Hope is gone. Someone has taken my Hope."

CHAPTER 19

SACUMED

As Jippers led the three others up the staircase, back in Cambel the sun had already risen, but the company still slept, all except Helge who kept guard.

Sim lay alone in the tent he usually shared with Wim, tossing and turning in his sleep. With a start, he awoke to a memory of a meeting at Tobin's castle a month earlier and a visit at the Black Dog in Southport a few days previously.

"Don't worry, mother," he whispered to himself. "I will deliver Squire and the precious shield to you."

Sim went first to the place, not far away, where Faithful and Conny were tethered. He untied them and whispered for them to wait for his signal.

His next job was to overcome the tall woman. She sat a few metres from his tent, whittling a stick with her knife. With stealth aided by magic, he crept up behind her. Whispering, "Sleep," he applied a gentle touch to her neck, and she crumpled to the ground. He bound and gagged her before dragging her limp form towards the tent she shared with Vylin.

Dealing with Vylin proved easy since she still slept soundly. He had no difficulty in overpowering the diminutive Luchorpan, and tied and gagged her in the same way. Then he dragged Helge into the tent and laid her next to Vylin. He had achieved all this without showing his face. Nevertheless, he took the precaution of blindfolding them before moving on to the next tent, the one Squire shared with Alvin.

HOPE

The drain of energy from the use of magic and the physical exertion began to make Sim feel weak. Alvin and Squire began to stir, so he knew he must act quickly. He crept up behind them, whispered the magic word and applied the same deft touch of the hand to each of their necks. Then he bound and gagged them both and blindfolded Alvin.

Sim went outside and whistled. A few moments later Conny and Faithful trotted to the young wizard's side. He gave each of them a reassuring pat. Then he quickly gathered his own belongings and those of Squire, including the shield. He put these into Faithful's side packs, and crammed some food and water bottles into those of Conny.

When everything was ready, Sim touched Squire once again to awaken him from his induced sleep. A look of surprise came over the latter's face as he recognised his abductor. Sim untied Squire's legs, but left him gagged and his wrists tied. The strain on Sim really began to take its toll, and it took a final effort of will, aided by his staff, for him to coax Squire out of the tent and force him to climb onto Conny's back. With a quick look around to make sure that he hadn't forgotten anything, the wizard mounted the mule and left the camp, leading the pony by a rope tethered to her bridle.

They set off on the road northwards which led to Tee Crossing. This was the beginning of a journey that he expected would take them to Wellborough, Rivermeet, Swanborough, and then through the Caves of Boggart to Boggarton.

*   *   *   *   *

Jippers, Wim, Perkin and Vinny found the return walk to Cambel somewhat easier to endure than the outward journey. Their mission accomplished, the discomforts of the marshes – the cold, the wet, and pungent gases – seemed of lesser significance than before. Only Jippers felt heavy of heart, for he had sensed that something had happened, that his Hope had disappeared.

When they arrived back at Cambel late in the day, they could see no sign of their friends. Nobody stood on guard, and the tents were shut up as if the occupants already slept. The four friends exchanged worried glances. Moreover, they noticed the mule and pony were not tethered where they had been before they left.

"Something's happened," cautioned Jippers. "You know I had that funny feeling about the shield. Well this strange sight only reinforces my belief that something is wrong. We must approach the tents with care."

Oblivious to the warning, Wim rushed to the tent he shared with Sim, thrust aside the flaps and looked inside.

"It's empty," he cried. "All Sim's clothes and personal belongings are gone!"

"I'll go to see if I can find Faithful and Conny," said Vinny.

Perkin put his finger to his lips. "Sh … Did you hear that?" he said. "There's a noise coming from Alvin and Squire's tent?"

Perkin opened the flap of the tent a fraction and peeped inside where he saw Alvin, tied hand and foot, gagged and blindfolded. Jippers quickly cut the bonds and removed the gag from Alvin's mouth.

Wim grabbed Alvin's shoulders and looked into his eyes. "Who did this?" he asked.

"I don't know," Alvin replied. "Whoever it was, they came up behind me and touched me on the neck. I don't remember anything else. It was some kind of magic that sent me to sleep. Who could have done this?"

"My brother's missing. Only Gordeve could be responsible for that."

"Where's Squire?" asked Alvin. "He was sharing the tent with me."

HOPE

Wim looked around. "His things are all gone," he said, "including the shield. Gordeve must have taken him too."

"I heard a cock crow last night," Alvin told them. "As soon as I heard it, I knew that it was a sign of bad luck to come. You all laugh at me when I mention these things, especially Sim, but this time I've been proved right."

Soon afterwards, they found Helge and Vylin. After Perkin had cut the ropes around Vylin's wrists and ankles, she threw herself into his arms.

"Oh, Perkin, thank goodness you're here," she said. After she had recovered, she told them, "I don't remember a thing."

Helge rubbed her sore wrists. "Me too," she said. "I didn't see them. What did they want, and how are we going to rescue Squire and Sim?"

"They must have been after the shield," said Jippers.

Meanwhile, Vinny had rejoined the others. "They've taken Conny and Faithful too," he said. "I found tracks leading off towards the north."

"They must be on their way to Tee Crossing," said Helge. "That's the only road. Wim, can you transform and go in search of them?"

Wim scratched his head and thought for a moment before replying. "It seems likely that Gordeve must have flown in to assist her Kobalos friends with the abduction of Squire and Sim. Once she had overcome everybody and handed the other two over to the Kobalos, she probably flew back to her castle. However, we cannot be sure of this. She may still be close by. This could be a trap. If I leave you alone and she's still out there, we might all be in danger. No, the only way is for us to stick together and follow them on foot."

"But it's too late to start tonight," said Helge. "We must set off first thing in the morning and follow them to Tee Crossing, then make some enquiries and try to find some more tracks."

"Besides," Vinny interrupted, "the instructions for finding the next tooth suggest that we should follow the same road leading to the Air Mountains."

"They have Conny and Faithful," said Vylin. "How can we possibly hope to catch up with them?"

"Maybe we'll be able to purchase a horse at Tee Crossing," said Vinny, "but, until we know more about the intentions of their abductors, we have little hope of finding them."

The following day when they arrived at Tee Crossing, they visited the inn where they had slept a few days previously.

The innkeeper scratched his chin. "I haven't seen anything of your friends, or anyone suspicious," he told them. "I'd love to help you, but I'm sorry there are no horses for sale."

He had hardly finished speaking before they heard a patter on the iron roof.

"Rain," said Wim. "It's starting to rain."

Moments later, the patter had intensified to a roar like the beating of drums.

"How are we ever going to find the tracks now? My poor brother!"

"I think it's unlikely they would have taken the western road," said Helge. "But they could have gone north towards Wellborough or east towards Southport. What are we going to do?"

"I suggest," said Perkin, "that we must continue our quest for the last tooth. When we get to Wellborough, a couple of us can go to seek help from Tobin. He'll know what to do."

Wim shook his head. "That will take days," he said. "I need to help Sim now, but I daren't risk flying when Gordeve might still be around. It's too dangerous."

HOPE

"I'm sorry, Wim, but Perkin's right," said Helge. "We can't do anything for our friends without Tobin's help. I'm the leader, and have decided we must continue with our quest. No arguments. Now let's look at the instructions for finding the last tooth?"

Vinny handed the piece of paper to Helge, who began to read the instructions once again.

"In Air's shadow stands a town,
Surrounded by fertile land,
With rills dancing down,
And hills planted with fruit, olives and grapes ... "

Alvin interrupted her. "That sounds familiar," he said.

"Isn't it the town Trumper described to us, the town where he grew up?" said Vinny. "What was its name?"

They racked their brains for several seconds, before a broad grin appeared on Vylin's face. "I've got it," she said. "It's Veca. We must travel to Veca and find this place of prayer. It's only a day's walk west of Rivermeet. We must set off at once for Rivermeet. We'll be so happy to return to our home, won't we Alvin, Perkin?"

"Yes," affirmed Alvin. "In that case we'd prefer not to be the ones to go to Tobin's castle to seek his help."

"I'll go to Tobin," volunteered Helge.

"No," said Vinny. "You're the leader. I'll go."

"And I will accompany you," said Jippers. "The sooner we get there, the sooner we can get my Hope back."

* * * * *

SACUMED

On the third day after their departure from Cambel, late in the afternoon, Sim and Squire approached Wellborough from the south. Sim had removed the gag from his prisoner's mouth, but his hands remained bound.

When they rounded a bend in the road, silhouetted against the evening sun, they saw a stooped figure walking ahead of them. As they got closer, Squire noticed that the man had long grey hair and a grey beard.

The old man turned when he heard the sound of the approaching pony and mule. A ragged cloak hung from his hunched shoulders and the trousers covering his hobbling knees had patches on them. Squire thought the wrinkled face looked familiar.

The man smiled. "Good day to you, sirs," he said. When they approached more closely, his old eyes focused on the face of Squire. He tried to recall where they had met before, when the mule nuzzled up to him and brayed.

"Faithful!" he exclaimed. "It's my old friend Faithful. Aren't you one of the people who bought him from me?" he asked, addressing Squire.

"Yes indeed. We gave you thirty shillings for him."

As he was about to reply, the old man's eyes lit upon the ropes around Squire's wrists.

His mind raced while he considered what he had seen. *Why is he a prisoner? This man and his friends were very kind to me. Who is the stranger who has bound his wrists, and why? And, it wasn't thirty shillings they gave me, it was sixty. He's trying to tell me something. I know what to do. I'll pretend I've seen nothing, and go on my way. Then I'll go home, gather a few things together and get to Tobin as quickly as possible.*

"Yes, that's right, thirty shillings it was," he said. "And a good price it was too. Well, I'll be wishing you a good day, sirs. I must be getting back home."

HOPE

The old man scuttled away and turned off the main highway into a side road leading towards the west. He didn't hurry too much to avoid rousing suspicion from the other stranger, but he did not want to tarry either.

*   *   *   *   *

Sim watched the old man pass out of sight over the brow of a hill. *It was a mistake to let him see Squire's tied wrists*, he thought. *I mustn't make that kind of blunder again. I don't think he noticed anything. He's very old and probably can't see clearly. However, I must take every precaution not to let anyone else see that Squire is my prisoner.*

Since departing from Cambel, they had not booked into any inn, but had always slept rough close to the roadside, in a small copse of trees, or concealed behind some rocks. After the meeting with the old man, they now hid when anyone approached them on the road, and skirted around the perimeters of the towns and villages.

*   *   *   *   *

The old man was a slow walker. During his journey, he made frequent stops to rest his weary bones, and it took him four days to reach Tobin's castle. He arrived there just as the sun set. The drawbridge was up, but he found a bell on the outside of the moat, which he rang. After about ten minutes, he heard the sound of approaching footsteps on the cobblestones inside the castle walls, and then a thin face appeared in a small opening in the gate.

"May I help you?" asked Digbee.

"I urgently need to speak to the wizard Tobin," said the old man.

"My master has already retired to his chambers, and will not see anyone else today."

SACUMED

"It's very urgent. I must see him at once. Please tell him that Sacumed is here."

Digbee glared. "Very well," he said. "Wait here."

The servant returned a few minutes later. "My master will see you now," he said. He let down the drawbridge and opened the gate. Sacumed crossed the moat and passed through the gate. Digbee invited Sacumed to follow him and led him through a series of courtyards and along narrow stone passages until they reached the foot of the stone spiral staircase that led to the wizard's study. Sacumed found the ascent very exhausting and had to stop every few steps to catch his breath. When they arrived at the top, Digbee knocked on the door.

The booming voice of Tobin bade them to enter. Digbee turned the huge brass knob and opened the heavy timber door into the wizard's study.

"Sacumed!" exclaimed the wizard. "It's good to see you, my old friend." They embraced. "But you look tired. Have you had a difficult journey?"

"I need to talk with you in private," said Sacumed. "It's a matter of great urgency."

"Of course," replied Tobin. "Digbee, please leave us."

"Yes, master," said Digbee. As he turned to leave, he cast a nervous glance towards the old man. *Sacumed? I'm sure Gordeve has mentioned that name to me before*, he thought.

After the door had closed, Digbee descended a few steps, making sure that the wizard could hear his footsteps. Then he turned and crept back up to the door. He pressed his right ear to the keyhole and listened. Sacumed began to relate the story of the encounter with Squire and the other man whom he had not recognised.

"Can you describe him to me?" asked Tobin.

HOPE

"He was not very tall," said Sacumed. "He had short, brown hair and just a wisp of a beard. He had a roundish sort of face, and a flat nose. He wore a cloak like yours, and no shoes."

"Did he carry a staff?"

"I didn't see one, but he might have kept it hidden to conceal his true identity."

"It sounds very much like one of the twins," declared Tobin. "But did you not say that Squire's wrists were tied as if he were a prisoner? How can this be?" Tobin paused. "Not unless my evil sister has corrupted one of them. However, the twins are always together, so if she has corrupted one, then why has she not also corrupted the other? Except … " He paused again. "There was one time when Sim was on his own, the time when he looked after my castle while I attended the council at Fort Holt. However, Gordeve could not have made contact with him then unless ... unless Digbee also knew of it. There can only be one explanation – Digbee is in the service of Gordeve."

Digbee's right ear was burning. He jumped up from his crouched position, climbed onto the sill of the window at the top of the staircase, said the familiar words that Gordeve had taught him, and transformed into a bat.

"It looks very likely," agreed Sacumed. "I never trusted him. That's why I requested an audience with you alone."

Tobin strode to the window overlooking the courtyard and flung it open. "Digbee," he shouted. There was no reply, only the sound of the flapping of wings as a bat took off towards the east.

"Sacumed, you wait here," ordered Tobin. "I'll be back in just a few minutes." With that, the wizard transformed himself into the form of the giant eagle and took off in pursuit of the bat.

SACUMED

A quarter of an hour later the eagle returned and alighted on the windowsill, a wriggling bat held firmly in his beak. The eagle flung the bat onto the study floor, and then transformed himself back into the wizard. At the same time, a shaken Digbee appeared writhing on the floor.

"Explain yourself, Digbee," Tobin commanded.

The servant clasped his hands together. "Have mercy on me, master," he pleaded.

"How long have you worked for my sister?" demanded the wizard.

"For more than twenty years, ever since the twins came here to study with you," replied Digbee. "She forced me to work for her. She said she would turn me permanently into a bat, skin me alive, and eat my flesh if I did not do as she commanded." As he spoke, he wrung his hands together and cowered into a corner of the room.

The wizard glowered. His red face showed no sign of sympathy for the treacherous servant.

"You foolish man," he cried. "Did you not know that I could protect you from her threats? Did your former loyalty count for nothing?"

The servant appeared confused and frightened. "Yes, no, I mean ... please forgive me."

"Now tell me about the time I was away at the council of Fort Holt," demanded Tobin.

Digbee hesitantly related the story of Gordeve's visit, the revelation that she was the mother of the twins, and the details of how she had succeeded in corrupting Sim. Sacumed gasped as he heard for the first time the news that the twins were the sons of the wicked wizard.

Tobin raised his staff and banged it down onto the floor with a crash. "This is very serious," he declared. "Sacumed, I need your help. I'll lock this rogue up in the dungeon beneath my castle. I need you to guard him and provide for him, and also to look after the castle while I go in pursuit of Sim and Squire. I will leave first thing in the morning. I will only be gone a few hours. Do you think you can do that for me, my old friend?"

The old man nodded. "Of course I will help you, my dear fellow," he replied. "But don't be long. I'm not a wizard and have no defence against Gordeve if she should come to try to rescue Digbee."

"Don't worry," said Tobin. "She won't yet be aware that we've exposed him."

*   *   *   *   *

Early the next morning, just as the sun's first rays streamed in through the east-facing window of the tower where Tobin lived and studied, he departed. Though reluctant to leave the safety of his castle, he felt that the situation was so serious that he had no choice. With Digbee incarcerated and his old friend Sacumed to look after things, he was willing to take the risk of leaving the castle for a few hours. However, he did not go at once to find Sim and Squire, but took the opportunity to investigate developments in other parts of Thorland.

First, he flew north-eastwards to assess the situation on the other side of the wall. Landing on the wall north of the Oasis of Yedi, he was aghast to see a multitude of tents housing Gordeve's army, both men and Kobalos, as they slept during the day. The tents were well concealed from the view of any who should chance to look from the top of the wall, but not from the eye of the eagle. *There must be at least a thousand of them*, he thought.

Without hesitation, he took off once again and swiftly flew eastwards to Dunton where he landed outside the tent of Ben Lei and transformed himself back into the form of the wizard.

SACUMED

Ben Lei's guards recognised the renowned wizard and sent a message at once to their chief. At Tobin's request, Ben Lei immediately called a meeting with Yohan and his other chiefs.

"Gordeve's army is on the move westwards towards Boggarton," the wizard reported. "It looks like they're force-marching their way along the northern highway, travelling by night and resting by day. I estimate they will arrive there in two or three days' time. I don't know for sure what is the purpose of their advancement, but it would seem likely that the secret way through or under the wall must be situated somewhere near Boggarton. Is there any word from Queen Sofee?"

Yohan replied, "The queen herself led the contingent travelling in a westward direction from Dun Wood, and she and her group should by now be north of the western extremity of the desert, about three days away from the place where the wall meets the Air Mountains near the caves of Boggart. The latest message we received told us that so far they have discovered nothing. Similarly, the other group, which travelled south and east from Dun Wood, has found no breaches in the wall. They are reported to be south of Patumann's Tunnel and expect to reach the coast near Ash Wood in another two or three days."

"If I am correct and there is a secret way somewhere near the western end of the wall, we must expect an attack in the northern part of West Thorland close to Swanborough," said Tobin. "The enemy is relying on surprise, but we must outwit them. Ben Lei, I urge you to rally some of your men and ride with haste westwards to Swanborough. With your strong horses you should be able to cover the distance in three or four days."

"It shall be done," replied the chief. "Yohan will lead a company of five hundred Telekai. I cannot spare more since we must also be prepared to defend the gate through the wall at Dun Wood."

HOPE

"It is well," declared the wizard. Before leaving, he briefed Ben Lei and the chiefs on his other news. "I must go at once now to intercept my nephew and Squire before it's too late," he said.

*   *   *   *   *

The day before Tobin's flight, Sim and Squire had arrived on the outskirts of Swanborough, a small ancient town on the upper reaches of the Swan River. By the time the wizard left Dunton, they had departed from Swanborough and begun the ascent to the Caves of Boggart. Gordeve had told Sim that a secret way through the caves to the other side of the wall existed, but he didn't know exactly where to find the entrance. However, she had promised him that friends would be there waiting to show him the way. The path to the caves, narrow and in parts very steep, was strewn with small rocks that made their progress slow.

In the middle of the day, despite the coolness of the winter sun, they were sweating from the exertion of the climb and fighting fatigue, when Tobin caught up with them.

The only warning Sim had was a last minute gust of air from the giant bird's wings, followed by a screech. He looked up. The cold winter sun dazzled him, and then dust flew into his eyes as the eagle came in to land a few metres in front of him. Before Sim had time to recover, the eagle had transformed once again into the shape of the old wizard. The mule was also startled and kicked its rear legs and the pony tugged hard on the lead held by Sim. Finding it difficult to control both animals, he let go of the lead and Conny trotted off with Squire on her back.

When Sim had regained his composure and calmed the mule, he addressed the older wizard.

"Uncle!" he exclaimed. "How nice of you to drop in. But how did you know where to find us?"

SACUMED

"You foolish boy," boomed Tobin. "What do you expect to gain from this treachery?"

"Treachery! You, Uncle, are the traitor. My mother has told me all about how you stole us from her soon after we were born. She's the good one, and *you* are evil."

These words so angered Tobin that he raised his staff and pointed it towards Sim, intending to teach the young wizard a lesson he would not forget. As he did so, he noticed too late, that Sim held something in his hand, as if to protect himself. A beam of energy had already passed from Tobin's staff before he saw that his nephew held the Shield of Squire. The force of the beam hitting the shield knocked Sim over and he lay stunned on the ground. Before Tobin could grab him or the shield, he had disappeared.

Tobin reached for the shield himself, and moments later, he too had passed through to the world of Squire and Jippers.

When Theresa awoke, she saw her father a short distance away, tied up and gagged, blood still pouring from a gash to his head. Then she became aware of another man bending over her and peering into her eyes. Earlier, when she had grabbed hold of the log that careered towards the waterfall, she had just caught a glimpse of this man before she had lost consciousness. The man bending over her now was the same strange, spirit-like man who had carried her from the water to the safety of the riverbank; the short man with the roundish face and flat nose. "What's happened to my daddy?" she asked. "Why is he tied up?"

The man did not answer, but bent down and roughly lifted her into his arms, and started to walk away from the spot where Grant lay. After a time he put her down and allowed her to walk, but his strong

HOPE

arms held her as he pushed her along the path that led away from the river.

"Let me go," screamed the terrified girl. "Before you were kind to me, but now you are being cruel. I don't understand."

The next moment, another stranger appeared on the path in front of them. He looked similar to the one who had abducted her, but much older, and he had a long grey beard. She felt the grip on her arms relax, and managed to escape from the hold of the wicked man. She ran into the forest and hid behind a tree.

From the safety of her hiding place, she observed that the two strangers were fighting each other, but they were not using their fists or any kind of conventional weapon. Each of them held a strange looking stick in his hand and beams of light came from the end of each stick. More like the kind of weapon you see in a science fiction movie, she thought.

For several minutes the two men fought, each of them knocked down from time to time as light from the other's stick struck him. Nevertheless, each time one of them was struck, he quickly jumped to his feet and held his staff ready to ward off another blow. They seem to be evenly matched, she thought, and neither of them is quick enough to press home the advantage. The light coming from the sticks seems to hurt them without doing any real harm – something like an electric shock.

After the struggle had continued for some time, the younger stranger fell again, but this time he did not get up immediately. Then she saw the older man offer his hand to the younger. He helped him to his feet, and the two embraced. The next moment they vanished.

SACUMED

Theresa rubbed her eyes thinking it had all been a dream. Then she ran to her father's side and shook him.

"Daddy, wake up," she implored. "Guess what I've just seen?"

A shrill whistle from Sim brought the pony trotting to his side. Squire still sat on Conny's back, tied up and gagged. As Sim cut the ropes, he noticed that Squire's wrists were raw and bleeding. Then he removed the gag and held out the shield to Squire.

"Here, this is yours," he said. "Sorry I had to borrow it."

Squire accepted the shield and glared at Sim. "What's going on?" he asked. Then he turned in surprise as he recognised another familiar voice.

"Don't worry, my friend. You are safe now."

"Tobin! What's going on?"

"Sim will explain everything to you."

After Sim had finished relating the story of his corruption by Gordeve, and Squire's abduction and release, he concluded, "Please forgive me for tying you up. You see, my uncle has come to us and freed me from the spell my mother placed on me."

Squire looked at Tobin. "Your uncle ... your mother?" he said.

"Yes, it's true," the old wizard replied. "Gordeve is the mother of Sim and Wim, and therefore I am their uncle. I rescued them from her wicked clutches when they were babies, and brought them up. I have taught them since they were very young, and have indoctrinated them only with good. Unfortunately, Sim's mother came to him when I was away at Fort Holt. Thankfully, I just caught you two in time before you reached the Caves of Boggart. Sim and I fought. After a struggle, I overpowered him, and revoked the spell that had bound him."

HOPE

"Where are the others?" asked Squire.

"The last I heard they were approaching Wellborough," replied Tobin. "When I leave you, I will go to check on their progress. It's not necessary for you go back to try to find them now. They can manage without you. Gordeve is amassing her troops at Boggarton, just on the other side of the wall from here, and we are expecting an attack from her army in the next few days. You and Sim are needed here."

"Uncle," said Sim, "an advance party must already be on this side of the wall waiting near the entrance to the caves. Gordeve … my mother … told me that friends would be waiting to lead my prisoner and me through the caves."

"Then you must deal with them at once," commanded Tobin. "I'm sure you can do this without my help. I've been away from my castle too long already and must return there at once. Squire, you must pretend that you are still Sim's prisoner. After you have dealt with your 'friends', I want you two to return to Swanborough and wait for the arrival of Yohan and the Telekai. They should be arriving there in about three days from now. You must assist them in the battle. The other members of your company can find the last tooth, and we will all meet back at my castle when your work is done."

"Yes, uncle," replied Sim, "we will do as you say … Uncle," he continued, "if Digbee is proved to be a traitor, who is looking after your castle?"

"Sacumed."

"Sacumed. Who is Sacumed?" asked Squire.

"He's an old friend. You know him as the old man who sold you the mule, Faithful. But, he has yet an even more important part to play in the battles ahead. Now I must bid farewell to you both."

SACUMED

Squire mounted the pony and Sim replaced the gag and retied the ropes around his former prisoner's wrists, but not too tightly, so that he could easily free himself when required. Then they resumed their climb up the narrow path towards the Caves of Boggart.

An hour later, as they rounded a bend in the track, they heard a challenging cry of "Halt". They found themselves surrounded by a group of twelve gruesome Kobalos.

CHAPTER 20

RETURN TO TOBIN'S CASTLE

"Friends, I am Sim, son of Gordeve," said the young wizard, using the language of the east. He spoke calmly, without his voice betraying the nervousness he felt. "I bring the prisoner, Squire, and his shield that my mother craves. I'd been expecting you to meet us. Can you lead us through the caves so that we may find a safe route to my mother's castle?"

"Welcome, Sim," said the leader of the Kobalos. "Please follow us. You must leave the mule and pony here."

Sim dismounted from Faithful and one of the Kobalos pushed Squire roughly from Conny's back. Sim tied the two animals to a branch of a small tree and followed the Kobalos. One of the Kobalos, a huge brute with a high forehead, snatched the shield from Squire and grabbed hold of him by the neck. He raised his fist as if preparing to smash it into Squire's face, but stopped when he felt a cord around the latter's neck.

"What's this?" He yanked on the cord, which broke. "Aha, a pouch!"

"What's inside?" asked another, who had only one eye.

"Teeth, gold teeth." He popped the pouch into his pocket. The one eye followed the pouch's passage into his friend's pocket.

After ascending for a few hundred metres, they arrived at the southern entrance to the caves and passed inside.

"Wait a minute," said Sim before they had left the entrance behind. "I will place a spell of binding at the cave entrance so that none may follow us." The Kobalos leader nodded his compliance.

RETURN TO TOBIN'S CASTLE

Sim raised his staff. Just at that moment, a scuffle broke out as the Kobalos with one eye tried to wrest the pouch from the one with the high forehead. In the confusion, the pouch fell to the floor and several Kobalos rushed for it.

Instead of creating the spell of binding, Sim spoke the words of a spell of changing. As light shot from the tip of his staff, he rapidly rotated it in an arc to envelop all the Kobalos and commanded, "Kobalos writhe."

Within a few seconds, the swing of the arc had transformed all of the Kobalos into a group of angry, hissing snakes. The wizard raised the staff once again and spoke to the snakes. "Find a hole in which to hide," he ordered, "and don't come back." One by one, the snakes silently slithered into holes and crevices in the rock floor of the cave, and that was the last anyone ever saw of them.

Squire removed the ropes from his wrists and picked up the shield that lay undamaged on the floor of the cave. Nearby he found the pouch containing the teeth.

"Let's go to Swanborough," he said.

*　　*　　*　　*　　*

Queen Sofee and her group had set up camp near the western end of the wall due south of Boggarton and some fifty kilometres north-east of Swanborough. They had now almost accomplished their mission, and so far had found no place where the wall could be breached, nor any tunnel under the wall.

"Our last hope is where the wall meets the mountains," said the queen to her aide. "Maybe we will find some track across the mountains, or caves beneath them, that will lead to the other side of the wall."

They were preparing their supper when the silence was disturbed by the sound of hooves, many hooves, approaching from the east.

HOPE

A sentry rode into camp, jumped from his horse and burst into the tent of the queen's aide with the news, "A large group of Telekai warriors is drawing near to the camp."

The aide took the message to Sofee who emerged from her tent to await the riders. As the sounds got nearer, clouds of dust heralded the arrival of the army of five hundred Telekai.

Even at a distance, she could recognise Yohan at the head of the army, riding on Windracer, his long blond hair blowing in the wind. As he approached, the queen's heart raced. *It's him,* she thought, *my love. He looks so young for his years, so handsome and strong of character. He's the one who will be my regent.*

He reined in his horse in front of Sofee's tent, and dismounted. The Telekai warriors also dismounted at a distance and prepared to set up camp for the night.

As Yohan approached the queen, he lowered himself onto one knee and bowed his head. "Your Majesty," he said.

"Please stand up, sir," commanded the queen. "Enter my tent, so that we may have counsel." After they had seated themselves inside the royal tent, the queen continued, "What brings you and your Telekai army to this remote corner of West Thorland?"

"Your Majesty," he replied, "three days ago the wizard Tobin visited us at Dunton. He brought news that the enemy is on the move north of the wall heading towards Boggarton, and that we should expect an attack on West Thorland through the Caves of Boggart."

"It is as I suspected," said Queen Sofee. "There is a way, and there are caves."

"Tobin urged Ben Lei to send an army to quash the enemy, and I was charged to take command of this army of five hundred. However, there is

RETURN TO TOBIN'S CASTLE

more news," he continued, "the wizard Sim has been corrupted by Gordeve, who is his mother, and is even now approaching the Caves of Boggart from the south with Squire as his captive. He intends to deliver Squire and the shield to Gordeve."

"His mother did you say?"

"Yes, it's true, Gordeve is the mother of Sim and Wim. Your Majesty, we must depart at first light for the Caves of Boggart. Will you and your people accompany us?"

"We are not trained for fighting," replied the queen. "However, we will come and wait for you at Swanborough."

*   *   *   *   *

Meanwhile the army of Kobalos, cougars and men from East Thorland, more than one thousand altogether, had already left Boggarton on their way to the northern entrance to the caves.

From Boggarton they had a twenty-kilometre hike up into the mountains along a rough track that rose steeply at times, until they reached the northern upper entrance to the caves, an entrance large enough for the men to walk inside without stooping.

Some of the Kobalos and cougars had made forays into West Thorland before, and the way through the caves was familiar to them. The Kobalos leader, who was one of them, said, "For speed we will take the upper level. It is much drier than the lower level and should take us no more than a day. Follow me."

From the northern upper entrance to the caves, he led them along a series of low narrow passages, past an ancient catacomb, and along more passages until, after about an hour, they reached one of the wonders of the Caves of Boggart. Some of the men stopped to marvel at the vertical limestone shaft that stretched high above them to some point in the upper reaches of the mountains. Beams of light from above reached down the limestone walls to produce a myriad of bright sparkling colours. The same shaft plunged far below them to the subterranean Boggart River at the lower level – the course of an ancient waterfall, now dry except at times of heavy rainfall.

"What are you waiting for?" said the leader. "We haven't got time to waste gawping at some wonder of the Creator. Move yourselves."

They continued along another series of narrow tunnels until they reached an enormous cavern adorned with several large stalagmites and stalactites, and hundreds of smaller ones. Some of the stalagmites stood erect like sentinels, some stalactites reached down like giant fingers from the roof above. In other parts of the cave, after thousands of years of reaching out to each other, stalagmites and stalactites had joined to form limestone columns.

Urged on by their leader, Gordeve's troops did not stop to admire these wonders, but proceeded into another series of narrow tunnels, some with ceilings so low that the men among them were forced to stoop, though the Kobalos and cougars had no such problem.

Soon afterwards, the leader took them through a group of three large interconnected caverns. One wall of the third cavern, where water must have seeped down from above over many generations, was adorned with festoons of stalagmites, stalactites and columns. The people of Swanborough had named this cavern 'The Pipe Organ'. From this cavern, a narrow passage led off towards the west.

"That passage leads to a dead-end," said the Kobalos leader who had been there before. "We must follow that tunnel." He pointed to a slightly wider tunnel that led southwards and downwards towards the southern exit, and into West Thorland. He had hardly finished speaking before some of the

RETURN TO TOBIN'S CASTLE

Kobalos and men, eager to reach the open air, pushed past him and rushed down the tunnel.

The southern exit, marking the route of a dried up stream that had once run into the Swan River, was much smaller than the northern one. From the narrow entrance a path, the former bed of the stream, dropped steeply down towards the south.

However, Sim, Yohan and the Telekai had already arrived and had planned their ambush. The first part of the plan comprised an illusion created by Sim. He used magic to replace the steep downward path with a much gentler looking track that wound its way lazily down towards Swanborough. The leaders of the group, who had been through the caves before, knew about the sudden drop, but were too late to warn the ones who had rushed ahead.

As the first few dozen of Gordeve's army emerged from the exit, glad to be free of the claustrophobic caves, they charged out expecting to run onto a gently sloping path. Instead, their feet trod on air and they found themselves tumbling helplessly down the steep slope. They then proved easy prey for the Telekai warriors who waited for them below.

The enemy troops who came behind the first group pulled up abruptly as they saw what had happened to their fellows.

"Where did they go to?" asked one. "They fell, and then … disappeared."

"How could they just disappear?" asked another.

"It's a trick, an illusion," said a third.

They stood helplessly at the exit, not daring to go forwards, yet being pushed and jostled by others coming from behind. Those at the front could not hold on as the sheer weight of those coming behind forced them to lose their balance. They toppled over and rolled down the slope.

HOPE

Eventually the shouts of some of them reached the ears of those behind and they managed to arrest the forward surge. The armies of Gordeve now stood motionless and vulnerable inside the narrow tunnels at the southern end of the Caves of Boggart, not knowing what to do next.

The next moment, more shouts of warning came from deep inside the caves. The surge of panic resumed and more of the Kobalos and men were pushed down the slope.

The cause of the shouts was the result of the second part of Yohan's plan. He and the remainder of the Telekai warriors had waited silently in the narrow passage that led westwards from 'The Pipe Organ'. After the last of the enemy had passed by, the Telekai stole along the narrow passage and into 'The Pipe Organ' to cut off their means of retreat, thus trapping the enemy.

On two fronts, the Telekai warriors attacked with their sharp, curved blades. The enemy were unprepared and found it difficult to move to defend themselves in the confined spaces. In the confusion the cougars, who detested being trapped in these narrow claustrophobic passages, turned on their own troops in an attempt to escape. Chaos ensued in the narrow spaces as snarling cougars pitted against fierce Kobalos. Through advantage of numbers, the Kobalos and men succeeded in overcoming the cougars, and slaughtered every one of them, but there was no escape. Though some of them fought bravely and the Telekai suffered a number of casualties, the latter had the strategic advantage. It was only a matter of time before the enemy surrendered.

When Sim removed the illusion he had created earlier, the defeated troops of Gordeve were relieved to step out onto firm ground and to breathe freely again. As they left the cave, they surrendered their weapons. A sorry file of Kobalos and men wound its way under guard down towards Swanborough.

RETURN TO TOBIN'S CASTLE

Queen Sofee and her volunteers had waited at Swanborough, together with Squire. The queen was jubilant when she saw the proud Telekai warriors mounted on their horses herding the captive enemy troops towards the town. Finally, she caught sight of Yohan on Windracer bringing up the rear. When he reached her tent, he dismounted and approached, preparing to kneel once again. As their eyes met, the queen felt a surge of emotion, signalling both relief that Yohan was unharmed and a strong desire to embrace him. Ignoring etiquette, she jumped up, ran towards him and threw herself into his arms.

"Your Majesty!" he exclaimed. "It is not fitting that you should hold me thus."

"Sir, it befits a future prince to embrace his future bride," she replied. Yohan did not comment, but held her tightly in his arms.

*   *   *   *   *

Three days earlier, after Tobin had left Sim and Squire near the Caves of Boggart, he had flown southwards to check on the movement of the rest of the company, and found them making slow progress on the road north from Tee Crossing not far from Wellborough. He did not land, but looked down with satisfaction to see that they progressed unhindered.

When they arrived at Wellborough, they stayed for only a few hours, just enough time for Vinny to catch up with his old friends Reddy, Xoe and Jillijon. There wasn't time for him to fulfil his promise to give them another 'pasting' in field archery, but they were very interested to hear about all the adventures that the company had experienced over the last six months.

The time came once more for the company to separate into two groups. Vinny and Jippers set off towards the west on the road to Tobin's castle. Helge, Wim and the three Luchorpans headed northwards towards Rivermeet.

HOPE

Both groups arrived at their next destinations at about the same time on the afternoon of the same day. It was the day of the routing of the enemy at the Caves of Boggart.

Vinny and Jippers arrived at the wizard's castle and rang the bell. The old man who came to open the gate looked familiar to Vinny.

"What are you doing here?" he asked. "And where's Digbee?"

"It was I who brought news that your friend Squire was a prisoner of the wizard Sim," replied Sacumed. "As a result, the traitor Digbee was also exposed."

"Squire is a prisoner of Sim! Digbee's a traitor?"

"I think you had better come in and let Tobin explain everything to you," said Sacumed.

He led Vinny and Jippers through the passageways and courtyards and up the staircase to Tobin's study. The old wizard spent the next half an hour explaining everything that had happened, right up to the moment that he had left Sim and Squire on the approach to the Caves of Boggart.

"So you see," he concluded, "although your reasons for coming here to seek my help were laudable, they have proved unnecessary. Thanks to my old friend Sacumed, I already knew what was going on. By now, the Telekai and my nephew will have defeated Gordeve's army. Sim and Squire may well be on their way back here already."

*   *   *   *   *

Meanwhile the other five members of the company had arrived at Rivermeet and decided to stay for a couple of nights in the Luchorpans' own homes. Helge was the guest of Alvin and Vylin at the Shoemaker's home, and the Goldmaster family at Perkin's house entertained Wim.

The Luchorpans did an impromptu dance when they discovered that they had arrived at Rivermeet on the eve of the winter solstice.

RETURN TO TOBIN'S CASTLE

"Do you remember the midsummer solstice?" Alvin asked Helge. "We have a similar celebration for the winter solstice. There are differences, though. One is that the sun's rays don't stream through the hole in the rock as they do at sunrise on the morning of the summer solstice. Nevertheless, we have a celebration just the same. There will be dancing and lots of ale."

That evening the five companions travelled to the grassy embankment between the two rivers situated two or three kilometres to the west of the town. More than three hundred Luchorpans also travelled to the site outside Rivermeet where they had traditionally met every year, twice a year, since the migration from Luchor. Each of them carried a torch, and they noticed that a sea of bonfires already covered the embankment.

Unlike the midsummer festival, which started early in the morning before sunrise, at the time of the winter solstice families arrived on the day before and kept vigil throughout the night with fires burning brightly.

"The purpose of the fires is, we believe, to aid the sun in its battle against darkness," explained Alvin as they approached. "The passing of the winter solstice is also a symbolic celebration of growing light and a commemoration of spiritual rebirth."

"Look, it's almost time for 'The bowl of fate'," said Perkin.

"What's 'The bowl of fate'?" asked Helge.

"It's another popular tradition at the time of the winter solstice. All those present at the festival write their names on slips of paper and place them in a large bowl. One of the elders, or sometimes a specially invited guest, draws the slips of paper from the bowl two at a time. We believe that the two people whose names are drawn together will forever remain friends."

"You have been chosen as the special guest this year," Vylin said to Helge, "and given the honour of drawing the slips of paper from the bowl."

HOPE

After Helge had drawn several pairs of names, she selected Alvin's name together with that of Daykin, the Luchorpan they had met at the Festival of Music and Dance at Jackville. Then, a little later on, she drew Perkin's name together with that of Vylin. When Helge called out their names, Perkin blushed once again and glanced furtively towards Vylin who smiled, and giggled.

"Now we know your secret," Alvin whispered to Perkin, "the secret that Percival mentioned. Don't worry, my friend. I shall not stand in your way if you wish to marry my sister."

* * * * *

The following day, the five friends left Rivermeet and took the westward road towards the small hill town of Veca, arriving there late the same day. As they approached the town, they passed through fertile farmland and alongside hillsides planted with grape vines, fruit trees and olive groves. Small streams ran down from the mountains above to the valley of the Butterfly River below.

"It's just as Trumper described it," said Vylin, "– twenty stone houses lying in the shadow of the Air Mountains, all clustered together around a central marketplace."

"Yes, it's not difficult to imagine the young boy genius roaming these hills, gleaning his first knowledge about the natural world around him," said Helge.

Veca had no inn, so they were obliged to sleep once again in their tents. Ever since they had left Cambel, without the aid of the mule and the pony, they had carried their tents and provisions in their backpacks and they were always very tired by the end of the day, especially the diminutive Vylin. As she rested, the savoury aroma of roasting rabbits reached her nose, and she was once again grateful for the expertise of Helge with the sling. She peeped out of her tent and observed with pride that Perkin was the chef that evening.

The next morning, they completed the short walk to Veca Monastery, on the northern bank of the Butterfly River. To reach the other side they had to pass over a narrow suspension bridge. It reminded Perkin and Vylin of the suspension bridge over the Hom River, but this one was much shorter and closer to the water's surface. They had no fears as they crossed, and arrived safely at the monastery soon after midday.

At the main entrance to the monastery, another monk greeted them. Like Brother Beghlin, he was clean-shaven and the hair on his head was cut very short. He also wore a simple orange robe tied at the waist with a rope, and sandals on his feet, but there the similarity stopped. This man, who introduced himself as Brother Ferrin, was tall and skinny and walked with a limp.

"Welcome to Veca Monastery," Brother Ferrin greeted them. "What can I do for you, my friends?"

Helge spoke on behalf of the group. "Thank you for your welcome, brother. My name is Helge. I hail from Hanlin Forest. My three Luchorpan friends Perkin, Alvin and Vylin are from Rivermeet, and this is the wizard Wim, lately apprentice to the wizard Tobin. We are on a mission for Tobin, seeking out the golden teeth that belong to the golden skull."

"I've heard tell of Tobin," said Brother Ferrin, "and have some knowledge of the golden skull of which you speak, but how can *we* help you?"

"The instructions which we follow tell us to seek out a cloistered courtyard with a fountain," replied Helge. "We believe these may be found within the walls of your monastery."

HOPE

"Yes indeed," said the monk. "We have such a fountain in the inner courtyard of the monastery. Please follow me inside to see whether or not this is the one you seek."

The five friends followed as Ferrin limped through two rooms and along a short passage that opened onto a courtyard surrounded by a cloistered corridor. The courtyard was resplendent with foliage.

"When spring arrives and the flowers bloom, this courtyard is a beautiful sight," said Ferrin.

In the middle of the courtyard, they saw a concreted area, and at its centre a fountain. The fountain was an unusual one, made in the shape of a volcanic mountain. Water overflowed from the lips of the crater of the volcano.

"It was a gift from the brothers of Atmos Monastery," explained the monk. "Their monastery sits in the foothills of the mountain on which this one is modelled."

Helge looked into the monk's eyes. "If you don't mind," she said, "I would like to feel inside the crater of that mountain."

He raised his eyebrows and shrugged his shoulders. "By all means. Be my guest."

Helge hauled herself up onto a ledge that surrounded the fountain and, standing on tiptoes, just managed to stretch her arm to reach inside the crater of the mountain. She had to search around for some time with the tips of her fingers before she found what she was looking for – a small corked glass bottle. She removed the cork and pulled out the tooth, the final tooth of the upper jaw. She found no instructions with it, for they already knew their next destination, Tobin's castle. In the absence of Squire and the pouch, Helge carefully placed the bottle containing the final tooth in her tunic pocket intending to deliver it safely to the wizard's castle.

RETURN TO TOBIN'S CASTLE

The return journey to Tobin's castle, which was uneventful, took them six days. However, there were many surprises waiting for them when they arrived there.

* * * * *

Sim, Squire, Yohan, Queen Sofee, and the volunteers from Atmos had left Swanborough a few days earlier, travelling south to Rivermeet. They had just missed meeting up with the other five members of the company returning to Rivermeet from Veca Monastery, preceding them by half a day.

The group from Swanborough continued to travel together until they reached the branch in the road fifty kilometres south of Rivermeet. There the volunteers had taken the road south towards Wellborough on their way home to Atmos. Sim, Squire, Yohan and the queen had followed the other road to the south-west towards Tobin's castle. The betrothed were also on their way to Atmos to be married, but had decided to visit the wizard first. These four arrived at the castle a day ahead of the others.

The Telekai and their prisoners had left Swanborough at about the same time as Yohan's group and for a while followed the same southward route. They were taking the prisoners to Fort Holt where they intended to detain them and interrogate their leaders. However, the prisoners made their progress slow, so the others soon left them behind.

* * * * *

Finally, the company was together again, and Tobin could reunite the teeth of the upper jaw with the golden skull housed inside the cabinet in his study. Vinny, Jippers and Squire already knew the surprise news about the mother of the twins and the way she had tricked Sim, but the three Luchorpans, Helge and especially Wim greeted the news with amazement.

HOPE

"How can it be that these fine, honest young men are the offspring of such an evil woman as Gordeve?" Helge asked.

"The character of the children doesn't come from that of their parents, but rather from the upbringing they receive," Tobin replied. "Fortunately for the twins, I was able to rescue them from their mother when they were yet babies and before she could influence them. However, as the incident with Sim verifies, I made the wrong decision to leave him on his own. Gordeve must not be underestimated. Although the twins are now wizards, she is still much more powerful than they are, and was easily able to corrupt Sim with her evil."

"That is really the hardest part to believe, that they are Gordeve's children, I mean," said Helge.

"It's true," Tobin reiterated. "But there's more to the story, eh Jippers?"

"Yes," replied Jippers. "It's now time for me to reveal my secret to you all, the one Percival referred to. I am the father of Wim and Sim." There were gasps when Jippers paused before continuing. "Thirty years ago, Gordeve summoned me to Thorland, just as Tobin summoned Squire. She must have mistakenly thought that I was the saviour referred to in the prophecy. Soon after my arrival, she took me prisoner and held me for over a year. During that time, she corrupted me into believing that she is a good person and gradually won over my confidence, and my heart. Then the twins were conceived. After they were born, Tobin took them and brought them safely here, so that he could teach them the right way.

"It was during Gordeve's time of grief and anger over the loss of her children that I recognised her true character, and resolved to escape from her evil clutches. One day, when I saw her transform into an eagle and fly off towards the west, I took my chance. I told the Kobalos guard that I intended

RETURN TO TOBIN'S CASTLE

to travel to Wichtlein to purchase some provisions for Gordeve. They did not doubt me since I had made this journey for the same purpose many times before. When I reached Wichtlein, I continued westwards towards the wall. At that time, Patumann's Tunnel was open and I bribed the guards to allow me to pass through. I travelled to Bunbury where I managed to get a job as rat catcher to the king." He turned to face Squire. "I stayed in the service of the king until you and your friends arrived, and the shield brought me my Hope."

"That is indeed a strange story," said Helge. "Your desire, your hope, to return to your own world is obvious, but is it possible?" She turned to face Tobin. "Can the shield help Jippers and Squire find a way back to their homes and loved-ones?"

"It's possible," replied Tobin, "but will require more than just magic to accomplish. When the time is right, the way will be revealed to Squire. As for Jippers, I am not sure. It was never his destiny to come here in the first place. It was only the result of a foolish mistake by my sister."

"How could Gordeve make such a mistake?" asked Helge. "They don't even look similar."

"I have a small scar above my top lip on the left side. My moustache conceals it," Jippers replied. "And when I was younger, I more closely resembled Squire. I believe that is why she made the mistake."

"It was indeed an unfortunate mistake for you, Jippers," Tobin concluded.

*   *   *   *   *

They all stayed at the castle for two days before going their separate ways.

"Well," said Tobin. "It's now time for us to separate once again. Vinny, Alvin, Perkin and Vylin, you may return to your homes for a well-

HOPE

earned rest. Helge, you still have a promise to keep after you return to your cottage. The mule, Faithful, shall go with you on your journey to Ash Wood. Squire, the twins and the pony will remain with me here. Jippers, you may also stay if you wish. I charge you all to meet here again in three months' time, so that you can begin 'The Quest for the Teeth of the Lower Jaw'."

Finally, he turned to the queen and Yohan. "Your Majesty, my Lord Yohan," he began, "it has indeed been a pleasure to have you stay at my castle. I rejoice at the announcement of your betrothal and I wish you both a safe passage to Atmos and good fortune for your imminent marriage. As you may have guessed, each of you will have a very important part to play in the battles ahead in the struggle to free our lands from evil. Now go in peace, all of you, until we meet again."

EPILOGUE

Thus concludes the first book of 'Windows on Our World'.

'The Quest for the Teeth of the Lower Jaw' continues in the second book of the trilogy, called 'Faith'. This sees our company encounter a new set of adventures in the lands to the west of the Air Mountains. Meanwhile, the enemy has regrouped and its strength is increasing once again as war looms in the Land.